REPORTAGE PRESS

ABOUT THE AUTHOR

Adam LeBor is an author and journalist based in Budapest, Hungary. He writes for *The Times*, the *Sunday Times*, *The Economist*, the *New York Times*, *Literary Review*, *Monocle*, *Condé Nast Traveller*, *Prospect*, the *Jewish Chronicle* and numerous other publications and websites. He is the author of six critically-acclaimed non-fiction books, published in nine languages, two of which, *Hitler's Secret Bankers*, and *City of Oranges*, were short listed for literary prizes. *The Budapest Protocol* is his first novel.

# The Budapest Protocol

BY ADAM LEBOR

REPORTAGE PRESS

REPORTAGE PRESS

Published by Reportage Press
26 Richmond Way, London W12 8LY United Kingdom
Tel: (0044) (0)7971 461 935
e-mail: info@reportagepress.com
www.reportagepress.com

*The Budapest Protocol* was produced under the editorial direction
of Laura Keeling.

British Library Cataloguing in Publication Data.

A catalogue record for this book is available from the British Library.

ISBN-13: 978–1–906702–12–0 paperback

ISBN-13: 978–1–906702–20–5 hardback

Cover design by Daniel Pudles.

Layout by Florence Production Ltd

Printed and bound in the UK by CPI Mackays, Chatham ME5 8TD

## Advance praise for *The Budapest Protocol*

"A well-paced Eurothriller that rolls today's headlines – terrorism, loss of liberty, political subterfuge and racial tension – into a conspiracy from the past that threatens the future of the continent. Fans of the late Robert Ludlum will be happy to learn that in Adam LeBor they have a worthy successor." – Mark Burnell, author of the Stephanie Patrick thriller series.

"A superb thriller from a talented writer. LeBor weaves together a gripping tale of Hungary's complex wartime past and her corrupt, post-communist present. A stylish and atmospheric debut." – Charles Cumming, author of *Typhoon*.

"With a tale that intrigues from the start, Adam LeBor is a deft guide to a central Europe where the shadows of the past still hang heavy and an alarming future beckons." – Jonathan Freedland, writing as Sam Bourne.

"*The Budapest Protocol* is a first class political thriller. Only an exceptionally sharp-eyed and knowledgeable foreign correspondent like Adam LeBor could have written this book – he's been there, he knows eastern Europe and the suspense is the real-life thing." – Alan Furst, author of *The Spies of Warsaw*.

"*The Budapest Protocol* is in every way a superior thriller: tense, intelligent and thought-provoking. One of those books which flies by when you are reading it but stays with you long after you've finished." – Boris Starling, author of *Messiah*.

For everybody at *Budapest Week*. *Azok voltak a szép napok, barátaim.*

# Acknowledgements

My grateful thanks go first to Rosie Whitehouse and Laura Keeling at Reportage Press for their belief in this book. Their sharp eyes and inspirational suggestions helped turn a manuscript into a novel. I first started writing the story that would become *The Budapest Protocol* in Paris more than a decade ago. Adrian Brown and Patrick Bishop were stalwart friends and allies, always encouraging, supportive and ready to spend an evening over couscous royale and a carafe of vin rouge at Chez Omar. Special Parisian thanks also to Chantal Agueh and Alex Chester. I am grateful to many friends and colleagues who have helped along the way. They include: Rick Bruner, Mark Burnell, Chris Condon, Dora Czuk, Charles Cumming, Simon Evans, Bob Green, Peter Green, Gerald Jacobs, Anthony Julius, Rudy Kennedy, Bea Klukan, Tony Lang, Justin Leighton, Nir Livay, Sam Loewenberg, Dr Jancis Long, Mark Milstein, John Nadler, Laszlo Ney, Boris Starling, Erwin Tuil and Diana Tyler.

Thanks to Danny O'Brien of the Electronic Frontier Foundation, Janet Haven of the Open Society Institute and Solana Larsen of Global Voices Online, who all helped with invaluable technical advice about secure communications on the internet. Fiammetta Rocco and Helena Douglas at *The Economist* provided a steady supply of thrillers for review, which helped me hone this book. Nick Thorpe generously shared an anecdote about his brushes with Hungary's communist era authorities. David Chance, Katalin Korompay, Desmond McGrath, Bill Swainson and Olen Steinhauer read early versions of the manuscript and made valuable suggestions, as did my agent Laura Longrigg. Many thanks to my colleagues at *The Times* foreign desk for sending me on numerous reporting trips across the former Yugoslavia and eastern Europe. I am especially grateful to Dr Istvan Fenyo and Kriszta Fenyo who some years ago took me on a memorable walk through Budapest's Jewish quarter, site of the wartime ghetto, which helped inspire this book. Alan Furst and Roger Boyes have been consistently helpful and encouraging over the years. And thanks most of all to Kati, Danny and Hannah.

*"I am convinced that in fifty years' time, people will no longer think in terms of countries."*
Josef Göebbels, September 1940.

## PROLOGUE

### Budapest, November 1944

Only the lucky were buried.

Miklos Farkas stepped over the woman's frozen corpse and opened her suitcase, still held tight in her hand. It was empty. He walked quickly along Karoly Boulevard, his thin coat pulled around him. The survival instinct had long replaced any vestigial shame at foraging among the dead. The pavement was coated with ice and the snow fell hard, the wind slashing at his face. He smelt smoke and cordite, tasted the brick dust of pulverised apartment blocks. A dead horse lay splayed across the road. The ghetto gate at Dohany Street was a hundred yards behind him. He was seven minutes walk from his destination, the SS headquarters at the Hotel Savoy.

The gunmen stepped out of the darkness, smiling greedily when they saw Miklos. There were two: one was tall and thin, with a pointed nose and droopy moustache. A silver *mezuzah*, the door ornament on a Jewish house, was pinned to his jacket. The other was short and red-faced, hopping nervously from foot to foot. They wore army caps and greatcoats, their armbands emblazoned with a four pointed cross. Their boots were wrapped in layers of yellow parchment, the ink of the Hebrew letters running into the snow.

The tall gunman slammed his rifle into Miklos' stomach. He gasped and staggered forward, stumbling on the icy pavement. He righted himself and raised his right hand, his heart pounding. "Courage, brother," he said, using the Arrow Cross greeting. "I

1

didn't see you there." He handed him his documents, willing his hands not to shake.

The short man walked around Miklos. He looked him up and down, prodding him with his pistol. "Brother? I don't think so. Looks like a Jew to me," he exclaimed in a high-pitched voice, like an excited schoolboy.

"Me? A Jew? You're joking. If anyone looks like a Jew, I think it's you. Shoot me if you want," said Miklos scornfully. He spat on the ground. "But you'll have the SS to answer to."

"The SS?" sneered the tall gunman. "We'll see about that. This is Hungary, not Germany." He jammed the rifle barrel under Miklos' chin, pushing upwards into the soft flesh around his throat. Miklos grunted in pain as his head was forced back.

"Head back, up, up, that's good. Papers here say you are Miklos Kovacs. One point eighty-five metres tall, light brown hair, blue eyes," he continued, peering at Miklos. He glanced down at the documents. "Special dispensation from German staff headquarters to be out after curfew because of your *valuable* war-work at the Hotel Savoy. Nice. But not nice enough, Miklos Kuhn," he said, pushing the rifle barrel harder.

"My name is Miklos Kovacs. You can see there, it's clearly written," Miklos said, trying to swallow as the barrel pressed into his throat.

"Kuhn, Cohen, whatever. Let's see who you really are. Say your prayers, Kuhn-Cohen," he said, taking away the rifle barrel. For the Germans, killing Jews was business. For the Arrow Cross, their Hungarian Nazi allies, it was a pleasure, one ever more frenzied as the Russians steadily advanced.

"Our Father, Who art in heaven," Miklos coughed, a loose, hacking rattle, and continued. "Hallowed be thy Name. Thy kingdom come. Thy will be done, On earth as it is in heaven. Give us this day our daily bread. And forgive us our trespasses . . ."

"Finish it," the gunman growled. A shell exploded near the river, its boom rattling nearby windows. "And quickly."

Miklos recited fluently until the end, "For thine is the kingdom, and the power, and the glory, for ever and ever. Amen." He crossed himself decisively.

The tall gunman lowered his rifle and twirled his moustache as he looked at Miklos. "Not bad. Not bad at all. But anyone can learn a prayer. Drop them."

"Yeah, you can't learn that," squealed the short trooper.

"Are you crazy? It'll freeze and fall off," Miklos protested.

The tall gunman slammed his rifle butt hard into his chest. "Don't – argue – with – me," he said, slowly and deliberately.

Miklos reeled from the blow. He stumbled back against the wall and slipped on a patch of ice. He fell onto the pavement, his cheek hitting the ground. They yanked him up by his arms so that he was kneeling. The short trooper twisted Miklos' arm behind his back and forced his head down, laughing as he forced his pistol into Miklos' neck.

"Whose turn is it?" he asked.

"I can't remember," said the tall gunman. "I think I did the last one. Or did you?"

Miklos shivered violently as a trickle of ice-cold water ran down his back. He tried to conjure up an image of his wife, Ruth, but all he could see was the grey, icy pavement. A cold fury surged through him. *Not now, not like this.* He tried to twist away from the pistol barrel but the gunman jerked his arm up higher. Knives of pain shot down his back. The tall gunman pointed his rifle at Miklos' head. He braced himself, closed his eyes and bit his lip, his breath coming in short ragged pants.

"Do yourself a favour, Kuhn. Keep still, and we'll be done here nice and fast. Otherwise it's going to get very messy," the short gunman said, as he again twisted the gun barrel into Miklos' neck.

A Grosser Mercedes, sleek and black, drove towards them, two Nazi flags fluttering over its headlights. The car stopped suddenly by the pavement, sliding on the icy road, and the door flew open. An SS officer in full dress uniform jumped out. His adjutant emerged from the other side, machine-pistol at the ready, and stood facing the Hungarians.

"*Halt*! Put your guns down," the SS officer ordered.

The Hungarians lowered their weapons and stepped back. Miklos stood up slowly, his hands in the air. The German marched over.

The tall gunman gestured at Miklos, smiling nervously. "Please, be our guest. A Jew."

The SS officer took his Luger from his holster and pointed it at the two Arrow Cross men. The crack of the bullet echoed across the streets as it gouged a large hole in the wall beside them. The gunmen jumped back, shock and fear on their faces. The SS officer fired twice more into the ground, a bullet in front of each. The short gunman shook with terror, a yellow puddle forming in the snow next to his leg.

Miklos dropped his hands and wiped his mouth, tasting blood as he stared at the German. He was tall and pale, his hair so blond it was almost white, with sharp features and intelligent blue eyes. His left sleeve was empty, pinned to his tunic. Friedrich Vautker was the youngest Colonel in the Waffen SS. War had accelerated his promotion. He nodded at Miklos. Miklos nodded back warily, his heart still thumping.

"This man works for us. Is that clear, you Hungarian jackasses?" Vautker snapped at the Arrow Cross men. "You stink of drink. No wonder the Russians are at the gate."

Vautker put his pistol back in his holster. He yanked off the silver *mezuzah* from the tall gunman's coat, tearing the cloth. A military truck rumbled by. Two rows of German soldiers sat facing each other, wrapped in their winter greatcoats, headed for the front. The driver slowed as he approached, looked briefly at the scene, and stopped.

"Any trouble here?" he asked, gunning his motor. The engine juddered, trying to fire cleanly on the watery petrol. Several German soldiers turned to stare.

"Not now, no," said Vautker. "Where are you headed?"

"The eastern sector. The Reds are pounding us. HQ says we are stretched too thin there."

Vautker flicked his hand at the Arrow Cross men. "Take them. For the first front-line."

The Hungarians tried to protest. Six burly troopers jumped down and pushed them on board. The lorry lurched off, the short Arrow Cross man mewling like a kitten.

The SS officer weighed the silver *mezuzah* in his hand and handed it to Miklos. "Have it, Herr *Kovacs*. It should fetch something. Now get in the car."

\*   \*   \*

Miklos' arms ached under the weight of the silver tray laden with champagne glasses. His head hurt, his neck throbbed and his knees pulsed with pain but he tried to focus on his work. The dinner was served in the Savoy's cellar. Heavy black drapes lined the walls from floor to ceiling. Candles sputtered, dripping wax onto the tablecloths. A pianist played snatches of Frank Lehar's *The Merry Widow*, Hitler's favourite operetta. A couple of dozen people were gathered in the chilly room. Some wore black SS uniforms, or army grey, but many seemed to be civilians. A handful of women shivered in cocktail dresses. Two men in suits stood on the edge of the group. Both waved away the offer of champagne. They spoke with Zurich accents, Miklos noticed.

Miklos stopped in front of a famous Budapest actress, a redhead in a blue-silk dress. She looked at Miklos quizzically, drank a glass of champagne in two gulps and immediately grabbed another, her blue eyes glazed and unfocused.

The Savoy's headwaiter beckoned Miklos over as the other waiters brought food from the kitchen. Aladar Nagy had been the Farkas family butler, in charge of their city residence, a fifteen room villa at the top of Andrassy Avenue. He was a short, chubby man, with a round face and lively brown eyes.

"She ought to remember you. I served her dinner at your house often enough," he muttered.

Miklos smiled grimly. "Yes. When we had a house."

The Farkas family villa had been appropriated by the Germans in March, the day after they invaded. Nagy was sacked but quickly found new work at the Hotel Savoy, where he arranged for Miklos to work as a waiter. This gave Miklos access to the most precious commodity of all in Budapest that winter: food.

"Your father?" asked Aladar.

Baron Lajos Farkas, friend – he thought – of Hungary's ruler Admiral Horthy, had been arrested after his house was seized and not seen again. The family had received a single postcard from somewhere in Austria called Mauthausen a couple of weeks later, but it had been written in another's hand.

Miklos shook his head. "No news."

"And Ruth?"

Miklos smiled. "Alive. I wonder how sometimes. Whenever I bring her something to eat she gives it away. And with you?"

"They sent my boy to the front," said Aladar, his voice cracking. "He's sixteen. They gave him a rifle from the first war. He's never fired a gun in his life. His mother can't stop crying."

Miklos shook his head and laid his hand on Aladar's shoulder. He walked back into the throng. The air was thick with cigarette smoke, perfume and alcohol fumes, the room loud with laughter now, tinged with hysteria. Miklos stared in wonder at the men and women gorging themselves at the table. His mouth flooded with saliva: goose liver and crisp potatoes, fried in fat, roast ducks with piles of vegetables, beefsteaks slathered in creamy pepper sauce. Dusty bottles of fine wine were lined up in front of the food. A minute's walk away they were starving to death.

Colonel Vautker beckoned him over, as he poured himself a large glass of red wine. "So, Kovacs, the Russians will probably be here soon. You'll put in a good word for me, won't you? Tell them how I saved you from the Arrow Cross? I might need it."

Miklos nodded. "Of course, sir. Anything I can do to help," he replied, his voice deadpan.

Vautker turned to the redheaded actress sitting at his side, putting his arm around the back of her chair. She smiled invitingly.

Miklos walked back to the Savoy's kitchen. The room was hot, airless and stank of fat and cooking. The walls began to wobble and Miklos felt he would faint at any moment. He poured himself a glass of water and sat down until the meal was over and what Colonel Vautker called the "evening's business" began. The doors were closed, and the waiters left, bringing in the leftovers. Miklos reached across the table for a goose leg, barely touched. A thin, stooped man snatched it away before him, his eyes triumphant as he jammed the greasy meat into his pocket.

Something snapped inside him and Miklos lunged forward, raising his right fist. The thin man grabbed a kitchen knife. Aladar stepped between them. He put one hand on Miklos' chest and held out his palm to the thin man. He handed Aladar the knife. Aladar said: "There's enough fighting outside. None in here if you want to work another shift. Now shake hands."

The two men did as Aladar ordered. Aladar took Miklos' arm and led him away. "Don't worry. There will be plenty for you. Come."

Aladar thanked the staff and sent them home, each with a package of leftovers. Miklos cleared some space among the debris of dinner and sat down with a plate of chicken and potatoes. He chewed slowly and carefully. The rich food was hard to digest after the ghetto diet. Aladar poured them both a glass of red wine.

"How much time do you think they have?" Aladar asked.

"Not long, thank God. The Russians have surrounded the city. They have no shortage of shells, as you can hear. The German supply lines are being cut off. I heard some generals want to surrender, but Hitler won't let them. The Arrow Cross are fleeing westwards. The Russians are capturing the city house by house, room by room. Could be weeks. Could be days."

Aladar nodded. "I've no love for the communists. But I just want this to be over as soon as possible, and for my boy to come home. What will you do when the Ivans get here?"

Miklos shrugged. "Try and rebuild our lives, I suppose."

"You'll stay? After this?"

"Of course. We are Hungarians." Miklos carefully speared a chunk of chicken breast and a slice of potato. "But what are these lunatics doing, having a party now?"

"It's strange. The two Swiss suits arrived a couple of days ago." Aladar paused. "We had quite a show this morning. They made us turn the hotel inside out."

"Why?"

"Some documents went missing. The suits were hysterical."

"And did they find them?" asked Miklos.

Aladar smiled and poured more wine. "Drink up. Soon there'll only be vodka."

# ONE

## Budapest, winter, present-day

Alex Farkas jerked awake, his body slick with sweat, his heart racing. He lay still in the semi-darkness, forcing himself to breathe steadily, listening to the low roar of the early evening traffic.

"Why you did wake me? I was having such a nice dream," a sleepy female voice asked indignantly. "You were shouting. What's the matter?"

Alex sat up, shaking his head, willing away the memories. "Nothing. I'm fine." This was reality, he told himself: here, now, her skin warm against his, her blond hair tousled with sleep.

Zsofi Petcsardy stretched and propped herself up on her elbow, green eyes full of concern. "You don't look fine. You look like you just saw a ghost." She turned and reached for the bottle of mineral water next to the bed.

It was warm and stale, but he gulped the water down. He looked at his watch. "Thanks. I'm sorry, Zsofi, I have to be at Kultura at eight, then I'm meeting my grandfather."

She glared at him. "Is that my thanks for looking after you? Throwing me out?"

"You can wait for me here if you like," Alex offered, as he kissed her head.

Zsofi shook him off and looked around the one room, fifth floor corner flat. The walls, once white, were grey and peeling. The 1970s furniture was faded brown and orange. Boxes of books were piled in every corner, their contents spilling onto the worn parquet floor, whose loose slats rattled when walked on. The flat overlooked

Kossuth Lajos Street, a busy four lane road stretching from the Great Boulevard that encircled the inner city, down to the Elizabeth Bridge and the river. French windows opened onto a small balcony which offered a view of the Danube in one direction and the Hotel Savoy, on nearby Ferenciek Square, in the other, but the panorama was now partially blocked by a cordon of browning plants. "No thanks, I don't like. At least make me some tea," she said, pulling the quilt around her.

Alex clambered out of the bed and walked into the bathroom. He stepped into the claw-footed bath-tub, where a hand-shower attachment reached from the mixer tap. He was too tall to stretch out, so he sat and sprayed himself with the hottest water he could bear, washed quickly, and jerked the lever to cold, gasping and shivering as the freezing water coursed over him. His head clear, he stepped out, wrapped a towel around his waist and walked through to the kitchen. Tea was more complicated than it sounded. The cooker pre-dated the collapse of the Berlin Wall, if not the wall itself. The fridge roared like an airplane, when it worked. The electricity board had declared the wiring a health hazard and only a bribe of 10,000 forints, thirty-five euros, had stopped the inspector cutting off the supply.

He touched a worn photograph taped to the wall. He was younger, his face thinner, standing with his arm around a tall, Slavic-looking young woman with her long dark hair tied back in a ponytail. They both wore flak jackets and helmets and were grinning nervously. 'Welcome to Hell' was painted on a wall nearby, the letters pockmarked by shrapnel scars.

Alex looked away, filled the electric kettle and plugged it in. He looked in the two kitchen cupboards for some tea. One was empty, the other contained a packet of sugar and an ancient jar of plum jam. A pizza box poked out of the rubbish bin. Inside was a single, curling slice, and a used tea bag. He had rinsed the teabag and placed it in a cup when the socket popped and the kettle went dead. He turned to see Zsofi struggling with the zip of her black leather biker's jacket. Zsofi was a ballerina, a rising star of Hungarian dance. They had met in the summer when Alex profiled her for the

*Budapest News,* an English-language weekly newspaper, where he worked as associate editor. An interview over drinks had stretched to dinner and more.

"Thanks, but I'll pass on the tea. I'm going," said Zsofi, walking into the kitchen as the zip finally slipped into place. She walked over to the photograph. "A new picture."

"It's not new. It's Sarajevo, in the war," said Alex, fiddling with the kettle.

"You were skinnier. Who is she?" Zsofi asked, pointing at the picture.

"Everyone was skinnier then. Her name is Azra."

She looked closer. "Attractive Azra. Was it really hell there?"

He smiled. "Not always."

"So I see," she huffed.

"It was a long time ago," he said, half to himself. He reached inside the pizza box and took out the remaining slice. "How about dinner?" The pizza slice broke in half and flopped onto the floor.

Zsofi glared at him. "Ask Azra. Maybe she's hungry."

He bit his lip. "I doubt it." He stepped towards her. "Zsofi, I'm the one who should be jealous."

"Forget it, Alex. Call me when you can fit me into your busy schedule," she said, slamming the door behind her.

\* \* \*

Alex lived on the corner of Petofi Sandor Street and Kossuth Lajos Street, a few minutes on foot from the Danube. Kultura was fifteen minutes walk away, in the heart of District VII, Budapest's historic Jewish area. Many of its streets, squares and markets had been untouched since 1945. Students, artists and expatriates had moved in, and District VII was now the city's hippest and most bohemian quarter. Its central location and grand but dilapidated apartment houses made it a prime target for foreign property developers. Numerous buildings were on the verge of collapse, as their new owners waited for them to become uninhabitable so they could demolish them. Once the developers received their construction permits there were usually several months before the work began. Then the squat-bars arrived. The owners brought in a lorry-load of used chairs and tables, drinks and a sound system, and the party started.

Alex walked away from the river, up Kossuth Lajos Street, glancing at the tourist coaches parked outside the Hotel Savoy. The traffic roared past him towards the Elizabeth Bridge, the exhaust fumes mixing with the smell of doner kebabs from the Turkish fast food place on the corner of Karoly Boulevard. The freezing wind blowing towards the Danube made his eyes stream and he huddled into his leather jacket. He was tall and lean, with thick, unruly black hair and a long, straight nose over a full, wide mouth that he chewed when nervous. His eyes were his most unusual feature, one blue, the other green, both framed by long, curved eyelashes.

He turned left onto Karoly Boulevard, walked past the Great Synagogue, crossed the tramlines on Deak Square and into Kiraly Street, the heart of District VII. A giant poster, four stories high, covered the front of a building being renovated. It showed a well-built, suntanned man, standing next to an attractive blonde woman. Three children stood in front of them, all smiling with perfect teeth. The poster proclaimed: "Vote Sanzlermann: Family, Work, Unity."

Kultura's security guard greeted Alex and moved aside to let him pass. A wide entrance opened onto a maze of bars and smoky alcoves. A raw brick wall was covered with advertisements for room-mates, bicycles for sale, jobs for English teachers. Alex walked through to the main courtyard, covered with a plastic sheeting roof and warmed by garden heaters. Roma Party, a popular Gypsy group, played on stage, the music surging across the courtyard. The owner greeted Alex with a loud "*Shalom, habibi*," and handed him his regular glass of chilled *szilva palinka*, plum brandy. Ehud was an Israeli, a sinewy former commando, the grandson of Hungarian Holocaust survivors, with a pierced nose and shaven head. He had dropped out of medical school in Budapest after his first year and now ran the city's hottest bars and clubs.

Alex thanked Ehud, sat down at an empty table and picked up a copy of *Magyar Tribün*, the former Communist Party newspaper that was now a left-wing daily. Six people had been killed, including a deputy minister, and forty injured by a car bomb outside the Bundestag, the German Parliament. The bombing was the third attack in recent weeks, after Paris and Rome. The Immigration Liberation Army, a terrorist group, claimed responsibility. Alex put the newspaper down and called his grandfather on his mobile phone to let him know he would soon be there. No answer. That was strange, he thought, for Miklos rarely ventured out in the evenings. Perhaps he had gone to see his friend Peter Feher for a game of chess and a cup of tea.

A well-fed man in his fifties walked up. Istvan Kiraly looked around with interest, like a naturalist who has discovered a new species of tropical plant. "You do find the most *fascinating* places, dear boy. I had no idea that there was a secret universe behind that drab door."

Kiraly spoke English with the careful enunciation of a 1930s BBC newsreader announcing the scores of a cricket test match. A wily survivor of vicious political infighting under the communist regime, and a former spokesman for Hungary's last communist President, Kiraly was nicknamed 'Teflon'. After the change of system in 1990, he reinvented himself as a 'strategic lobbyist and communications strategist'. He had lines into every political party and was friendly with every Cabinet Minister. He advised western companies how much was needed to bribe the old communist networks that still ran much of the economy, and guided Hungarian businesses in milking EU subsidies. He was of one Alex's best sources.

Kiraly pulled out a flimsy metal chair from under the rickety table. He positioned himself carefully, as though the chair was about to collapse under him.

Alex stared at Kiraly. "You've changed." He looked the PR man up and down. The familiar hand-tailored navy Italian suit, the monogrammed cufflinks and hand-made shoes. The same wary blue eyes, set deep in a lined face, under a carefully trimmed head of grey hair. But the lines stopped abruptly above Kiraly's eyes.

Alex touched his forehead. It felt hard and taut. He laughed. "I don't believe it."

13

.iraly blushed and moved back. 'What are you talking about?"
.e blustered.

"You know that there have been cases of people getting Mad
Cow Disease after a botox? Something to do with the extracts they
use in the injections," Alex said, nodding solemnly.

"Don't be ridiculous. And I would like a drink." Kiraly waved
at a waitress, a willowy brunette. "Now I see why you come here.
A glass of Bailey's Irish Cream please, my dear." The waitress
looked at Alex. He picked up his glass. "Another *palinka*. Thanks."

"Tonight we are celebrating," Kiraly proclaimed.

"And why's that?"

"Firstly, because it's your birthday."

Alex looked surprised. He didn't feel like celebrating. He had not
even told Zsofi.

"Don't think I didn't know. Happy Birthday, dear boy. And
secondly, because I have just signed up the future President of
Europe."

Alex sat up straighter. "*Sanzlermann*?"

Kiraly nodded. "That's right. Frank Sanzlermann. Presidential
candidate for the European National Union, Austrian Foreign
Minister, intellectual godfather of the drive for European unity, and
devoted husband and father. He arrives tonight to start his election
campaign. "

Alex looked doubtful. "That's the same Sanzlermann who has
called for all Gypsies to be fingerprinted?"

"Alex, every country needs to keep track of its citizens. The
fingerprinting is part of a proposal for a Europe-wide census. These
are dangerous times. There are bombs going off all over Europe.
You're a journalist, a born cynic. Herr Sanzlermann is a thinker, a
writer, like you. You would have plenty to talk about. He has
repeatedly stated his commitment to the values of European
integration." Kiraly tapped his fingers on the table top in time to
the music. "This is rather good. What is this group called?"

"Roma Party. Maybe they could play at one of Sanzlermann's
rallies. That would show a real commitment to European
integration. Can Gypsies still vote?" Alex asked, deadpan.

"Don't be ridiculous," said Kiraly indignantly.

Alex sipped his *palinka*. He could not allow Kiraly to escape that easily. "Did you see that article in *Ébredjetek Magyarok!* about you?" *Ébredjetek Magyarok!*, which meant "Hungarians Awake", was a new conservative newspaper that had just been launched by the Volkstern Corporation, a German media conglomerate with extensive holdings across eastern and central Europe. The papers' editors saw communist conspiracies everywhere, but as ex-party members themselves they knew what to look for. Kiraly looked alarmed. Few things made him more nervous than press coverage that he could not control.

"I know it's a dreadful rag, but they had dug up one of your old speeches," Alex continued. "I quote from memory: 'Under the guidance of the party leadership, and the implementation of Marxist-Leninist principles, we build the new socialist future.' Or something like that."

Kiraly spluttered into his drink. "My dear boy. We are none of us gifted with perfect foresight. That was a long time ago. Another world."

"October 1989, actually. The wall came down two weeks later."

"A low blow, Alex. Times change and we must move with them."

"I'm sorry, Istvan, you are quite right," said Alex, mock contrite. His nose twitched at the strong smell of burning rope wafting over from a nearby table. Two young women were passing a badly-rolled joint back and forth, giggling as scraps of tobacco mixed with marijuana spilled on to the table. They sat dreamily as the music suddenly speeded up, the violinist sawing at his instrument as though he was trying to cut it in half. The notes soared, plunged, capturing the whole open space. Conversations faded as the audience watched, entranced. The violinist played a long, drawn-out note, and bowed. The applause exploded, Kiraly too clapping enthusiastically.

The waitress brought their drinks, and the two men clinked glasses.

"Happy Birthday. And here's to the new Europe," exclaimed Kiraly.

"The New Europe," echoed Alex. He looked at the entrance. "And here it is."

A large black van pulled up outside the bar. Its windows were black, covered with a thick wire mesh, "Gendarmerie" painted on its sides. Hungary's paramilitary national police force had been disbanded after the Second World War. But the government had just reconstituted it, with sweeping powers of arrest and detention for nebulous offences such as "disturbing citizens' tranquillity" and "insulting national pride". Local police forces reported to the Ministry of the Interior, but the Gendarmerie answered solely to the Prime Minister, Tibor Csintori, and the Interior Minister.

Csintori's government described itself as "moderate conservative" but was under increasing pressure from the far-right Hungarian National Front. Every concession Csintori made only increased the National Front's power and confidence. Even with the Gendarmerie, few believed Csintori, a middle-aged former dissident sociologist, would remain in office much longer. Across eastern Europe membership of the European Union had turned sour. Authoritarian nationalists had already taken power in Romania, Slovakia and Croatia. Poverty and unemployment were soaring as state-owned industries were sold off on the cheap. Rocketing inflation ate away at the value of wages and pensions.

Riots had erupted in impoverished eastern Hungary, and Budapest's decaying inner city. A Romany family had been killed the previous week after someone had hurled half a dozen petrol bombs through their windows. The police force seemed ever more ineffectual, mired in a turf war with the Gendarmerie. A new far-right group, the Pannonia Brigade, whose members wore paramilitary-style uniforms, held rallies and marches every weekend across the country. The Brigade even policed these itself. There was a growing sense that the state was no longer in control of the country. The government only survived the Hungarian National Front's vote of no-confidence by boosting the Gendarmerie's budget by fifty per cent.

Alex watched two Gendarmes saunter in. They wore paramilitary khaki fatigues and narrow pointed caps, topped with a bright cockade of red, white and green feathers, Hungary's national colours. Each was armed with a machine pistol and a long billy club. A Sam Browne leather belt stretched across their chests, studded with clip-on cans of CS gas. They ignored Ehud's protests. Four more Gendarmes soon followed.

Kiraly's lips pursed in distaste. He watched the two students nearby stub out their joint and empty the ashtray into a plastic bag. They walked quickly to the bathrooms. "I hope those toilets flush properly." He paused, "And Miklos?"

"I'm a bit worried about him. He seems very distracted lately. He was insistent that I come over for a birthday drink to talk about 'family things'. I just called him but he didn't answer."

"Don't worry about Miklos. He's probably visiting a lady friend," said Istvan lightly. "And how is your prima ballerina?"

"Who told you about that?"

"Very little is confidential in this town, dear boy. Especially from me. A word to the wise, if I may. Mr Karoly Petcsardy. The lissom Zsofi's husband."

"I know who he is. They're separated. She wants a divorce."

"Does she?" Kiraly's voice was sceptical.

"He has his own lovers," said Alex, feeling a sudden stab of acid jealousy.

"Yes, he does. But Mr and Mrs Petcsardy are not divorced. Nor have any papers been filed, or lawyers hired. There is nothing like the appearance of a rival suitor to make a previously unappreciated woman suddenly worth fighting over. Frankly, Alex, I think you deserve better. She is very pretty, but this is a dead-end relationship."

Alex finished his *palinka*. "Istvan, you are absolutely right."

He knew Zsofi would never leave her husband and in his heart, he probably didn't want her to. But how long was he going to keep running from any potential commitment? He put down his glass, watching the Gendarmes. They slowly checked the identity papers of everyone entering and leaving. Their commander stood nearby, smoking a cigarette as he watched approvingly. The party atmosphere quickly evaporated. A group of boisterous students heading towards the entrance fell silent, crossed the road and briskly walked by when they saw the Gendarmerie bus.

Kiraly called the waitress over and paid the bill. "Alex, I'm sorry, but I also have to meet someone at 9.00pm." Alex reached into his pocket for his wallet, but Kiraly waved his money away. "Enjoy your birthday, Alex. And give my best to your grandfather."

They shook hands as Kiraly departed, flashing his identity card at the Gendarmes, who made way for him. The Gendarmes spread out across the bar. Alex checked his watch. It was 8.45pm, and definitely time to go. He walked over to the entrance where a Gendarme blocked his way. He was well built, his head shaved under his cap, his face pitted with acne.

"Papers," the Gendarme demanded, one hand resting on his billy club.

Alex reached into his back pocket and took out his press card. The Gendarme carefully read Alex's name and held on to the card. "Go back and sit down," he ordered Alex.

"Why? And I would like my press card back," Alex said, not moving.

The Gendarme signalled to the commander. He was tall and dark complexioned, with thick black eyebrows. He dropped his cigarette, crushed it out on the ground and walked over. The Gendarme handed him Alex's press card. The commander checked it and glanced at his watch.

"I need to be somewhere at 9.00pm," said Alex, his voice insistent.

"Unfortunately, Mr Farkas, you will have to make your excuses."

"Why?"

"It's nothing personal. Just a random identity check. I am sure you are who you say are. But the regulations are that nobody is allowed in or out until we have finished. It will be no more than half an hour. Here is your press card," he said, handing it back to Alex.

Alex bit his lip and returned to his chair, anger and anxiety curdling inside him. Any further protests, he knew, would earn him a trip inside the Gendarmerie van. He called his grandfather again. There was still no answer.

## TWO

Frank Sanzlermann slowly sipped his single malt whisky as the executive jet crossed into Hungarian airspace. The aeroplane was fully fitted with a complete office including satellite telephones, a high-speed internet connection and an open line to party headquarters in Vienna.

He picked up a freshly printed copy of his new book, smiling with satisfaction as he leafed through its glossy pages. Before Sanzlermann had entered politics a decade ago he had taught Philosophy and History at the University of Vienna. *'From Charlemagne to Schengen: The Invincible Drive for European Unity'* was the culmination of his intellectual career, cementing his reputation as both a thinker and a politician.

Published in twelve languages, its twenty chapters, each densely footnoted, traced the development of the European ideal from the Holy Roman Empire to the Schengen Accords which had abolished border controls between member states. His basic argument was simple, accessible and endlessly repeated: the traditional concept of national sovereignty was an anachronism and the greatest cause of suffering in European history. The only remedy was the abolition of that sovereignty and the construction of a European super-state with common government, financial markets, laws and institutions. The book's front cover was the same photograph as his campaign poster, showing Sanzlermann and his family, while the back was covered with numerous endorsements from European politicians, hailing Sanzlermann as an "Aristotle for the modern age" and "The leading intellectual of the 21st century."

19

Sanzlermann's writing on the necessity of the euro, that abolishing financial autonomy was a worthwhile sacrifice, as nations who shared a single currency would never go to war, had been especially acclaimed. He had just won that year's Brussels Prize, 250,000 euros, for the greatest contribution to European unity. His arguments about the essentially Christian nature of European identity, and its Greco-Roman heritage – like his proposals for fingerprinting Roma – had triggered considerable controversy, angering many Muslims, Jews and those on the left, but his robust defence seemed to only strengthen his support. There was increasing talk of a Papal audience. After the recent Immigration Liberation Army bombing in Berlin most polls gave Sanzlermann at least an eight per cent lead over his main rival, Edith Leclerc, the French schoolteacher standing for the Social Democratic Alliance.

The plane banked slowly as the pilot announced preparations for landing at Budapest's Ferihegy Airport. A young, handsome flight attendant walked down the aisle and offered Sanzlermann some more whisky. He shook his head, and pulled out a pen from his pocket.

"Klaus, isn't it?" Sanzlermann asked, looking into his eyes.

The steward nodded. Sanzlermann signed his book and handed it to him. The steward thanked him, blushed and walked quickly to the back of the plane, holding the book and whisky against his chest. Sanzlermann smiled to himself, turned and looked out of the window. The plane flew over acres of concrete pre-fabricated apartment blocks, the drab "panel flats" that were built all over the former eastern Bloc, from Bulgaria to Berlin. The Danube was a black ribbon snaking through the city, its banks marked by orange streetlights. The same river that flowed through Sanzlermann's home town of Linz, from where he had first been catapulted onto the national, then the international stage.

The European Union now had thirty members, including all the central European post-communist countries, Macedonia and Croatia. As Austrian Foreign Minister, Sanzlermann had played a pivotal role in expanding the union eastwards. The remaining former Yugoslav countries were scheduled to join within five years. The post of President of Europe would not be ceremonial. After intense lobbying by Germany and Austria, and hints from Switzerland that it may soon consider its own referendum on eventual membership, it was agreed that the President would be directly elected by universal franchise in each member state. The President would chair the finance, economics and foreign relations committees of the European Parliament, with veto rights over all new laws. The post would be an unprecedented hybrid of executive, legislative and ceremonial powers. That much was public information.

Behind the scenes, the future President's potential for deal-making and breaking, awarding contracts and peddling power and influence was almost unimaginable. Brussels had decided that voting would take place on a country-by-country basis, over a three-month period, to allow the candidates an opportunity to campaign across the continent. The eastern members were first on the trail, to show Brussels' commitment to the new, expanded Europe. With Sanzlermann's help Hungary had been chosen to open the voting, to the chagrin of its neighbours, on November 9, the anniversary of the opening of the Berlin Wall. November 9 was also the date of *Kristallnacht*, the Nazis' 1938 pogrom against the Jews that marked the start of the Holocaust, although that anniversary received less attention.

He checked himself in the back of the seat vanity mirror: ski-slope tan, a firm chin, well-trimmed light brown hair streaked with grey, blue eyes, cool and assessing. The years on the piste had preserved his looks. Satisfied with what he saw, he steadily scratched the back of his left hand, closing his eyes with pleasure as his nails dug into the flaking skin. The plane began its descent. Sanzlermann's Chief Political Adviser returned to his adjacent seat as the seatbelt lights came on. Reinhard Daintner was a thin man in a grey suit, somewhere in early middle age – Sanzlermann had never been able to find out the details – a near-albino, with snow white blond hair, eyebrows and eyelashes, above very light grey eyes. He had the unnerving habit of licking his lips like a lizard contemplating a particularly juicy insect.

"Back to Budapest again. How many times is it now?" asked Daintner, as he buckled up.

"I've lost count. It will be good to see Attila again. He seems to have things under control," Sanzlermann replied, reluctantly ceasing his delectable self-torment.

Daintner said: "There are half a dozen television crew waiting for you on the tarmac when we land, including CNN and the BBC. Do you want to give a quick press conference?"

Sanzlermann shook his head. "No, not tonight. They will be broadcasting live and we cannot control the questions or the setting. Let them wait until the rally and the press conference on the weekend."

Daintner agreed. "You are right. Just a brisk wave hallo, and then straight to the hotel. Have you decided what to do with the Brussels Prize money?"

Sanzlermann swirled his whisky around his glass. "How is the Roma fingerprinting proposal playing out?" he asked.

Daintner reached into his briefcase and pulled out a file. He quickly leafed through the pages until he found a long list of tables. "Among socio-economic groups E, D and C2, very well, especially in the post-communist states. But it is not so supported among groups C1, B and A, notably among those with higher education, and in western Europe. Leclerc is seen as having more social compassion. The repeated slurs against you and claims of racism are gaining some traction." Daintner paused and licked his lips. "Some counter ammunition would be useful."

Sanzlermann traced his fingers over his raw left hand. "That's why we are launching the European National Union Foundation for Roma Education with the Brussels prize money. Speak to our friends, they will contribute at least as much again. Scholarships, grants to local schools, you know what to do."

Daintner scribbled rapidly in his notebook. "Excellent."

\* \* \*

Alex looked at his watch: 9.30pm. He had been sitting there for more than half an hour, phoning his grandfather every five minutes.

There was still no answer. The Gendarmes were moving from table to table at a snail's pace, ignoring the increasingly vocal protests of the crowd. All Kultura's back entrances were also blocked. There was no other way out. The anger and tension rose up inside him. He walked over to the commander to demand that he be allowed out.

The commander was talking on his mobile telephone. He looked at Alex and turned away. "Yes, yes," he said, nodding, and hung up. Alex prepared to protest when he spoke. "Good news, Mr Farkas. We have completed our identity checks. You and everyone else are free to go."

Alex controlled his fury and sprinted up Kiraly Street, skidding on the wet pavement. He barely missed crashing into two Chasidic Jews, oblivious to the world in animated discussion, and stopped at 23 Dob Street, on the corner of Klauzal Square. The heavy wooden door was open. The building had once been magnificent, with a huge hallway that stretched back several metres and a wide curved marble staircase adorned with plaster figures. But decades of neglect had exacted a high toll. The stair edges were crumbling, the walls were coated with grime and dirt. The entrance was dark. Alex felt his way along the wall until he found the light-switch. He pressed it several times. Nothing. He bounded up the stairs as fast as he could to the third floor. Alex knocked on the door, a great wooden slab with a brass lion's head knocker. Silence.

Miklos Farkas had lived in the same flat since 1945. After the ghetto was liberated, he studied medicine, but when the communists took over Hungary in 1948 he refused to join the party. He was expelled from university, decreed a "class enemy" because of his family background. He scraped a living as a journalist, writing about culture, while his wife Ruth worked as a French teacher. During the 1956 revolution Miklos broadcast on the rebels' radio station, for which he received a ten year sentence. He served five and was released in an amnesty in 1961. Miklos and Ruth had one son, Edward, Alex's father who had defected to England on a student exchange trip in the 1960s, a decision they had encouraged, despite its personal cost. During the 1980s Miklos joined the dissidents' movement, editing their samizdat publications, and liaising with western human rights activists. He was arrested and imprisoned for several months, and only released after repeated international protests. Once Hungary became a democracy the Liberal party asked Miklos to stand for Parliament, but he refused. Ruth had died a decade ago.

Alex knocked on the door again. Still no movement inside. His heart thumped from the exertion, his anxiety turning to fear. A door across the hallway opened a fraction. Alex glimpsed a mess of grey hair, two bright blue eyes and the arm of a pink nylon housecoat belonging to Erzsebet, Miklos' neighbour and keeper of his spare keys.

"No answer?" she asked, emerging from behind her door, stuffed with enough locks and iron bars to keep out a division of the Red Army, should the Russians ever return to Budapest. "I saw him yesterday morning. He seemed fine. He said you were coming today." She waddled out onto the landing, a barrel on legs, perturbed that something was disrupting the peace of her realm.

Alex pounded on the door, repeatedly. Silence. Where was Miklos' dog, Berta, a lumbering crossbreed who doted on her master, and galloped to the door as soon as the bell rang? Perhaps Miklos had forgotten that Alex was coming, and had taken Berta for a walk. There was one way to find out. The twisting sensation in his stomach became more intense.

"You can get into the flat can't you, Erzsebet?" he asked.

"Yes, of course. It's my responsibility to look after the building. There might be a flood, or a fire. I have a set of keys for every flat in case something happens," she replied, puffing up with the weight of her duties.

"That's fine. Why don't you get them? Maybe Miklos is ill, or has fallen over. Have you heard anything funny? Did you see anyone strange?"

"Some music last night. But that's nothing unusual. I thought it was probably just those people downstairs who have just moved in. Foreigners, I think. They're always having parties, you should see the mess they leave, bottles and cigarettes everywhere, all over the staircase, on the landing. I don't know where they think they are living, like Gypsies they are, always making chaos. Who knows the kind of people they are bringing into the building . . ."

Alex took a deep breath before he spoke, interrupting her flow, which once started was always difficult to staunch. "Erzsebet, please get the keys."

She rushed inside and shouted at her husband to fetch the keys. She returned and handed them to Alex, expecting to come in with him. Alex motioned for her to wait outside.

The flat was dark and still and his heart began to pound. He called out for his grandfather several times, but there was no reply. His stomach churned. Alex inched along the dark hall. He felt along the wall for the switch. The flat filled with light as he entered the lounge.

Miklos was slumped on the ancient green sofa. His blue eyes stared sightlessly at the ceiling and his hands gripped the arms of the sofa. He looked surprised and his white hair was dishevelled. Above his head, the word "AVO" had been painted on the wall in red paint. *Allami Vedelmi Osztaly*, the State Security Department, the brutal communist era secret service. Berta lay dead in the entrance to the room. Drips of paint had trickled down the wall. In front of Miklos' bare feet sat a pig's head on a plate, eyes staring blankly across the floor. The room was wrecked, bookshelves toppled over, books strewn across the floor, furniture overturned, vases smashed, pictures askew, drawers opened and tipped on the floor. A record revolved on a turntable, the needle clicking with each revolution.

Alex rushed to his grandfather. He touched the side of his neck. The skin was still warm. There was no pulse. Iron bands snapped around his chest. He could not breathe and began to hyperventilate. The pressure built inside until it burst. He lashed out with his foot, kicking the pig's head off the plate. It flew across the room, hit the wall and bounced back, rolling at his feet. Two glassy eyes stared up at him. Alex kicked the pig's head again, and it landed in a corner.

He inhaled steadily through his nose and told himself to keep calm as he carefully straightened Miklos' twisted hands. He closed

Miklos' eyes, and stroked his hair, smoothing it back into position. His fingers slid down the old man's cheeks, scraping against something sharp. He leaned forward, looking closer, and switched the nearby reading lamp on, shining the light straight onto Miklos. A strange blueish tinge to his face and lips.

Alex looked again at his hand. Tiny fragments of glass stuck to his fingertips. He bent down and sniffed his grandfather's mouth. A faint odour of bitter almonds. A window rattled and he jumped up. He looked around for something to use in self-defence and grabbed a large glass paperweight. His hands were sweaty and he almost dropped it as he went to check the other rooms. The bathroom, bedroom and kitchen were all empty, but one of the kitchen windows was open, rattling in the breeze. He closed the window and opened the kitchen cupboards: each was crammed with cans of meat, tinned vegetables and bottles of preserves, carefully arranged four lines deep. There was more than enough to feed a family for a month. The memory of ghetto privation never faded. Three large loaves of fresh bread sat on the kitchen table, far more than Miklos could eat before it went stale, together with six cartons of cigarettes.

Alex returned to the lounge. The repeating click of the revolving record sounded loud in the quiet of the room. He picked up the turntable arm from the record: a Hungarian singer from the 1960s singing "Happy Birthday", a favourite song from his childhood. He sat next to his grandfather, holding the gloves to his nose as the music filled the room. He tried to compose himself but his hands shook. A ball of grief and pain welled up inside him before it exploded. It felt like someone had pulled his insides out. The tears ran down his face as he sobbed for several minutes. He kissed his grandfather's cheek, stroked his hair, and went outside.

Erzsebet was still waiting on the landing. She looked aghast at his tear-stained face and dishevelled appearance. She moved toward the door, but Alex held his hand up, and shook his head as he called the police on his mobile telephone. Erzsebet pushed past him and into the flat. Her screams echoed through the building.

## THREE

Cassandra Orczy poured her first cup of green tea of the day and bit delicately into a crescent-shaped pastry stuffed with ground walnuts. It was 8.30am and the State Security Service headquarters on Falk Miksa Street was already filling up, the officers and secretaries pouring in. The communist era office block was five minutes walk from the Danube and Parliament Square, in the heart of the city's historic centre, but was one of the ugliest buildings in Budapest. Six stories of unadorned concrete loomed over the wide, tree-lined street, but there was no need for the repository of Hungary's murkiest secrets to look attractive. As chief of the Threat Assessment and Analysis Department, Orczy had her own spacious office, with a view of the river, furnished with Art Deco pieces from the nearby antique shops.

She brushed the crumbs from the pile of files on her desk. Each had a small white label in the top right hand corner. The top two were marked: Farkas, Miklos and Farkas, Alexander. The dossiers contained transcripts of telephone taps, snatched photographs, biographies, bank statements, work histories, medical records, the everyday details that make up a life. Miklos' file was four times as thick as Alex's. Orczy had ordered the records up from the registry as soon as she woke and heard the radio reports of Miklos' death. Her job was to assess potential threats to national security for the government, and recommend appropriate action. The violent death last night of Hungary's most famous dissident definitely came under her purview.

A wary, determined career-woman in her mid forties, Cassandra lived alone with a cat in a spacious Secessionist-era apartment overlooking Parliament. She was petite but curvaceous, her over-indulgence in fine food and wine concealed by French and Italian designer outfits. With her well-coiffured dark blond hair and blue-green eyes, she liked to think she looked like a young Catherine Deneuve, and was an avid reader of celebrity and Hollywood gossip magazines. But work was a deadly serious matter. Whether choosing which business suit to wear, or deliberating on matters of state security, her decisions were taken slowly and carefully. Which was one reason why she had steadily risen up the ladder of the security service, and her tea, flown in by diplomatic bag from the Hungarian embassy in Tokyo, was now served in a blue cup of fine Zsolnay porcelain. Others made do with the white. The gold-rimmed porcelain, she thought, was in sight, but still out of reach.

The Farkas files lay on top of a detailed report on the economic activities of two major German investors: KZX Industries and the Volkstern Corporation. KZX, Germany's largest industrial conglomerate, had already taken over Hungary's food processing industry and now was rapidly buying up much of the Hungarian pharmaceutical sector, a key part of the country's economy. The Volkstern Corporation, a media group that owned hundreds of newspapers, magazines and radio stations across eastern Europe, had purchased half a dozen regional private television stations in Hungary, which it wanted to turn into a new national channel. It had just launched a new national cell phone network, Magyar Mobile. Cassandra planned to recommend that the government block any further investments from KZX and the Volkstern Corporation, arguing that they were buying up so much of the economy and media that their activities were a threat to Hungary's national interests, even sovereignty. But this morning KZX and the Volkstern Corporation would have to wait.

In theory, Cassandra had instant access to whatever information she needed, either from her employer, which dealt with domestic national security issues; the foreign intelligence service which operated abroad, or the police. In practice, the police's response for information had recently been increasingly sluggish. There had always been a rivalry between the police and state security, but at least they cooperated. Now reports arrived late, or incomplete, sometimes not at all. Numerous senior police officers had transferred to the Gendarmerie, tempted by the salaries, more than double their previous wages, and a direct line to the Prime Minister's office, which made them virtually untouchable.

She opened Miklos' file and winced at the picture of his body, attached to a copy of the scene of crime report. This one at least was detailed and accurate. The District VII police chief was an old friend of hers, from their time together in the Communist Young Pioneers. The report told her some of what had happened, but not why. For what reason had an elderly, apparently harmless man been brutally killed and 'AVO' painted on the wall? Miklos Farkas had never even joined the Communist Party, let alone the secret police. Who was his grandson, and what was he doing here? Cassandra began reading.

Ten minutes walk away, in the *Budapest News* office on the Great Boulevard, Alex stood staring out of the window. The sky was still grey and dark, the passersby bundled up against the rain. The office looked out at the wrought iron façade of the Nyugati, western railway station. The Art Nouveau waiting room was now a McDonald's. Alex could see the commuters inside lining up for their take-away coffees. A tram trundled by, covered in election posters of Sanzlermann's grinning, chiselled features.

Alex picked a greasy Big Mac box off his chaotic desk and threw it into the nearby dustbin. Old press releases, back issues of the *International Herald Tribune* and *The Economist*, cold cups of coffee, half a banana and recent editions of *Magyar Tribün* and *Ébredjetek Magyarok!* all competed for space. The only tiny patch of order was around the three framed photographs in one corner: Alex holding hands with Miklos and Ruth; a formal portrait of his parents; and a blurry snapshot of Alex and a gang of foreign correspondents in the bar of the Holiday Inn Sarajevo, wearing flak jackets and helmets, bottles raised to their lips. He bit into the banana but couldn't swallow. Ronald Worthington, the editor, had called and told Alex not to come in for the rest of the week.

But he couldn't sleep and the last thing he wanted was to sit at home on his own. He felt very alone.

Alex's father, Edward, and mother, Caroline, had been killed in a car crash on the way home from a dinner party when Alex was eight. He had grown up in boarding schools, and was sent to Hungary every summer, to stay with Miklos and Ruth, where he had learnt fluent Hungarian. They were the only family he knew – both his parents were only children and his mother had been estranged from her family. He picked up the photograph of him with Miklos and Ruth. Summer at Lake Balaton. The lake shimmered turquoise in the heat, and yachts sailed past in the distance. Miklos held one of his hands, Ruth the other, as the three of them stood on the shore, squinting into the sun. He remembered the day very clearly: chocolate ice-cream and *langos*, a deep-fried Hungarian doughnut, greasy and delicious; the cool grass under his feet, the clean smell of the water, and his ninth birthday present, a red kite.

He wiped his eyes, put the picture down and switched on the television. CNN showed Russian tanks lumbering down a bomb-damaged street. Another former Soviet republic finding out the hard way that where Moscow was concerned, independence was just a word. Alex had never been there, but he did not need to witness the carnage to know its reality.

*The smell of cordite, and the way the buildings shake and tremble. Nothing feels permanent or solid. His second day in Sarajevo. On the surface he tries to be like the other reporters: nonchalant, cynical, but the fear twists inside him like a living thing. He has already seen three of his colleagues wounded: one shot in the face, another in the leg, a third covered with blood from glass splinters. He does not want to die here. He is walking up Martial Tito Street when a window shatters in the next building. As one the crowd rushes for the entrance of an apartment building. He flattens himself against the wall. The old lady sits in the middle of the street, moaning with fear. The bullet smacks into the tarmac, a few feet in front of her. Another shot, this time nearer. The sniper takes his time, playing, taking out the nearby windows one by one, raining glass on to the street, on to her. She wriggles and flails as each bullet comes a bit closer. The sound of the glass as it shattered and tinkled onto the pavement. The ripe, stale-sweat smell of the crowd. It was surprising how loudly an old lady could scream.*

He still remembered the headline: "Under Fire on the Streets of Sarajevo." It took up most of the front-page, complete with a photo by-line. He had watched and taken notes as two men had dashed out into the middle of the road to rescue the woman, while a soldier had opened fire on the sniper's position. He had travelled with her in the ambulance on the way to the hospital. She had not been hit, but died of shock.

Journalism had been an obvious career choice for someone who always felt an outsider, looking in. In Hungary, he missed Britain: its stability, moderation, and basic assumption of reasonableness. In Britain, he missed Hungary: its passionate, exuberant people, with their wild mood swings from elation to despair and back again. Studying History at the University of Manchester, he spent most of his time working on the student newspaper. He posed as an illegal immigrant and worked as a cleaner, and won a student journalism award for his exposé of the exploitation of migrant workers. That got him a coveted place on the *Daily Sentinel's* graduate trainee scheme. He quickly specialised in human interest articles. He instinctively knew how to listen, when to probe further and when to keep silent, teasing out often startling confidences.

Alex was twenty-three when he was first despatched in the early 1990s to Vukovar and Sarajevo for the *Daily Sentinel*, burning with righteous indignation to tell the world the human cost of war. Older hands scoffed that he was too young, but his despatches were vivid, capturing potent images: a Croat farmhouse abandoned in mid-meal, the soup still steaming on the kitchen table; a teenage Muslim fighter wide-eyed with shock after his best friend had been shot dead beside him; the charred remains of a Serb icon in a demolished Orthodox church. After Bosnia came Kosovo, Chechnya and Afghanistan. He learnt to draw out the details of a massacre from a single survivor or negotiate safe passage with the warlord whose men had carried it out, to memorise a scene of carnage with a single mental snapshot, to drive slaloming under fire. The countries changed but everything else remained the same: the envious looks from the home news reporters before he flew out, the fat wad of dollars in his money belt, the airplane to the nearest capital, briefings from aid organisations and diplomats, nights in dingy 'hotels' with no hot water or heating in a hamlet unmentioned on most maps, the frantic front-line couplings.

By the time he realised that the world didn't care about the horrors he chronicled, he was addicted. The rush kicked in at the S-shaped curve of mines, sandbags and tank traps that marked the start of no man's land. Then came the drive into the killing zone, the very air thick with menace, adrenalin pumping so hard his senses were on fire. He could taste the gun smoke curling skywards a kilometre away, hear the bullets sliding up into a Kalashnikov's barrel, see the soldiers crumple as the shells exploded. Getting in, and getting out with the story was the greatest high, better than sex. Part of him even came to love the stink of war: wood smoke and decay, cordite and sweat. Best of all was the camaraderie. No-one lived like they did. Anywhere that buildings burned and people were killing each other, he would find his friends and colleagues, half-crazy, passionate and generous, ready to share everything, from the notes of their interviews, to their final drop of whiskey. It almost felt like a family; especially at the funerals.

After the fourth, he stopped. He refused Iraq and asked for a transfer from the foreign department to the home news desk. He had taken six months sabbatical, spent most of it lazing on a small Greek island, before starting in Westminster as a political reporter. Once he would have relished being on the inside track to Parliament's intrigues. But the Byzantine, self-interested manoeuvrings left him cold, and his workaday reports reflected that. One afternoon he realised that he had spent three hours silently staring out of the office window at the River Thames. The managing editor had refused his resignation and called him in for a talk. The *Daily Sentinel* had just bought a newspaper in Hungary, the *Budapest*

*News*. The staff needed training and the paper needed a makeover. Alex's Hungarian background made him a natural choice for secondment. He offered Alex a year's contract on his London salary. Alex accepted. The work was easy, but what reason was there to stay now that his grandfather was dead?

His phone bleeped. An SMS: My deepest condolences. Come at four. M.

\* \* \*

Natasha Hatvani sat down at her desk, a cup of coffee in one hand, a large manila envelope in the other. She rested the coffee on top of a bulky report on money-laundering in eastern Europe, put the envelope aside, and checked her email. She immediately deleted six long missives, all from the same address, and added "nearsuicidal@webmail.com" to her blocked sender list. All six would now be bounced back, marked "address unknown". There was only one person on the blocked list, but he already had twenty-two email addresses. Every few days Gabor Urban opened another webmail account with a new pseudonym and continued his cyber bombardment. Changing her email address was pointless, as reporters' contact details were listed on the paper's website. She clicked on the spam filter button. A new window opened, entitled "block keywords". She quickly tapped in "heartbroken Hungarian", and "I beg you to come back". She sat back, sipped her coffee and ate half a chocolate bar she found next to her telephone. Any email containing those phrases would automatically bounce back. And nobody else was likely to be writing such declarations.

Natasha had started work at the *Budapest News* a year earlier as a receptionist, on the understanding that she would be considered for a reporter's job. She was first into the office at 9.00am, and last out, at 7.00pm or later. She never complained and her work was fast and accurate. Nor did she socialise at the paper's frequent parties, although lately she had become friendly with Kitty Kovacs, the advertising manager. Tall and slender, her bob of black hair framed luminous grey eyes, while angular cheekbones gave her the appearance of a Slavic Nefertiti, a legacy of her Russian grandfather. Fluent Russian and decent Slovak and Polish helped get her a trial as a researcher, working on an investigation into a Moscow mobster who had set up in Budapest. She proved talented at extracting information from both cops and *biznissmen*, none of whom took her seriously because of her looks, and revealed all kinds of information in the erroneous hope of first impressing, then bedding her. She was soon promoted.

Natasha checked the news websites. "Former dissident found dead at home: Murder suspected" announced *Magyar Tribün*, "Pig's head horror at home of dead ex-dissident" screamed the tabloids. She read the details of how Miklos' body had been found, and that the police had launched a murder investigation. She stood up, shocked and dismayed. Natasha remembered meeting Alex's grandfather once in the office, a courteous gentleman with an old-world charm. She picked up the envelope and walked over to Alex's room.

"I just heard. Alex, I'm so sorry. What happened?" She hesitated at the door.

"Thanks. I don't know exactly. I suppose the post-mortem will tell us," Alex said, feeling once again the glass granules under his fingers, seeing his grandfather motionless under the red letters spelling out AVO. He turned down the television and gestured for her to come in.

After Natasha was promoted Alex had taken her for a coffee. He had learned almost nothing about her personal life, except that she lived at home with her mother. Intrigued, he had invited her for lunch twice more. After two refusals he gave up and made sure to be as businesslike as she always was. The other reporters dressed in casual clothes, unless they had a major interview, but from her first day at work Natasha had always worn trouser suits. She only had two, Alex had noticed, one dark blue and the other black. Today's was the black, a well cut jacket, and slightly flared trousers. Its repairs were sewn skilfully enough to be almost invisible.

"Do you need anything, Alex? Can I help at all?" she asked, standing away from his desk.

Alex cleared a pile of newspapers off a nearby chair and gestured for her to sit down. She sat on the edge of the chair, her back straight and her knees together, as if waiting for instructions.

"Thanks, I'm managing," Alex said. After several seconds of awkward silence, Alex asked: "What's in the envelope?"

She reached inside and unfolded a sheet of A3 paper. An election poster showed Attila Hunkalffy, leader of the Hungarian National Front, and Frank Sanzlermann standing together, staring resolutely forward. A slogan proclaimed: "Family, Work, Unity." She handed it to Alex.

He leaned forward and looked at Natasha. "How did you get this?"

"You told me to develop contacts. So I did."

"Well done. This is a story," said Alex, sitting back in his chair. Focus, he thought, perhaps work could dull the pain. So Sanzlermann would be campaigning with Attila Hunkalffy. Where did that leave Csintori? Out of a job soon, probably. Istvan Kiraly had kept that quiet. Hunkalffy was an ardent nationalist, a handsome, charismatic professor of Hungarian poetry in his early fifties, scion of a famous literary family. His ponytail of long black hair, now streaked with grey, was the only reminder of his bohemian past. Hunkalffy had personally introduced the parliamentary vote of no-confidence that almost brought down the government. Several of Csintori's MPs had already defected to his party, including the powerful Interior Minister.

Alex continued: "We need to get this up on the website immediately. Ask the art department to scan it. I need a 500 word news story, and then the same length analysis of what this means for Csintori's government. This afternoon please, news first."

"Yes, the government is finished. You will have them both by lunchtime," said Natasha. She turned and looked at the chaos on the television. An elderly lady sat on the ground, her legs splayed, blood seeping through her white hair. She held her hand to her head and rocked back and forth, pushing away a soldier trying to help her get up. "What are you watching?"

"The Russian air force strafing civilians, somewhere in the Caucasus."

Natasha bristled. "Russians pilots don't kill innocent people."

"Maybe not on purpose, but they don't care if they do. Did you see Grozny after the Russians' retook it?"

Natasha shook her head. "I did," said Alex. "What was left of it."

"My grandfather was a Soviet fighter pilot in the Second World War," Natasha replied, her voice tight. "He shot down eleven German fighter planes. The rebels must be using innocent people as cover. They always do."

"Maybe they are. But Russia is a state. It should observe the rules of war."

Natasha laughed derisively. "What rules? The Germans shot down my grandfather and sent him to Dachau. He left a wife and three young children, including my mother. They never saw him again. At least you had some time with your grandfather. There are no rules, Alex. Don't you know that by now?" She picked up the election poster and walked out.

\* \* \*

Café Casablanca was a dark hideaway on Akacfa Street, about ten metres long and half as wide, jammed between a shop selling 'second-hand' mobile telephones, digital cameras and laptops, and a locked-up garage. A badly-lit restaurant nearby offered a cheap lunch of soup and noodles. No foreign property developers had yet ventured to this part of District VII, which bordered neighbouring District VIII, the Gypsy quarter. The buildings were still gouged with shell and bullet holes from fighting during the siege in 1944, their stucco façades peeling off. A homeless man, his thin, undernourished face encrusted with dirt, lay fast asleep on a bench, hugging a plastic shopping bag with his meagre belongings.

Alex stepped inside the half-empty café. It fell silent, as though a switch had been turned. A clutch of dark-looking men in leather jackets hunched over packets of cigarettes and mobile telephones turned to look at him. The barmaid stared, unsmiling. The air was thick with tobacco smoke, and an Arabic chanteuse crooned in the background. A heavy set man with a shaved head raised his hand in greeting. The room seemed to breathe again, and the conversations restarted. Alex smiled at the barmaid and ordered a coffee. She filled a brass pot with water, spooned in some finely-ground Turkish coffee and put it on to boil. The rich, burnt aroma filled the room. The café's owner appeared as the thick mix bubbled up.

"Alex, my friend. Come, sit down," he said, leading Alex to the back of the room.

Mubarak Fonseca was a half-Palestinian, half Cuban leftover from Hungary's communist era. His father and mother were engineering students, who had met and fallen in love at Budapest University in the 1960s, when Hungary was carrying out its fraternal internationalist duty, educating students from the developing world. His parents had long since divorced, and gone home, but Mubarak had stayed. He had inherited coffee-coloured skin from his father, dark curly hair from his mother and engaging brown eyes from both. Someone along the line of ancestral Palestinians and Cubans had passed him down a business sense as sharp as his dress sense was atrocious. He was wearing pink flared trousers, a tight black shirt, and a maroon velvet jacket.

Mubarak was also a former national karate champion, which had proved useful in his struggle to remain king of Budapest's black market money changers. Mubarak's rate was always better than any bank. He never short-changed his customers and always paid off the police on time, which was why they let him stay open. Even the Russians used him, once a peace agreement was drawn up after an unsuccessful attempt to muscle in that ended in several of their foot soldiers returning to Moscow for lengthy periods of convalescence. Very little of significance took place within Hungary's black economy, and its darker criminal offshoots, without Mubarak's knowledge. The two men sat down at a corner table.

"Alex, firstly my sincere condolences on the death of your grandfather," said Mubarak. The barmaid brought a plate of pistachios and coffee in tiny cups. "It is a terrible tragedy."

"Thank you," said Alex. He took out his mobile telephone and showed that he was removing the battery. Mubarak followed suit, and reached into the plate of nuts. He cracked one open with his teeth and dropped the shell into the ashtray. He was an addict and usually ate a bag a day.

"I had us swept for bugs yesterday," he said, gesturing at the ceiling. "But soon they will find a way to listen to us, even without the battery in, you know."

"Perhaps they already have."

"You know, you are probably right," said Mubarak, shaking his head wearily at the difficult ways of the world. They chatted for a while, exchanging pleasantries, as ritual demanded.

"You said you may have some news for me," said Alex, sipping his coffee.

Mubarak sat up straight, scooping up a handful of pistachios. "I hear things, that money is moving. A lot of money, coming from the west. From Austria, and from Germany especially. Old friends, coming home to where they always felt comfortable, bringing lots of old money, money that nobody even knew they had. Hungary is a democracy now, of course. But still a young one, impressionable. Like a teenager, easily swayed by fast cars and rolls of money. Follow the money trail, my friend," he said, offering the plate of pistachios to Alex.

Alex took several. "If you know something about my grandfather's death . . ."

"Nothing concrete, just my intuition. Something is happening. I just wonder if it is connected," Mubarak said, rubbing his thumb and forefinger together and crinkling his nostrils. "I know I am a black marketeer, but people need euros and dollars. They don't want to fill in lots of forms and papers. Who knows on what desk they will land? My rates are reasonable, generous even. And I hand over real money, not rolls of Yugoslav dinars or toilet paper. Of course, the authorities know about me. We have a modus vivendi. I meet a social need. Like George Soros, I am a capitalist building a free market society."

"And you bribe people," said Alex, amused at Mubarak's remodelling of himself as a social philanthropist.

"Well, yes – that as well. But recently my contacts, those who permit me to operate for a percentage, have become so greedy. These people do not think for the future, only what they can get immediately. My margins are terrible. The Socialists were cleverer. They had a long-term view. All those five-year plans give you a perspective. Maybe I will relocate to Cuba. Listen to Buena Vista Social Club, drink rum and smoke cigars with Fidel. They are still communists there, they need dollars."

Mubarak leaned back, lit a cigarette and blew a plume of smoke at the ceiling. He laid his hand on Alex's arm and his voice turned serious. "Be careful, my friend."

## FOUR

Peter Feher knew he looked his age. He walked with a stoop and his skin sagged on his bones, as though he had been wrapped in a casing of soft parchment one size too large. His face was pale, and thin white hair lay in carefully-combed strands over his pink scalp. His huge beak of a nose seemed to precede him by several seconds. Over-exertion triggered a watery rattle in his chest. But his pale blue eyes missed nothing, and the years had not dulled his lawyer's brain. He scanned the rows of black-clad, sombre-faced mourners, crowded around the grave at Budapest's Jewish cemetery. The turn-out was impressive: MPs from all the mainstream parties, former dissidents who had landed comfortable posts teaching at the Central European University, the theatre crowd, and numerous journalists, some come to pay their respects, others to report. Even Csintori's Minister of Culture had turned up. Miklos, you would be proud, Feher thought.

The cemetery was near Budapest's Keleti, the city's eastern station. The clatter of the carriages as they trundled along the railway lines, north towards Poland, was a faint murmur in the funeral's background, carrying over the Rabbi's prayers as he recited the *Kaddish*, the prayer for the dead. The Rabbi was young and confident, with a clear baritone voice. Feher joined in, carefully reciting the Aramaic words with which Jews have mourned their dead for thousands of years.

"*Yisgadal, veyiskadash, shemey rabo*, May his illustrious name become great and holy," he intoned, and the liturgy still came easily to him. Eight-two years on this earth and how long before it's my turn, he mused. He watched the Rabbi hand Alex the shovel. Alex

40

took it firmly in his hand. He dug it hard into a pile of earth, before lifting it over the grave and dropping the soil over the coffin. It landed with a quiet thump, spilling over the sides. Alex wiped his eyes. Others followed, until it was Feher's turn. One by one the mourners thanked the Rabbi, and filed out of the cemetery. Alex and Feher were the last to leave. They stood together by the grave for several minutes, each lost in their own thoughts, and walked back together into the clamour of the lunchtime city. Alex shook Feher's hand and said goodbye.

"Alex, no, surely you're not leaving already," Feher protested. "What's the hurry? Come and take a coffee, perhaps even something stronger. Of course, if you have the time," he said, hailing a taxi which stopped a few metres away. Alex followed him to the car.

\* \* \*

The Margaret Patisserie stood at the bottom of St Stephen's Boulevard, near the Danube. Named after the nearby bridge, it offered not just drinks and snacks, but time travel back to the socialist era. Ranks of brightly coloured cakes were displayed in glass cases, all topped with artificial cream, a brilliant, impossible white. The coffee was thick and tepid, a burst of high-calibre caffeine, fired out of an ancient steam-driven contraption into short, stumpy glasses. Blowsy waitresses smoked listlessly at the counter, between flirtatious strolls among the cheap wooden tables and their mismatched chairs. The walls were brown wood, stained with decades worth of nicotine, and the floor a worn linoleum. It was a glorious dinosaur and would probably be a hamburger restaurant within six months.

They sat at a corner table. Feher smiled at a waitress with a black beehive hairdo that seemed to defy gravity. She quickly brought a tray of coffees and glasses of sticky Hungarian brandy, together with a plate piled high with chocolate cake and apple strudels.

"These are on the house. He was a regular here, and we'll miss him," the waitress said. Alex and Feher chatted for a while about the funeral. Feher turned his attention to the cakes. Alex tried not to stare as Feher wielded his fork with rapid precision, eating silently with a look of intense concentration. Two pieces of chocolate cake and a slice of apple strudel disappeared in a few minutes. Alex looked up to see an elderly man with thick horn-rimmed glasses wearing a threadbare army greatcoat approach their table. He clutched a bundle of different newspapers, some so fresh that Alex could smell the ink.

Feher put his fork down and greeted the newspaper vendor. "My old friend Eduard Szigeti. Good day to you."

Alex stood up, shook hands and introduced himself, surname first, in the Hungarian manner.

"Farkas. A relative?" asked Eduard.

"He was my grandfather," said Alex.

"My condolences. I just saw the funeral on television. A fine turn-out."

"What's this?" asked Feher, waving at the papers.

"Special edition. *Magyar Tribün* Friday lunchtime extra. Eight pages. Tibor Csintori is no more. Parliament is in emergency session, arguing about how to form a new government. And I've got all the others, if you're interested."

Alex's hunch had been correct. "Csintori's resigned?" he asked.

Szigeti looked amused. "In a manner of speaking. He keeled over in Parliament in the middle of a speech about the European presidential election. He's dead. A heart attack, they say."

"A heart attack?" asked Alex, amazed. "He was forty-six."

Szigeti tapped the newspapers. "Are you buying, or you want all the news for free?"

Feher bought two copies of the special edition of *Magyar Tribün* and asked for that day's *Ébredjetek Magyarok!*. Szigeti raised his eyebrows but handed both newspapers over. Feher handed one of the special editions to Alex. It was full of long think pieces about what Csintori's death meant for the future of Hungary, several of which referred to Natasha's article on the *Budapest News* website about Hunkalffy and Sanzlermann. There was silence for several minutes as they both read. Feher looked thoughtful.

"He was a Professor of Cultural Aesthetics, you know," he said, sipping from his coffee.

"I thought he was a sociologist," said Alex, puzzled.

"Szigeti, not Csintori. He taught for forty years at Budapest University. They sacked him last month with two hours notice to clear his office. His replacement is teaching a new course on 'The Lifetime Achievements of Admiral Horthy.' Apparently, he had no choice but to ally with Hitler and hand over half a million Jews in six weeks. Well, it's one point of view," he said, dryly. "As for Csintori, he had no history of heart trouble, did not smoke and had an excellent ECG reading from his last medical . . ."

"How do you know?" asked Alex, looking anew at the elderly lawyer.

"I hear things." Feher took a cigarette from a packet made of cheap white paper. The label showed a cogwheel, and the Hungarian word *Munkas*, worker. A leftover from the days before advertisements and fast-food. Alex noticed a long smear of blue ink on the arm of Feher's white shirt, near his wrist, as he lit up. He realised the stain was not on the fabric, but on Feher's forearm. He tried not to stare, but like a roadside car crash, the tattooed numbers drew his eye with an irresistible force.

Feher saw Alex looking at his arm. He inhaled and blew out a cloud of pungent grey fumes. He offered the packet to Alex. "The train journey was indescribable. It took two days. When I arrived they asked me what my profession was. I was a law student. But I could see they didn't need lawyers there. I told them I was a metal worker. At home I was always in charge of getting the house and office keys copied for my father. Perhaps that qualified me. It was enough. I turned right, my parents and my sister went left," he said. He raised his coffee cup to his mouth. It rattled against his teeth. "But I'm still here," he said, smiling as he put his cup down.

Alex did not know what to say. He accepted a cigarette, lit up and breathed in. Something punched him in the throat. Coughing and spluttering, he put the cigarette down. The waitress, laughing, brought him a glass of water, which he sipped gratefully, and tried to sound composed.

"Who do you think killed my grandfather, Peter?" he asked.

Feher shrugged. "I suppose the post-mortem will tell us what he died of. A heart attack perhaps, after being beaten by skinheads who had broken into his flat, according to the speculation in today's newspapers."

"Do you believe that?" asked Alex.

"No. Do you?"

"There was a pig's head in the room, and someone had painted AVO on the wall in red paint," said Alex, trying not to think of the scene he had discovered. "But he wasn't in the AVO. He hated communism. The Soviets took his house, his factory, everything the family had. AVO officers arrested him after 1956. They put him in prison."

"And the Soviets liberated him and tens of thousands of other Jews from the ghetto. You should also remember *that*," Feher said archly, the smoke drifting from his nostrils. "But you are right, mistakes were made. That was another world. The point is, Alex, that your grandfather was a fine man, a brave man. Clearly someone doesn't want him to be remembered like that."

Alex nodded.

"So what better way to destroy his reputation than to accuse him of being a snitch for the communist secret police? There are still people here who think all Jews were communists, and even if they were dissidents they must have secretly been communist spies." Feher opened *Ébredjetek Magyarok!*. "Look. It's started already," he said, pointing to a banner headline: "Miklos Farkas: Dissident or Secret AVO Agent?", above a long article by Balazs Noludi, the newspaper's editor.

Alex glanced at the turgid prose, a skilful cocktail of lies, smears and distorted quotations from Miklos' samizdat publications. He shook his head wearily. "Unbelievable." He paused. "Peter, were you a communist?" he asked, carefully.

"Yes, I was, for a while. The Red Army liberated me from Auschwitz. They fed me and brought me home. It seemed completely natural. We thought we were building a new world then. I argued about it all the time with Miklos. He was right, I was wrong. I left the party after 1956. Tell me, how many members do you think the Hungarian Communist Party had in 1989?"

"I don't know."

"Eight hundred thousand. That's a lot of party cards in a country of ten million people. This was the softest regime in the Soviet bloc, and they still clamoured to sign up." He flicked through *Ébredjetek Magyarok!*. "Our friend Balazs Noludi was party secretary in his home village. Poor Balazs, he is a quite sad story."

"Why?"

"He is a Hungarian from a village in northern Serbia. He wrote a novel about countryside life. It was very promising, full of poignant vignettes and good characters: a lonely farmer in love with the village shopkeeper, a mayor whose brother was executed after 1956 who was forced to join the Communist Party, even a Holocaust survivor who was the last Jew in the village."

"And what happened?"

"He moved to Budapest when the war in Yugoslavia started. He thought he would be invited into the literary elite. But those clever urban liberals ripped his book to pieces. They laughed at the countryside boy with his funny accent. And now he takes his revenge."

Feher paused and seemed to take some kind of decision. He looked around the room, and moved closer. Alex could smell the cognac on his breath. "He doesn't matter. This does. In 1944, your grandfather worked as a waiter at the Savoy, with false papers. We had some friends then, not so many, but some. Waiters are invisible, but he watched, and he listened."

"What did he hear?" asked Alex.

"All through the autumn of 1944, many German and Swiss businessmen appeared at the Savoy. They would stay one or two days, and have long meetings with the Nazis. Then in December the Russians sealed off the city, and nobody could get in or out anymore."

"What kind of German and Swiss businessmen?" asked Alex.

"The same companies that ran on slave labour then and still control the German economy now, and the Zurich bankers that laundered their blood money. Do you know that the next President of the Federal Monetary Authority will be German? He or she will be able to control the monetary policy of every country in the euro-zone."

"Yes. But what did Miklos tell you about these meetings?"

"Just that they happened. He wasn't invited to attend. I worked for the Germans during the war. The conditions were very poor. Most of my co-workers died. The government wrote to me a few years ago, to give me what they called 'compensation'. One thousand deutschmarks. I tore up the cheque and sent it back."

Feher's voice was hard, edged with anger. His hands shook as he lit another cigarette. "Miklos did not die by accident."

Alex replied: "There were tiny fragments of glass around Miklos' mouth. He looked almost blue. I smelt bitter almonds. If he died of a heart attack it was induced."

"Yes, I know," replied Feher. "The question is, did he decide himself to bite the cyanide capsule, or did someone help him?"

Alex started with surprise. "Is there anything you don't know?"

"Yes. Why this happened now," said Feher. He looked hard at Alex. "Go to work."

\* \* \*

Alex stood for a long while that evening on his balcony, staring out at the night-time city. The Hotel Savoy had recently been renovated, and its Art Nouveau façade was softly illuminated. He watched the excited tourists climbing out of their taxis while uniformed porters picked up their baggage, and doormen helped them inside. The Elizabeth Bridge arched gracefully over the waters, casting a golden glow over the Danube. A boat floated by full of tourists on a night-river cruise. He could see the revellers, distant figures eating, drinking, and dancing. He opened a bottle of red wine, and a book of poems by Miklós Radnóti, a Jewish poet who had died in Serbia in 1944, shot by his Hungarian guards. His body was later exhumed, his last verses found hidden in his coat. His early work was full of joy and light but Alex turned to the end, verses full of death and anguish. Fifty years later, nothing had changed in the Balkans. Alex saw a Muslim home in a remote Bosnian village. It was seared into his brain.

*The orthodox cross is daubed on the white wall of the kitchen, a Cyrillic letter 'S' in each corner. The letters are an acronym: 'Only Unity Can Save the Serbs,' the slogan for Greater Serbia. The whole family is dead: grandmother, grandfather and their daughter where they sat. The old man had thrown himself across his womenfolk in a vain attempt to protect them. The young woman's husband lies outside, twisted in the dirt, still holding his green prayer beads. Blood seeps from his head. A chicken pecks the ground near his corpse. The little girl is hiding in the barn. Alex covers her eyes as he leads her to the car. She says nothing on the journey into Sarajevo. Even when a bullet pings off the car roof, she just rocks back and forth.*

Alex gulped some more wine and switched the television on. The newsreader on CNN announced that a German bank had proposed several senior executives as candidates for the next President of the Federal Monetary Authority. The bank's press officer stood outside its headquarters. "Our bank is one of the motors of European unity. We believe our personnel can contribute so much more to European financial stability and continent-wide economic integration," she proclaimed, before being ushered into a Mercedes.

Alex switched to Hungarian television news. A red-faced, male middle-aged newsreader wearing a black armband was speaking. "The Hungarian Parliament has just voted to form a new government." Alex sat up straight and turned up the volume. The newsreader continued: "Attila Hunkalffy, President of the Hungarian National Front, will be Prime Minister of a minority government, in coalition with the Hungarian People's Party, of the late Prime Minister Tibor Csintori. Despite the fact that almost half of the People's Party MPs announced that they will refuse to serve under him, Mr Hunkalffy said he was confident that he would be able to form a cabinet. Opposition Social Democrat and Free

Liberal MPs condemned the parliamentary announcement as 'a stealth coup', and walked out of the chamber. Interior Minister and National Front MP Csaba Zirta, who served as Interior Minister under Tibor Csintori, will remain in his post, Prime Minister Hunkalffy has already announced."

The broadcast switched to Parliament where Attila Hunkalffy was standing on the steps of the sprawling neo-Gothic building, dressed in his trademark leather jacket, flanked by two stone lions, several bodyguards and a clutch of aides holding Hungarian flags, and the blue European Union flag, with its fifteen yellow stars. "The death of Tibor Csintori was a national tragedy. But I am honoured to have been chosen to lead my country at this vital time, when the eyes of all Europe are upon us, in the coming election for European President," intoned Hunkalffy.

The newsreader continued, "We'll be returning to that story as we receive more information. Also today, does Hungary need a new self-defence force to defend its national values? We have an exclusive interview with Istvan Matonhely, the leader of the controversial Pannonia Brigade."

The screen showed a small village, where Matonhely and several dozen followers stood under a large Hungarian flag, waving placards demanding "No More Gypsy Crime" and "Send the Roma to Work". A line of police on the other side of the street held back twenty or so Gypsies, who were shouting abuse at Matonhely and his followers. The Pannonia Brigade wore the traditional Hussars' uniform of black brocaded jacket and riding trousers. Behind the Pannonia Brigade dozens of bikers wearing black leather and German army helmets roared up and down the village main street.

"Please tell us what the Pannonia Brigade stands for, Mr Matonhely, and why it's needed," asked the reporter, respectfully. Aniko Kovacs was state television's star reporter, a pretty blonde from a village on the Ukranian border, who made no secret of her nationalist leanings.

Matonhely, a thin man in his early thirties, was a former Liberal MP. He was dressed in a well cut black suit, a white shirt with a cutaway collar and a striped silk tie in red, white and green. His black hair was neatly styled and he looked like a successful banker. He leaned forward, his voice calm and reasonable. "Pannonia was the ancient name for Hungary. We want a return to those proud Magyar traditions, not the mess we have now. We aren't against all Gypsies, only those who commit crimes and live off our taxes. We stand for common values, shared by everybody: work, family, discipline and respect for our culture and heritage. I go to work every day. So should the Roma."

Aniko nodded enthusiastically as he spoke. "Yes, the Gypsy question is certainly very difficult," she said, as the screen switched to stock footage of Romany children playing barefoot in a village street and a woman in a bright floral headscarf begging on the Great Boulevard. Aniko turned to the camera. "Something certainly needs to be done about Hungary's biggest social problem, and many people believe Istvan Matonhely has the best answer."

Alex's mobile telephone rang. "Can you believe this?" an indignant Welsh voice demanded. "Is this a news report or a recruitment advertisement?"

"Both, I think," said Alex, laughing. David Jones, Reuters Budapest bureau chief, was Alex's drinking partner. A veteran reporter with curly red hair and sharp blue eyes, David managed to retain a dry wit, even under fire in Bosnia, where they had first met. They had worked together in war-zones around the world, until Jones' wife had threatened him with divorce and he had finally asked for a quieter posting. "Thanks for your letter, David. It's a long time since someone bothered to write to me with a pen and paper," Alex continued. The Reuters journalist had written Alex a hand-written note, expressing his condolences at Miklos' death.

"You're welcome. Some things aren't for email. Anyway – Aniko is a dangerous little minx. She'll do anything to get information for Balazs Noludi. I'd love to listen to their pillow talk."

"Pillow talk?" asked Alex, looking askance at the telephone.

"You are out of the loop, aren't you? Hungarian TV's star reporter is the girlfriend of the editor of *Ébredjetek Magyarok!* And now their friends are in power and have the whole country to play with."

"How are they going to hold a government together, when they only have 185 out of 400 seats? They could get voted down at any moment," said Alex.

"Think . . . Csaba Zirta."

"I see a short fat man with a big moustache who boasts that he has never been abroad. And?"

"Zirta is now a member of Hunkalffy's party, and has been Interior Minister for six months. That's six long, leisurely months to take out each MP's file, and read all about sticky fingers in European Union pies; long-legged secretaries flown to Strasbourg and Brussels for the weekend on business-class tickets at public expense; not to mention the secret portfolios of shares and government bonds secreted away in Switzerland and the Cayman Islands."

"He's going to blackmail them," said Alex.

David sighed down the line. "Bingo. Pour yourself another drink. And I owe you one for the heads-up on the Hunkalffy-Sanzlermann poster story. We beat Bloomberg and Associated Press by more than half an hour." Alex had called David as soon as Natasha had filed her stories to let him know they were going up on the website and emailed him the scan of the poster.

"So when are we going running?" asked David. He was a marathon runner, whose idea of a quick jog was three laps of Margaret Island, a total of sixteen kilometres. Alex often tagged along, usually retreating after one lap.

"When ever you like. One lunchtime next week?"

"Sure. I'll call you." His telephone bleeped with another incoming call. He looked at the screen: Zsofi. "Gotta go," he said to David, and pressed the answer button.

Zsofi spoke: "Dearest Alex, can you forgive me? I so wanted to be with you today."

Relief and annoyance competed. Still he smiled, despite himself.

"Where are you?" he asked.

"Standing outside your flat. Your doorbell's broken. Are you going to let me in?"

He opened the door. She strode inside and handed him a large bouquet of yellow roses.

"Darling," she said, as she took off her coat, and hugged him. "I'm so sorry about Miklos. I know how close you were. But I can't stay long. I'm taking the dawn train to Vienna tomorrow. I'm auditioning at the state Opera House for Juliet."

"Congratulations." He willed himself not to ask if Karoly was going too. Zsofi nuzzled his ear. He kissed her lightly on the cheek. She responded eagerly, her tongue darting into his mouth.

Alex sat back. "I thought you couldn't stay long," he said.

"I can't," she said, running her hand up his thigh.

He sipped his wine and took her hand off his leg. "Zsofi, I've been thinking. I don't think this is what I need right now, sharing you with someone else."

"Is that an ultimatum? You know the rules. We agreed: no questions, no demands, no breakfasts. You know my situation is very complicated. We always have fun together don't we?"

"Yes. We do." But on days like these, he thought, when you didn't feel like 'fun', what else was there between them?

She sensed the change in his mood. They sat silently for several minutes, and she held his hand. "I'm sorry, I just thought you might need some tender loving care."

"It's OK, really," said Alex.

Zsofi picked up the book of Radnoti poems and recited in a clear, musical voice.

"That's my favourite, 'Whistle in the wind'," he said.

She smiled at him. "And the last line is?"

"Oh, I love you," said Alex.

"Well, then." Zsofi kissed him chastely on both cheeks and walked to the door. "I'll phone you tomorrow from Vienna."

His landline rang as Alex sat down. "Zsofi? Is that you? Did you forget something?"

Silence. "Hallo, *Jó estét*, good evening," Alex said. He clicked the receiver on and off. A hum of static, and a crackle. He pressed the handset closer to his ear. A familiar tune sounded. He slammed the receiver down, his hand shaking, a Hungarian version of "Happy Birthday" echoing in his ears.

## FIVE

Cassandra Orczy looked at her watch: 2.30pm. Her appointment was at 2.00pm, and she had been sitting on an antique chair in a wood-panelled corridor in Parliament for thirty-five minutes. What a way to spend Saturday afternoon, she thought, although in truth her diary was not exactly bursting with social invitations. Still, she had heard that Prime Minister Hunkalffy had already kept the American ambassador, a close personal friend of the U.S President, dangling for forty-six minutes that morning, so Cassandra was in good company. At least the ambassador probably got a cup of coffee.

She picked up that day's issue of *Ébredjetek Magyarok!* from a nearby table. The front page proclaimed: "National Salvation: Hunkalffy Takes Power." The usual toxic mix, she thought and put the newspaper down. She took out the new edition of *Grazia* magazine from her handbag, keeping one eye on Hunkalffy's door as she flicked through the paparazzi shots. One of his flunkies walked by, giving her a disdainful glance. Hunkalffy's camp loathed the security service as a nest of communists. But she was still at work. It had immediately been made clear to Hunkalffy that any attempt at a wholesale purge would result in the release of information currently held in the pages of his own file in the basement registry. So the balance of forces in Hungarian power politics was maintained, for the moment at least.

"He will see you now," said a gangly youth, ushering her into a room bigger than most Budapest apartments.

Attila Hunkalffy stood at the window, looking out over the Danube, his trademark ponytail of long black hair resting on his shoulders. He stood close to a tall, athletic-looking man. They both turned round as Orczy entered the room.

Hunkalffy bade her a cursory good afternoon. He was dressed in a black suit and white shirt, without a tie. His dark eyes and olive skin exerted a hypnotic power, like a panther in a cage. He looked like an Italian film star, she thought. A fine black down covered the back of his hands. Frank Sanzlermann was dressed for the weekend in jeans and a light blue designer polo shirt that set off his sun-tan. He made himself comfortable on a nearby leather sofa and poured himself a brandy from a crystal decanter. He offered the drink to Hunkalffy. Hunkalffy shook his head, and sat down behind his desk.

"I'll speak English, so Herr Sanzlermann can understand us. Now this memo, Miss Orczy, about the supposed 'threats' to our pharmaceutical industry and media," said Hunkalffy.

Cassandra sat upright. "Prime Minister, I must protest. Herr Sanzlermann does not have clearance, and he is also a foreign national. These are matters of national security. As an experienced statesman himself, I am sure he will understand," she said in English, her voice emollient as she turned towards him.

Hunkalffy shook his head. "Herr Sanzlermann is an old and trusted friend. We see eye to eye on many, even most issues."

"I am sure you do. Nonetheless, I repeat these are classified matters. I must ask that Herr Sanzlermann leave the room."

"You were not so fussy about foreign nationals when you were a student in Moscow, studying under the KGB at the Dzerzhinsky Institute," sneered Hunkalffy.

"I was sent to Moscow by the Hungarian security service. I served, and continue to serve my country. You didn't complain twenty years ago when my predecessors smuggled you over the border into Romania after Ceausescu announced that all Hungarian villages in Transylvania were to be turned into concrete agro-complexes. We took you in, dodged the *Securitate*, brought you out, and then introduced you to our contacts in the west. You even met Prince Charles. All of which established your reputation as a valiant fighter against communism. I am sure you agree, Prime

Minister, we are all patriots in our own ways."

Hunkalffy remained silent, although his eyes glittered.

Still angry at the implication she was a traitor, she plunged on, unable to stop herself. She examined a mother of pearl button in her blouse as she spoke. "Your uncle was a veteran member of the party in your home town of Gyor, was he not? He joined in 1957. I believe he even once stood for a post on the Party's Central Committee."

Sanzlermann listened to the exchange with growing interest, gently stroking his left hand. "Really, Attila, I didn't know that your relatives were communists."

Hunkalffy forced his face into a smile. "Ach, every family has its black sheep. Frank, let us meet later. As you see I have things to arrange."

"That was perhaps not very wise of you, Miss Orczy," said Hunkalffy, switching back to Hungarian after Sanzlermann had left. "But not as much of a mistake as this report of yours that arrived on my desk last night."

Hunkalffy leafed through the pages stamped "Secret". "Are you seriously suggesting that KZX Industries and the Volkstern Corporation represent a threat to our national interests?"

"Yes, Prime Minister, that is exactly what I am saying. We believe that under cover of the economic liberalisation that followed our accession to the European Union, neighbouring countries, especially Germany and Austria, are attempting to take control of our drugs manufacturers, and our print and broadcast media. You will see that we have found evidence of telephone and email intercepts, as well as surveillance by operatives of unknown origin."

Hunkalffy sat back, picked up a pencil and chewed its end. "Miss Orczy. Please, look at a map. We are a small country, we need foreign capital. Germany and Austria are our neighbours, our historic friends. The European Union has brought peace and security here, for the first time in our history. The borders are open. People can say whatever they like, travel wherever they like. There are no more tanks in the street, no more torturers in the basements. Nobody knocks on our doors in the middle of the night any more.

Do you miss that? I don't. Or perhaps you would prefer your friends in Moscow to buy up the country."

"And what friends are they?" she demanded.

Hunkalffy sat back. He put her memo aside, and opened a drawer. He took out several photographs, and placed them face down in front of him on the wide antique table. He turned over the first and handed it to her. She was driving a red open-top two-seater sports car.

"Mazda RX-7. Sporty, fast, compact, easy to park," he said.

She nodded. His eyes drew her in. "And?"

"A present, wasn't it?" he asked.

She blushed. "It's not a crime for a woman to receive a gift."

"No, it is not. We have not yet lost our politesse. Women are honoured and respected. Treated with courtesy, given flowers on their birthday and their saints' days. But what if this car was less of a gift than an exchange, for something equally valuable," he said, passing her the second photograph. "Such as information."

A well-groomed man in his early forties, with a wide Slavic face, smiled ironically at the camera.

"Your classmate at Moscow University," said Hunkalffy. "Formerly regional director of a Soviet oil company. Now chairman of a new Moscow firm, which last year took a significant minority stake in the Hungarian state oil company. After several rival bidders dropped out at the last moment. A week later Miss Cassandra Orczy was driving her new Mazda RX-7 down Andrassy Avenue. The state oil company, you will agree, is one of our *most* important national assets."

"That deal was completely transparent and above board," she replied, her voice agitated. "Everything was public. Parliament raised no objections."

"No, it did not. Hungarians are realists, first of all. Russia supplies most of our oil and gas. But I'm still interested in your car. Considering your salary you live very well. You drive a sports car, and have no mortgages on your flat, or your other properties, do you?" Hunkalffy asked.

Cassandra looked away.

Hunkalffy picked up the framed photograph on his desk. It was an old-fashioned formal portrait of a young man in his best suit. He turned the picture round so that she could see it. He looked like a younger version of Hunkalffy, with shorter hair. "Do you know who this is?"

Cassandra shook her head.

"You mentioned my uncle, so I'll tell you more of my family history. This is my father, Jozsef Hunkalffy. When he was seventeen, he was a street fighter in the 1956 revolution. His first and only girlfriend, my mother, tried to make him to flee to the west. He refused. The AVO arrested him soon after. He was sentenced to be hanged, but the sentence was postponed," Hunkalffy continued, still holding the photograph. "They told him in prison that his girlfriend was pregnant, but refused to let her visit. One day my mother received a letter saying she had permission, as it was his eighteenth birthday. She was overjoyed. When she arrived they told her my father had been hanged that morning. Just half an hour earlier. They let her see his body. It was still warm. So she had her visit. She was pregnant with me." His hand shook as he put the picture down.

Hunkalffy took a sip of brandy, and turned over the last photograph: a double-winged ochre-coloured Art Nouveau villa on the shore of Lake Balaton, set in landscaped gardens.

"Beautiful, isn't it?" he said, picking up the picture. "Built in 1885. After 1948, the holiday home of the steel workers. Twenty rooms, with views of the lake, a swimming pool and an orchard of cherry and peach trees. Do you know who originally owned the villa?"

Cassandra shook her head.

"Because I am sure, Miss Orczy, that you are basically a moral person. And you would not wish to personally profit from the horrors of the Nazi era. Would you?"

"No, of course not," said Cassandra warily.

"Did you ever think to ask who originally owned this lovely property?"

"No," she said, the sinking feeling in her stomach growing heavier by the minute.

"The villa was built for the Farkas family. Most of them perished in the Holocaust. Its rightful owner was Miklos Farkas. He is now dead, so his grandson Alex should receive the keys." Hunkalffy put the photograph down and pulled out some papers from a file. "But sadly, that seems unlikely. The steel workers union sold it in October 1989 to a company in the Bahamas, for the equivalent of $5,000. It is now worth at least fifty times that, probably 100 times. You travel to the Bahamas regularly, don't you, Miss Orczy?"

She looked down at the floor, her face burning red.

Hunkalffy picked up the photograph of the villa. "So don't lecture me on the correct disposal of strategic national assets. We are in charge now." Hunkalffy gathered the papers on his desk, as she stood up to leave.

\*　　\*　　\*

From: hatvanin@bnews.hu
To: farkasa@bnews.hu
Alex, can we meet for a coffee this afternoon at the Hungry Postman? I know it's Saturday, but I want to talk to you about something.

From: farkasa@bnews.hu
To: hatvanin@bnews.hu
OK. Let's say 3.00pm.

The Hungry Postman was a small café near the *Budapest News* office, located in the pedestrian underpass that led to Nyugati Station and the Great Boulevard. Alex had walked past the café many times but had never stepped inside. He breathed in the familiar smell of dirt, kebabs and urine and stopped to give 500 forints, about two euros, to a homeless woman who sat nearby selling yesterday's newspapers. She gave him a beatific smile and tucked the money under the three overcoats she was wearing.

Natasha was waiting by the door. A weathered red plastic sign showed a postman tucking into an enormous plate of schnitzel and chips. A smell of frying wafted out.

# Adam LeBor

"*Szia*. You go first," she said, ushering him in front of her.

Alex looked at her questioningly. "*Szia*. In Britain, it's ladies first."

"We're not in Britain. Here the man goes first. If there is a fight, he can protect the woman."

"Are there usually many fights in the Hungry Postman?" he asked.

"Why don't we take a look?" asked Natasha, her voice brisk. Alex walked in, Natasha following him.

The Hungry Postman was dimly lit, with a dozen rickety wooden tables covered in red and white plastic tablecloths, and a glass display case full of questionable cakes. A short, elderly man with grey hair and sloping shoulders, wrapped in a grubby waiter's apron, was leaning at the aluminium counter, reading that day's sports newspaper. There were no other customers.

Alex turned round. "We're safe, no fights at the moment," he said, beckoning Natasha inside.

The waiter came over and greeted her by name. She kissed him on each cheek. "Sani, this is my colleague Alex. Sani is an old family friend," she told Alex.

Sani shook hands with Alex, looking him up and down suspiciously. He turned to Natasha: "How is Irina?"

"My mother is," Natasha paused, "the same. She'll be glad you asked after her."

Sani directed Alex and Natasha to a window table where they sat opposite each other. He brushed down the tablecloth with a great show of ceremony, and they ordered coffees. Natasha also asked for a *meleg szendvics*, a toasted sandwich covered in cheese, ground meat and tomato ketchup. She passed Alex that day's *Magyar Tribün*.

## OPPOSITION MPS DEMAND INQUIRY INTO KZX INDUSTRIES AND VOLKSTERN CORPORATION ROLE IN HUNGARY

### By Magyar Tribün staff

Social Democrat and Liberal MPs are to table a motion in Parliament this week calling for a full inquiry into the growing holdings in Hungary

58

of the giant German industrial and pharmaceutical company KZX Industries and its allied media conglomerate the Volkstern Corporation.

Following its purchase of the joint Hungarian-Slovak company Mediconpex, near Kosice, in Slovakia, KZX Industries recently completed a controversial acquisition of a pharmaceutical works outside Miskolcs in the east of the country, and has immediately announced that fifty per cent of the staff are to be made redundant with no compensation. Rival bidders for the formerly state-owned company complained that they were not properly informed of the terms of the tender, and their bids were rejected on obscure technical grounds.

The Volkstern Corporation, which shares several board members with KZX Industries, and is also based in Munich, has recently bought numerous local television stations, and is launching a new mobile telephone network, 'Magyar Mobile', promising tariffs twenty per cent lower than its rivals. The Volkstern Corporation is also believed to be lobbying for Hungarian state television to be privatised. It also has extensive holdings in Slovakia, Croatia and Romania. Liberal chairman Peter Herzog said: "KZX Industries and the Volkstern Corporation are taking controlling interests in several important sectors of the Hungarian economy. They are completely unaccountable."

A Volkstern Corporation spokesman told *Magyar Tribün*: "We are committed to maintaining editorial freedom for our new acquisitions, within the confines of market realities." KZX spokesmen were not available for comment.

Alex read the article and put the paper down. "Interesting. But the *Budapest News* comes out at the end of next week. When they table the motion in Parliament we'll put it on the website. So what's the big rush? It's Saturday afternoon."

Sani brought the coffees and set them on the table. Natasha thanked him and turned to Alex: "When I was promoted to reporter, you told me that journalism was a vacation."

He laughed, not unkindly. "A vo-cation. A profession, which takes over your life. A vacation is a holiday."

"Excuse me for my bad English. It is not my first language," Natasha said defensively.

"No, no, there's nothing wrong with your English," Alex protested.

"A *vo*-cation. Not a Monday to Friday, nine to five job. 'News knows no office hours,' you said. 'Otherwise get a job as an accountant.'"

Alex sipped his coffee. It was thick and bitter. She had no sense of humour at all. And had he really been that pompous? He looked at her. "OK. We're here. What have you got?"

Natasha took out a notebook from her bag and flicked through to the middle. "One: last year KZX buys Mediconpex. Two: in July this year, KZX buys another drugs factory in eastern Hungary, near the Slovak-Hungarian border. Three: in September this year KZX Industries is fined for dumping out-of-date drugs in eastern Slovakia. They were bribing doctors to prescribe them for completely inappropriate illnesses. In one case in the village of Novy Marek, five members of the same Romany family died after being given anti-cancer drugs for a throat infection."

"Yes, I remember," said Alex, drinking more coffee. "It was a huge scandal because the doctor was fined 200 euros and suspended for a month. KZX only had to pay 10,000 euros." The room wobbled and his skin prickled. Alex put his hands on the table to steady himself. He had eaten nothing all day and the coffee, heavy with caffeine, had gone straight to his head.

Natasha looked alarmed at Alex's pale face. "Are you OK?" she asked, pouring him a glass of water from the jug on the table.

Alex drank the water slowly, breathing carefully. "I think I need to eat something."

Sani reappeared and placed a foot-long slice of toasted bread, covered in grilled meat and cheese, and a bottle of ketchup, on the table in front of Natasha. She pushed the *meleg szendvics* across to Alex and ordered another one, ignoring his protests. "Take it," she said. She took out a packet of Marlboro Lights. "Do you mind?" she asked. Alex shook his head as she lit up, blowing smoke to his side.

He bit into the crispy bread. It was surprisingly tasty, and he suddenly realised how hungry he was. "Thanks," he said, squirting ketchup along the length of the sandwich. The food began to revive him. "What's point four?"

"Wait," said Natasha. "I am interested in KZX and the Roma, so I made several calls. I found out that Slovak health workers have recently been reporting a substantial increase in the number of Romany women either suffering miscarriages or having stillborn babies. There were two in 2006, five in 2007, nine in 2008 and fifteen this year. And many other Gypsy women are complaining of infertility, even though they usually have many children. I don't have those statistics yet. "

"Five, nine and fifteen aren't very big numbers," said Alex.

Natasha put her cigarette down and leaned forward, her voice intense. "They are all in the *same village*. Less than two thousand people live there, about half are Gypsies. The corresponding figures for neighbouring settlements of the same size are about one or two miscarriages or stillbirths a year."

Alex put his sandwich down. A familiar tingling coursed through him. "Novy Marek."

Natasha nodded, triumphant. "Yes. Which is just outside Kosice, site of the Mediconpex pharmaceutical plant. That's point four."

"I need a memo from you, outlining everything you just told me, and where you think this story could go. I'll talk to Ronald." Alex knew Natasha was sharp when he recommended her for promotion. Now she was turning into the best reporter on the paper. But could he trust her to help with what he needed to do that evening?

Sani arrived with another sandwich. Natasha stubbed out her cigarette and took a hearty bite, sending butter and ketchup down her chin. Alex handed her a napkin. She wiped her face and smiled. "Thanks. Tell me, what do you see out there?" she asked, gesturing at the underpass.

Alex looked out of the café's window. Four tunnels radiated out in different directions, their shabby orange tiling covered with graffiti. Strip lights flickered on and off. Kiosks sold cheap t-shirts, greasy kebabs and doughnuts. Bolivian musicians were setting up in one corner, while two policemen watched and smoked cigarettes. The homeless woman selling newspapers had fallen asleep, her mouth wide open. Several wiry, dark-skinned young men stood at the row of public telephones.

"The usual flow of shoppers. Young guys hanging around, homeless people. A western man, well-dressed in a long green coat, maybe German or Austrian, waiting to use the telephone."

"That's a start. See over there?" Natasha pointed at the telephones. Alex turned to look.

"Those young guys are Romanian male prostitutes. They are here in the same place every day. If a cop appears they pay him off. Mr Green Coat is deciding which of them to take to his hotel. That's why he keeps looking over at them. If he is staying in a five star hotel he will have to give the doorman 100 euros to get the boy to his room, fifty euros in a three-star place. Different groups of homeless people control each entry and exit, because they are the best begging points. They also keep an eye for the cops, and when one turns up, they signal to the Romanian boys so they can disappear. The homeless people get a cut of the rent boys' deals in exchange."

"I'm impressed." He took a gamble, relying on his gut instinct. She was smart, hard-working and reliable. And most of all, professional. "Natasha, are you free tonight?" he asked.

She blushed, and sat up straight. "Alex, I asked to meet you to talk about work, not . . ."

Alex interrupted. "This is about work. Well, sort of. But don't misunderstand me." He watched the man in the green coat beckon over a short, black haired youth and press something into his palm. The boy smiled, zipped up his leather jacket and followed him out of the underpass.

Natasha looked at him coolly, as if calculating possibilities. "I could be. If it's really important."

"It is," said Alex, leaning forward to outline his plan. He removed the battery from his mobile telephone and gestured for her to do the same.

Natasha put her battery aside and listened carefully as he spoke. "I'll help you, Alex.' She paused. "If I'm covering Sanzlermann's campaign rally on Sunday."

Alex smiled. "It's a deal."

# SIX

Peter Feher was dozing off at home in front of the Saturday evening arts and culture programme on Hungarian state television. Like Miklos, he was a widower. He lived alone on the first floor of a once grand villa in the Buda hills that the communists had chopped into numerous small flats. The lounge was lined with history books, and a large flat screen television dominated one wall. He awoke to see Aniko Kovacs, the presenter, praising a new biography of Admiral Miklos Horthy, entitled '*Horthy: A True Hungarian Hero.*' The backdrop to the studio was a life-size photograph of Horthy shaking hands with Hitler. The book's author, Laszlo Munnich, was a columnist at *Ébredjetek Magyarok!*. Munnich had no previous teaching experience but had just been appointed Professor of Modern Hungarian History at Budapest University, sitting in the office formerly occupied by Peter's friend, Eduard Szigeti.

"Congratulation, Professor Munnich. This is a major work of scholarship," trilled Aniko, holding the book's cover up to the camera. "We could even call it a rehabilitation."

Munnich, a cadaverous man in a baggy grey suit, nodded. "Absolutely. The liberals and neo-communists have maligned Admiral Horthy for far too long. That's why the Ministry of Education has just ordered 250,000 copies."

"Finally, our history will be correctly taught!" exclaimed Aniko.

Feher shook his head wearily when a mobile telephone began ringing. He scrambled to pick it up before he realised he had the wrong handset. He grabbed the second one, which was larger and heavier, and punched a code into the blue plastic keyboard. The screen flashed.

"He's on his way," a distant, metallic voice said. "You must have hooked him yesterday."

"It wasn't difficult. He loved his grandfather." Feher held the telephone away from his head and looked at it. "You sound strange. Are you sure it's safe to talk on this?"

"It's scrambled. It's completely secure," the voice said, exasperated but affectionate.

"Is he alone?" he asked, watching film footage of Horthy triumphantly riding a white horse into Budapest in 1920, after the Romanian army returned home. There was no mention of the pogrom that had followed, when two of his uncles had been killed.

"No, he should be meeting the girl. She was there earlier."

"Good," said Feher and hung up. He sat back and switched to Eurosport.

\*   \*   \*

Klauzal Square was the heart of Budapest's old Jewish quarter, flanked on four sides by run-down Habsburg-era apartment blocks and a market. Even at eleven o'clock on a freezing Saturday night it was crowded with revellers bar-hopping from Kultura, five minutes walk away, to the numerous nearby clubs and cafés. Light and music spilled out from Groove, a ground-floor jazz café on the facing corner of the square. Alex watched two young men, arm in arm, laughing loudly as they walked across Kisdiofa Street to a new sushi bar. The row of facing buildings was covered in scaffolding and green builders' sheeting. However thoroughly the developers scrubbed and repainted Klauzal Square they could never wash away its history. After the Nazis invaded in March 1944, Budapest's Jews were forced into two ghettos. Much of District VII was walled off, and tens of thousands of people jammed into its narrow streets. Others were moved to the 'International Ghetto' in the riverside District XIII, across the Great Boulevard, where they were protected by the Swedish, Swiss and Spanish embassies. In the winter of 1944, as the Russians advanced, Klauzal Square was an open mass grave, the frozen bodies stacked up in piles. A children's playground now stood in the centre.

Alex walked over to the young woman sitting on a swing, smoking a cigarette. "I used to come here as a kid," Natasha said, rocking back and forth.

He looked at the serious young woman sitting in front of him, her head wrapped in a black scarf that highlighted her grey eyes and austere beauty. "Me too. I still do, sometimes, when I need to think," he said, his voice wistful. He felt his grandfather's hand on his back, pushing him forward as he held tightly onto the chains holding the swing, his legs tucked under the seat as he flew into the air, the memories triggering the now familiar ache.

Natasha handed him an envelope and he peeked inside. "Thanks. Let's go."

He slipped the envelope into his shoulder bag and they walked across the square. Natasha had visited Miklos' building earlier that evening. The apartment door was sealed with printed paper strips announcing 'Police – scene of crime: entry forbidden'. She had taken numerous close-up photographs of the seals with her digital camera. Back at the office she had scanned the photographs onto a computer. Alex could email and use the internet, but that was about it. Natasha's computer skills were far more advanced. Using a photographic software programme she then manipulated the digital images to reproduce the exact colour, typeface and lettering of the police seals onto a template the same size as the original. It was then simple to print out the copies and cut them to size. The result: several forged police scene of crime seals, identical to the real thing.

The door to Miklos' building was open as usual, the staircase unlit. Alex had copied the set of keys he had borrowed from Erzsebet, the neighbour, on the night of Miklos' death. The only tricky moments, he anticipated, would be actually getting in and out of Miklos' apartment. Most of the inhabitants were elderly, and even nosy Erzsebet went to bed about 10.00pm, so there was little danger of bumping into someone. Luckily Miklos had lived on the top floor. Natasha kept watch over the stairs, while Alex put on a pair of thin black leather gloves, cut the seals and opened the door.

As soon as he closed it behind him, Natasha began to paste the new strips in place. Less than a minute later, she stepped back to admire her handiwork. Only a very scrupulous professional could ever tell that the door had ever been tampered with, she thought, as she waited on the staircase.

\*　　\*　　\*

Miklos' flat was spacious and airy, with high ceilings, two bedrooms, a massive walk-through lounge, and a large balcony that looked over Klauzal Square. But over the years he had retreated, sleeping on a fold-down sofa in the lounge where he spent most of the day. The room was still in chaos, with books hurled all over the floor. Thankfully his body, together with the pig's head and the plate, had been taken away. The painted slogan 'AVO' remained on the wall.

Alex damped down the anger and grief that once again surged through him as he walked back inside. He began his search methodically, starting in the room that his grandfather had slept in while his wife Ruth was still alive. A large bed, a dressing table and two mahogany wardrobes, one still full of her clothes, suits and dresses from the 1940s, a hat, huge, pink with a giant ostrich feather stuck jauntily in the band. The clothes smelt of mothballs. The faintest hint of perfume? Then his grandfather's closet: rows of suits, sharply cut, with wide double-breasts and oxford trousers. They must have been, in their day, quite a stylish couple. A picture of Ruth at the beach, posing demurely in a 1950s swim-suit, was stuck on the inside of the door.

Nothing there, the boxes on top of the cupboards filled with old bills and letters from various ministries. Under the bed only a few pairs of shoes. The next room had served as a sort of office, and an ancient handsome desk stood by the window. Alex sat down on a Beidermeyer chair, and opened the drawers, one by one, rummaging through the detritus of two long and turbulent lives. There were photographs, sepia tinted, of young men and women grinning happily at a camera. At the beach by Lake Balaton, at a party in a smoky night-club, a dark-haired girl pulling a silly face at the camera as she held tightly onto the arm of the proud-looking young man sitting next to her.

Like several of the people in the pictures, the happy couple looked vaguely familiar, and he supposed them to be distant relatives who had died in the war, for he had never met any of them. He pocketed several photographs and the bundles of letters. The bottom drawer of the desk was locked. There was no key in sight, so he went to look for a sturdy knife in the kitchen. He slipped the knife between the top of the drawer and the cupboard and levered it upwards. The knife bent, but the drawer refused to give way. This was craftsman's work, hand-built by artisans, of aged hardwood, solid brass and not about to surrender to some mass-produced socialist blade.

The problem was, he realised, as he tried to force the desk open, that he was getting in deep here. Now it would be obvious to even the most dull-witted policeman that someone had tampered with the crime scene. Well, he thought, it's too late to go back now. The drawer creaked, groaned in protest and eventually splintered. The lock had come loose in its setting, and with the remnants of the kitchen knife he managed to lever it out, and the drawer opened.

Inside lay a pile of yellowing letters, carefully wrapped in a rubber band. Perhaps here then. The envelopes were old, with wartime stamps, and they crackled as he took off the rubber band. He opened one, and read an account of Ruth's trip to see her aunt in the summer of 1943 in the southern town of Pecs, and how worried she was that all her male cousins had been drafted for forced labour in Transylvania, and hadn't written home for three months. It was carefully written, in an educated cursive script, and filled with loving endearments. He scanned the rest of the envelopes, all written in the same hand, and put them in his bag before returning to the lounge.

Books were scattered everywhere, works in German, French, Hungarian, Russian, even a couple of Sherlock Holmes novels in English. Alex sat down in the chrome and leather chair and scanned the titles, spread across the carpet. An intellectual's books, and there were times in eastern Europe when that had been a dangerous thing to be. He started sorting through the books – perhaps Miklos had hidden something inside one of them, or why would they be strewn all over the floor – *Madame Bovary*, *Crime and Punishment*, a collection of verses by Hungarian poets, works by Camus and Sartre, a history of the Soviet Union, a biography of Janos Kadar, Hungary's last communist leader, a copy of the Talmud. Alex picked up a leather-bound edition of the *Karma Sutra*, well read by the look of it, and the telephone rang. He sat up with a jerk and grabbed his mobile phone, but this was the flat telephone ringing.

Alex looked at his watch. It was 1.10am. Who rang a dead man in the middle of the night? Perhaps it was Natasha. Maybe there was a problem with his mobile and someone was coming. The phone was an ancient contraption, black and curving with a loud, piercing bell that resounded through the flat. His heart began to beat faster. Desperate to stop the noise, he grabbed the Bakelite earpiece and said hallo. There was no reply, only silence.

"Hallo, hallo. Who do you want to speak to?"

He tried again, in both Hungarian and English. No reply came. Alex waited a few seconds and put the telephone down, feeling very rattled. He decided to leave in a few minutes, whether or not he found anything. You could push your luck so far, he knew. It had been a stupid mistake, he realised, to pick up the receiver. He had just confirmed that someone was in the flat.

He flicked through a pile of newspaper clippings on Miklos' desk. Some of the yellowed strips of paper dated back to the 1950s: Nazi judges appointed to the German supreme court; Nazi doctors appointed professors at universities; Major General Reinhard Gehlen, former chief of Nazi military intelligence on the eastern front, setting up the West German intelligence service with the help of the CIA; the relentless growth of KZX Industries through the 1970s; a picture of the Berlin Wall coming down with a question-mark drawn over it. There was also more recent material on the Volkstern Corporation's expansion into eastern European, and a cutting from the *New York Times*, about legislation compensating

Holocaust survivors for lost properties. Alex gathered the clippings and put them in his bag.

He glanced around the floor for the last time. A thick red book lay by the sofa: *Seventy Years of Progress: The Achievements of the Soviet Union*. Miklos had showed him it on a previous visit. In fact he had made a point of explaining that it was a family heirloom, and should always be taken care of as it held 'special, and precious memories'. He thought that his grandfather, a famous anti-communist, was being ironic. But what if he was telling him something else? Alex picked the book up. Colour photographs of tractors ploughing the fields of Kazakhstan, grinning Muscovites skating on the ice-rink at Gorky Park, rockets, missiles, astronauts. A vanished world. The covers felt odd, bumpy and too thick. There was a ridge running along the edge of the inside leaf that was stuck to the red hardboard, on both the front and the back. He pulled at the corners, tentatively at first, then quickly. They tore, and then both came away easily.

Underneath lay a clump of thin grey paper, held together by rusty paper clips, hand-written in the faded blue-grey ink of an ancient fountain pen. Alex's heart thumped as he held the papers, and read the first line: *The Ghetto Diary of Miklos Farkas*. His mobile phone rang in his pocket.

"Hurry up, I can hear voices downstairs, I think it's the police," Natasha whispered urgently. "Get out of there."

He grabbed the papers, stuffed them in his shoulder bag, together with the book. He turned at the front door, and dashed backed into the lounge. He snatched Miklos' boxing gloves, stuffed them into his bag and left as fast as he could. Natasha was outside. He closed the door gently behind him. She pulled off the torn police seals, quickly replaced them with a new pair. Alex scrunched up the paper strips and stuffed them into his trouser pocket.

He showed her the book and the grey papers, gesturing at her to keep silent as they descended the stairs. A blue light spun around the walls and entrance on the ground floor.

"Shit," exclaimed Alex, "Now what?"

"Shut up and come here," Natasha said, grabbing Alex. She pushed him against the wall, her hands snaking around his neck. Alex looked at her in amazement.

"Just shut up and let me do the talking now," she hissed as a torch was shined on them.

"Hey, you two lovebirds, what's going on up there? No home to go to?" They broke apart as the policeman approached. He was burly and overweight, a cigarette dangling from his mouth.

Natasha smiled, holding Alex's arm as she spoke. "I'm sorry Captain, we were out walking, and we just stepped in out of the wind, and then we, well, you know, started to get carried away. You must know how that can happen, so easily, sir."

The policeman looked doubtful. "You both stay there. Have you seen anyone else here tonight? We had a report that someone was inside that flat where that Jew was murdered. Someone heard someone moving about, or so they said. Have you seen anything suspicious? Perhaps I should wake up the housemistress to see what she knows."

"No sir, nobody at all. We've only been here a couple of minutes," said Natasha, her eyes wide and innocent.

Alex prayed the policeman would not follow his instinct, for the prospect of dealing with Erzsebet Kovacs at this time of night, and explaining to her what he and Natasha were doing there was too awful to contemplate. Especially as she would almost certainly, even if inadvertently, give his identity away.

"Identity card," the policeman ordered Natasha. "Who is he?"

"He's British. We met at a bar tonight. He doesn't speak any Hungarian," said Natasha as she handed over her card. The policeman turned it over, checking her face against the photograph.

"You met at a bar tonight and you're kissing him already," he grunted.

"Passport," the policeman demanded of Alex. Natasha caught Alex's eye. He shook his head imperceptibly. Now they had a problem. If he showed the policeman an ID, and he saw that he had the same family name as Miklos, he would radio into headquarters for instructions. He would certainly ask Alex to open his bag and order him to empty his pockets. They could make a run for it but how far would they get?

Alex shrugged and showed his empty hands. The policeman stared at him, his eyes narrowing with suspicion.

"This is a problem. A very big problem," said the policeman. "You must come with me. You too," he added, looking at Natasha. But he did not move towards the car, where his partner sat reading a tabloid newspaper.

Natasha smiled at the policeman. "Perhaps we could sort things out here, sir."

The cop shook his head. "It is a very serious problem. This is a crime scene, he is a foreigner and he does not have any papers."

"Surely we can *arrange* things here?" persisted Natasha.

"What kind of arrangement were you thinking of?"

"This kind," said Natasha. She reached inside her handbag and took out a 10,000 forint note.

The policeman shook his head and put the money in his pocket. "This is a very big problem."

She handed over another 10,000 forint note. The policeman took it, but still shook his head.

"How big is this problem exactly, do you think?" asked Natasha.

"Fifty thousand forints big."

"Thirty."

"Forty. And quickly," the policeman grunted, holding out his hand.

Natasha reached into Alex's jeans and took out his wallet. She opened it up and removed two 10,000 forint notes, handing them to the policeman, who swiftly pocketed them.

"Wait here. And don't try any funny business," he ordered.

He clomped up the stairs to the top floor, his heavy boots echoing through the entry hall. Alex looked at her in amazement, bursting with questions, but she put her fingers on her lips. Back in his war correspondent days, he and his colleagues judged their fellow journalists with the SUF test. SUF stood for Steady Under Fire, someone who could be trusted not to freak out in extreme circumstances. Not everybody passed, but Natasha was certainly

SUF. He had chosen the right accomplice. She had forged the police seals, taken his word that it was worth committing a crime to get into his grandfather's flat and was handling the policeman superbly.

The policeman reappeared. He walked over to the car and told his partner that there was nothing happening here. The flat was closed and sealed, there was nobody around except these two lovebirds, he grumbled, and it was nearly 2.00am, almost the end of their shift. He radioed into headquarters that everything seemed to be in order.

"Go on," he said, waving at Alex and Natasha. "Get out of here. Fucking foreigners."

Alex's heart was pounding from adrenalin and nervous tension as they walked down the side of the square towards Groove. Natasha looked calm and unconcerned.

"You did brilliantly. How did you know he would take a bribe?" asked Alex.

"Cops always work in pairs. If you get stopped and the other one moves away out of sight, or doesn't come forward it means they are open to be bribed. Plausible deniability. The other cop didn't see anything, because he wasn't there. The one who pockets the money gets sixty per cent and the other forty per cent."

"That would make a great article. A guide to bribing Budapest police officers," replied Alex enthusiastically.

"Yes, it would. But Alex, I must apologise to you," said Natasha formally.

"What for? I should apologise to you. I nearly got us both arrested," he protested.

"No, I was wrong. In the office, I was disrespectful of your grandfather, and to you. When I said at least you had some time with him."

"You don't have to apologise for anything, but thank you anyway. Let's have a drink. I think we deserve one," said Alex, taking her arm and steering her towards Groove.

Natasha walked briskly ahead, pulling her arm forward so his hand fell away. "No thanks, Alex. I have to go home now."

"It's Saturday night," protested Alex. "You were a star. Please let me buy you a drink."

A group of tipsy teenagers clambered over the playground, laughing and shouting. Natasha shook her head. She took out a packet of cigarettes and lit one, puffing quickly. "Alex, I was glad to help you with this. But I really have to go now. I need to be fresh for the Sanzlermann campaign rally tomorrow."

Alex shrugged, his face burning with embarrassment and confusion. "You're right. Call me later tomorrow night and let me know how it went."

Natasha walked away. "I'll try if I'm back in time. Or I'll see you in the office on Monday."

## SEVEN

Alex stood on the grassy shore of Lake Balaton, fighting the wind that violently buffeted his red birthday kite. Miklos watched nearby, smiling and nodding encouragingly. The kite pulled harder, the string cutting into his palm. A sudden gust dragged it away, spinning red across the water as it disappeared into the distance. He felt the tears well up, but when he turned to Miklos he had vanished. Alex woke with a jolt, disorientated, his hand tingling. The clock showed 9.30am. He switched on the radio. Schumann played gently as he lay in bed. A church bell tolled and a tram trundled past along the riverbank. The ambient noise of weekend Budapest was both calming and painful. He had always spent Sundays with Miklos, and sometimes took him out for lunch. He had been planning to show him Kultura. Now the day yawned empty in front of him.

Alex glanced at Miklos' diary, lying on the kitchen table, next to the book about the Soviet Union. He replayed the previous night in his mind. On a practical level it had been extremely successful. They had got in and out of the flat. They had escaped arrest. Nobody even knew they had been inside, except perhaps whoever telephoned. How idiotic he had been to pick up the handset. But that was not why he felt so low. Part of it was grief, he knew, as it was not even a week since he had found his grandfather's body. But it was also more than mourning. He stared at the grey, cracked ceiling. He was thirty-nine years old. He had some money in the bank but owned no property; there was a woman in his life, who even said that she loved him, but she was married to someone else. And he was starting to fall in love with her, so it could only

74

end badly. His friends and colleagues were married, with kids, mortgages and obligations. Part of him sneered at that bourgeois routine, and part of him – especially on mornings like this – hungered for familiar faces at the breakfast table. Was this the famed mid-life crisis?

There was a faint smell of Zsofi's perfume on the sheets. Alex tried not to think of her waking up next to her husband. Istvan Kiraly was right. His relationship with Zsofi was a dead-end. He felt his face flush red with embarrassment as he remembered trying to take Natasha for a drink and how swiftly she had shaken off his arm. One part of him said there was nothing wrong with inviting a colleague for a drink, especially when you had just broken into a crime scene together. But even after their clinch against the wall Natasha had made it abundantly clear that she was not at all interested. Holding him so closely was strictly business, it seemed. In his younger days he would have regarded her froideur as a challenge, a Siberian permafrost to be melted with his oh-so-winning smile and a bottle of wine or vodka. The other part of him remembered another Slavic girl, with longer hair and just as striking cheekbones.

Alex swallowed hard, got up and walked to the bathroom. He stared into the mirror at his stubbled cheeks and bleary eyes. His mouth tasted sour from the whisky he had drunk alone at home the previous evening. "The unexamined life is not worth living" Socrates had written, but there was also a point when the examination became an excuse for not doing anything, he thought. This was not any kind of crisis, but maudlin self-indulgence, he decided. It was time for the hot and cold cure. He sat in the bath, yanking the lever on the mixer tap back and forth as the near scalding then freezing water coursed over him, yelping at the sudden change in temperature. His skin tingled as the pores opened and closed and he willed the gloom away. He would finish with Zsofi. More importantly, he would find out who had killed Miklos, and why.

He shaved, dressed in clean clothes and stood in his kitchen, considering the breakfast possibilities. The pizza slice was still on the work surface. He threw it in the bin, rolled up his sleeves and blitzed the grimy space, scrubbing the dishes, wiping down the surfaces, brushing and sweeping the floor. His reward was a packet of Mubarak's Turkish coffee, a bag of pistachio nuts and some digestive biscuits he had brought from England, discovered at the back of a dusty shelf. He boiled the coffee in a small brass pot Mubarak had given him and watched the water rise slowly up, ready to foam over. He would spend the day reading Miklos' testimony. He sat at his desk and reached for the thin grey papers, covered with his grandfather's elegant, copperplate handwriting.

## THE GHETTO DIARY OF MIKLOS FARKAS

### November 2 1944

*I have decided to keep a diary. I will write of how we live and die, but I am going to start with a question. One I have been thinking about for a long time. What did we do to these Hungarians to make them hate us so much? We are – were – good loyal citizens. We paid our taxes, built factories, schools, hospitals. We wrote books, plays, films, newspaper articles, poems, founded literary journals. We fought in their wars, died in their revolutions, built up the economy, provided jobs and work. We even made shells and bullets for the Germans and uniforms for the Hungarian army.*

*What was our reward? That the Hungarians watched and cheered as the Germans rounded us up and send us to Poland, for work supposedly, but none return. And what kind of work can children and the elderly do? No, let me correct myself. The Germans did not round us up. The Hungarians did. Hungarian clerks drew up the lists of Jews for deportation. Hungarian Gendarmes cleared the towns and villages of their Jews, and forced them into ghettos. Hungarian Gendarmes tortured the young and old to find where they have hidden their gold. Jewish gold, of course we have it, even when we don't, and we collapse bloody in front of them, and still they seek and seek. And still they kill us, even now. Why? Everyone knows the Germans have lost the war. The western Allies are* halfway through Europe, on the road to Berlin. The Russians are advancing from the east and have Budapest surrounded. Even the Romanians have changed sides. But not us. No, we have a new government, of the true believers, even worse than the Nazis: the Arrow Cross who murder us for pleasure.

## November 5 1944

I am writing this in an apartment on Dohany Street, not far from the Great Synagogue, by the gate to the main Budapest ghetto. We live twelve Jews in one room, sometimes more, sometimes less, as people die off and others take their places. Nobody is buried any more, and the frozen corpses pile up in the synagogue courtyard. For light and heat we have a few candles. The walls shake when the American planes drop their bombs, but we cheer inside to hear the sound of the explosions and the thunder of the Russian artillery as the shells fall into the city. My wife Ruth is here with me, working at the communal kitchen – if such is the word for a place from where comes very little food – trying to help as best she can.

We huddle together at night for warmth, young and old, men and women, it doesn't matter anymore. A few have blankets, but most only their clothes. The air is thick and fetid with the smell of unwashed bodies. When the detonations sound too loud, we hide in the cellar with the rats. There at least we are safe from bullets and shrapnel. A fire burns inside me, that somehow helps keep me alive. I rage against this war, the stupidity of this country's leaders, and the passivity of its people. Where are the partisans? Where is the resistance? Where are the police and the army while the Arrow Cross runs wild? They have surrendered our homeland to butchers and do nothing to stop them. So much anger, but what do I actually do? I could buy a gun and start shooting. But I do not. I want to live. Does that make me a coward? Perhaps.

## November 6 1944

I feel calmer today. Perhaps I should still count myself lucky. I am alive, after all, when so many are not. So is Ruth. And some of us at least are resisting. The Zionist youth groups can move across the city between this ghetto, and the so-called International Ghetto, in District XIII, by the Margaret Bridge, using neutral papers. Help came from a most unlikely quarter: the Swedish and Swiss embassies. The Swedish diplomat Raoul Wallenberg and his Swiss colleague Carl Lutz are issuing papers placing Hungarian Jews under their protection. They use these papers to move around the city, and print their own forgeries. I even go to work when I can, thanks to our former family butler. Aladar Nagy is now head waiter at the Hotel Savoy, favoured billet of the SS, one of the last places in the city where food, alcohol and tobacco are still available. And he is a member of the resistance. Nagy recruited me as a waiter and arranged something even better than a Wallenberg paper – a laissez-passer from the SS itself. Ironic that I know how to serve the Nazis – precisely how lunch or a cup of coffee should be presented: only a few months ago my needs were still met by servants. Now I live on the Nazis' leftovers. How the world turns, not just around but also upside down.

### November 7 1944

Today I again brought coffee to Adolf Eichmann at the café of the Hotel Savoy. He is a strange figure, quite softly spoken. He speaks some Hebrew, which he learnt when he visited Palestine before the war, and knows all the Jewish festivals and customs well. He looks much more like a civil servant than a hate-filled fanatic. Because I am quite skilled in my new occupation, Eichmann asks for me by name, or rather, by the name on my false papers: Miklos Kovacs. "Kovacs," he announces at 11.00pm, as he strides into the café, expecting me, naturally enough, to jump to his attention, "Coffee! Strong and black!" I would rather pour the boiling liquid over his head. But of course I do not. Instead I try to eavesdrop on Eichmann's conversations as much as I can, although it is a delicate task, for if he suspected my intentions he would surely have me shot. He was sitting with SS Colonel Friedrich Vautker, and I am sure that Vautker knows I have false papers, for he takes a dark amusement in being friendly with me. He even saved my life once, *from the Arrow Cross. Eichmann and Vautker spend much time meeting with businessmen. Considering that the Russians are advancing on the city day by day, they do not seem unduly concerned about the military situation.*

### November 9 1944

*The bombardment is getting worse. Corpses lie in the street of the ghetto, sometimes for days, before they are taken away. The Arrow Cross launch drunken raiding parties, and drag out whomever they please, before marching them down Rakoczi Street to the Danube. They are running out of bullets, and tie the Jews together three at a time before shooting one, who topples into the water, taking the others down as well. There are rumours that Wallenberg's people hide on the riverbank, and then dive into the river to try and untie some of those still alive and bring them out. Not just Jews, but all of Budapest now lives underground most of the time. Tonight I have been summoned to work at the Savoy for a 'special gala dinner'.*

### November 10 1944

*The 'gala dinner' was indeed a special occasion. I had not seen such food for months. True to his word, Aladar Nagy gave me a substantial package. I shared the food with Ruth and the others in our flat, and gave some potatoes to a child crying from hunger. There were several men in civilian clothes at the dinner. I looked at the hotel's guest book – even in the inferno of war bureaucracy still turns – and saw that businessmen from Zurich were registered, together with many German industrialists, the barons of the steel, chemical and car industries. Halfway through the dinner there was a power cut and the only light came from candles. Eichmann was not there, but Vautker, the "friendly" SS Colonel, was. His bony, shadowed face, illuminated by the flickering Flame of a nearby candle, looked as though it contained a terrible secret hidden under the surface, a premonition of a dark and terrible future for mankind.*

## December 25 1944

*Christmas Day. I have neglected my diary, but there is little new to report. The Hotel Savoy has closed, and most of the SS have fled. The Russians are advancing steadily, driving the Arrow Cross into a frenzy. They have killed everyone at the Jewish hospital, shooting the doctors and nurses and murdering the patients in their beds. Yesterday I met a young boy, fourteen at most, who had somehow made his way here with his sister from the Jewish childrens' home on Maros Street on the Buda side. They had hidden in the cellar while the Arrow Cross raided the place and marched the youngsters down to the riverbank where they had set up machine-guns. He had pulled off his yellow star and his sister's, and walked across the city at dawn to find his parents. Incredibly, he succeeded.*

*Here everyone is sick, feverish, and the doctors can do nothing. Still our communal kitchens keep operating, and distribute meagre food supplies: bread made of flour and sawdust and sometimes a thin stew of peas or beans. But our teeth are loose in our mouths and we cough and spit blood. They call this illness the Ukrainian disease, but its name doesn't matter. There is no medicine to cure us. The only cure is the Red Army.*

## January 1 1945

*The start of a new year. I heard today that a gold watch will buy a lump of rotten horsemeat. A man with a packet of cigarettes is a millionaire. The rats are becoming fatter and no longer fear us. A few brave ones amongst us still venture out under the ghetto gates through the sewers into the city, and bring us back news of how Budapest is slowly dying. I too used to sneak out by bribing the Arrow Cross guards, but they have been sent to the front. Their replacements are even worse, political commissars, true believers in their leader Ferenc Szalasi's madness and there is no dealing with them. So now I sit and wait. We know not what terrible fate they have planned for us when the Russians advance into the city. There are rumours that the Arrow Cross will torch the whole ghetto, with us trapped inside. We have a few weapons, guns, stolen pistols and a rifle or two. We have pledged to die fighting, as our fellow Jews fought in Warsaw. At least now we all shelter and starve together, Jew and gentile.*

## *January 3 1945*

*Today I received a present: a piece of bread. It arrived courtesy of the SS, in a roundabout way. Someone knocked on the cellar door, quite politely, about 11.00am. In the doorway stood a man in SS uniform, smart black jacket and trousers, even a cap perched on his head with the twin flashes, holding three loaves. Then a strange thing happened. The SS officer smiled. The woman next to me jumped up, sobbing and laughing with joy. "Don't worry, don't worry everybody. It's my husband, my husband." They embraced, and she kept saying his name, "Laszlo, Laszlo." She had last heard from him six months before when he was serving with the Hungarian army in Romania.*

*Our great generals have lost whole armies, but he had survived. He walked back, travelling by night, sleeping by day, for six weeks, and somehow crossed the Russian front-lines. A friendly SS officer – can such a creature exist – had drafted him as his driver, and even given him, a Jew, a Nazi uniform. A privilege to wear such fine clothes, and the Arrow Cross does not bother him. But then, as I know myself, strange things happen in war. I made the bread last as long as possible, for it was a taste from another world, a reminder of breakfasts served on Meissen china, of fresh pastries and strong, hot coffee in our dining room at home on Andrassy Avenue. I have heard that the SS has requisitioned it. Antal Noludi too is quartered there, the former manager of the Farkas steel works on Csepel Island, to whom my father gave trusteeship. The mills and factory are gone from us forever, that much I know. But I would surrender them willingly just to know the fate of my parents.*

Alex sat back trying to digest what he had read, leafing through his grandfather's testimony with a kind of awe. The faded ink, the thin wartime paper only served to highlight the power of Miklos' words. He walked over to the window and stepped out onto the balcony. It was a cold and blustery winter day, pedestrians wrapped up in hats and scarves against the wind blowing in off the Danube. He felt the air buffet him, as he watched a well-dressed family emerge from a Ford estate car, mother and father in their Sunday best, two young children in hand. The mother carried a bunch of flowers, and a parcel of cakes, carefully wrapped in dark green paper and topped with a ribbon. A Budapest Sunday lunchtime, a Mittel-European snapshot, following family rituals established over a century ago. Take away the new cars and modern shop signs, and the street must have looked exactly the same then. He felt as though he had somehow travelled back in time.

Who knew what had happened here, in front of his apartment building, or a few yards away, down by the river? A powerful longing surged through him. Alex's grandfather had rarely spoken of the war, and then only in general, vague terms. If only he had sat him down with a tape recorder. But now it was too late. Yet perhaps Miklos was telling him more with his diary than he ever would have said in person. Alex tapped idly on the keys of the antique typewriter on his desk. Black and gold lettering on the carriage, a faint smell of ink. It was a present from Zsofi, dating from the 1930s, and still worked. Outside the grey sky darkened and thunder rumbled. A sudden gust of wind rattled the windows, and rain began beating down on the pavement. He turned up the heating and returned to his grandfather's testimony.

\*  \*  \*

Natasha looked around the audience at Frank Sanzlermann's campaign rally at Budapest's central sports arena. She was surprised at how many young people there were, almost all fashionably dressed and clearly prospering. The atmosphere was electric. Sanzlermann was a masterful speaker, thoroughly briefed, never patronising, asking and answering rhetorical questions. He frequently used phrases in Hungarian, and made repeated reference to points of Hungarian culture and history. He spoke in English, while

German and Hungarian subtitles flashed up along the bottom of
the two video monitors flanking his lectern. A giant banner behind
him proclaimed: "Family, Work and Unity: Forward to a Christian
Europe."

He was halfway through his speech. "I'm sure that by now, many
of you are thinking there is a paradox here. How can a federal
Europe, with a common currency, political and legal institutions,
protect Hungary's national interests? I know what you are asking:
for the first time in its proud 1000 year history, Hungary is finally
free, sovereign and independent of foreign rule. We *Magyars* can
decide our own destiny. Why should we give that up?"

The audience sat still and attentive. "It is a good question, and
here is the answer. Because you are not giving up anything. You
are gaining, not losing. In the new Europe Hungary can protect
its national interests as never before. Hungary's interests are
Europe's interests, and Europe's interests are Hungary's. You will
no longer be a *Magyar* island in a Slav sea, no longer be isolated,
misunderstood, unappreciated. You will be surrounded by friends
and allies, at the very centre of a strong, united Europe."

He paused, while the cheers echoed around the stadium. "But
enough of politics. Let me turn to an even more important theme.
And that is family. I never knew my parents. I was raised in a
children's home in the mountains of Carinthia. My father was killed
in a car crash on an icy mountain road when I was four. My mother
died soon after. She just faded away. Friends of my father paid for
my stay at the home," he said, with a faraway look in his eyes.

Natasha felt the sympathy ripple around the auditorium. There
was a press box, with a good view, and copious supplies of
refreshments and food, but she preferred to sit among the public,
to better take its mood. Which was hugely enthusiastic. The young
woman on her right, a heavily-made up tall brunette with a copy
of *Ébredjetek Magyarok!* poking from her black mini-rucksack,
kept turning to Natasha, nodding enthusiastically. On her left
a pale young man with a long ponytail of blond hair stared
as Sanzlermann spoke, yelping his approval. Both wore plastic
wristwatches emblazoned with a picture of Sanzlermann.

Sanzlermann waited, as though gathering his strength before recalling the poignant memories. "It is family that gives us a sense of self, of who we are and what our values are. I am now blessed with a family of my own," he said, gesturing at the screen over the stage. A picture flashed up of Sanzlermann, flanked by his German wife Dagmar, and their three children. "I believe in family, work and unity, for all Europeans, no matter what their ethnic origin. For some of our fellow citizens desperately need our support."

The picture of Sanzlermann's family was replaced by a picture of a Romany settlement. A mother breastfed a baby in the doorway of a flimsy shack, children played barefoot in the mud. There was muttering in the audience. Sanzlermann continued: "My friends, I see some of you are uncomfortable with this picture. But we can, we must, help the Roma, to overcome prejudice and misconceptions, to overcome unemployment, and lack of education, or we will continue to pay a high price for our neglect. We will pay in crime, in delinquency and lawlessness."

The settlement was replaced by a photograph of a group of inmates at a young offenders' institution, all dark-skinned and obviously Gypsies. "The Roma have slipped so far through the net that we don't even know how many of them there are. Births are unregistered, deaths unreported. That is why I am calling for a Europe wide census, and as part of that, the Roma would be fingerprinted, so we know where they live, and can help them live full and productive lives." The prisoners vanished, and the screen showed two swarthy men brawling in the middle of a village main street. "Sadly, violence is all too common, but it is never the answer. Education is. Which is why I'm personally donating the 250,000 euros I received from the Brussels Prize to launch the European National Union Roma Education Fund," he proclaimed.

Natasha scribbled in her notebook while the audience clapped enthusiastically. Sanzlermann stopped and drank some water. "I am proud to say that I believe in Europe's Christian heritage. I have been accused of being racist. Race is not the issue. The issue is values, European values. Some argue that we should let Turkey join the European Union. Turkey is home to a rich culture, a moderate

Islam that can guide the rest of the Islamic world. But look at a map. Turkey borders Iran and Iraq. Their values are not our values: 'honour killings', stoning adulterers, executing teenagers. For whatever the multi-culturalists argue, Christian values are the pillars of our civilisation, from the renaissance to the internet, pillars on which we are building the new Europe. And you *Magyars* know what it means to live under Islam."

A slow murmur of assent.

"You suffered for 150 years, under the rule of the Sultans."

The murmur grew louder. The screen showed the bloody aftermath of the Berlin bombing.

"The shadow of foreign terror once again falls over Europe. Immigration Liberation Army bombers are murdering the innocents in Berlin, Rome and Paris. Peace loving immigrants are welcome of course. But what of the extremists? Who claim asylum in the democracies that they seek to destroy? They despise us, our freedoms, and our tolerance. Many times I have asked, why do we give sanctuary to those who wish to destroy our way of life, and impose the values of an alien religious system? Nobody can answer. Nobody. But not only do they despise us, they also kill us. That's why we say no. No to the Immigration Liberation Army. No to its leader Hasan Al-Ajnabi, and no to terrorism and extremism. *Nem, nem, soha*, no, no, never. Do I hear you?"

A muttered, *nem, nem*.

"Do I hear you?" louder, this time. Natasha looked round as the chorus erupted across the hall. "*Nem, nem, soha. Nem, nem, soha.*" Hundreds of voices thundered across the hall as the audience rose to its feet. "*Nem, nem, soha. Nem, nem, soha.*"

She sat silently, looking straight ahead as her neighbours shouted their approval, stamping their feet, waving Hungarian and European Union flags and campaign placards. Sanzlermann stepped back, waved and disappeared behind the stage.

## EIGHT

Alex put Miklos' diary down and exhaled slowly. He was three quarters of the way through, but it was too much to digest all at once. Rimsky Korsakov's *Scheherazade* had replaced Schumann's piano and the surging music echoed through the flat. It was a morning of storytellers. Sentenced to die by the Sultan, Scheherazade had spun a web of stories to live, keeping him entranced with cliff-hanging tales for 1001 nights, of Sinbad the sailor, menaced by fantastic beasts and stormy seas. Alex's grandfather's adversaries were real, and far more murderous. That Miklos did not know if he would ever live to see at least the arrival of the Russians only rendered his testimony more powerful. He needed a break. He poured himself some more coffee and checked his email. Two messages. He opened the first:

From: zpetcsardy@webmail.com

Dearest Alex, can you ever forgive me? It's already Sunday lunchtime and I am absolutely stranded in Vienna. So many people to see. I GOT THE PART! Meet the new Juliet. Can't wait to see you (tomorrow hopefully) and we will go out and celebrate. Or maybe even stay in . . . :-) your only Zsofi.

He smiled, despite himself. He would miss her. He clicked on the next message.

From: hatvanin@bnews.hu

As you say in English, great minds think alike. You may find the attached article from yesterday's Magyar Tribün of interest. No tariff listed for our encounter, but I think we got a good price. Natasha.

Alex clicked on the attached file. The article was a report on a recent conference on police corruption in Budapest. So the Siberian ice-queen did have a sense of humour. He laughed out loud as he read. One of the conference speakers, from the police's own Internal Affairs Department, had caused a scandal by publicly listing the tariffs for different levels of bribe. The prices were clearly defined. At the top end, getting a criminal case dropped by a senior officer, for 'lack of evidence' or other reasons would cost half a million forints, or about a couple of thousand euros. At the bottom of the scale, a traffic violation would be forgotten or ignored for about ten thousand forints, thirty-five euros. Definitely a story for the *Budapest News*. He tapped out a brief reply, thanking her for sending over the article.

His mood sobered as he sat back down and read through the rest of Miklos' testimony. He knew that his grandfather never saw his parents again. The steelworks manager Antal Noludi had brokered a deal for Baron Laszlo to hand over the foundry to the SS, in exchange for safe passage to Switzerland. But Miklos had never trusted Noludi, let alone the SS, and decided to take his chance in the ghetto under false papers. Once the deal was signed, the rest of the Farkas family was quickly despatched to Auschwitz and killed. Noludi had quickly appointed himself General Manager and taken over the steelworks and the family villa.

## January 15 1945

*The Red Army advances steadily. We count the days, the hours, the minutes. Every second we survive brings us nearer to salvation. And revenge. Sweet, cold revenge. A Russian soldier will surely sell me a gun. A revolver, black and heavy. Or perhaps a rifle. I dream of a line of Arrow Cross men, unarmed, fearful and begging in front of me. Or Gendarmes. Shall I be merciful and quick, or shall I play with them, taunt them, as they did us? My anger has curdled to hatred. Pest is wreathed in smoke and flames and I rejoice. The shells pour in, raining death and destruction. The Russians fire their barrages of Katyusha rockets. Stalin Organs, they call them.*

*Whoosh, bang, whoosh, bang, goes the chorus of the Red Army. Encore, Jozef Stalin. Play on!*

## January 18 1945

*This morning the shelling stopped, and an eerie silence descended, although a few shots still echoed in the distance. After a couple of hours a few of us ventured outside. Everywhere was deserted, and the ghetto seemed somehow different, no longer full of fear, but still and expectant. Ruth came with me, and I held her hand tightly. A few blocks away we saw some soldiers, moving warily, darting between doorways, sub-machine guns in hand. They wore grey uniforms. The gate to the ghetto was destroyed, and deserted. Corpses lay nearby, dead Germans and Arrow Cross. The troops were ragged and filthy, faces blackened with the grime of war, a red star on top of their caps. They advanced warily, shouting. In Russian. I shook from excitement but stood still, with my hands in the air, for they were tense and nervous.*

*By some magic process, the news spread, and all around Jews suddenly appeared. They crawled out of the basements, and many were too weak to even stand up so just lay in the street. Some were laughing, others cried in their joy while most just stood and stared, half-starved, unable to believe that the day had finally arrived. The Russians looked at us, appalled at the parade of human skeletons. A few of the soldiers started handing out bread, which the Jews wolfed down. The Russians pushed two Arrow Cross men forward, ordering them to stand against the wall. A Russian offered me his sub-machine gun, waving the barrel at them. They were mere teenagers. They stared at him, then at me, their eyes darting back and forth, terrified. One began to cry, calling for his mama. Here was my chance for revenge, the moment of which I had dreamed. But I felt no anger, only a weary numbness. I shook my head. The Russian shrugged. The boys were cut almost in two by the hail of bullets. The Russian kicked their bodies each once, and started going through their pockets, shouting with delight at the treasure trove of watches and jewellery. A Soviet officer appeared.*

*"What shall we do, where shall we go?" I asked him.*
*"You can go wherever you like. You are free now," he said.*
*He told me to put my arms down and took a knife from his belt.*
*He cut through the thread holding my yellow star on my coat. It*
*fell on the ground. I stared at the cloth. I could not speak. He*
*handed me some bread which I gave to Ruth. I held her close and*
*wept, as though I would never stop.*

It hit him then, the power of what he held in his hand. Alex felt as
though Miklos was there in the room, reading to him in his warm,
wry voice. He felt his grandfather's loss keenly. He had to get out
of the apartment, get some fresh air. He grabbed his jacket and
walked down to the river. He strode fast along the embankment,
past the five star hotels, the Chain Bridge and towards Parliament.
A thin winter rain spattered his face and clothes but he didn't feel
the cold. There was a memorial near Parliament, dozens of iron
shoes spread along the riverbank, to commemorate the Jews that
the Arrow Cross had shot into the Danube. Womens' shoes, mens'
shoes, childrens' shoes, dress shoes, work shoes, casual shoes, all
black and made of metal. He stopped, knelt down and touched
a sculpture of a woman's boot. It was coated with a thin layer
of ice.

A number two tram trundled by, Sanzlermann grinning from the
posters on its side, and stopped by Parliament. Alex jumped on and
took it two stops to the Margaret Bridge where the line ended. He
walked away from the river, down Pozsonyi Way, once the main road
of the International Ghetto, under Raoul Wallenberg's protection,
and went into a courtyard. Even on the brightest summer's day it
was always dark and gloomy. For some reason it was here that he
always imagined them. They stood in a line, four or five people wide,
yellow stars on their coats. Arrow Cross and SS troops shouted
orders, and they stood frightened, gripping suitcases, that held,
what? Clothes, food, a crust of bread, sandwiches even – *don't forget*
*the packed lunch, it's a long ride* – valuables or family heirlooms
stashed in the suitcase lining. Fathers, reciting platitudes, trying to
reassure their wives and children; screaming babies; trembling old

people, who knew they were never coming home; children holding a favourite teddy bear. Neighbours watching silently.

In Jerusalem, at the Yad Vashem Holocaust Memorial, he had seen a photograph of Hungarian Jews lined up at Auschwitz. One face stood out: a man in his late twenties. He was dressed in a crumpled suit, and he had sensuous, Semitic features, and large, intelligent eyes. He looked like an intellectual, a writer perhaps, who had spent his days arguing about politics, the course of the war, who would arrive first to kick out the Nazis, Russians or Americans. His face was resigned, as he stared sideways at the camera. He knew he would never see the Danube again. *So this is how it ends, but please, just tell me, for what am I to die*? The same question that Stalin's victims asked as they walked along the corridors of the Lubyanka. *Zasto?* For what? It was the question of the twentieth century. There was no answer.

He walked down to the embankment by the Margaret Bridge and looked out over the river flowing fast under its arches. The water ran high and brown, waves breaking its surface, whirlpools spinning. He heard the crackle of rifle fire, smelt acrid cordite, saw the bodies bound together by barbed wire bobbing in the water, their faces bleached white, their clothes swirling in the current. The Danube in 1944, the Drina in 1994, even now, somewhere the guns were being reloaded, the shots echoing across the water, the dead tumbling in. This world, he thought, this city, was a giant graveyard, and he lived in its heart.

\* \* \*

Two tables had been laid with a lavish cold buffet in Sanzlermann's pressroom. Salads, rare roast beef, even caviar. Attractive young hostesses circulated, some with trays of champagne and canapés, others handing out press packs. Natasha accepted a press pack: copies of Sanzlermann's speech, campaign literature, badges, the plastic watch the young people next to her at the rally had worn, a digital recorder and a USB memory stick. Giant posters of Sanzlermann covered the back wall, above the buffet, several showing him and

Attila Hunkalffy with their arms draped around each other's shoulders. She dropped the watch in a nearby dustbin, took a glass of champagne, and sipped slowly as she looked around the room.

The assembled journalists had broken up into three groups. The Hungarians writing for the nationalist press broke into applause as Sanzlermann entered, but there were mutterings and sneers from those working for the left standing on the other side of the room. A few foreign correspondents stood in the middle, talking animatedly in a babble of languages. David Jones was deep in conversation with a French television reporter, waving his cigarette in the air as he spoke. He smiled when he saw Natasha and raised his hand in laconic greeting. She waved back, and watched Istvan Kiraly march up to Sanzlermann. The two men shook hands briskly.

"Herr Sanzlermann, congratulations. An excellent speech. Complex and important ideas, but expressed clearly and simply," said Kiraly, radiating bonhomie.

"Thank you, thank you. But please call me Frank. And I could not have done it without your help. *Nem, nem soha!* What a brilliant idea. Certainly arouses that fiery *Magyar* spirit. Remind me please of its origin."

"It dates back to the 1920s, after the Treaty of Trianon, when Hungary lost two-thirds of its territory to the neighbouring countries like Romania, Yugoslavia and the Soviet Union. It was the national catchphrase: *no, no, never*, we will never accept Trianon," explained Kiraly. "You are a new face, but the message is that you understand Hungary, 'you feel its pain'."

"Or, Istvan, it means that you take one of Hungary's greatest historical traumas, an injustice that still reverberates today, and manipulate national sentiment for partisan political point-scoring," a female voice said. "And I have a question."

Sanzlermann and Kiraly turned to their right.

"Herr Sanzlermann, it's my pleasure to introduce Natasha Hatvani, from the *Budapest News*," said Kiraly, smiling brightly and nodding at Natasha, who was standing poised with pen and notebook. "Natasha always says, and writes, what she thinks."

Sanzlermann shot him a puzzled look: she was certainly attractive, but was this newspaper important?

Kiraly jumped in. "An English language publication, with a wide readership among Hungarian opinion-formers, politicians, diplomats and, of course, the expatriate community." He could hardly have anything *but* important journalists at his reception.

Sanzlermann bowed slightly. "Ms Hatvani, a pleasure to meet you. Please, go ahead with your question." Reinhard Daintner materialised by his side.

"Greece," she said.

"Greece? That is a country, not a question. Although some may think differently," Sanzlermann laughed and scratched his left hand.

"My question is, have *you* looked at a map recently?" she asked. "Turkey also borders Greece. Part of Turkey is in Europe. It's called Thrace. So why shouldn't Turkey join the EU?"

"Only a part, my dear, only a part. Perhaps we could let a slice of Turkey join the EU," said Sanzlermann. "Yes, that's a good idea. A slice of Turkey. Maybe at Christmas, ha ha. What do you think of that," he asked Daintner and Kiraly.

The PR consultant smiled politely. Daintner nodded slowly, as though this was a serious policy option to be considered.

Natasha pressed on: "Your opponents say you are deliberately whipping up hatred against the Roma. How do you respond?"

"With amazement. As you heard, we have just launched a new fund for Roma education," exclaimed Sanzlermann. He felt a tug at his elbow and Daintner murmured in his ear.

Sanzlermann moved away. "It was a pleasure to meet you, Ms Hatvani. We should discuss these issues at length when I have more time. Here is my card, just call my office if you would like an interview," he said, as Daintner directed him to the throng of reporters.

\* \* \*

Alex lay on his bed, wondering if he had chosen the best hiding place for Miklos' diary. He had photocopied it, and posted the duplicate by recorded delivery to an old friend in London. He then wrapped the original in thick plastic and brought in the largest plant from the balcony. He slid a knife around the edge of the pot, carefully removed the plant and its packed-in compost and placed the diary on the bottom, before covering it with soil and returning the plant to the balcony, where it looked as brown and dead as ever. He switched on the television and flicked through the afternoon programmes. CNN showed footage of the recent Bundestag car bomb. The newsreader, a slim African woman, announced: "In a videotape passed exclusively to CNN, Hasan Al-Ajnabi, leader of the Immigration Liberation Army, promised further outrages after last week's car bomb in Berlin, threatening strikes at targets across Europe."

A lean, hawk-faced man, dressed in camouflage fatigues stared at the camera. His eyes were the colour of obsidian and he spoke slowly and deliberately. "We are the Immigration Liberation Army. We live among you but we are invisible. We clean your offices. We cook your food. We care for your children. We sell you sex, all manner of pleasure. But you give us nothing, beat us, arrest us and deport us. We gave you no permission to plunder our lands in Africa, in Asia and the Americas. Now we will reclaim what is ours. By whatever means necessary."

The programme returned to the studio. "An ominous warning," said the newsreader.

Alex pressed the off button and walked over to the windows that opened onto the balcony. The plant shimmered in the wind on the other side of the glass. He stared out at the river. A police launch roared under the Elizabeth Bridge. Miklos' testimony had unleashed powerful emotions and filled in a piece of his family history. But Alex had read nothing there that could account for his death. The ghetto diary raised more questions than it answered.

\*   \*   \*

Natasha put her bag down and pulled up a chair in Kitty Kovacs' office. Even though it was Sunday, many of the staff were working, as the Presidential election campaign was generating extra pages and advertising. She poured two glasses of red wine from a bottle on the filing cabinet and handed one to Kitty. The advertising manager came from Pecs, a city in southern Hungary, near the Croatian border. Kitty was as ambitious as she was vivacious. She had no qualms about exploiting her shoulder-length raven hair, dark, come-hither eyes and Rubenesque figure to entice advertisers into buying space. She flirted outrageously but the nearest she ever got to her clients was the other side of a restaurant table.

"Want a new phone?" asked Kitty, putting down the glass and reaching into a box marked 'Magyar Mobile' next to her desk. She took out two handsets and tossed one to Natasha. "Two dozen just arrived, pay as you go, loaded with 100 euros worth of credit. The network's already working. It's a barter deal. Magyar Mobile get page five. We give away a dozen as prizes in a competition, and keep the rest. It's their own model, but quite good. It's even got GPS."

"Thanks," said Natasha, putting it in her bag without looking at it. "I'll give it to my mother."

"You're both very welcome. You don't look very happy. How was the rally?" asked Kitty.

"Sanzlermann is an incredible speaker. He was really well briefed, hitting all the right notes. It's amazing, watching him play the audience like a violin. If he carries on like this in every country I'm sure he'll win. I asked him for an interview. Do you think I'll get one?"

"Did you flirt with him?"

"Of course not," said Natasha indignantly. "That's not professional."

"Professional means getting the interview. It's a man's world out there, Natasha. You need to use everything you've got. And you've got a lot. I'm sure Alex thinks so. Let's call him and ask," she said, tapping out some numbers on her new handset, smiling mischievously.

"Stop it. We're colleagues, and that's all." Natasha took her press pack from her bag and put it down on Kitty's desk. Natasha moved over to check her email at Kitty's terminal. There was one email in her inbox, from Alex, thanking her for the *Magyar Tribün* article. It included the text of her email to Alex. Nothing from Gabor. Maybe he was finally getting the message.

"Only colleagues?" asked Kitty. "So why are you blushing?" She turned towards the screen.

"I'm not. And that's private," said Natasha.

"Not while you're using my computer. Hmm, very businesslike, but he did write back to you immediately. That's a good sign." Kitty scrolled down and continued reading. "An 'encounter'. When was that? Tell me everything." She turned to look at Natasha, grinning. "Encounters are *much* more interesting than sending each other boring articles from *Magyar Tribün*."

"It was work. And it's an interesting article," said Natasha, taking a gulp of wine.

"Who cares? I don't know why you are making life so difficult for yourself. He's not bad looking, he's intelligent, charming when he wants to be. And he's keen on you, don't pretend you haven't noticed the special attention your articles get," she said, laughing.

Natasha gathered her things and started for the door, her face set like stone.

"Natasha, wait," said Kitty, her voice rising in exasperation. "You can't keep yourself locked away for the rest of your life, just because of Gabor. It's been six months. Why are you punishing yourself like this? There's a whole new world out there."

Natasha stopped at the door, turned and sat down again. She lit a cigarette, inhaling deeply and blew a plume of smoke at the ceiling. "I keep remembering opening the front door and hearing the noises from the bedroom."

Kitty poured her some more wine. "Did you go in?"

"Yes. I wish I hadn't. He was with my best friend. I've known her since I was ten. Gabor and I had been together for five years. We were engaged. I would have been married by now. I moved straight back to my mother's."

"Then you had a narrow escape. He'd be doing the same now

and it would be much worse." Kitty clinked her wine glass against Natasha's. "Here's to new 'encounters'."

Natasha smiled cautiously and drank her wine. Maybe Kitty was right, she thought. She wasn't a nun. Her career was on track but her personal life was a disaster. At university her fellow students, the gilded-youth of the *Uj-gazdagok*, the new rich, spent their days and nights partying and sleeping with each other. At the end of each academic year they left 50,000 forints in their examination papers. Natasha had worked her way through college as a waitress in the pubs near the university, sometimes serving her classmates, who delighted in leaving her ten forint tips. In her spare time she had read English books out loud to hear the rhythm of the language, copied articles out of British newspapers to see how each story was put together, and taped BBC television programmes to perfect her pronunciation.

Unlike most of her classmates, she had never even been to Britain. But she had won the prize for English when she graduated, scoring the highest grades the university had ever awarded. Her fellow graduates now worked for banks and public relations companies, earning three or four times her salary. Natasha hadn't been to a proper restaurant since Gabor took her out on her birthday, last year. She couldn't remember when she had last bought new clothes. She told herself that she didn't care. She gave almost all of her salary to her widowed mother Irina. Her father, Professor Pal Hatvani, a world renowned authority on Pushkin, had taught at Budapest University for two decades but was sacked after the change of system. He was not interested in politics, and was hurt and bemused that his knowledge was suddenly judged worthless because there was a new government. Irina and Natasha found him one afternoon, sitting in his favourite armchair, his last cigarette smoking in the ashtray.

The door opened and Natasha turned to see a lean young woman with alert blue eyes and a wild mop of frizzy brown hair bustling in, two cameras draped around her neck. She held a sheaf of photographs in one hand, a mobile telephone clamped to her ear in the other.

"Yes, we'll be there. Try and ensure the models turn up on time with the right clothes this time will you?" Edina Draskovitz put her phone down and handed Kitty the photographs. Natasha offered her the wine, but she shook her head.

"The shots for your advertising supplement on the Budapest fashion industry," she said, her smoke-cured voice deep and husky. "One more designer to go, then I'm done. Hopefully onto something a bit more challenging."

Natasha looked Edina up and down. She was wearing baggy green army trousers, a fisherman's waistcoat and grey t-shirt. She might dress like a soldier but she was certainly a live wire. A couple of trips to the hairdresser, some decent make-up to high-light her bone structure and she would look very presentable. The photographs were very good indeed, and Edina had a fine eye for lighting and detail.

Kitty's telephone rang. "*Istvan*. Lovely to hear from you. I'm just hearing all about your rally. Of course, we must have lunch," she said, rolling her eyes at Natasha. "Istvan Kiraly," she silently mouthed. Natasha nodded. "Yes, she's here," said Kitty, handing the phone over.

Natasha perked up instantly as she spoke to Kiraly. "He does? When? Tomorrow? Tomorrow is fine, ten o'clock at the Hotel Savoy."

She hung up and turned to Kitty. "I've got an interview with Sanzlermann."

"A real story," interjected Edina. "You will need pictures. Call back and tell them you're bringing me as well," she demanded, lighting a cigarette and blowing smoke through her nostrils.

"Sorry, Edina. They only use their own campaign photographs," said Natasha, without pausing for breath. "But I'll ask again tomorrow, once I get there, and I'll call you if need be."

Edina looked doubtful as she left. "Ok. My phone will be switched on."

Kitty waited until the door was closed. "You are a dreadful liar. He wouldn't care if you brought a female photographer," she said, sounding amused. "He'd probably enjoy the attention. Poor Edina. Why are you trying to sabotage her career?"

"I'm not trying to sabotage anything. I just don't want to be distracted from my interview, that's all. She'll use up all the time, getting him to pose." She examined a glossy calendar on the wall. It showed two young women in leopard skin bikinis draped over a red sports car.

"What's this? A gift from a male admirer? Very sexist for a modern career woman."

"I don't know, I think it's quite entertaining," said Kitty. "Maybe we should get Edina one of those bikinis. She's skinny enough, she would look quite good."

"Why do you think she always wears those army clothes?" asked Natasha.

"She's a woman in a tough profession. She has to show she is as good a photographer as any man. You two should team up."

Natasha looked doubtful. "Maybe. She and Alex always have lots to talk about."

"Edina lived in London for years. She knows Britain. They can discuss the Queen, how to make cups of tea. Why don't you call Alex on your new phone, tell him about your big interview. Perhaps you can arrange another 'encounter'," said Kitty, smiling wickedly.

"Very funny," said Natasha, gathering her belongings and her press pack. "Now I really am going. Thanks for the wine and the phone. See you tomorrow. I've got a *very* important interview to prepare."

"Wait," said Kitty, "You forgot your USB stick, it's fallen out," but Natasha was already out of the door. Kitty inserted it into her computer, and clicked on a video file. Frank Sanzlermann appeared, outlining his vision of the new Europe. She yawned and moved to close the file, when her telephone rang again.

## NINE

### ROMA WOMEN IN EASTERN SLOVAKIA
### COMPLAIN OF INFERTILITY

**By our correspondent**

Kosice (SNSA) – There are repeated reports here among Romany women in the villages outside Kosice that they cannot have children. The problem is worst in the settlement of Novy Marek and its surrounds. Within the last two months, six Romany women have complained to their doctors, and appeared at hospitals, demanding to know why they are no longer conceiving. Romany women traditionally have up to six or more children.

"At first we thought that this was just coincidence," said local health official, Dr Veronika Husakova. "But non-Roma report normal levels of fertility. It is very mysterious, as when we examine the Romany women they have no gynaecological abnormalities."

Alex searched for the print out of the Slovak news agency report on his desk but it had disappeared into the pile of Monday's newspapers. The story was trickling out and they needed to move quickly. Natasha had already sent him her briefing about Novy Marek, cc-d to the editor, Ronald Worthington, and the news of her interview with Sanzlermann. Quite a scoop, but fifteen minutes meant four or five questions at the most. Alex had agreed with Natasha's suggestions that she focus on the Roma and xenophobia. He looked at his watch. It was 10.05am. The interview should have started by now. There was still no sign of Zsofi, who presumably was still in Vienna. Alex had sent her a text message, but there was no reply, or even a signal that it had been received. It was time, he knew, to implement his decision.

Kitty Kovacs stopped by his desk as he finally fished out the report. "Don't worry, she'll be in later," she whispered in his ear, winking as she walked off.

"Who?" Alex asked, as innocently as he could.

He walked through to the editor's office. It made his desk look positively tidy. Polish, Czech, Slovak, Hungarian and Romanian newspapers were heaped across the floor. A stack of invoices on a filing cupboard were held in place by a can of beer. A sack of pet food rested next to a case of wine and a cricket bat. The office had its own peculiar smell, a gamey but not unpleasant cocktail of coffee, alcohol and dog. Ronald Worthington sat with his feet up perusing the company's latest book: *High Living in Hungary*. He ran a relaxed regime. An easy-going but astute Fleet Street veteran approaching retirement, he had been despatched by the *Sentinel* to knock the paper into shape. With his bald shiny head, substantial girth, stentorian voice and baggy suits, he resembled a modern-day Sydney Greenstreet. Apart from newspapers, cricket and restaurants, Ronald's main interest was his loyal red setter, Ferrari.

"Alex, old chap. Have some coffee. There's a pot of Jamaican Blue Mountain on the go," he said, gesturing at a glass jug hissing gently in the corner. Ferrari looked up before returning to sleep in his favourite corner.

Alex poured himself a cup and picked up a ten day old copy of *Mlada Front Dnes*, the Czech daily. The pneumatic new Miss Czech Republic looked out from the front page. "You can't speak Czech," he said mock-accusingly.

"That picture's worth at least a thousand words. And look at this," he said, proudly holding up the thick glossy book. The cover showed a fat jolly chef in full whites, in a steamy kitchen, happily slurping soup from a large ladle. Two good humoured small blue eyes beamed out from a shiny, pudgy face.

"I didn't know you moonlighted as a model," said Alex.

"Now you do. So, to work. We've got a busy news week. There's Natasha's Sanzlermann interview, and now she's uncovered these murky goings on in eastern Slovakia. It's all very impressive. We're lucky that I spotted her journalistic potential."

"Really? I thought it was my idea to promote her. You said she should stay on the reception desk as she was so decorative," said Alex, as he handed Ronald the SNSA story.

Ronald speed read the report. The jolly fat man was replaced by a thoughtful professional. His pudgy fingers moved swiftly over his keyboard and he turned his screen towards Alex.

### GERMAN DRUGS COMPANY FINED FOR DUMPING OUT OF DATE DRUGS, ESCAPES MANSLAUGHTER CHARGES AFTER DEATH OF ROMA

#### By David Jones

Budapest (Reuters) – KZX Industries, Germany's biggest pharmaceutical company, has been fined 10,000 euros for distributing out of date drugs in eastern Slovakia.

The scandal emerged after five members of the same Romany family from the eastern Slovak village of Novy Marek died after being prescribed medicines that were at least three years past their use-by date and completely unsuitable for their illnesses.

Liberal and Socialist members of the European Parliament have introduced a motion protesting against the small size of the fine.

"That was a year ago. Nobody's ever heard of this place, and now it is in the news again," said Ronald. He walked over to a map of eastern Europe on the wall. "Right in the very back of beyond," he said, pointing at a tiny speck in eastern Slovakia, by the Polish and Ukrainian borders. Ronald returned to his desk and typed in www.slovakiatriumphant.com on his internet browser. The homepage offered streaming video with Czech, Polish, Hungarian or English subtitles. He clicked on English. The computer screen filled with the doughy face of the new Slovak Prime Minister, Dusan Hrkna. A bulky former Olympic boxer gone to seed, Hrkna had enjoyed a meteoric rise through the ranks of the Slovak Patriotic League. He had won a landslide election victory, despite repeated scandals over party officials giving voters beer emblazoned with the SNU symbol. Hrkna was speaking at a public meeting, pounding the podium while the audience roared its approval. English subtitles flowed across the bottom of the screen: "The Roma understand one thing," he proclaimed. The screen showed him slowly forming his fingers into a fist and punching the air. The crowd roared its approval.

Ronald paused the video and chewed a pencil. "Slovakia: the Prime Minister you can see for yourself, German pharmaceutical companies are dumping drugs there and Gypsies can't have kids. Pack your overnight bag. Take Natasha, she understands Slovak. And we'll need some photographs of the families in Novy Marek. See if Edina is free."

Alex looked doubtful. "We would be a bit mob-handed, with Edina as well. I'll also need someone to take us in. The Roma won't talk to us if we just turn up. That's already four."

"OK, go with Natasha but take a digital camera and make sure you get some pictures." Ronald gave him a wry look. "Alex, your considerations here are purely professional?"

"Of course," he replied, careful to keep his voice deadpan.

\* \* \*

The Hotel Savoy's presidential suite was on the top floor. Her mother's flat would have fitted comfortably inside, thought Natasha, as she walked in. There were three large rooms, all painted light green: a bedroom, lounge and office area. The furniture was original Beidermeyer, an elegant nineteenth century style. Oil paintings hung on the walls: a stag in a forest, a young woman in a ball-gown. Silk rugs covered the polished parquet floor. Stepping inside was like time travel back to Berlin or Vienna a century ago, to an age of deference, respect for authority and carefully graded social distinctions. The view was magnificent: the grey curve of the Elizabeth Bridge arching over the Danube, the Buda hills rolling into the distance. It was a sunny winter's day, the sky blue and flecked with clouds, but the heating inside was overpowering. The room smelled of cigars and aftershave. Natasha fought off a powerful urge to open a window.

Sanzlermann sat on a sofa in the middle of the lounge, and Reinhard Daintner sat next to him on an armchair. A bottle of Hungarian sparkling wine stood in a silver ice bucket on a nearby coffee table, flanked by two crystal glasses. Natasha walked over to an armchair but Sanzlermann stood up and beckoned her to come and sit next to him, on the sofa. She hesitated, then sat down at the other end, and placed her digital recorder on the coffee table. Reinhard Daintner walked over and placed an identical model next to hers. "So we both have an accurate record of Herr Sanzlermann's statements," he said dryly. "Would you like some tea or coffee, Miss Hatvani? Or something stronger?"

Natasha declined and opened her notebook, trying to sound efficient, businesslike and not at all nervous. This was the most important interview she had ever done, and she was still not quite sure why Sanzlermann had offered it. One reason might be the way he was smiling at her. He moved slightly nearer the middle of the sofa.

"Interview on the record with Frank Sanzlermann, for publication in the *Budapest News*," she began. "Herr Sanzlermann, your critics accuse you of whipping up hatred against the Roma. For example, in your speech yesterday you showed three pictures of Roma: of poverty and squalor, young criminals and two men fighting. You have also called for compulsory fingerprinting of Roma. Why only Roma? Isn't that racist?"

Sanzlermann leaned forward as he spoke. "I also announced the launch of our new Roma Education Fund, to which I have personally donated 250,000 euros. These claims of racism are baseless, but might be open to misinterpretation. So Miss Hatvani, I am happy to tell you that you now have a scoop. Our policy now, which I am pleased to make public here, is that everyone in Europe will be fingerprinted, and their prints, together with a DNA sample, stored on a secure database."

Daintner immediately sat up, a look of alarm on his face, and whispered rapidly in Sanzlermann's ear. He waved him away.

"What does it matter," he muttered, scratching his hand. "We were going to announce it this week anyway."

Natasha's heart thumped. She had not been expecting that answer. This really was a story. She looked at her notebook and back at Sanzlermann. She needed a follow up question. "Everyone? Every European citizen?"

"Everyone," said Sanzlermann decisively.

"And what if someone does not want to provide their fingerprints and a DNA sample?"

"Law-abiding citizens have nothing to fear. But to answer your question, anyone refusing will be subject to sanctions, initially civil, and ultimately criminal," he replied.

"Meaning what, exactly?" asked Natasha, the adrenalin coursing through her body as she scribbled notes in case the recorder failed. She looked down at the machine. The red recording light glowed comfortingly.

"Fines, then imprisonment, and ultimately being stripped of citizenship, which would render refusers liable to deportation," said Sanzlermann, his voice calm and reasonable as his fingers dug into the skin on his left hand.

Natasha's brain was whirling. "Deport them where? And how will you obtain DNA samples from people who don't want to give them?"

Reinhard Daintner interjected. "Miss Hatvani, as I am sure you understand we are still working on the policy details of this complex and hitherto *confidential* policy," he said, staring hard at Sanzlermann as his tongue flicked out over his lips. "Let us move on."

Natasha glanced at her watch, an antique timepiece that had once belonged to her grandmother. She had nine minutes left. "What is your opinion of the new Gendarmerie?"

"A new national police force that combines intelligence gathering with law enforcement? It sounds like an excellent idea," said Sanzlermann.

"But we already have national and regional police forces. Why do we need an unaccountable paramilitary militia?"

"Frankly speaking, these are internal matters for your government. But let me speak in general terms. Hungary, like most of Europe, suffers from increasing levels of crime. A new approach is certainly needed, to unify the various law enforcement agencies under a cohesive efficient leadership. And as far as I understand the Gendarmerie is absolutely accountable. It reports to the Prime Minister, who is elected by universal vote in a free and fair election."

"But why 'Gendarmerie'," demanded Natasha. "The word has terrible historical associations here. The Gendarmerie put the Jews on the trains at gunpoint in 1944."

"Nineteen forty four was a long time ago. What I think, what the European People's Union thinks, and Prime Minister Attila Hunkalffy agrees, is that we must move on. We cannot allow Europe to be forever haunted by events that took place more than sixty years ago, no matter how regrettable they might have been."

"*Might* have been?" said Natasha.

"Were. I mean were, of course." She watched him gouge his hand again, deep enough to leave red marks across the skin. "But this is a different age, and difficult times call for strong measures, and strong leadership." He caught her watching him and immediately stopped scratching. He smiled, sat up and looked into her eyes. "Some *sekt*?" he asked, as he picked up the bottle. His blue eyes seemed to glow from within as he leaned forward to fill her glass.

There was no denying how handsome he was, Natasha thought. It had been a long time since a good-looking man had offered to pour her a drink. She steeled herself. "No, not for me, thank you." she said, putting her hand over her glass just as Sanzlermann began to pour. The wine splashed over her hand and onto her trousers. She jumped up and knocked over the coffee table. Wine, ice-bucket, and digital recorders tumbled to the floor. Natasha stepped back and apologised, her face red with embarrassment.

Sanzlermann picked up several napkins and handed one to Natasha. "It's nothing. Really, don't worry. A minor accident. Shall we call room service to help with your wet clothes?"

Natasha shook her head, and patted her trousers with the napkin. "There's really no need, thank you." Daintner handed her the digital recorder, which she placed on the table. She checked the light: it still glowed red. "Again, I do apologise for that. But let's proceed." Natasha looked down at her notebook. "Isn't your party encouraging xenophobia against Muslims?"

Sanzlermann looked shocked. "Xenophobia? How? I am fully committed to ensuring the rights of all minorities, of whatever colour or creed, as long as they accept our modern European values. It is not us who are encouraging anti-immigrant prejudice, but the outrages perpetrated by groups such as the so-called Immigration Liberation Army."

The telephone rang, cutting Sanzlermann off. Daintner answered, and handed it to Sanzlermann. "Attila, a pleasure to hear you. In ten minutes? Yes, that's fine."

He turned to Natasha. "I apologise, but I have to cut our interview short. Your Prime Minister summons me. I hope you have something you can use."

"I certainly do. Thank you for your time," she said, and quickly left.

* * *

From the outside the Sphinx Egyptian Restaurant looked unremark-able, even unwelcoming, and the owners seemed to like it that way. Grimy windows, a hand-written menu in Arabic taped to the glass, a tattered poster of the Red Sea Riviera. Inside, shipped Formica tables and canteen chairs. Tucked away in the run-down Seventh district, not far from Keleti, the city's eastern railway station, the Sphinx looked out over Garay Square market. By day Chinese stall-holders sold imitation Nike trainers and stale shrink-wrapped German Chocolate cakes; robust countryside women offered vast jars of pungent, home-made pickles and live squawking chickens. Other goods could also be obtained: a U.S. or E.U. passport complete with valid visas; a new BMW; a crate of Kalashnikovs, still packed in factory grease. At 10.00pm on a Monday the square was deserted.

Alex and Mubarak sat at the back of the restaurant's corner. A bottle of Lebanese arak, a carafe of water, an overflowing bowl of pistachio shells, humous and salads sat on the table between them. Mubarak's minder Hamid sat a few metres away, reading an Arabic newspaper. Despite its dilapidated appearance, the Sphinx served the city's best Middle Eastern food. Alex dipped a piece of pita bread into the rich, nutty humous. The smell of grilling kebabs, rich and spicy, wafted through the restaurant.

"Something I've been meaning to ask you," he said. A lone backpacker diligently spooned up lentil soup, a guide book resting on the bowl.

Mubarak poured them both some arak. "How can I help you, Alex? My prediction for the dollar rate against the euro? Good buys on the FTSE or the New York stock exchange? The Romanian property market is booming."

Alex had met Mubarak soon after his arrival at the *Budapest News*. The paper had been in the midst of one of its periodic cash-flow crises. The promised funds from the *Sentinel* had not yet arrived, and even the pile of ten thousand forint notes that Ronald Worthington carried in his back pocket were spent. The printer was demanding payment within twenty-four hours, or he would pulp that week's paper, with its biggest ever advertising spend. It would have been the last issue. Spurred on by Ronald Worthington standing on his desk and delivering a resounding version of Henry V's speech at Agincourt, the staff rallied. Bank accounts were emptied, credit cards maxed-out, relatives tapped for loans. Alex had been despatched to Café Casablanca with a briefcase full of euros and dollars. The room had fallen silent as he walked in, like a scene from a bad western. Alex asked a man dressed in a purple velvet jacket and orange trousers if he knew what the forint exchange rate was. Mubarak did. As a loyal reader of the *Budapest News* he donated an extra 50,000 forints. The paper was saved, a friendship born.

"What do you know about the ILA, the Immigrant Liberation Army?" asked Alex.

"Very little," said Mubarak, pouring more water onto the arak, turning the drink an oily milky-white. He paused while the waiter, a bald giant with a long moustache, who looked as though he should be guarding a harem, set down a plate of kebabs on the table with a flourish. Mubarak piled several on Alex's plate before serving himself. "The curious thing is that nobody seems to know anyone with any connection at all to them. Setting up a terrorist organisation is expensive, and time-consuming. You need funds, organisation, recruiters, and safe houses, secure communication networks. There is usually a supporters' organisation, like the IRA's Sinn Fein. A website, something. Inevitably, there are leaks. Someone talks, people hear things. Except with the ILA. Off goes the bomb, and silence. Until Hasan al-Ajnabi – his name means something like 'the good foreigner' you know – is back on CNN, promising us more blood and death."

Mubarak paused and speared another kebab. "And you?"

Alex shrugged. "The same. Mostly what I see on television."

Mubarak sipped his arak. He laid his hand on Alex's arm. "What about your grandfather? Is there any news?"

"The post-mortem results will be released at some stage. I am also looking into it myself."

"Anything I can do to help, Alex, you know. We have to stand together against these *mumzers*," he said, using the Yiddish word for bastards.

Alex laughed. "Where did you learn that?"

"Not far from here actually. At school, from Eszter Weiss. We were sixteen. She taught me several things," he said, nostalgia flitting across his face. "She lives in London now. Married to an accountant in Golders Green. I see that London is full of Russians now. Which reminds me, we are being invaded by Ukrainians. Some old faces, many new. The new ones are very violent."

The waiter appeared and cleared away their plates, before murmuring in Mubarak's ear. Mubarak answered: "*Aiwa, min-fadlik*, yes please."

Coffee appeared, thick and dark, together with sticky pastries drenched in sugar syrup. The two men leaned back companiably. The waiter brought out two water-pipes, elaborate constructions of glass and polished brass. He prepared them: the tobacco packed just so, the coals glowing a certain colour. Mubarak took a small cube from his pocket, wrapped in silver paper. He showed it to

Alex, who smiled. Mubarak broke off a small piece of brown resin and crumbled it over the coals. The smell of burning rope drifted across the room. The backpacker, by now the only other customer, looked up, happily surprised, less so when his bill arrived and he was ushered to the cashier and out of the door.

The waiter locked it and pulled the shutters down. The magnificent voice of Um Kulthoum, Egypt's most famous singer, filled the room. She sang, her voice vibrating with enough grief and longing to make the pyramids crumble. Alex puffed on the pipe, watching the smoke bubble through the water. It tasted cool and sweet, nothing like the throat-burning marijuana grown on Csepel Island that appeared at *Budapest News* parties. The music coursed through his body. He floated peacefully. Zsofi's face merged into Natasha's. Alex smiled and looked over at Mubarak staring into space, smoke wafting from his nostrils, lost in his thoughts.

Alex sat entranced, the music coursing through his whole body. He opened his eyes to a loud knocking on the door. He blinked and sat up. Mubarak walked over to Hamid, and murmured instructions into his ear. Hamid reached for his mobile telephone, and Mubarak walked to the restaurant's entrance. Alex moved to follow him, but he held his hand up and went alone. The waiter appeared with the keys and opened the door. The lights went on in several apartments overlooking the square.

"Horses' asses!" someone shouted. Two Gendarmerie officers stood outside, one male, with a narrow face, thin sandy hair and nervous eyes. The boss, it was clear, was a tired-looking middle-aged female, a chunky bottle blonde with dark roots. A loud bang sounded as something bounced off the police car roof. The young Gendarme jumped, and reached for his gun.

The female Gendarme sighed, bent down and picked a large potato from the ground. She handed it to her colleague. "Take it home to Mum, Geza," she said, wearily.

Mubarak laughed. "Sergeant Kovacs. A pleasure as always. I see you've joined the Gendarmes. What can I do for you tonight? Or rather for Captain Toth?"

She shrugged apologetically. "We all have, including Captain Toth. They pay double what I got before. Sorry, sweetheart. He says we have to bring you in. Maybe he wants to go on holiday again. Where was it last time? Greece?"

Mubarak snorted. "I wish. Two weeks in the Seychelles."

"Come on then, get your coat," said Sergeant Kovacs. "You know the form. The sooner you're in, the faster you can be out and back at home."

## TEN

Alex squeezed onto the early-morning metro to Keleti station. Sullen commuters pored over their free newspapers, and a gang of schoolchildren chattered excitedly. He found a space pressed against the rear door of the carriage, his overnight bag between his legs. A bearded homeless man sat a metre away, exuding a powerful odour of stale sweat and urine. Budapest's Soviet-built metro was cheap, fast and reliable. But the outside of the carriage was covered with graffiti and the hard plastic chairs were cracked and battered. 'Gypsy Free Zone' – the name of a new far-right rock group – was scrawled along the top of the door. Frank Sanzlermann grinned down from the advertising placards. Alex had yet to see a single poster for his main opponent, Edith Leclerc. Sanzlermann's camp seemed to have bought up every empty hoarding in the city.

Alex tried not to breathe the stale, pungent air too deeply. The train rolled out of Blaha Luiza metro station, picking up speed as it headed towards Keleti train station, the next stop. He looked at his watch: 7.42am. The train to Kosice left at 8.06am. He was cutting it fine. No word from Mubarak, but he had seemed nonchalant when he drove off with the police officers. Hamid had assured Alex there was nothing to worry about. The bribes were 'business expenses', even written off by Mubarak's accountant. Zsofi had called when Alex was drifting off to sleep. She was back from Vienna and wanted to come over. Not tonight, he told her. "Why not?" she asked, almost indignantly. "Because I'm going to Slovakia tomorrow with a colleague. I'm meeting *her* – he knew it was juvenile but could not resist a slight emphasis – at 8.00am." Silence had followed, for several seconds. "Enjoy yourself," Zsofi snapped. "Thanks, I'll try. Good night," he said, and hung up. He felt quite proud of himself, and enjoyed his first good night's sleep in days, helped by Mubarak's water-pipe.

Two vivacious young women, a plump redhead and a tall brunette with a noisy laugh, stood nearby. They had well-styled hair and were carefully made-up. Even though it was winter, they were dressed in figure hugging skirts and well cut heavy coats. Hungarian women certainly knew how to use every asset they had, thought Alex admiringly. They both worked at a car assembly line and were gossiping about their German boss, Helmut, who had repeatedly asked the redhead out to dinner. So far she had declined, worried for her job if it all went wrong.

"You're absolutely right, Ildiko. Keep work and play in separate compartments. What if he just wants a bit of fun?" said her brown-haired friend. "He's not very good-looking, And he's got a moustache! It would tickle."

"Depends where," said the redhead, laughing.

The train juddered and stopped in the tunnel. The lights flickered, it crawled forward a few metres, then stopped again. Alex's heart thumped faster. He told himself that it would move any second. The lights flickered again and went out. The darkness was absolute. Nervous laughter coursed through the carriage. The schoolchildren joked and fell silent. Several passengers reached for their mobile phones, cones of light cutting through the blackness. The rumble of trains echoed in the distance. The homeless man began moaning, his smell seemingly getting even stronger. Alex felt the tunnel walls steadily close in, as though they were inching towards him. Someone lit a cigarette lighter and shadows danced on the anxious faces. There was no way out. No way out. The words bounced around Alex's head. He tried to control his rising panic but his hands were wet with sweat.

*He is locked in a dark, windowless cell in Mostar prison. He hears a key turning in a lock, sees the heavy door open. The Bosnian Croat soldier is drunk, almost staggering, the brandy fumes coming off him in waves as he walks. He has a torch in one hand and an*

*AK-47 in the other. He shines the torch on Alex, laughing as he prods him with the barrel of his gun. Alex blinks and recoils, trying to shield his eyes from the sudden light.*

*"You, journalist. Muslim lover. We will deal with you, like we dealt with them," he says. "One shot, maybe two. In the head, if you are lucky." The soldier jabs him in the stomach with the end of the gun barrel. Alex gasps in pain. "Or maybe here, if you are not." The soldier raises the gun and fires several shots into the ceiling. The noise is thunderous. Chunks of concrete fly around the room. A jagged lump smashes into Alex's shoulder, sending him reeling against the wall. The soldier fires once more and staggers out. The cell door shuts. Alex touches his shoulder. His shirt is ripped, the skin torn and bleeding. A warm trickle slides down the inside of his leg to the floor.*

Alex felt the dread straining in his chest. It was a living thing trying to burst out, to force its way into the carriage, into the tunnel. It would gallop along the tracks until it found a station, with escalators that rose into the air, and open spaces, until it was free and could evaporate. Sweat slipped down his forehead. He began to hyperventilate. He willed himself not to try and force the carriage doors open. A light shone on his face and he jerked away in fright.

"Are you all right, love? Don't be scared," asked the redhead, using her mobile telephone as a torch. "It's only a phone. You don't look very well." She put her hand on Alex's shoulder.

Alex blinked and swallowed. "Please don't shine it in my face," he said, trying to smile.

"Sorry, love. These trains are always stopping in the middle of nowhere. Nothing to worry about. Where are you off to today then?" she asked brightly, bringing the handset down.

"Slovakia." She was being kind, Alex knew, trying to distract him from the panic attack. The fear fed itself. Think about something else and it would fade. "Kosice. I'm going with a friend."

"Lucky you, at least you won't be stuck in a factory all day, with Helmut," she laughed.

Alex took a deep breath, breathing slowly through his nose. He had been released from the Mostar prison. The train would soon move. He wiped his hands on his trousers. The train would soon move. Wouldn't it? The lights flickered on and a tinny voice apologised. The carriage lurched forward and pulled into Keleti station.

"There now," said the redhead. "I told you there was nothing to worry about."

"Thank you. You're very kind," said Alex, gratefully.

He picked up his bag and headed into the station. Despite its seedy appearance Keleti's familiar yellow departure hall had never looked so welcoming. The platforms were lined with fast food stalls, offering fried meatballs of doubtful provenance and cheap wine ladled out from aluminium barrels into plastic cups. Pirate taxi drivers wearing home made badges proclaiming 'Official Taxi' touted for passengers among disorientated tourists. Swarthy men in tracksuits stood around smoking, guarding woven plastic bags filled with cheap clothes and sports shoes. Alex weaved past a peasant lady, swaddled in flowered skirts and laden with bags overflowing with peppers and tomatoes, and just missed bumping into a very overweight Gendarme.

The newspaper stands were piled with copies of *Ébredjetek Magyarok!* and local language editions of *Playboy, Hustler* and *Penthouse*. He glanced at the cover lines on the women's magazines: 'Magyar Mothers Prefer Home to the Office', was one article's offering, while another offered advice on 'How to Keep Your Hungarian Husband Happy'. None displayed the *Budapest News*. Lately he had asked several kiosks around the city without success for a copy. It was not sold out, but rather, the stallholders said, was 'unavailable'. A crowd of humanity speaking a babble of languages surged underneath the information board. Alex heard Romanian, Serbian, Russian and even Turkish. Trains left south from Keleti for Belgrade, before going on to Sofia and Istanbul, and east to Lvov and Kiev, before trundling north to Moscow and St Petersburg. The train to Kosice departed from platform five, a few yards away.

The Gendarme barred his path. His giant belly strained against his jacket and rolls of fat rippled over his collar. His grubby cockade drooped over his cap. "Destination?" he demanded.

"Slovakia. That's my train. Just over there." He glanced at his watch: 7.55am.

"Your train? I don't think so. Papers," he grunted.

Alex handed over his press card, smelling the stale tobacco on his rank breath. A stubby finger prodded his chest. "I'm talking to you," the Gendarme said.

"I just gave you my identification."

"Don't get clever. Passport. Or I'll have you in the station. And you wouldn't want that."

Alex looked over to Keleti's small police station, now run by the Gendarmerie. Two Gendarmes were manhandling a young Romany man in a shiny shell-suit. His protests were cut off with several slaps around his face and the Gendarmes threw him into the foyer. Alex handed over his passport. The Gendarme looked through its pages and scribbled in a grubby notebook when a policeman walked over. He was slim, in his late twenties, with buzz cut blond hair, and intelligent blue eyes behind rimless designer glasses.

"Is this man bothering you?" he asked.

"No, it's all under control," the Gendarme replied, not bothering to look up.

"I wasn't asking you," the policeman said. He turned to Alex. "Is he?"

"Yes. Immensely."

The Gendarme bristled. "What the fuck is it to you?" he demanded, turning to the policeman. "This man is," he said, rustling in his pockets, and pulling out a laminated sheet of paper, "disturbing citizens' tranquillity."

The policeman laughed mockingly. "Horseshit. He's trying to catch a train. You and your Gendarmes are the ones disturbing citizens' tranquillity."

Alex watched with pleasurable fascination as the Gendarme looked around for help. Six more policemen walked over and surrounded him. Two took out their billy clubs and began smacking them into their palms. The blond policeman held out his palm. The Gendarme reluctantly handed him Alex's passport.

The policeman flicked through its pages and gave it to Alex. "Bon voyage, Mr Farkas."

Alex thanked him and ran down the platform. Natasha waved at him from the window and the whistle sounded as he clambered aboard. She had found an empty compartment, with two rows of seats facing each other. It looked like it had not been cleaned since the collapse of communism. The windows were caked in dirt, their rubber seals cracked and peeling, the upholstery on the seating grubby and torn. It smelled of dirt and tobacco. Natasha sat by the window, that day's *Magyar Tribün* and *Ébredjetek Magyarok!* next to her. Alex flopped down on the facing bench, near the door.

"Good morning. That was close," she said dryly.

"Closer than you think," said Alex. He flicked through his passport. A business card fell out: Captain Jozsef Hermann – Criminal Intelligence. He put the card in his wallet, puzzled. Why would such a high ranking officer be hanging around at Keleti station at eight in the morning?

Natasha rummaged in her bag. "I brought you the Sanzlermann interview transcript, and my article. I've emailed them both to Ronald."

She handed Alex the print-outs as the train began its slow trundle east, past the blocks of grey communist era flats. Alex quickly read them through and looked at her in admiration. The news story was perfectly structured, explaining how Sanzlermann wanted to take DNA samples, by force it seemed, if necessary, from everyone in the European Union and store it on a central database. She even had quotes from a human rights organisation about civil liberties. They had a major international scoop. David Jones would be green with envy.

"Brilliant," he said enthusiastically. "Well done."

A half-smile flickered on her face and she picked up her newspaper. Alex's telephone rang and he scrabbled in his pocket.

"Alex, old chap," said Ronald. "Dusan Hrkna has just announced that Novy Marek has been sealed off. A closed medical zone, while they investigate. Can you still get in?"

"We'll already on the train, so we'll have to try. I'll call you." He hung up and sat back, pondering his unlikely guardian angel before drifting off to sleep.

*   *   *

Vince Szatmari was troubled. He couldn't concentrate. He recognised the words, but they were just swirls and squiggles of ink. He usually enjoyed the lunchtime bible study class, at the St Korona church, not far from the Hungarian National Bank, where he worked in the state privatisation department. It was tricky trying to juggle spiritual values and success. He admitted that he also wanted a comfortable life and why shouldn't he? An only child, he had studied hard for his degree in economics, supported himself through college and sent money home to his mother, alone and widowed in their home village. He was certainly proud of his job, but Bible study was a reminder that material success was not everything.

The high-roofed Gothic church usually brought him a sense of tranquillity, and he loved to gaze at the delicate stained-glass scenes from the lives of the Apostles, but today they did nothing to calm his inner agitation. The site had served many religions: a Roman temple had first stood here, when Hungary was known as 'Pannonia', then one of the country's first churches, turned into a mosque under the Ottomans – a *mihrab,* a prayer niche facing Mecca – survived, still inscribed with Arabic script, and now it was a place of Catholic worship.

There were half a dozen of them, sat in a semi-circle around the priest. A trio of earnest university students, a young girl who worked in a grocery shop and an elderly lady who lived nearby. The priest, Father Gabor Fischer, was a softly spoken giant with a neatly trimmed beard, and warm, kind eyes. A former Olympic discus champion, he brewed his own powerful *szilva palinka*, plum brandy.

The priest looked at Vince, who was usually so attentive but now seemed lost in his reverie. "Perhaps Vince can help us with that one. Vince?"

"Help with what?" Vince jerked up, plucking at his tie as though it might answer for him.

"Well, my son, as an important man in the world of finance, I thought you might be able to give us some of your thoughts on a question that has bothered Christian thinkers of many centuries," Father Fischer's voice was affectionate as he regarded the young man's confusion.

"Is it really easier for a camel to pass through the eye of a needle than for a rich man to enter heaven? Nowadays we see many rich people. That, they say, is the price of freedom. But how much does one have to give away, to become a person worthy of entering the Lord's domain?"

"That is a difficult question, Father. I think, as much as one can, but still be able to live in comfort and support his family. It is a question of individual conscience," said Vince.

"So many things are," said the priest. "Every day I see an old lady going through the dustbins for food. I give her money. But how much should I give her? Enough for bread, enough for meat, or enough to go to a restaurant? I love restaurants. Should I give her the money I would spend there?"

The discussion carried on for a few more minutes, until Father Fischer closed the session with a brief prayer. Vince was almost out of the door, when the priest called him back.

"Vince, can you spare a couple of minutes?"

Father Fischer regarded the young man. He was a good lad, always willing to help out when an old person needed some shopping or an errand running. Tall and skinny, with untidy blond hair that flopped over his heavy black-rimmed glasses, he often seemed distracted, today even more than usual. But he knew that Vince had a probing mind and a strong moral sense.

"Come, sit down for a moment," he said, leading the young man to a long wooden pew. "Is something bothering you, my son?"

Vince stared at the stained-glass window. Jesus fed a crowd with loaves and fishes. He was silent for several seconds. The priest waited patiently.

"Father, if you knew that things were happening at your workplace, which could, almost certainly will, eventually, lead to a lot of hardship for innocent people, would it be your duty to do something about it? Especially if you have to support someone else who relies on you for money to live. Because you might lose that job. Or is it better to just concentrate on your own responsibilities and forget about things you have seen or heard that were not meant for you?"

Father Fischer looked at him sympathetically. "I think we had better talk in my office."

*   *   *

Alex jerked awake as the train stopped at the Slovak frontier. Both Hungary and Slovakia were part of the Schengen Zone, so in theory there were no border checks. An ancient Lada wheezed past, belching exhaust fumes. A young thin Romany woman, her face already lined and drawn, hawked cold drinks and snacks through the carriage windows. Alex bought two cans of cola and cheese sandwiches and gave one of each to Natasha. They unwrapped the food and began to eat.

The carriage door banged open. *"Passport!"* demanded a moon-faced border guard as he marched in with an unmuzzled Alsatian on a lead. His belt was loaded with handcuffs, a pistol in a leather holster, a truncheon and a can of pepper spray. Alex put his sandwich down and handed his passport over. The guard leafed through it carefully, slowly checking every page. He looked at the photo and at Alex several times. He punched the document's number into a small handheld computer. After a few seconds the screen flashed.

"Alex, Alex," the guard said into his radio. "A – l – e-x-a-n-d-e-r," he said, slowly spelling out the letters, "F– a – r – k – a – s. *Ano, ano,* yes, yes." The Alsatian growled.

The guard turned to Alex. "Open your bag." He went through it methodically, unfolding Alex's clothes, even opening his soap bag. "What is the purpose of your visit to Slovakia?"

"Holiday," said Alex. Rule number one when lying, he thought: never over explain.

The guard shook his head. He kept Alex's passport in his hand and walked across to Natasha. She was eating and reading *Magyar Tribün*. She glanced up, handed over her Hungarian passport and returned to her newspaper. The guard thumbed through it, reached for his handset and spelled out her name. A burst of crackly Slovak came over the radio. Natasha put her newspaper down as the guard stared at her. He looked her up and down as though she was the star offering at an Ottoman slave market. He began to unpack her clothes, carefully examining her salmon-pink silk knickers. He held her knickers up to the light, leering at Natasha and twirling her brassiere round on his finger.

"Just your colour. Why don't you see if it fits?" she asked derisively.

"We'll see how funny you are in ten minutes," the guard said, smiling coldly. The dog barked, straining against its leash.

Alex stepped forward, his heart pounding.

\* \* \*

*He is sitting in a car with his interpreter, waiting at a checkpoint just behind the Croat border, not far from Banja Luka, epicentre of Serb ethnic cleansing. It is a sweltering summer's day. A wave of Muslim refugees pours out of the city towards the barricades. He smells the cordite, hears the rattle of machine gunfire nearby. The refugees are nearly all women, some so old they can barely walk, and children. The women wear brightly coloured headscarves. They carry a few scattered belongings in plastic bags, babies in their arms. The children cry as they try to keep up. Where are the men? The womens' stories are garbled, incoherent once they have crossed over to Croat-controlled territory. Names, places, times, all are jumbled up in a kaleidoscope of terror. But each tells of executions, husbands taken away at night. Of screams and pleading. Of neighbours who pointed their houses out to the Serb militiamen, neighbours they had invited to weddings and family celebrations.*

*He sees the Bosnian Serb soldier, drunk, staggering up to the procession of terrified humanity. The young woman is just a few steps from no-man's land and sanctuary. Alex wills her to move forward, to go faster. The soldier grabs her arm, and pulls off her headscarf. She had covered herself to try and disguise her beauty. The soldier leers at her high cheekbones, and dark eyes. He laughs and grabs her long black hair. Her mother wails and sobs. Alex watches the young woman pray, her lips moving quickly, as the soldier drags her away, towards the woods.*

\* \* \*

"That's enough," said Alex.

He walked over and lifted the underwear from the border guard's finger. The guard said nothing, too amazed to react. Alex picked up Natasha's clothes and began to place them back in her bag. Natasha watched silently. The guard reached for his handcuffs and pepper spray.

Alex turned to him, speaking calmly. "This is an open border between two European Union member states. Free and unhindered travel is guaranteed by agreements signed by Slovakia. Either you arrest us, in which case you must inform our embassies – and we have notified people that we are crossing here, so enquiries will be made if we do not arrive – or you must let us travel on. It is up to you. If you continue this harassment and intimidation I will make an official complaint. I will notify the British and Hungarian embassies and the international media. And I will name you."

He looked at the name patch on the guard's uniform. "Mr Pucak."

The border guard glared at Alex for several seconds, his hand hovering over the pepper spray. He grunted and handed their passports back.

"Enjoy your holiday," he sneered, as he left the carriage.

Alex handed Natasha her brassiere. "Thanks," she said, looking curiously at Alex, before folding it and putting it in her bag.

Alex sat down. He squeezed his eyes closed, his hands under his legs so she would not see them shaking.

## ELEVEN

Vince Szatmari walked over to the *Budapest News* office on Monday lunchtime. He had talked at length again with Father Fischer after Sunday Mass. The report he had found lying on a cistern in one of the toilets at the National Bank was stamped 'Confidential'. Normally he would have handed it in to the receptionist. But when he saw the name 'Ignac Akardy' at the top of the document he read it. By the time he reached the end he was puzzled, and very worried. Akardy was Vince's boss. Portly and pompous, with a taste for ostentatious gold watches, Akardy had twice dropped unsubtle hints to Vince about share buys, that in other countries might have led to charges of insider trading. Vince had not acted on them, but in both cases he noted that the prices leapt after a massive investment by a consortium of Swiss banks.

But that was not why he wanted to talk to the *Budapest News*. He didn't trust the partisan Hungarian press but the foreign journalists seemed accurate and objective. Akardy had banned the newspaper from the office after its series on corruption in Hungarian banks. He walked up to the front door of the grand apartment building opposite Nyugati station. The newspaper's office was on the fifth floor. What was it they called what he wanted to do in English? Blowing? Whistling and blowing? Whistle blowing, that was it. He pressed the buzzer by the entry-phone.

"Hallo, my name is Vince Szatmari and I want to blow a whistle."

He groaned inside. Hungarians always announced themselves by their name. But this was not the time to broadcast his. He was anyway not that confident in English, and it sounded all wrong.

A female voice sounded through the speaker. "Are you looking for a sports shop? There's one around the corner."

"No, no, you misunderstand me. I want to blow a whistle, not buy one."

"This is a newspaper office. We don't sell whistles," said the voice before breaking the connection. Vince turned on his heel in frustration.

\* \* \*

Alex watched from the window as the train trundled into Kosice. "Dusan Hrkna: King of Slovakia" was crudely painted on the station wall in letters three metres high. Three burly men in leather jackets stood on the platform, walkie-talkies in hand. His telephone beeped twice and he looked at the screen: an empty text message from a blocked number. It beeped again: another blank screen. Alex quickly pulled the curtains closed and picked up his bag, gesturing for Natasha to follow him out of the compartment. They ran down the corridor to the end of the carriage, continuing through the cars to the end of the train. As soon as it stopped they climbed down and clambered over the railway lines until they came to a concrete embankment. Narrow, steep steps were cut into its side, leading to a busy highway, twenty metres above. A rusting fifty litre drum of motor oil stood at the top of the stairs. Alex turned round to see the three men running down the tracks towards them, shouting into their walkie-talkies.

"Go, quickly," he told Natasha, following her as she ran up the stairs. She stumbled on the crumbling concrete but quickly righted herself. They stood at the top, catching their breath. Cars rushed by, weaving from lane to lane, drivers honking impatiently. Alex looked back. The three men were a hundred metres from the embankment. He scanned the motorway but there was no sign of a grey Volkswagen Golf.

Alex pointed at the oil drum. "Help me with this." They pushed the container towards the top of the stairs. Alex levered off the lid with a fifty forint coin. The first pursuer sprinted up the embankment stairs. Natash held the drum while Alex tipped it forward. A tide of thick, filthy motor oil gushed down the steps, splashing over the man in the leather jacket, drenching his trousers and shoes. He cursed and toppled backwards, his walkie-talkie flying in the air. Alex lifted the drum higher and the last of the oil flowed out down the steps. He looked around again – where *was* she?

Natasha stood laughing. Two more security agents arrived at the foot of the stairs, staring at Alex and Natasha with fury. One tried to scrabble up the side of the embankment, away from the oil, but slipped back down. He pulled out a mobile telephone, punched the keyboard and barked angrily into the handset.

"When do you think your friend might get here?" Natasha asked brightly, as though enquiring about the time of the next bus.

A battered Volkswagen Golf pulled up, tyres skidding. Alex pulled the doors open, gesturing for Natasha to sit in the back, and jumped in next to the driver. Svetlana Todorova slammed the car into first gear and shot off into the traffic, triggering a chorus of outraged hooting. "So you got the messages. We put the oil there this morning. That is the only other way out of the station. Here, wipe your hands," she said, passing Alex a box of tissues. "We heard that state security knew you were coming. Anyone asking about Novy Marek is added to a watch list."

Svetlana was a bustling and energetic woman in her mid-thirties with large brown eyes. Long curly russet-coloured hair cascaded around a round, intelligent face. She wore a shapeless blue skirt, a brown baggy jumper and a black fake leather jacket. But somehow the mismatched ensemble only added to the impression that the deputy head of the Roma Rights Action Group was a woman who knew her own mind.

"Welcome to Kosice," said Svetlana, looking at Natasha in the drivers' mirror.

"*Dakujem*, thank you," she replied in Slovak, to Svetlana's delight. The two women immediately switched to Slovak, chatting like old friends. Svetlana slowed down as she drove through Kosice's pleasant, spacious old town. A Habsburg spirit and the remnants of empire lingered – an imposing cathedral, an opera house and public gardens. The Art Nouveau main street was dotted with terrace cafés.

"It looks nice, doesn't it" asked Svetlana, not waiting for an answer. "It's not. No Roma are allowed to live here. They cannot even go to any of those pretty cafés or they will get arrested, beaten up or both. The Roma have all been moved to Lunik IX, a ghetto on the edge of the city. It was built in the communist era as housing for police and soldiers but now the local municipality uses it as a dumping ground. We think at least 10,000 people are crammed into housing built for 2,500. There is 100 per cent unemployment, and the authorities have cut off electricity and gas, so everyone lives off pirated supplies."

Svetlana speeded up and drove over a concrete flyover, out of town. Road signs showed the way east, towards the Ukrainian border. They passed through a wasteland of abandoned factories and half demolished industrial buildings until she pulled over, in front of rows of concrete tower blocks. "And now you can see for yourself. Welcome to Lunik IX."

Romany men stood on street corners, smoking and watching suspiciously as they got out of the car. Dismembered vehicles rusted away, engine parts scattered across the walkways. Children chased each other around piles of smoking rubbish. The outside of the tower blocks were spotted with black scorch marks. Empty window frames gaped. Lunik IX looked like Sarajevo without the shell damage, Alex thought.

"The police won't come to Lunik IX so you are quite safe here. And if they did, they wouldn't get very far. Especially not with Maria around," said Svetlana, as she parked the car and stepped out. Half a dozen children immediately ran up to her, shouting her name. She picked up two young girls, and walked towards the entrance, the other children chattering excitedly behind her. A plump, dark-skinned matriarch dressed in a brightly patterned floral skirt and thin acrylic jumper emerged from the housing block. She hugged Svetlana tightly, and ushered her, Alex and Natasha into a ground floor flat. The chairs and sofa had clearly been rescued from a rubbish dump, and a broken television stood in the corner, but despite the overwhelming poverty, it was warm and spotless inside. The children followed them in, yelping with excitement as Svetlana handed over sweets and chocolate bars.

A boy of six or seven walked over to Natasha and stroked her hair. His thin frame showed under his oversized t-shirt as he jumped on her lap. Maria moved to sweep him off, but Natasha protested that he should stay. He whispered in her ear and she answered him in a language Alex did not recognise. The boy giggled delightedly.

"What language are you speaking?" Alex asked Natasha as Maria put a tray of coffee on the table in front of them.

"Lovari. It's a Romany dialect," said Svetlana, a look of surprise on her face. She looked at Alex. "You picked the right one."

\*　\*　\*

Vince Szatmari stood outside the *Budapest News* office building, watching the hordes of commuters descending into Nyugati underpass. It was now six o'clock and he had decided to try once more. He reached for the buzzer when the door suddenly opened, and two secretaries came out, absorbed in their gossip. He held it open for them, wishing them a good day, and stepped inside and took the lift to the fifth floor. A bored-looking young woman with dyed black hair sat behind the reception desk, chatting on her mobile telephone. She looked at him, turned away and carried on talking. He waited for a couple of minutes, his doubts rapidly growing.

"Excuse me," he said, leaning forward, momentarily distracted by her impressive cleavage.

"One moment, I am occupied," said the receptionist.

"Miss, my time is also valuable. I have some valuable information for the editor. I think he will be very interested indeed in what I have to say."

She sighed and put down her mobile phone. "Who shall I say wants him?"

"I don't want to say at this stage."

"How can I tell him who wants him if you won't say who you are?"

"Look, why can't I just talk to him?" he said, exasperated.

"We are closed," she snapped. "There is nobody here. Come back tomorrow."

Well, he had tried. How did these newspapers ever find out anything, if you couldn't get past the receptionist? He turned on his heel to leave, when a deep voice boomed across the room.

"Young man, are you looking for me?"

Szatmari turned to see an enormous English gentleman strolling towards him.

"Ronald Worthington. Why don't you come through to my office."

\* \* \*

Slope-shouldered, with large brown eyes and a hooked, crooked nose and almost bald apart from a monk's fringe of hair, Mike Jakub drove as fast as he talked. Romany himself, the director of the Roma Rights Action Group was one of the tiny minority who managed to get a university education, which had led to international scholarships, bursaries and grants. A regular guest on Slovak television and radio shows, Mike was now a celebrity in Kosice, profoundly unpopular with the police and Slovak nationalists. Fame, he argued, was his best protection against police or other harassment, and he made sure to keep his name in the papers. Married, with a one year old son, Mike had been offered a seat on the Social Democrats' candidate list for the European Parliament, an offer he was still considering.

Alex leaned forward as they spend down the motorway through the night. It was 10.00pm and the four of them were finally headed to Novy Marek. He sat in the back next to Natasha. They had spent the afternoon at Lunik IX, waiting for Mike, playing with the children and sharing the family's meagre supper of bread and jam. Maria's husband Jozi was in prison, but she had refused all offers of money. Alex had surreptitiously left 100 euros on the table when they left. The road was almost deserted. A few lights flickered in the tiny hamlets that dotted the surrounding hills. "How are we going to get in, if the village is now a closed zone?" Alex asked.

"Stop worrying. Have you been to one of the Romany settlements?" Mike replied. "*Un-believ-able*, in Europe in the twenty-first century. It's like India. Not that there's anything wrong with India, after all that's kind of our homeland. The neo-Nazis keep telling us we should go back there. We got firebombed the other day," he continued, overtaking an ancient East German Wartburg. "Idiots, they didn't know that we have a metal door. One of them threw a petrol bomb and it bounced back and blew up on him. Set his trousers on fire. He's only twelve, so the judge said he's below the age of criminal responsibility. No punishment at all. He's back at home, convalescing. I saw him yesterday in the main square. He gave me a Nazi salute, so he must be getting better."

A torch flashed in the night. A policeman stood at the side of the road, waving them down. Mike pulled over to the hard shoulder. Alex's stomach lurched. There would definitely be an alert out for them after the incident at Kosice station.

"It's nothing," said Mike. "They are just checking that we have paid for a motorway permit."

"And have you?" asked Alex.

"Yes. For 2006."

The policeman was a policewoman, a chubby brunette, bundled into a padded jacket, gloves and boots. She checked the permit stuck on the windscreen and shined a torch into the car, lingering on their faces. Her breath hung white in the cold night air. A lone car swished by on the other side of the motorway.

"You do know that this is long past its expiry date," she said, pointing at the motorway permit. "It is illegal to drive on the highway without a proper permit. Please show me the car papers and your identification documents."

They handed their passports to Mike, who passed them to the policewoman. The police radio crackled and a voice spoke. Alex thought he heard their names in the burst of Slovak. He looked at Natasha, who shrugged. Svetlana bit her nails. Mike looked unconcerned.

The policewoman looked through their documents, checking their photographs against their faces. Alex's heart began thumping.

"Alexander Farkas, Natasha Hatvani, Svetlana Todorova and Mikhail Jakub. Two Slovaks, an Englishman with a Hungarian name and a Hungarian woman with a Russian name. Perhaps I should check in with headquarters. We have been told to watch out for suspicious foreigners in this area. Where are you going at this time of night?"

"For a drive," said Mike. "I am showing my friends Slovakia."

"Is that so?" said the policewoman. "It's good of you to be such a diligent guide. Slovakia is a beautiful country. There is a lot to see, although it's hard to appreciate in the dark. I have seen you on television Mr Jakub. You are not very popular among my colleagues."

"I regret to hear that, Madame," said Mike, his voice conciliatory. "Perhaps you have heard the old Turkish proverb."

"I think I am about to," said the policewoman.

"He who told the truth was chased from nine villages."

The policewoman guffawed. "Even from Novy Marek. There are lots of police checkpoints on the motorway, especially approaching the main turn-off. But we don't have enough manpower to watch every tiny side-road."

"Thank you, Madame," said Mike.

"I do not agree with everything you say, Mr Jakub," said the policewoman, shaking her head as she handed the documents back through the car window. "But someone has to speak out."

Taking the policewoman's advice, they turned off the motorway, and drove down a narrow tarmac road that turned into a dirt track for several kilometres, narrowly avoiding two peasants driving a horse and cart. The only signs of habitation were lights glowing a kilometre or so away.

"The Roma at Novy Marek live on an island. The village is split into two," explained Svetlana, showing a crudely-drawn map. "The Slovaks live on the hill. That part looks like a normal place anywhere. Nice big houses, gardens. The river, a stream really, runs around the bottom of the hill, and it splits around this bit of land. That's where the Romany settlement is. Apartheid here is very simple. The local government refuses to allow the Roma to register as official residents in the village. So they cannot buy land to build a proper house, they cannot apply for electricity, running water or sewage to be installed in their houses, because they shouldn't be there in the first place. So they stay on the island, build their own houses and dig their own toilets. You will see for yourself, we cannot drive any further. We have to walk now, through the woods, to the top end of the island."

"What about the police in the village?" asked Alex.

Mike looked at his watch. "It's almost midnight. The Roma know you are coming. The cops on the night shift are all local boys. My people have been filling them full of home-brewed brandy for the last two hours. "

She was a Romany Madonna, painted by Titian and illuminated by candlelight, thought Alex. The dingy surroundings only highlighted her iridescent beauty. Waist-length black hair framed an almond shaped face. Her black eyes shone in the candlelight, while her son Mario lay fast asleep on her shoulder. Her name was Teresa Sandori and she was seventeen.

Alex and the others had arrived after a twenty minute walk through the woods. Just as Mike had predicted, the two policemen were fast asleep, and they had strolled right past their car. Teresa's house was a one-room shack barely larger than a prison cell. When Alex stood up his head brushed the ceiling. Teresa and her husband Virgil had built their home from mud and wattle, held together with the odd splash of concrete. The wind whistled through the gaps. There was no running water, and no heating. There was one chair, and two home-made beds, mattresses on warehouse pallets. The toilet was an outhouse, dug in the earth a few yards away, sheltered by some scraps of wood. They drew their water from the stream which ran around the island.

Alex remembered reading a report by the European Union on the situation of the Roma in Slovakia. "The country has made considerable progress in integrating its Romany minority, although some work remains to be done." Whoever wrote that had clearly never been to Novy Marek. He caught Mike's eye in the dim light, sitting on the bed, next to Teresa and Virgil. A picture of Jesus was tacked on the wall, together with a photograph of Nicole Kidman, torn from a magazine. Jakub looked weary and depressed, his earlier ebullience now gone.

Teresa began to tell the story of what happened to her after she gave birth. "I don't read Slovak very well. So I didn't really understand what was happening to me in the hospital. I had just given birth to Mario, and the nurse pushed this paper at me, yelling at me to sign it. I can't write, so I just put my cross there."

"What do you think the paper said?" asked Natasha.

"I don't know. All I know is that I cannot have any more children."

Teresa was the third woman they had spoken to. All the stories were similar. A coerced signature, soon after giving birth, a series of injections and a course of pills. The doctors, said Teresa, had been most insistent that she take the pills. As she finished speaking, Teresa blinked and wiped away a tear.

Virgil brought out a bottle of Johnny Walker Red Label whisky, which he placed on the table, with several chipped china cups. He put his arm around Teresa. Virgil was short and wiry with slanting cheekbones and curly black hair. Pride, hurt and anger competed in his eyes. "You know the white people say we do not want to work. That we are lazy and we steal. I have stolen, sometimes, it is true. I stole food for my wife and my child. Bread, and a bottle of milk. I am not proud to be a man, a father who cannot provide for his family, who has to take, who cannot pay for what he needs."

Virgil's hands twisted as he spoke. He looked at his wife. She nodded encouragingly. "Do you think that we like to live this? And what shall I do with my darling, my little dove now? Who will look after us when we are old? We have one son, our Mario. For us it is important to have many children. I have four brothers and three sisters. But there will be no more sons, no more daughters. Because

I will stay with my little dove," he said, running his hands through his wife's hair. She smiled at his touch.

"Because I love her, more than the children we would have had, than the sons and the daughters we will never have. They have done something to my wife. They have damaged her inside." Virgil's voice began to crack. He poured the whisky into the cups, and passed the drinks round, leant over and briefly murmured to Mike.

"Of course you can," he said. "It's your house."

Virgil reached up to the shelf and brought down his violin.

"It is a love song. A *cigany* melody. I play it for all of you."

A single chord filled the room, rising and falling. Virgil's eyes were closed shut as he teased and cajoled the violin, his bow caressing then attacking the strings before once again soothing them. It was the sound of longing, of poignant, doomed love. Alex thought it was the most haunting music he had ever heard. Goose-pimples rippled down the back of his neck, and the hairs on his arms stood on end.

Teresa sang softly as her husband played. Mario stirred on her shoulder, burrowing further into her neck. The candle sputtered and flickered. Natasha took up the second verse. The two women sang, one verse after another and embraced when the song was finished. Alex stared at Natasha, transfixed. Her eyes were luminous in the dark. She looked straight back at him, unblinking as she sang. Virgil leaned forward and grasped Alex's hand in an iron grip. His fingers were worn and calloused. Virgil spoke in a low, urgent voice.

"Write about what is happening to us, to the Roma. Tell the world. They stop us from having children. They try to finish what Hitler started. Not with the killing rooms, but with pills."

Virgil reached under the bed and handed two medicine boxes to Alex. Each held two empty blister packs, embossed with the name 'Czigex'. Alex examined the pill packaging. Inside the box tiny printed letters announced: 'Birkauchen Pharma.' He slipped a blister pack and a box in his pocket and took out his digital camera.

"Can I take some photographs?" he asked Virgil. Virgil smiled and pulled his wife and son closer to him. Alex stepped back and took a dozen shots from different angles.

The hovel's door suddenly swung open as an enormously obese man lumbered in. A gust of night air, sharp and cold filled the room. Virgil and Teresa looked alarmed and stood up. The fat man patted Mario's cheek with one hand, and snatched the remaining box and Czigex blister pack with the other. Considering his bulk, he moved with surprising grace and speed.

"Where are the rest?" he demanded of Virgil. Virgil shrugged. "In the river."

The fat man sat down on the bed and stared suspiciously at the visitors. He was dressed in a purple and white sports suit, and wore two thick gold rope chains around his neck. His face was sallow and sweaty, and the whites of his eyes were almost pink. Mario woke up and began to cry.

"I am Mihaly Lataki," he wheezed. "Chief of this clan. I heard that we had visitors."

He picked up the bottle of whisky, poured himself a generous measure and drank it down in one. He leaned back and burped with satisfaction. He glanced at Todorova, looked Natasha up and down, ignored Mike and stared at Alex.

"What do you want here, *gadje*?" he asked, using the Romany word for non-Gypsy. He made a hissing sound as he spoke, as though air was escaping from a puncture.

"We are journalists," said Alex, handing him his business card. Lataki peered at the card. Alex saw that he was holding it upside down. Lataki put the card in his pocket, and lit a cigar.

"More journalists. Coming in our houses, asking questions, day and night. We are not animals in the zoo. How about if I ask you so many questions?" He turned towards Natasha, puffing out clouds of smoke. "Are you married? How many children?"

"It's none of your business," she snapped, waving away the fumes. Mario began to cough.

"It is very much my business. You are here in my village. My son needs a wife. You are too skinny, but we can fix that. And it is a Romany tradition that the wives of sons must also keep fathers happy."

"What tradition is that?" asked Mike.

Lataki looked at him with disdain. "Who asked you, *gadje*-lover? I think I will call my son," he said, reaching into his tracksuit pocket and pulling out an ultra-modern mobile telephone.

"Wait, hold on a minute," said Alex. "We are investigating why Romany women in this area cannot have children. We are trying to help your people."

Lataki guffawed: "We don't need your help. We are sick of reporters. We are sick of all the do-gooders destroying our traditions, giving our women ideas."

He pointed at Virgil. "Look at him, and you can see why his wife can't get pregnant again. He makes one son, and cries and moans like a woman about how hard things are. But maybe not hard enough. Too much drinking and not enough of this," he said, making an obscene gesture with his hand and forefinger.

"Poor Teresa. I will have to come and visit you," he said, patting her behind. Her face froze as his hand slid down her backside.

Lataki waved for more whisky. "And get some more candles. I can't see a thing in here."

Virgil brought a pack of candles and placed several on the table, lighting them with a shaking hand. Lataki took out his mobile phone, holding it still for several seconds before he put the handset down and reached into his bag. He pulled out a carved wooden Madonna and placed it on the table.

"Handmade. By our Romany artisans," he said, slurping some more whisky.

Alex picked it up. It was a crude rendition, but possessed of a simple, graceful, power.

"Our craftsmen should be better known. That's what you should write about," said Lataki.

"Very nice," Alex replied, his voice bland and neutral, as he examined the Madonna.

"Two hundred euros. A bargain," said Lataki. The others watched silently.

Alex sighed. "I don't think we have enough cash with us to buy this today, Mr Lataki. Maybe next time," he said, putting the statue back down on the table.

Lataki's eyes glittered. "That is unfortunate. Then I will sing a song for you, a real Gypsy lament. For nothing. The song wakes the dead from their graves, they say. The way I sing, it will be heard across the valley."

Alex quelled his rising anger. There was nothing he could do. They had their interviews, and the priority now was to get out as quickly and quietly as possible. He reached into his wallet and handed the Romany chief a 100 euro note. Lataki examined it in the candlelight and flicked it twice with his fingers. Small puffs of smoke escaped from his nostrils as he drew on his cigar.

"A good start," said Lataki, looking at Alex expectantly. He drained the last of his whisky and crumpled the Birkauchen box and blister packaging into a ball, dropping it into his glass.

Alex handed over another 100 euro note. He showed Lataki his wallet, now empty. Lataki lit a match. He dropped the match into the glass with the packaging. The plastic popped and melted, sending out foul-smelling smoke.

Lataki opened the door and threw the glass into the stream that ran by the house. "Goodbye, *gadje*," he said.

## TWELVE

Alex swallowed a deep draught of Ronald Worthington's Jamaican Blue Mountain coffee, hoping it might kick-start his brain. It was 3.00pm on Wednesday, half an hour into a special editorial meeting. Alex, Ronald Worthington, Edina Draskovitz and George Smith, the surprise new deputy editor just seconded from the *Daily Sentinel*, were discussing Vince Szatmari's information. That week's edition was already at the printers. Ronald had decided to publish a day earlier than usual, splashing on Natasha's interview with Sanzlermann and his plans for compulsory DNA testing for every European citizen. Alex had sent a copy of her story to David Jones, together with the transcript, under strict embargo until they both went up on the *Budapest News* website early on Thursday morning.

Alex stifled a yawn and tried to concentrate. The journey home from Novy Marek had passed without incident. Mike had driven them to a little-used border post that was technically closed after 8.00pm. They had simply lifted up the red pole across the road, and crossed into Hungary. Mike had dropped them at the eastern city of Miskolcs. From there they caught a dawn train back to Budapest. Natasha had slept most of the way. He had dozed on and off, his head full of images: the poverty and squalor of Lunik IX and Novy Marek; Maria's family and the laughing children; Virgil and Teresa's shack, where there would be no more children; the way Natasha had stared at him while she sang with Teresa. And why had Lataki, the clan leader, been so keen to ensure that all the Czigex packaging was destroyed? Alex checked his jacket pocket: the box and the plastic wrapping were still there.

Alex considered Smith's corpulent form with distaste. Smith had been imposed from above, a sudden, unwanted gift from the Sentinel's London management. He had flown in that morning, and checked into a suite at the Hotel Bristol, the city's most luxurious. Smith was soft, pink and chubby, an over-upholstered man in his early fifties with small, perpetually wet lips, who spoke with a pronounced lisp. A cherubic mop of blond curls, now streaked with grey, and two small but alert blue eyes, made for an apparently friendly manner. But Alex knew him of old. The Bunteresque appearance concealed a Machiavelli. Smith had briefly served on the foreign desk while Alex had been in Bosnia. He urged him on to the most dangerous places, so he could boast in editorial conference about how expertly his staff were deployed. The most perilous thing he had ever done was pad his expenses.

"Szatmari sounds like he's flying a kite to me," said Smith. "When I was business editor on the Sentinel we wouldn't have let someone like him past the front door, let alone granted him half an hour with the editor to spin out his fantasies."

"I thought you were night business editor," said Alex.

"I was in charge of what went into the paper on the business pages while it was going to press, which is the same as being business editor," snapped Smith.

"Yes, OK, I see your point. But you did only edit the business pages at night," said Alex, careful to keep a straight face as he took another slurp from his coffee.

"I'll have you know, that *I* decided . . ." said Smith, leaning forward, giving Alex a good blast of stale wine breath.

Ronald Worthington tapped the table twice. "I don't think this approach is very productive, Alex. Let's return to Szatmari. He works in the privatisation department of the National Bank. He says he saw bank documents, secret guidelines on responding to tenders, that every bid is to be rejected on spurious technical or legal grounds, unless it comes from a company on a short, classified list. Remember the opposition made a huge fuss about KZX Industries buying up the pharmaceutical firm in Miskolcs. There were claims that perfectly good bids were rejected on very dodgy grounds. If what Szatmari says is true, then this is a major story."

"*If* it's true, and Szatmari can prove it," said Smith. "Where's this so-called secret list? We can't run this on the word of one disgruntled employee."

"He said he will bring it as soon as he can. Then we will have a story."

Smith scribbled in his notebook. Alex noticed that he drew several rings around Szatmari's name.

"Szatmari also said that the National Bank is planning to issue a new thirty day security. It will be called the 'Patriot Bond' and will pay fifteen per cent interest a year."

"Fifteen per cent is pretty high," said Edina, polishing a long telephoto lens. "I'm sure there will be a big rush to buy. We could get some great pictures of the launch, and the scramble."

"I can check that out," said Alex. "It should be fairly straightforward."

"So we are agreed. We will wait for more confirmation from Szatmari, and check the Patriot Bond," said Ronald, looking around the table. Alex and Draskovitz nodded, and Smith eventually did as well. "Now Alex, could you please update us on the Presidential election campaign."

Alex flicked forward through several pages in his notebook and summarised the current state of play. In an effort to make Europeans feel more involved in the political process, the EU had decided that each member state would hold a nationwide poll for President. The results would be collated over the next three months. The winner would be calculated by a complicated weighting procedure based on the population of each EU member state. Over a dozen candidates had managed to gather the necessary million signatures to enter the race, but only two counted: Sanzlermann, and Edith Leclerc, of the Social Democratic Alliance. Sanzlermann was leading the polls in Germany, Austria, Belgium, northern and eastern Europe. Leclerc was ahead in France, Spain, Italy and the Mediterranean basin and was expected to arrive in Budapest in the next day or so, having delayed her trip after a severe bout of food poisoning. Most analysts agreed that the eastern member states would prove crucial. The Hungarian polls gave Sanzlermann thirty-nine per cent, and Leclerc thirty-six per cent, but with over forty per cent of voters saying they were undecided, there was still everything to play for.

Ronald sat back in his chair which creaked alarmingly. "Thanks. I also have some news, all bad. Firstly, my sources tell me that the Information Minister is about to announce that all state advertising will now only appear in certain newspapers, basically pro-government ones. We are not among them. So we are going to lose a massive amount of recruitment advertising, and those full page government ads encouraging foreign companies to invest in Hungary. That's thirty per cent of our advertising budget. We need to think about how to replace that lost revenue."

"Maybe we should invest in some Patriot Bonds," quipped Alex.

Smith frowned. "Or maybe we should just be a little more balanced in our reporting. I think that the Hunkalffy government could be just what this country needs to get up and running properly. And we might get the advertising back."

Ronald looked annoyed. "Well, we'll have to agree to differ on that, George. Secondly, I received this registered letter this morning," he said, unfolding a notification from the newly formed Financial and Economic Police Force, a subdivision of the Gendarmerie.

"At some unspecified time next week, inspection teams will arrive at the office for a full audit of the last year's books. They want to check all VAT receipts since we launched. They want to see the customs importation documents for every computer, or an official VAT receipt if we brought the machines here, and an individual licence for every software programme that we are using. I'm starting to think that someone doesn't like us," said Ronald.

"But this is ridiculous," said Edina. "Nobody can produce all that documentation."

"Where did you get your Photoshop software from, Edina?" asked Smith. She resumed her lens polishing and mumbled something unintelligible.

He looked concerned. "Is it the case, Ronald, that this newspaper is produced using pirated software?"

Ronald sighed. "It's not all pirated. We do have some legal copies."

"How many?"

"Er, one copy of Microsoft Word, circa 1996."

\*　\*　\*

Cassandra Orczy swung her RX-7 through a tiny gap between two cars, sped down the wrong side of the road, and turned into an eighteenth century courtyard. The Museum of Catering and Domestic Science, on the far side of the Castle district, was obscure enough to be discreet. He was waiting for her, leaning against the window in the first room, as agreed, reading the *Financial Times*. The paper's Budapest correspondent had filed a detailed story about the steady slide in value of the Hungarian currency, run next to similar reports from its correspondents in Zagreb, Bratislava and Bucharest. The forint had recently dropped from 240 to the euro to almost 400. The Croatian kuna, Slovak koruna and the Romanian lei were also plunging in value, while the Polish zloty and the Czech koruna were starting to slip. The reports from the security service economics section were increasingly alarming. Foreign money was pouring in, buying up commercial property, as the region turned into a bargain basement for those paying in euros.

She greeted him, and they kissed each other on the cheeks. "Why are you wearing sunglasses?" she asked. "It's November. And we are indoors."

"I'll tell you soon," he replied. They walked up to a glass display case. Inside was a curiously shaped pair of small tongs. He bent over to read the caption. "It's for curling your moustache."

"I don't have a moustache. At least I hope not."

He pretended to check. She brushed him away, laughing. "Doesn't this remind you of our student days?" he asked. "All these pots and pans, and recipes."

"You know, I don't remember that either of us cooked very much. We lived on cheese and salami. When we remembered to buy anything to eat."

"A loaf of bread, a jug of wine, and thee. Omar Khayyam said it best. You still look as youthful and as beautiful as ever," he said, reaching for her hand. She blushed, and gave his hand a long squeeze before extricating hers. She looked around the room before she spoke. "Tell me what you are hearing. The economy is going haywire."

He took off his sunglasses. Cassandra gasped. She leaned forward to touch Mubarak's face, but he jerked back. His right eye was a slit in a brown and green mound of bruised puffy flesh.

"A doctor told me that with luck I will eventually be able to see out of it."

"Who did it?"

"The Gendarmes raided the Sphinx last night. I thought it would be the usual routine, a quick trip to the station, pay off the captain and I would be back at the Sphinx for dessert. Not this time. They held a telephone book to the side of my head and hit me with a truncheon. Then they removed the book."

\* \* \*

It was a bracing winter afternoon; the kind that Budapest did well. The Habsburg apartment blocks looked stately and majestic, the Danube grand and sweeping. The sun shone brightly, white cotton-wool clouds scudding across a turquoise sky. The wind was clean and sharp. Alex's cheeks tingled as he walked down the Grand Boulevard to the Margaret Patisserie. He passed a legless man sitting in his wheelchair, holding out a battered hat to the passersby. One or two dropped him a few coins. Alex gave him 200 forints. A crowd had gathered around a nearby stall, its walls plastered with posters of Sanzlermann and Hunkalffy shaking hands. It was less than two weeks to the start of the Presidential election. Alex walked over to the stall. Well-dressed young men and women were handing out campaign baubles: badges, canvas bags and coffee mugs. Many of those walking away stared at their wrists, now proudly bearing a plastic Sanzlermann campaign wristwatch.

The welcoming aromas of roasting coffee, cakes and tobacco greeted him at the café. Peter Feher sat perusing a newspaper, a *Munkas* cigarette smouldering erratically in the ashtray by his coffee cup. The coffee machine hissed and wheezed in the corner, and Eva the waitress waved at him. Alex sat down and picked up Feher's newspaper. A two-day old copy of the *Daily Telegraph*, open at the Court and Social page. Her Majesty the Queen was taking tea with the Prime Minister of Tonga, it announced.

Feher smiled, and gestured at Eva. She quickly brought two coffees, and glasses of brandy.

Feher smiled ruefully at Alex, and they clinked glasses. "To the memory of your grandfather," said Feher. "I miss him every day," he sighed.

Alex drank the brandy, enjoying its welcome glow. "So do I," he said, smiling ruefully.

Feher folded the newspaper up. "I usually read the sports pages first, but there's no cricket today. I went to Lords once. On a cultural delegation to Britain. What a game," he said, shaking his head in wonder. "You have cricket and 'Court and Social'. We have this," he added, handing Alex that day's issue of *Ébredjetek Magyarok!*.

A two-page feature was headlined: "The Enemy Within: The Immigrant Menace Among Us." Written by Balazs Noludi, it called for all asylum seekers and would-be immigrants, legal or illegal, to be immediately interred in strict-regime detention camps, to be built in isolated areas as soon as possible. Children would either be interred with their parents, or taken into care. Attila Hunkalffy was liberally quoted: "We can no longer allow our countries to be used as a back-door to Europe for potential criminals and terrorists such as the so-called Immigration Liberation Army." There were supportive quotes from Frank Sanzlermann, the Croatian President Dragomir Zorvajk, Slovakia's Dusan Hrkna and the recently elected Romanian President, Cornelius Malinanescu.

"I've been in Slovakia. I just got back," said Alex, pointing at a photograph of Dusan Hrkna. "I went to meet some Gypsies. In Novy Marek. Something strange is happening there."

"How did you get into Novy Marek? I read it had been sealed off."

"It is."

Feher looked hard at Alex. "And?"

"The Romany women I spoke to think they are being sterilised by Slovak health officials. They give the women injections after they have given birth. And then a course of pills."

"I can believe that. How do they make them take the pills?"

"There is a special room at the welfare office where the women receive their social benefits. The money is only handed over after one of the officials watches them take them. They check the womens' mouths afterwards to check that they don't hide the tablets under their tongues, and have definitely swallowed them."

Feher sipped his coffee. "Like children and their medicine. But rather gruesome in this case. If you can prove it, it will make a powerful article."

"I hope so. If we don't get closed down by the financial police. They are coming to raid us next week."

"You too," said Feher. "Some friends of mine are expecting a visit today."

Alex nodded, his mind on Novy Marek. "The company that makes the pills is called Birkauchen Pharma. It's strange. I couldn't find anything about them on the internet, or on the newspaper databases. I called up the *Sentinel's* medical correspondent and the business desk, and nobody had ever heard of them."

Feher dropped his cigarette. "*What* did you say the name was?"

"Birkauchen. Birkauchen Pharma."

"Josip Birkauchen was the chief of the drugs research branch of AF Weizen industries. He was an ethnic German from Croatia," said Feher, picking up the smoking stub from the table and taking a long drag. "AF Weizen was Germany's biggest chemicals conglomerate before the war, specialising in pharmaceuticals, dyes and disinfectants. After Hitler came to power they moved into pest-eradication products. All Jews, Gypsies, disabled and anti-Nazis falling into that category. Birkauchen and AF Weizen ran a special 'medical research' institute at Auschwitz. All its records mysteriously disappeared in 1945. So did he and everyone working for him. The Allies supposedly wanted to arrest them all for war crimes, but there was plenty of interest in its 'research' in Washington and Moscow. Some journalists kept trying to investigate but with all the evidence gone, they got nowhere."

"Isn't there some kind of historical connection between KZX and AF Weizen?" asked Alex. "Same headquarters in Munich, same interests in chemicals and pharmaceuticals before KZX expanded into industry?"

Feher laughed. "There's nothing historic about it. KZX *is* AF Weizen. The Allies supposedly broke up AF Weizen after 1945. But that was just PR. AF Weizen continued business as usual, but was renamed and reconstituted as KZX. German industry was a necessary bulwark in the Cold War, don't you know? Most of the managers who ran the slave labour camps simply went back to work, with the Allies' blessing. KZX did a lot of business in Iraq, when Saddam was in power. You know what happened to the Kurds at Khalabja? Methods invented by AF Weizen. The commercial attaché at the German embassy used to work for KZX."

"How do you know all this?" asked Alex.

"Most of it is public knowledge, if you know where to look, or are interested enough. I was supposed to be transferred to Birkauchen's institute. Luckily the Russians arrived two days later," said Feher, his hand shaking as he puffed on his cigarette. "Nobody ever came out of there alive."

Alex leaned forward. "I'm very glad you came home safely. So was my grandfather. You were his best friend, you know." He squeezed Feher's hand and gave him an envelope. "Miklos' post-mortem results. They are very late. They arrived this morning."

Feher unfolded the letter inside and slowly read it. "They cut you open and pretend they don't know what killed you." He exhaled slowly as he put the paper back down. "An open verdict."

"It doesn't tell us much," said Alex. He slowly rubbed his fingertips together, remembering the feel of the glass crystals.

"It tells us that now they want the matter forgotten. I don't think they realised how much publicity Miklos' death would get, especially in the international press. A verdict of unlawful killing would trigger more news stories," said Feher, sipping his coffee. "A suicide also. An open verdict, who knows? He was old, maybe his heart just gave out."

"Because he crunched a cyanide capsule," said Alex.

"Yes, I know. The question is, why? I think you have some of his effects."

Alex looked at Feher. Was he talking about Miklos' testimony?

"There were some things your grandfather would never speak of. That much I know. Also that there are many ways to hide information. Alex, you will have to excuse me, I have another appointment," he said, summoning the waitress. "Eva, bring us the bill please."

*   *   *

Alex sat at his desk, flicking through the new edition of the *Budapest News*. It was 8.00pm and the office was empty. The crisp winter day had ended with a thunderstorm. A driving wind lashed rain against the windows, rattling the glass, and jagged lightning streaked across the sky, illuminating the city for a split-second as though someone was switching a giant lamp on and off. The printers had just dropped off an early bundle of papers, fresh from the presses. The front page proclaimed '*Sanzlermann plans Europe-wide compulsory DNA tests.*' It was a brilliant scoop but he couldn't concentrate on the story. His brain was a kaleidoscope, spinning with fragments of memories and images: his grandfather's ghetto diary, Novy Marek, his conversations with Peter Feher, KZX.

But how to put the pieces together? By starting with what you know, he told himself: names and places, dates and times. Dates and times, he thought. Miklos had died the night that Sanzlermann had arrived. An image flashed into his mind and he sat bolt upright. The Gendarme captain at Kultura. Why had the Gendarmes carried out an identity check at the bar he was at, preventing him from leaving precisely when he was supposed to be at his grandfather's? Alex stood up and walked over to the window. He stared out at Nyugati station, its intricate glass and iron façade now awash with water. An enormous boom erupted and he jumped reflexively, his heart suddenly thumping rapidly. Calm down, he told himself. This was just thunder. But what of the Gendarmes at Kultura? Was the raid another coincidence? Maybe, or just paranoia. Was it paranoid to think that the whole bar was checked as a cover, to stop him leaving? He remembered the Gendarme captain speaking on his mobile phone when Alex approached, looking at him, and saying "Yes, yes." Was he saying, "Yes, yes," Alex was still there?

He took out his notebook and drew a line down the middle of a page, writing Places on the left and Players on the right. The main players were obvious: Sanzlermann and Hunkalffy. But who was backing their campaigns behind the scenes? He wrote KZX and Volkstern, underlining both. Where was the money coming from? That was what he needed more information about: the role of the two conglomerates, especially if KZX was really AF Weizen reborn. Under places he wrote Munich, Novy Marek, Kosice, Budapest. He paused and scribbled Auschwitz? when his telephone rang.

"If you've got copies of the new edition, then the news is out, so I can put it on the wire," David Jones demanded.

"How do you know that I have?" demanded Alex, laughing.

"Reuters knows everything. Especially when your delivery man is our receptionist's brother-in-law."

"Ok, here's the deal. The website team come in at 4.00am. I've asked them to call me as soon as Natasha's story and the interview transcript are up. That will be around 5.00am. I intend to be asleep then, so I'll divert all calls to your number. Then you can put it on the wire. And what do I get for not extending this favour to AP and Bloomberg?"

"The chance to masquerade as the Panamanian ambassador again." Every couple of months David took Alex out for an epic three bottle lunch on expenses, claiming Alex was a diplomat. "We're running tomorrow?"

"You're on," said Alex, smiling as he hung up.

He switched on Hungarian television news. Twelve high court judges had been summarily sacked after it was discovered that they had all once held high-ranking positions in the Communist Party, Aniko Kovacs announced brightly. Investigations were underway to see if they had been guilty of human rights abuses during the former regime. If so, they could expect to be brought to trial. The new Financial Police had started their raids. The screen cut to a clip of Gendarmes kicking down the doors of "World Writers' Review", a small liberal literary publication. Two elderly men in crumpled suits were led away, looking frightened and bewildered, one with his glasses askew, the other holding a sheaf of papers.

"And now we go live to Novakpuszta, where our reporter has news of some disturbing events," said Kovacs. A tall male journalist was interviewing a frightened old lady in a village in eastern Hungary. The woman plucked at her headscarf as she spoke: "There were lots of them, Israelis, shouting in Hebrew, taking photographs. They banged on my door and rang my bell. Shouting how they were coming back to get everything and that I should start packing. I didn't know what to do."

The reporter smiled encouragingly. "Are you sure they were Israelis?"

"Absolutely. They told me they were from Tel Aviv. Terrifying, it was," the woman continued. "They were very aggressive. But these are our houses now and we are keeping them."

That was bizarre, thought Alex, even by Hungarian state television's standards. Why would Israelis care about Novakpuszta? Alex added Novakpuszta to his notebook, when there was a tentative knock on his door.

Natasha walked in, holding a bottle of wine and two glasses.

"What are you doing here?" he asked, smiling. "You should be out partying."

"I'm meeting Kitty later. I thought we should also celebrate together," she said, pouring two glasses of red wine. She pulled up a chair and sat down. Alex thanked her, and tried not to stare as they clinked glasses. She looked even prettier than usual, and he realised that it was the first time he had seen her wearing make-up: subtle mascara and lip gloss.

"Your interview will be all over the world tomorrow," said Alex, sipping his wine. "You'll get a glamorous job offer and then you'll leave us," he joked.

"I'm not leaving. I'm not going anywhere. Journalism is my *vocation*," she said, laughing.

"It certainly is," said Alex, as he switched the television off. "Can I ask you something personal?"

"Last time you did, we nearly got arrested. But OK."

"What drives you, Natasha? Lots of Hungarians hate the Roma. They would be pleased if they couldn't have any more babies. Why do you care so much? And where did you learn Lovari?"

She swallowed hard. "That is personal." She looked at Alex. "I've never told anyone this."

Alex knew enough to stay silent.

"My parents couldn't have any more children after me, so they adopted a Gypsy boy." She smiled, but her voice was full of sadness. "His name was Anton. He was five when he came to live with us, a lovely child, bright, happy. It was the usual story. His parents split up, his mother thought he would be best off in a children's home so she gave him up. She used to visit us sometimes. Anton did well at school. He wanted to be a teacher."

She paused, looked at the ceiling and inhaled deeply. "One day we all went out for Sunday lunch. Anton was hit by a car. The driver didn't stop. He died on the pavement. He was sixteen. I'm sorry Alex, it's not much of a celebration is it?" she said, her eyes brimming. "They caught the driver. But he was an important man, much more important than Anton. Nothing happened to him. He didn't even lose his licence."

"Who was he?" asked Alex.

Natasha stared into her wine glass. "Attila Hunkalffy."

## THIRTEEN

Alex contemplated the length of Margaret Island and wondered again about the wisdom of agreeing to a lunchtime jog. The running path looped around for more than five kilometres. Flanked at one end by its namesake bridge, and at the other by the Arpad bridge, named after the medieval Magyar king, Margaret Island was Budapest's loveliest park, filled with landscaped gardens, medieval ruins and pavement cafés. He and Zsofi had enjoyed several summer evenings here, curled up in a glade near the water tower with a blanket and a bottle of wine. But in winter it was less welcoming. The bicycles and pedal-carriages for hire during the summer were locked away. The paths that in warmer months were full of snogging teenagers were empty, the kiosks bolted shut. An icy wind blew in off the water, cutting through Alex's sweatpants and track top. The river moved fast, a cold gunmetal grey.

David Jones was already stretching and doing knee bends, his skin-tight lycra oufit highlighting his athlete's physique. "Hup, hup, let's go," he proclaimed, running on the spot, clapping his hands together.

"What about going for lunch instead," said Alex. "It is lunchtime," he added hopelessly.

David started padding down the path. Alex followed, and a gust of wind almost blew him sideways. He counted through the markers in his head: the canoe club, the children's zoo, the ruins of St Margaret's nunnery, the spa hotels and the Arpad bridge, that meant half a circuit. The zoo soon came into sight. The animals were relocated for the winter, but the pungent aroma remained. Alex took in a lungful of manure-scented air and forced himself forward. The trick was to think about something else, not how heavy his legs felt. Like Natasha's revelation about the death of her adopted brother Anton. She had quickly composed herself but left soon afterwards. He supposed she was embarrassed, but was pleased she had confided something so personal. He ran faster and caught up with David.

"Natasha's Sanzlermann interview was brilliant," said David. "Compulsory DNA tests. These people are really crazy. Our story went out on the wire at dawn. London put an 'urgent' on it. Last time I looked, it had been picked up sixty-seven times, everywhere from Auckland to Alaska. We're making the *Budapest News* famous around the world."

"I think we are making you famous," said Alex, jamming his hat down over his ears. "I didn't see any Reuters reporters in the Hotel Savoy on Monday morning." The news that Attila Hunkalffy was a hit and run driver he decided to keep to himself.

David grinned and pulled ahead. "Don't worry, Your Excellency. The Panamanian ambassador is about to get the longest lunch of his life."

Alex pushed himself on. Had someone put lead weights in his shoes? "We're going to get raided by the financial police," he panted.

"You too? They've promised us a visit as well. It's not just your paper and Reuters, you know. Virtually every foreign news organisation is getting a visit from these guys. Except the correspondents for media owned by . . ."

"Let me guess. The Volkstern Corporation," said Alex, a sheen of sweat forming as they came up to the Grand Hotel.

"Yes. And did you see the new law: directors and managers of companies defaulting on their tax, VAT or customs obligations are now personally liable for those debts, with the possibility of a five year prison sentence. What is the legal definition of a manager? Anyone would think they were trying to intimidate us."

Alex's calf muscles began to ache. It was getting harder to talk and run at the same time. They ran in silence for several minutes, past the hotels, until Arpad Bridge came into sight. It was a concrete monstrosity, flat and functional with six lanes of traffic. It had none of the grace of the Chain Bridge, or the Elizabeth Bridge. Fresh graffiti had been painted across its base: "Immigrants Out: Magyars Arise." They turned left through the trees and headed down the other side of the island and up towards the water tower.

Almost halfway around and Alex had his second wind now. He breathed easily and steadily, sprinted ahead of David and swerved around two old ladies in fur coats, walking small, yapping dogs. Sea gulls soared and squawked above him. There were moments, rare enough, but they did occur, when he felt he could do anything. Alex looked closer as he approached the water tower. A small figure sat on a bench with her arms wrapped around her legs, watching the river. She looked familiar. Very familiar.

Alex sat down, breathing hard.

"Back from your business trip?" asked Zsofi, staring out at the water. She looked waif-like and vulnerable, wrapped in a man's army parka. It was his, he realised, 'borrowed' several weeks earlier when she had left in the early morning hours.

"And you didn't call me, or send me an email, or even a text message."

He wiped the sweat from his forehead. "No. I didn't. Congratulations, Juliet. When do you start?"

"Next week." She paused. "Alex, I, we ... I just keep wishing that I had two lives," she said, her voice small and uncertain as she turned to him.

He reached for her hand. She wrapped her fingers through his.

"I know, Zsofi. We won't be able to see much of each other. You'll be spending most of your time in Vienna." He watched an empty box bouncing on the waters, moving fast as the current pulled it towards Margaret Bridge. A running figure, wearing blue trousers and a hooded turquoise sweatshirt appeared in the distance, moving with graceful strides.

"You let me go that easily," Zsofi said, loudly sniffing and wiping her eyes.

Alex drew her close to him. They sat together silently for several minutes, his arm wrapped around her shoulders. He watched the box rush towards the bridge, bounce off one of the stanchions, and disappear into the distance.

"Alex," she asked. "We will always be friends, won't we?"

"Of course."

"Will you come and watch me dance in Vienna?"

He smiled. She really was incorrigible. "Maybe. But that's all," he said, pulling her close and kissing her cheek.

The runner drew closer and slowed down. Alex looked up to see Natasha staring at him as she passed the bench. She waved hallo, quickly looked away and sprinted off into the distance.

\*    \*    \*

Cassandra Orczy settled down to work late into the night again. As soon as one pile of papers on her desk went off to her bosses, suitably marked and annotated, another appeared. Budgets had been blown, agents dispatched before their training was finished, and still the questions came from on high: what were the implications of Frank Sanzlermann becoming the first President of Europe for Hungarian national security? Despite all her endeavours, the gold-rimmed Zsolnay coffee cups were no nearer, but somehow that didn't seem to matter any more. Even the quote from Sun Tzu framed on her wall failed to work its usual magic.

The truth was, she was lonely. She and Mubarak had broken up twenty years ago. He had proposed, but she had said no. She wanted a career, and an officer in the security service could hardly be married to a money-changer. So she had thought, until she found out how many of her colleagues were using their contacts abroad to run black market businesses, and their Communist Party connections to lavishly enrich themselves. As she had done, by buying the former Farkas family summer villa for $5,000. That was profiteering, pure and simple.

Of course she hadn't known then that the villa had once belonged to her father's best friend's family. But that was hardly the point. Her father had advised against marrying Mubarak, although of course he would never admit that he did not want his daughter to marry an Arab. Instead she had married Laszlo Orczy, rising star in the Hungarian theatre. Who, she soon discovered, rose to every opportunity to bed the fans who flocked to his dressing room. The marriage had not lasted. Perhaps if she had said yes to Mubarak, he would not have stayed a money-changer. What a hypocrite she was. What was the use of being chief of the Threat Assessment and Analysis Department when you woke up alone every morning?

She picked up the latest report on Frank Sanzlermann. It was raw intelligence, from an agent dubbed 'Voter'. Voter was their only source inside Sanzlermann's inner circle. Signals intelligence, microphones and radio transmitters had brought in a meagre harvest. They had bugged the candidate's room of course, placing tiny transmitters in the power sockets, light circuits, even the curtain rails. But his security people had swept the room and found every one; even the latest models that the British MI6 had said were undetectable. Sanzlermann's people did not use the hotel telephone other than to speak to room service. Their mobile phones were encrypted and the security service could not crack the code. Their emails were bland, confirmations of meetings, times and places. There was so much car and bus traffic around the hotel that laser bugging – bouncing the beam off the window to pick up speech vibrations – was not very effective, and the few smatterings they had gleaned up had too much background noise.

The Israelis had passed over some material on Istvan Matonhely, the leader of the Pannonia Brigade, and his international links. There was an interesting money trail, leading from Zurich to South America. The Americans had sent satellite pictures of Sanzlermann meeting senior executives of KZX and the Volkstern Corporation at a remote hunting lodge in the Austrian Alps. MI6's economic analysts had promised a report on Sanzlermann's campaign financing. What she needed, Cassandra knew, was to get people inside the hotel. Her watchers in the nearby buildings had reported a steady procession of Austrian and German businessmen passing through Sanzlermann's campaign headquarters, together with some very powerful figures in the Swiss banking world.

One of the Swiss had substantial interests in the Budapest property market. He had recently invested heavily in a riverside block of flats, bought cheaply from the state. But the development had run into difficulties. The son of the original pre-war owner had suddenly turned up alive and well, living in Hampstead, London. From where he was demanding the return of his family property, or substantial compensation. Reminded of this, and promised the security service's help in 'smoothing out legal problems' the Swiss banker had suddenly proved remarkably cooperative. Some kind of top-security gala dinner or party was planned for the evening of November 9, he had told her. Dignitaries would be flying in from Germany, Austria, Switzerland and South America. She reminded herself to tell the London station that 'Operation Hampstead' had proved most successful. Voter's report was flagged 'Top Secret'. So secret that it existed only in one paper copy. It would not be circulated to the former business partner of Attila Hunkalffy who had just been appointed director of the State Security Service. The secret service was now spying on its own Prime Minister and his associates. An inner cabal was keeping the chief out of the loop. Well, she smiled to herself, that's nothing new.

From: Voter
To: Head of Threat Assessment and Analysis Department
Cc: Head of Counter-Intelligence Directorate

1. Attention is respectfully drawn to the fact this agent's despatches have just been upgraded from 'Secret' to 'Top Secret'. This task and the information gained are highly delicate with possible ramifications at the highest level of national security, and the contents of this report should be handled with the utmost discretion, especially considering the increasing links between the government of ATTILA HUNKALFFY and FRANK SANZLERMANN's campaign staff.

2. This agent's report is based on material he has gathered first hand, from his own conversations and gleanings. The facts contained are not just based on talking with named individuals, but also on his personal

examination of documents, emails, letters and passports. A list of names and relevant business organisations is attached as 'Appendix A'. Where material has been indirectly learnt it has been marked with a *.

3.  Before proceeding, it is necessary to briefly restate the current political and diplomatic context of developments in post-communist Europe. Despite the rhetoric about returning the former Soviet bloc to the 'common family home' the reality is very different. There is growing resentment and disillusionment across western Europe at the costs of subsidising the fifteen new members. There is widespread anger that organised crime syndicates have retained their power and are linked to, and cooperate, with several governments. Ministers and senior police officers in accession countries are implicated in continent-wide networks smuggling women, drugs and even weapons from the Balkans to western Europe. Corruption is widespread and apparently unstoppable. Early enthusiasm to reform and modernise the accession countries has evaporated. Instead western governments are increasingly focused on the terrorist attacks by the Immigration Liberation Army, and their domestic political fall-out. The ever-louder calls for a 'crackdown' on illegal immigration and asylum seekers, means that little attention is given in Brussels and Strasbourg to political developments in the new member countries. Within this context, this agent believes he does not exaggerate when he says that a victory for FRANK SANZLERMANN in the coming election for European President, combined with the continuing administration of ATTILA HUNKALFFY, poses a substantial threat to national security and Hungary's continuing economic independence.

She rubbed her eyes, and read through the paragraph again, this time more slowly.

4.  ATTILA HUNKALFFY appears to be seen by the SANZLERMANN campaign as some kind of agent-in-place. It is unclear how much, if any, genuine autonomy he exercises. Concurrent with FRANK SANZLERMANN'S election campaign a parallel strategy seems to be operating on four, possibly more, fronts at once in Hungary. This closely follows the pattern of events in Croatia, Slovakia and Romania, the

wartime allies of Nazi Germany, where far-right governments have taken power. These fronts are: manipulating public opinion through control of the media, especially television, and, increasingly, websites; the sustained weakening of already shaky independent institutions such as Parliament, the police and judiciary; the use of violence against minorities to engender feelings of insecurity; widespread corruption, and a collapse in the value of the national currency (caused in part by the previous four steps) which opens the door for foreign investors to buy up national assets at prices far below their market value.

The strategy can be summarised as: Psychological/Media; Anti-Minority Actions; Police/Judiciary and Economy. All areas are interlinked. (It will of course be appreciated that many agents fall victim to self-projection and present their observations in a form intended to direct the reader to a certain conclusion. But I hope it is understood that this agent is concerned merely to present what he has discovered, rather than trying to draw premature and erroneous conclusions from this, or any other report.)

"Voter, you are one of the most pompous people I have ever encountered," said Cassandra out loud. *What you want to say*, she thought, *is that you don't know what it all means yet, but then neither do I*. She read on.

5. A breakdown follows of the four areas. The recently-launched Pannonia Brigade is of particular interest. As the general economic and political situation deteriorates, Hungarian society seeks a scapegoat. Traditionally, this has been the Jews. However since Hungary's accession to the European Union and subsequent growth of a young, more modern-minded middle-class, open anti-Semitism is no longer politically acceptable. There are few such constraints though with regard to the Roma. The Pannonia Brigade, which appears to be financed by émigré groups in South America, Germany and Austria, is focusing on what it describes as 'Gypsy crime'. Its choice of uniform, the traditional Hussars' costume, is psychologically masterful. The black outfits have a sufficiently militaristic feel, but are also part of Hungary's traditional dress, and so place the Pannonia Brigade firmly within the mainstream 'national community'. The subtext is that all 'true Hungarians' should be protesting

against 'Gypsy crime' and that violence is a legitimate form of national self-defence. The violence against the Roma serves a dual purpose: it engenders feelings of insecurity in the wider population, that state institutions can no longer protect society, but paradoxically, also makes them feel more secure, as non-Roma Hungarians are not being targeted.

The precise strategic relationship between these four areas and FRANK SANZLERMANN'S election campaign is so far unclear, but there are strong linkages of personnel, interests and financial backers.

She flicked through to the appendix. Sanzlermann's campaign was funded by numerous titans of German industry including of course, KZX Industries and the Volkstern Corporation. Hunkalffy had not heeded her warning about KZX buying a controlling stake in the Hungarian pharmaceutical industry, and was allowing the buy-out to go ahead. But was 'Voter' serious? Was he credible? She walked over to the window, and looked at the Danube. A barge moved slowly downstream, laded with coal, black as the night-time waters. She caught site of her reflection in the glass. Her blond hair was lank, dark shadows ringed her eyes. She poured herself some more coffee before returning to her desk. This would have be to flagged 'urgent'. She turned back the pages, to the detailed breakdown dealing with the media.

The use of the media is of prime importance. Ultra-nationalist websites such as pannoniabrigade.hu publish the names, telephone numbers and home addresses of political opponents. They organise 'flash-mobs', instant demonstrations, which frequently result in violence. The state media adopts more subtle tactics, such as the increasing number of stories about Israelis and property acquisition. Coded anti-Semitism, disguised as anti-Israel propaganda, is steadily increasing, through the use of terms such as the 'New York-Tel Aviv Axis', 'rootless cosmopolitans', media outrage over the 'blood-price' exacted by the Israeli army on its military operations, and increasing comparisons between the Hungarians and the Palestinians – meaning that Israelis/Jews are forcing the Magyars from their ancient homeland.

Such language and terms speak to an "underground community of the mind", that is, people who share values which are no longer acceptable in public discourse, but are still strongly held. The coded terminology is part of the campaign's 'psy-ops' or psychological operations. The language increases nervousness among those opposed to ATTILA HUNKALFFY. Another tactic is not to deny the Holocaust, but to minimise it, and blame the Nazi genocide on a regime long vanished, of little relevance to the present day. At the same time, extremist leaders such as ISTVAN MATONHELY are frequent guests on chat-shows and news programmes. Their views are never challenged by the journalists, but are accepted as part of the political mainstream, thus 'de-stigmatising' and legitimising the politics of hate.

This agent has discovered that LASZLO KENGODON, a Hungarian psychologist of Jewish background, has been charged with responsibility for psy-ops. KENGODON was briefly married to an Israeli medical student who left him and returned home, which seems to have triggered a violent psychological reaction, verging on self-hatred. He has been warmly welcomed as a 'Court Jew', who provides a useful alibi against charges of anti-Semitism. KENGODON is a close associate of BALAZS NOLUDI, who is a media advisor to ATTILA HUNKALFFY, and editor of *Ébredjetek Magyarok*! KENGODON uses his knowledge of Jewish history and culture to create as much havoc as possible. For example: KENGODON holds training sessions where he teaches young activists basic Hebrew. These groups are then despatched around the country to small towns and villages that were once home to Jewish communities. They pose as Israelis and march around the local streets, ringing doorbells and making loud and aggressive enquiries about property ownership. Local journalists are tipped off about their arrival, ensuring substantial media coverage. The pseudo-Israelis cause profound unease, especially as tens of thousands of homes, factories and other buildings were simply appropriated once the former owners were sent to the camps.

Cassandra flicked through to the end of the report before she put it down. There were another forty points, spread over seventeen pages. She lit another cigarette. It was going to be a long night.

## FOURTEEN

Alex strode into the *Budapest News* editorial office full of optimism and good cheer. It was Friday morning, a few minutes before 11.00am and the newspaper's weekly meeting. The editorial floor was usually crowded with reporters, designers and advertising staff, cracking jokes and taking friendly enjoyment in finding the tiny errors that inevitably crept into every issue. Alex was looking forward to taking the staff out for a celebratory drink after work to toast Natasha's scoop and to start the weekend. Which was why the tense, nervous atmosphere was even more puzzling. His 'Good morning' dried in his throat as he walked through the room.

Heads were bowed over computers, and the office was almost silent apart from the occasional click of a keyboard. Euan Braithwaite, a strapping former Rugby player from Hebden Bridge, who had recently joined the staff as sports editor, caught Alex's eye and shook his head. There was no music playing in the design department, and Ronald Worthington's office was dark and closed. Alex stepped inside the conference room. George Smith was the only person there, sitting in Ronald's chair. A copy of that week's paper lay on the table in front of him, with several paragraphs of Natasha's interview with Sanzlermann heavily marked in red ink.

"You're late," Smith snapped, his blue pin-striped shirt covered with a liberal sprinkling of crumbs from a bag of croissants.

"Where is everybody?" asked Alex, sitting down opposite him.

"Busy working, where they should be," he said, starting on a slab of sticky chocolate cake, and noisily slurping coffee from a familiar-looking mug. It was blue, with a picture of a dog jumping for a ball.

"Isn't that Ronald's? Where is he?"

Smith looked at the mug. "Ronald's in his room. London has made some changes."

"What changes?" Alex asked.

Smith wiped his hand across the back of his mouth and pushed a sheet of paper across the table at Alex. It was a joint press release from the Volkstern Corporation headquarters in Munich, and the *Sentinel's* head office in London, dated that morning. After many months of long negotiations the Volkstern Group was pleased to announce the launch of a new strategic partnership with *Sentinel* Newspapers. New opportunities, expanding market, and so on. And then the meat: while every effort would be made to safeguard the editorial independence of the group's media, some structural re-organisation and re-orientation would be inevitable, in light of the new economic reality, and the Group's financial interests.

Alex felt sick as he looked at the paper. How could this have been planned for so long? He hadn't heard anything on the grapevine. Several of his emails back to London, he suddenly remembered, had gone unanswered. He assumed his friends had been away or too busy to reply quickly. Maybe they were away for good. This was a disaster. New economic reality, he knew, meant PR fluff for favoured advertisers.

"No wonder everyone looks so gloomy outside. I didn't know about this."

"Well, you're not much of a reporter are you? You've been working for this company for long enough. I made an announcement to the staff. You would have heard it if you were here on time." said Smith, brushing crumbs from his hair. "I want to talk to you about this," he added, tapping his finger on the front page of that week's issue.

"Yes, we did well there. It's all over the world. Civil rights groups are up in arms."

"We are not a PR organisation for troublemakers. This is a very unbalanced article, giving a totally one-sided view of Europe's best hope for the future."

"No, it's not. It's an accurately reported interview. You can read the transcript on the website. I'm sorry you feel like that, but Ronald is the editor, and he has the last word," said Alex.

Smith smiled malevolently. "The article and the interview transcript have been removed from the website. And Worthington is no longer the editor," he said, pushing another sheet of paper across the table. It announced Smith's appointment as Group Editor in Chief of the new *Sentinel*-Volkstern regional publishing group, including the *Budapest News*. Sister newspapers were planned for Zagreb, Bratislava and Bucharest. Ronald Worthington, it noted, congratulated Smith on his appointment. His new role was 'special projects editor', overseeing the launch of a series of supplements on consumer lifestyles, starting with health clubs and gyms.

"And what's my new job?" Alex asked.

"You don't have one. You leaked company material to an international news agency. You've got half an hour to clear your desk. And don't come back."

\* \* \*

Alex walked into Ronald's office to find him sitting in the dark staring into space. His hands were folded, resting on his capacious stomach, a crumpled handkerchief on his desk in front of him. Ferrari, his loyal red setter, was lying beside him, looking up expectantly at his master. Alex switched the lights on and walked straight to Ronald's desk. He picked up a bottle of Johnny Walker Black Label perched on top of *Magyar Gasztronómia* magazine.

"*Ow*, that hurts old chap," Ronald exclaimed, his eyes red and watery. He whisked the handkerchief off the table and loudly blew his nose. "Heavy night last night," he added quickly.

Alex poured two large measures of whisky into a pair of coffee mugs. He handed one to Ronald.

"Here's to gyms and health clubs," said Alex, as they clinked mugs.

"What exactly *is* a health club, do you think?"

"The very opposite of the four course lunches and dinners you eat at Gundel."

"Lettuce leaves, shreds of carrot and a glass of mineral water, you mean," said Ronald, gloomily.

"Worse."

"How much worse?"

"Very much worse. You have to work for it. Exercise on machines, running and rowing. Ronald, you're not actually going to . . ."

"Of course not, old chap," said Ronald quietly, sipping the whisky. "They've offered me six months money to go quietly."

"And if you don't go quietly?"

"Smith was pleased to tell me about the new *Sentinel* –Volkstern corporate security department, whose regional office is opening in Budapest next week. On constant alert to deal with any 'difficulties'. First contract to provide close protection to the extra campaign staff arriving for . . . well, I think you can guess who."

"That's a good story."

"Which is why you won't see it in our paper," said Ronald, pouring them both a fresh slug of whisky. He sighed. "Of course it's not our paper anymore. And you?"

"I've been sacked." Alex did some rapid mental calculations. As he was seconded from London, he was paid a western salary. He had enough in his bank account to pay his bills for at least six months.

Ronald said dolefully: "I'm really sorry, Alex. It was on the cards as soon as Smith arrived. If we had just known about the negotiations with the Volkstern Corporation then we could have been better prepared. The thing about that bastard," said Ronald, letting Ferrari lick a spilled drop of whisky from his finger, "is that he's such a miserable sod. He never enjoys anything, except buggering things up for everyone else. So it's back to Blighty for us, eh Ferrari? And I think he's got my mug," he said, rubbing the dog's neck.

Alex was lost in thought. The new corporate security division would certainly go through his computer at work. His notes from

Novy Marek and the digging he had done into KZX were on his laptop at home. But there were numerous files, emails and contact numbers he wanted to get from his computer.

"Can I borrow your terminal?" he asked Ronald.

"Sure," said Ronald, clearing some space by the keyboard.

Alex sat down at his desk. He logged onto his computer and typed in his password. The screen flashed up: "Access Denied." He tried twice more, and both times was refused. The screen warned that the account was locked down and any further attempts to access it would trigger a response from the corporate security department.

"That bastard," exclaimed Alex angrily. "He's shut me out of my computer."

The telephone rang and Ronald waved his hand at Alex to answer it.

"I greet you, and I wish you a good morning," said a deep voice, in well-modulated formal Hungarian. "I am Father Gabor Fischer. I would like to speak to Mr Ron-ald Wor-thin-gton," he said, emphasising every syllable as though he was reading out loud a name that been transcribed into Hungarian.

"He is here, but he doesn't speak Hungarian. May I help you? I am Alex Farkas, one of his journalistic colleagues. *Mélyik ügyrol szeretné beszélni*, about which matter would you like to speak?" said Alex, switching to Hungarian.

"Oh, yes. Vince mentioned your name as well. He always enjoyed reading your stories."

"Enjoyed?"

"I am very sorry to be the bearer of tragic news, Mr Farkas, and also to your colleague Mr Worthington. Vince is dead. He was killed in a car accident last night."

\*   \*   \*

Alex bumped into Natasha on the building's grand marble staircase, on his way to Father Fischer's church. Ronald was already packing up his office. He was shocked and upset to hear of Vince's death.

They agreed that Alex should go to see the priest. Natasha was on her way out. She looked pale, he thought. Had she been crying?

"I suppose this is goodbye, Alex. We won't meet any more. I've resigned," Natasha said.

Alex's stomach lurched.

"What are you talking about? I know there have been a lot of upheavals. But you can't leave. You just had an international scoop."

"Yes, I know. Smith rewarded me with a new job. Typing up the cinema listings. So much for my career as a reporter."

They stepped outside onto the street. She looked around and began to head into Nyugati underpass, not waiting for Alex. He caught up with her as she walked past the Hungry Postman. It was almost empty, as usual.

"Natasha, can you please just stop rushing around for a minute. I want to talk to you. I can't do that if I have to chase you halfway across Pest."

She stood still, watching him. Ask, he thought, and then at least you will know, one way or the other. He heard his voice, as though someone else was forming the words: "Why don't we have dinner tonight. We can discuss things properly. We could go to . . ."

"No, Alex." She looked away from him. "I can't have dinner with you."

No. But what did he expect? He saw her jogging on Margaret Island, the surprise, perhaps something more, in her eyes, how she blinked twice, just as he kissed Zsofi's cheek.

Natasha twisted her hair in her fingers. "I need to be on my own for a while. I don't want to have dinner with anybody. This morning I had a career and a good job. I worked hard and did my best. Now I'm unemployed."

Alex tried again. "Look, Natasha, I wanted to explain. The other day when you saw me on Margaret Island. It wasn't what you think. She's an old friend. We're not together."

Natasha crossed her arms tightly. "I don't think *anything*. It's none of my business what you do, or who you do it with."

"Natasha, don't go like this. Look, let's have a coffee at the Hungry Postman. We're almost outside the front door," he said, almost pleading.

She stepped away from him. "Do what you want, Alex. I don't care. I have to go." Her voice was tight and controlled.

Alex flushed red. To his surprise, he felt near to tears. "I'm very sorry. I didn't want to upset you. It was a misunderstanding. There's been too many upheavals today. I wish you every success in the future." He proffered his hand to shake.

She shook his hand. Her lip twisted sideways as he quickly let go of her palm.

"*Djakujem*, Alex," she said, a catch in her voice.

He watched her walk off into the underpass. Trams and traffic roared by. She reached into her handbag, took out a tissue and blew her nose. He hailed a taxi. As the car pulled over to the side of the road, he saw her running back in his direction, waving. He was just about to get in.

"Alex," she said, her face flushed as she caught her breath.

He smiled. She had changed her mind.

"I'm sorry. I forgot to give you this. It's the recorder, with the Sanzlermann interview."

He stopped smiling and said nothing.

"I think there's something wrong with it. It doesn't work properly. I can't access the tracks. I had to use my notes to write up the interview," she continued.

There was a curious look in her eyes, thought Alex. And who cared if a digital recorder worked or not. "I think we already said goodbye," he said.

Natasha turned away and walked into the underpass. He didn't look back as he got in the car. The driver weaved through the lunchtime traffic like Ayrton Senna, lurching from left to right, tires squealing in protest. There was, he discovered, no satisfaction at all in having the last word.

\*　\*　\*

The church was cool and dark. Alex sat on one of the wooden benches, shined over the years by generations of worshippers. He wiped his eyes and blew his nose. He missed his grandfather. Miklos and Ruth had loved only each other and had been married for fifty years. Alex envied them that enduring love. He doubted he would find it here. Perhaps he should go back to London. What would Miklos advise? To stay until his business in Budapest was finished, Alex was sure, and every journalistic instinct he had told him that Vince Szatmari's death was no accident.

He leant back to take in the Gothic roof that soared towards the heavens, and the way the soft winter light diffused through the coloured-glass. He breathed in a pleasant smell of brick and leather. A few motes of dust floated in a beam of winter sunshine. What these walls had witnessed. Weddings and confirmations, funerals and memorials. There was a sense of peace, that life continued in its inexorable rhythm. An old lady sitting at the end of the pew smiled at him. She was from the countryside, dressed in a traditional embroidered Transylvanian skirt, with a headscarf tied neatly over her swept back grey hair. She had the clearest eyes he had ever seen, and weathered skin glowing with vitality. She offered him a shiny apple, which he accepted with a formal thank you. The windows were breathtaking, each one a work of art, an intricate tableaux of apostles and Biblical prophets. He saw a giant of a man approaching, with salt and pepper hair, and a neatly trimmed beard.

"Mr Farkas? I am Gabor Fischer. Thank you for coming. Let us go to my office."

It was a small room, the walls lined with glass-fronted book-shelves. Alex saw the cabinets contained several volumes about liberation theology, the doctrine that the Church must struggle against physical oppression as well as save souls. A small sofa was covered with several brightly coloured cushions and wraps. There was a pleasant smell of ground coffee, and a hint of something rich and fruity. A large photograph on the wall showed a younger version of the priest, in an athlete's leotard, standing on the medal winners' dias at the Moscow Olympics with a triumphant smile on his broad face.

The priest beckoned Alex inside. "Sit down, please. May I offer you something? Coffee? Something stronger? I brew my own *palinka*, from plums. You are familiar with *palinka*?" he asked, smiling.

"A black coffee and a glass of your home-made would be wonderful," said Alex, turning to look at the Moscow Olympics picture.

"I won the gold for the javelin," said the priest as he prepared the drinks, a nostalgic smile on his broad, handsome face.

They clinked glasses. The clear spirit worked its magic quickly. It was smooth and clean, with a tangy aftertaste of fruit. Alex licked his lips in appreciation.

"How does it compare to Serbia and Bosnia?" asked Father Fischer.

"Excellent." He picked up his coffee and drank. "Thanks. It's a long time since I had a real Balkan breakfast."

"I know. I used to read your articles," said Father Fischer. He shook his head, wearily. "Vince's death is a tragedy. His mother is devastated. The police said it was a hit and run. He'd been working late and was walking home across the Elizabeth Bridge, just a few metres from here. A car took the bend too fast, spun out of control, came up on the pavement and hit him at full speed, before driving off. He was killed instantly. They haven't caught the driver."

"Father, can I ask you a blunt question?"

The priest nodded.

"Do you think that Vince was murdered?"

Father Fischer leaned back in his chair, and picked up one of the cushions, coloured bright blue, green and red.

"I was in El Salvador. Twenty years ago. In the communist times. I knew your grandfather. My condolences on his death. We met several times. There were many things we agreed about. Long before Marx and Lenin, Jesus was fighting for social justice. We cannot just care for people's souls, when they live in misery and poverty. As Jesus went out among the poor, so did I. I was despatched to a small village in the jungle, some distance from San Salvador. We set up a weaving cooperative, a health programme, and taught the villagers to read and write. These are some of the products that the cooperative made. That was twenty years ago. The colours still haven't faded," he said, patting the cushion.

"The village got organised. They elected a mayor, Joaquin, a natural organiser. There was talk of a trade union, a school. And then there was an accident. A car hit Joaquin, while he was walking home at night. He was killed. A few days later the army came and shot half a dozen men at random, for 'aiding the guerrillas'. I was smuggled out, into Nicaragua, and eventually I made my way back here."

Alex sat back, trying to imagine this sturdy Hungarian priest tramping through the jungle with left-wing guerrillas. It was surprisingly easy.

"I pray for the soul of Vince Szatmari," the priest said. "I encouraged him to see you. Now he is dead. I encouraged the villagers in El Salvador to learn to read and write. Now most of them are dead and their village is destroyed. Perhaps the Muslims are right. Everything is recorded somewhere, and is God's will."

Alex finished his coffee and put the cup down. "Who wished to destroy Vince Szatmari?"

The priest looked hard at Alex, as if assessing him. "Vince told me he had found a document at the bank. It outlined the procedures for granting tenders in the new privatisations. Certain firms were to be favoured, others ignored. Everything had been arranged in advance. Billions of euros were at stake. Then he found the list of companies. Every firm was either part of, or connected to, two giant German media and industrial corporations buying up eastern Europe."

"Which two?" asked Alex, trying to keep the eagerness from his voice.

"I think you know that. Use the information wisely. It has already cost one life."

## FIFTEEN

The domed roof of the Rudas bath was inlaid with squares of tinted glass, framing coloured light sabres that cut through the steam, deep into the water. Built by the Ottomans in the sixteenth century, the Rudas had survived centuries of turbulent history. Empires rose and empires fell, swallowing and disgorging Hungary, but from Sultans to Soviets, the Rudas endured. A large hexagonal pool was kept at a steady thirty degrees, while its four smaller satellites varied from toe-clenchingly cold to hot enough to boil an egg, or so it felt. There were also two saunas and steam rooms. In short, the perfect way to spend a leisurely morning.

Now Alex was jobless he had plenty of time to take in the city's pleasures and join the poets, politicians and mobsters who colonised the Rudas. He lay back in the main pool and stared at the roof. He felt punch drunk, and not just from the steam and mineral tang of the waters. He had lost his grandfather, his job, his lover and any chance of getting together with Natasha. And he had just learned that as he was seconded to the *Budapest News* on a one year contract he would not even receive any redundancy money. Sixteen years of loyal journalistic service counted for precisely nothing with the Volkstern Corporation. He felt angry and betrayed. But even if he was unemployed he was still a journalist. Miklos had been killed. Vince Szatmari had died in a mysterious hit and run. KZX and the Volkstern Corporation were buying up the country on the cheap. And now he had time to dig deeper. As for Ronald Worthington, he was moving to Dorset to open a pub. He was, he promised, organising 'the mother of all leaving dinners'.

"You could always come and work for me," said Mubarak Fonseca, lolling companionably next to him as they soaked.

"As what? A waiter in Café Casablanca?" Alex laughed. "Actually I have worked as a waiter. I once had a summer job in a four-star hotel. I am fully trained to silver service standards. I know how to serve soup from a tureen without spilling it, and the correct way to fold a linen napkin." He nudged Mubarak as he spotted the country's most famous boxer, chatting to a former Foreign Minister in the cold pool.

Mubarak sat up and cupped water before pouring it on his head. "So, you see. You are ready to start. But I'm not sure that we need linen napkins at Café Casablanca. Maybe I could teach you how to be a money-trader. Although it seems that is a bit risky nowadays," he said, touching his black eye, now fading.

"Did you make a complaint?" asked Alex.

Mubarak snorted with derision. "To whom? My business is not exactly legal and transparent. But I did speak to a friend of mine who works for a different state agency. This might be interesting for you, Alex. There is some kind of power struggle going on in the Interior Ministry between the Gendarmes and the security service. I am not the only one this has happened to. The Gendarmes keep beating up their contacts in the more, let us say, eclectic sections of society. The crime rate keeps going up, the nationalist press is howling for a crackdown, and the forint is collapsing. Everything's for sale at bargain prices."

Alex smiled. "Including English-language newspapers. I think I'll get some steam. See you in a minute." Mubarak smiled and stretched out.

The steam-room was a small tiled space, about two metres by four. A notice was pinned to the metal pipe that carried the boiling vapour, warning customers that they used it at their own risk. An ancient thermometer showed the temperature: forty-five degrees. Two elderly gentlemen, pink and plump, were sitting on the wooden bench, discussing Hungarian literature. They made space for Alex. He sat back with his head against the tiles with his eyes closed, half-listening to their animated discussion. The sweat began to erupt from his pores and he felt the tension slowly drain away.

He did not see the door open as the two men came in. The literary critics quickly left. The first man was tall and well-muscled, heavily tattooed and completely bald. A crudely stitched scar stretched from his forehead to his right ear. His sidekick was a head shorter, but almost a foot wider, with a heavy, bony brow over tiny eyes. His head appeared to have been directly transplanted onto his shoulders, as though he was born of a new species that had eliminated the need for a neck. The tattooed man sat down next to Alex. His sidekick stood in front of the door with his arms crossed.

Alex sensed movement in the room, stirred and opened his eyes. Bolts of pain shot down his back. Iron claws gripped his right shoulder, forcing him down and his neck forward, as though he was held in a vice. He tried to twist away, but to no effect. The tattooed man smiled as he steadily increased the pressure. Alex arched his back in agony, staring at the spider's web tattoo across the man's neck and the giant lion's head roaring angrily in the centre of his chest. He opened his mouth to shout. A meaty palm suddenly slammed over his lips, pressing hard against his teeth.

"Easy now, Sasha. You don't mind if I call you Sasha, do you?" he asked, not waiting for an answer. "You can call me Yuri. We just have a couple of little questions for you. And don't think about biting my fingers. If you do, I will knock out every tooth in your mouth. Nod if you believe me," he said, his voice calm and assured.

Alex did as he was told, panting as fear and pain coursed through him. He looked around the room. Where was everybody else? The second man stood immobile at the door.

Yuri spoke again. "I will also do the same if you shout when I take my hand away from your mouth. Nod if you understand."

Alex nodded again. The pressure on his shoulder eased slightly.

"Good. Very good. Where is it?"

"Where is what?"

Yuri's eyes turned dull and distant. He yanked Alex forward and his right hand snapped back and forth. The slap cracked like a whip. "Carefully now. We don't want you to bang your head," he said, as he caught Alex's head and gently leaned him back against the tiles. A hose led from a nearby cold tap. He turned it on and drenched Alex with the cold water. He shivered violently, no longer knowing if he was hot or cold.

"That's better," said Yuri, soothingly. "Perhaps it will help your memory. I will ask you one more time. Where is it? Have you got it, or has she? A beautiful girl, your colleague. A terrible shame if anything happened to her."

"I – don't – know – what – you – are – talking – about," said Alex through gritted teeth. The heat was unbearable. His fingertips felt as though they were cooking. The sweat and steam poured off him as the room wobbled. The punch sent him spinning to the side. He felt that his head was exploding. Blood gushed from his lip, and he toppled off the bench onto the floor. Alex twisted round and hit the man hard twice in the groin. He gasped in pain and Alex dashed for the door. The thug standing there easily batted Alex back into the room and he crashed into the bench, sliding on the slippery floor.

"That was a mistake," said Yuri. "A big mistake." He picked Alex up and punched him in the stomach. Alex collapsed and threw up, the sour reek filling the tiny room.

"No sleeping on the job, Sasha," said Yuri. He sprayed Alex again with the ice-cold water and hosed the vomit into the corner. He slipped a knuckleduster over his fingers, a sculpted brass oval studded with metal points, with a short blade attached to the end. He knelt down next to Alex as he lay on the tiles. Alex tried to get up, but his limbs would not obey. Pincer fingers gripped his arm, forcing him back down.

Yuri slid the tip of the blade into Alex's upper arm, his movements quick and precise, as though he was slicing a salami. Alex twisted in agony, panting as the knife cut into his flesh. Drops of blood sprouted on his wet skin, mingling with the steam, dripping pink on the floor.

He stood back for a moment, admiring his work, as Alex's blood beaded along the incisions, before cutting him again. Alex screamed.

The door crashed open and Mubarak skidded across the floor. He turned and punched the thick-necked heavy hard and fast in the chest, slamming him against the wall. Mubarak span around with a back kick to his jaw. There was a loud crack as his jaw broke and his head bounced off the tiles. He grunted and slumped unconscious to the floor.

Yuri advanced, knife at the ready. When he saw Mubarak his hand dropped in surprise.

Mubarak looked at him with contempt and took the knife from his hand. "Yuri. Enforcer for the Ukrainians. You're a tough guy when it's two against one. How about one to one?" he demanded, holding Yuri's jaw in his right hand. Mubarak shoved him backwards and Yuri sat down hard on the bench.

Mubarak threw the knife between his legs. It stuck in one of the wooden slats with a dull thwack. "Does your boss know you are freelancing? I'm meeting him later tonight. I think he would be very interested to know that you have other employers."

Yuri looked alarmed. "Mubarak. Don't please. How was I to know he is your friend?"

Mubarak said: "Stay there. I want to talk to you." He turned to the Ukrainian's sidekick. "Get a clean cloth from one of the attendants, a medical kit, towels and plenty of mineral water."

Mubarak walked over to the steam pipe and switched off the valve. It clunked several times, hissed and fell silent. He helped Alex up, the room slowly clearing as the vapour evaporated.

*   *   *

Peter Feher wrapped his coat tighter around him as he waited at the skating rink in front of Vajdahunyad Castle, next to the City Park. Every winter the small artificial lake in front was frozen over. He smiled indulgently at the childrens' first faltering attempts to skate. Parents shouted encouragement, while their children wobbled onto the ice. Feher watched a young girl in her teens swish around the outer edge, lithe and smooth as a gazelle. She stopped in front of a proud father, her skates hissing as they sent up a little spray of ice, before he kissed her.

He felt a pang of regret. He could, he thought, have been a better father. The plan was to meet his daughter and go for a walk in the

park, take a look at Sanzlermann's election rally in nearby Heroes'
Square, and then lunch. Heroes' Square was an inspired choice for
Sanzlermann. Here King Istvan, the first king of Hungary, and his
chieftains were immortalised in two curved colonnades of
sculptures. Heroes' Square stood at the top of Andrassy Avenue.
Where had the Farkas family mansion been? No. 106. A vanished
world, servants graded by rank, fine china and silver polished until
it gleamed like platinum. No wonder Antal Noludi, the factory
manager, had appropriated it so quickly. His son Balazs, editor of
*Ébredjetek Magyarok!* was living there now. Did Alex know what
was rightfully his? Not that Feher believed in inherited privilege,
of course. But still . . .

\* \* \*

"Hallo Daddy," he heard a voice say. "Sorry I'm late." She offered
her cheek to be kissed.

He turned to look at her. She looked so much like her mother
that sometimes he did a double-take. Turquoise eyes, thick blond
hair cut short in a modern style, a ready smile. But there were
shadows under her eyes. He offered her his arm, and they walked
down to Heroes' Square. Giant red and white banners were draped
across the façade of the two art museums that flanked the open
space. One side proclaimed: 'Family, Work and Unity,' the other
'Forward to a Christian Europe.' Both were emblazoned with giant
pictures of Frank Sanzlermann. King Stephen stared out from his
plinth in the centre of the colonnade, unmoved. Workmen put the
last touches on a stage, to face straight down Andrassy Avenue.
Gendarmes were sealing off the roads around the square and
redirecting traffic, ignoring the vocal complaints of the motorists.

A small counter-demonstration was gathering in a far corner,
opposite the Yugoslav embassy. The demonstrators were mainly
young, students probably, he thought, dressed in denim, but also
some middle-class types. Wasn't that Krisztina Varga, the female
President of the Christian Democrats, a handsome woman in her
fifties, who had just resigned as Minister of Justice after Hunkalffy

took over? In fact there were several MPs and former MPs, including one or two who had been expelled from Hunkalffy's own Hungarian People's Party. A boy and girl stood together, holding banners in English: 'Hunkalffy is not Hungary', proclaimed his. 'And Hungary is not Hunkalffy,' announced hers.

He pointed at the banners. "Look at them. Maybe there is a chance."

"Let's hope so," said Cassandra Orczy.

\*   \*   \*

Alex winced in pain as the doctor stitched and bandaged the cuts on the side of his arm. They were shallow, and clean. Mubarak had called a taxi and wanted to take Alex to hospital, but he just wanted to go home. The doctor was a bulky, shambling man, with kindly eyes. He concluded his examination, shaking his head as he closed Alex's cuts. "You seem free of concussion or any brain injury. But you are to call me immediately if you feel nauseous, dizzy or confused, or if you cannot look at bright lights. Take your painkillers. You must rest and drink plenty of fluids."

Alex lay back on his bed. Mubarak showed him to the front door, slipping him two 5,000 forint notes before he left. He pushed the door hard to close it.

"Your front door is sticking. Looks like someone has been testing your locks. I'll send my security guy Zoran over to have a look."

"Thanks. And for rescuing me," said Alex. "You should go. You will be late. You have an appointment with Schevchenko's boss."

"I do. But not till next Wednesday," said Mubarak, laughing. "But I'll be sure to tell him that his chief enforcer is doing mysterious freelance work on the side. So mysterious that he has never met the people paying him. And paying him very well. I'll leave you now. Try and rest."

Alex slept for several hours after Mubarak left. The room did not wobble when he woke, but he could barely move his left arm. His face was scratched and sore and his stomach ached where the bruiser had punched him. He slowly made himself some tea and soup. The food and drink revived him and he picked up that day's copy of *Magyar Tribün*. A new law would allow the Gendarmerie to hold anyone for up to three months, or even longer with permission from the Interior Minister, without having to charge them with a crime. A planned demonstration against the new law had been immediately banned.

He turned on the television news. CNN showed the charred wreckage of a car in Vienna, while ambulances screeched by, sirens howling. A young woman staggered on the pavement, blood streaming down her face. The announcer said: "Nine people were killed today and seventeen injured in a car bomb several blocks from the Austrian Parliament in the latest in a series of terrorist attacks on European capitals. Hasan Al-Ajnabi, leader of the Immigration Liberation Army claimed responsibility. Riots erupted later on the outskirts of Vienna when a group of skinheads tried to attack a Turkish mosque and burn it down. In Strasbourg nationalist MEPs called for the immediate abolition of the right of asylum, and automatic internment in detention camps of anyone entering the Schengen zone without a visa."

Alex switched to Hungarian state television. Aniko Kovacs said: "Don't miss our live coverage of the historic rally in Heroes' Square where Frank Sanzlermann, guest of the Hungarian Prime Attila Hunkalffy, will be speaking. And now for some good news. The Volkstern Corporation today announced its internet expansion plans into central and eastern Europe. Volkstern is offering a free broadband internet connection for all customers who sign up for its multi-sector loyalty plan, covering consumer goods, mobile telephones and health insurance."

Alex picked up the digital tape recorder that Natasha had returned. It looked like an ordinary micro-cassette recorder, six inches by two inches, covered in chrome-coloured plastic, with a series of buttons down one side, above a speaker grill. A small LCD screen showed the date, time and current status of the machine. It recorded the data on an internal memory card, which could be transferred directly to a computer, stored on its hard drive and burned onto a CD. He pressed the data information button.

The display showed two tracks, taking up thirty-five minutes. He pressed play for track one. The LCD screen flashed once, but stayed silent. A second try produced the same result. He tried track two, also with no success. This was puzzling. He connected the recorder to his laptop computer. The screen showed a bar slowly filling a space until the connection was made. A software programme launched, with a range of options both to access the digital files in the recorder and transfer them to his computer. He moved the cursor over the graphic buttons and pressed 'play track 1'. "Encrypted. Access denied" the screen flashed up. "Enter your digital key password." He tried track two, with the same result.

Encryption was used for very sensitive or confidential data. It meant the data in the recorder had been scrambled, and was only available to those with a special password. The recorders the *Budapest News* had bought were the basic models. They did not have a digital encryption facility. He checked the connection: everything seemed fine. Had Natasha done this? Possibly. But why? Alex switched off his laptop and disconnected the recorder. If the data was encrypted, it might be set to self-destruct after a couple of unauthorised access attempts. Alex looked more closely at the recorder. A tiny trident logo on the bottom caught his eye. Underneath was printed in tiny letters: Property of KZX Industries.

Alex stared at the recorder in alarm. A voice sounded in his head. *Where is it? Have you got it, or has she?* He rapidly skimmed through his mobile's directory and called Natasha. Voicemail. He left a message to call him immediately. He tried her home. No answer. He left a similar message on the answering machine. Where was she? He called Kitty Kovacs.

"Alex, it's great to hear from you. It's awful at the office now. I don't know how much longer I'm going to stay. They've sent us a load of clones from London and Munich. Smith is marching around, ordering everybody about. Next week we're running two profiles: one of Hunkalffy, and one of Sanzlermann. And the business pages are just a plug for the Patriot Bond."

"Kitty, do you know where Natasha is?" asked Alex. "I need to find her."

"I don't know how you two survive this perpetual state of dramatic tension. And I thought you wanted to talk to me. Always the bridesmaid, never the bride." She laughed as she spoke.

"I do miss you Kitty, of course. But it's really urgent. She may be in danger."

"In danger? Are you serious?" she asked, no longer laughing.

"Completely. Tell her to call me as soon as she can."

"We think they've started killing people," said Cassandra. They were walking through the City Park, behind Heroes' Square. A grey squirrel nibbled at something before scampering up a tree.

"I thought that would happen sooner or later," replied Peter.

"A young man called Vince Szatmari died in a hit and run accident on Wednesday night. On Elizabeth Bridge. We had been keeping an eye on him."

"Not enough of one, it seems."

"I know Daddy," Cassandra sighed. "But half our people have been 'reassigned' to other duties by the new service head. I don't know what they're doing."

"Why were you watching Vince?" he asked. He looked up. The weather was getting worse, the sky turning the colour of dull aluminium. The wind blew harder, sending dead leaves whirling along the footpath. He belted his beige trench coat tighter.

"Because he worked at the National Bank, for Ignac Akardy, who has recently returned from a secondment at the Federal Monetary Authority in Munich. Akardy – who also once worked for KZX Industries – is in charge of privatisation now."

"Akardy worked for KZX Industries. It makes sense," said Feher, nodding to himself.

"It's not just KZX," Orczy interjected. "Swiss banks and German and Austrian companies are signing contracts to either purchase or take controlling interests in virtually every national industry, as well as the media. Hunkalffy is pushing this through. And look at that," she said, waving her arm at a giant billboard recently erected on the edge of the park. *"Magyars: Don't support international finance capital! Invest in the Patriot Bond!"* it announced.

"Fifteen per cent interest a year. How can they afford to pay that? And now Heinrich Vautker has been confirmed as the new President of the Federal Monetary Authority," she continued.

"Heinrich Vautker. The Good German. Let's rest for a minute," Feher said, reaching inside his coat for a packet of *Munkas* cigarettes as he sat on a park bench.

"I wish you would give those up. What about Vautker?" said Cassandra, sitting next to him.

"I'm sorry darling. You're quite right. I will stop soon. Vautker is one of the new generation of 'green capitalists'," he said, his voice tinged with sarcasm. "Former senior aid official, served as German Deputy Minister of Finance in the 1990s. Worked in Africa and South America on various development projects, funded by the banks. Saving the rainforests, giving out condoms. He makes a lot of noise about 'social responsibility' and using capital for 'empowerment', to help 'build our common European home'. Tell me more about Vince Szatmari. Was he in on this, whatever it is?"

"We don't think so. His record is totally clean. No convictions, no record of political agitation. He was a regular church goer. Even attended Bible study classes in his lunchtime." She paused and steeled herself. "Daddy, I've got something else to tell you."

Feher took her arm. "Yes, I know darling. But let's go and watch the Frank and Attila show first," said Peter, steering her towards the stage at Heroes' Square.

## SIXTEEN

The camera panned across Heroes' Square as Alex sat on his bed watching the Sanzlermann election rally on state television. Hunkalffy was due to speak first. A ring of Gendarmes stood around the stage, dressed in riot uniform: full body armour, helmets with dark visors and knee high boots. They held long truncheons, heavier than the usual issue. The camera cut to a close-up of Hunkalffy standing on the podium. He stood silently, his head bowed, for several seconds. The speakers blared out the finale of Beethoven's Ninth Symphony, the European anthem. The music stopped and he looked at the crowd. The camera zoomed in to show him holding a faded black and white portrait of a teenager in his best suit.

"This was my father. Jozsef Hunkalffy. This picture is all I have left," Hunkalffy said, in a strong, determined voice. "I never knew him. He died before I was born. He fought in 1956 against the Soviet invaders. The communists arrested him. They tortured him, to make him reveal the names of his contacts. But my father would not break. Eventually they hanged him. The same AVO torturers whose sons and daughters now sit in Parliament as 'Social Democrats'. The same AVO torturers whose friends and business partners in New York, and other cities far to the east of here, are buying up our land and our country."

The crowd stirred, murmuring its approval. An elderly man in a shabby raincoat shouted 'Down with the communists!"

"My mother died without ever being able to visit his grave," Hunkalffy continued. "His body was taken away, and buried in an unknown plot. I once asked a former member of the AVO, a

180

billionaire who now runs one of our biggest banks, where my father's remains were. He told me that he is encased in concrete under the foundations of the Communist Party headquarters, now the headquarters of the Social Democrats."

Hunkalffy paused and looked out at the crowd, from left to right. "He smiled when he told me that, this communist-turned-capitalist . . ."

The audience booed. A few demonstrators chanted "Death to the AVO".

Hunkalffy held up his hand, and the crowd fell quiet. "And then he told me, that it was the 'best place for him'."

An angry murmur ran through the crowd.

"Thank you, my fellow Hungarians. Thank you," said Hunkalffy. "There is no more AVO, and no more communists, they tell us. But their power lives on. Their networks still thrive. They seek to keep us under the dominance of international capital, instead of Moscow. But we did not surrender in 1848. We did not surrender in 1956. And we will not surrender now. These are great days in our country's history, when one of our greatest friends will soon be the first President of Europe. Frank Sanzlermann is our best guarantee of independence."

More applause followed, and some jeers. The camera zoomed in on the counter-demonstration: a couple of hundred peaceful protestors, standing silently with their placards, led by Krisztina Varga, the recently-sacked former Minister of Justice.

"They should have hanged you as well," shouted a heavy-set unshaven man in a leather jacket in the middle of the main crowd. An angry murmur ripped through the audience as they turned to look. The man pushed a middle-aged lady in her shoulder, and she stumbled and fell. The camera panned back to show several knots of hard-faced men weaving in and out of the crowds, knocking and scattering people out of their way, shouting more abuse. A can of drink landed on the podium. Hunkalffy's bodyguards looked agitated, and muttered into their lapel microphones. Alex sat up and stared at the violence. Who was throwing things? He could not imagine Krisztina Varga hurling missiles at her former cabinet colleague. The camera panned as pandemonium erupted and the men in leather jackets rampaged through the crowd.

Hunkalffy nervously glanced from left to right, and then down at his notes. He continued speaking. "A new dawn is breaking over Europe. When my friend, and our ally Frank Sanzlermann is President, Hungary will be in prime position to . . ."

A can bounced off his forehead. Hunkalffy stepped back, reeling in shock and surprise. He dropped the framed picture of his father. "My photograph," he shouted. The camera zoomed in on the blood trickling down his face as he tried to pick up the pieces of the broken picture from the stage. His bodyguards quickly hustled him off the podium.

The Gendarmes waded into the audience, lashing out with their riots sticks and firing tear gas canisters. Feedback shrieked and howled across the podium speakers and pandemonium erupted. The men in leather jackets quickly disappeared. The crowd ran in every direction, screaming and coughing as the clouds of gas gusted over them. The Gendarmes charged into the small counter-demonstration by the Yugoslav embassy, although none of the protestors had taken part in the fracas. An elderly man wearing a beige trench coat held up his arms to try and protect himself from a Gendarme wielding a riot stick. A blonde woman screamed at the Gendarme, thrusting a card in his face. A truncheon came down on the elderly man's shoulder. He slumped to the floor, his face contorted in pain. Alex sat up and looked closer at the television. The camera was far away but the elderly man's face looked familiar. Alex stared at the scenes of chaos as the programme cut back to the studio.

*　*　*

Sanzlermann smiled at the waitress as she cleared away the remains of dinner. He was sitting at the table in his suite with Reinhard Daintner and Attila Hunkalffy, feeling pleasantly replete, after sautéed goose liver, roast duck and poppy seed cake, and most of a bottle of red wine. Sanzlermann looked at her name tag, pinned above an impressively curved bust, and watched her tidy the plates, glasses and cutlery onto the serving trolley. With her wavy brown hair, freckles and lively green eyes, Eva made a very pretty picture, he thought, his fingers gently stroking the raw, cracked skin of his left hand.

"Would the gentlemen like anything else?" Eva asked decorously, looking from Sanzlermann to Daintner and Hunkalffy, as she held the coffee pot.

Daintner and Hunkalffy shook their heads. "Not now, thank you Eva. Perhaps you could look in a couple of hours time. I usually enjoy a nightcap," he said, lightly patting her bottom.

She smiled shyly. "Certainly, sir," she replied, refilling their coffee cups. She smiled at Sanzlermann before she left, her hips swaying as she pushed the trolley towards the door.

"Frank, we do have business to conclude," said Daintner, his voice brisk. "And whatever your plans are, I don't intend to be here in a couple of hours."

Sanzlermann sat up and lit a cigar. "And nor would I want you to be, Reinhard. But you are right. Let us finish our discussion. Attila?" he asked, turning to Hunkalffy, as the smoke trickled from his mouth.

The Hungarian Prime Minister sipped his coffee. "Stage one is going to plan. Csaba Zirta, our Interior Minister, is doing an excellent job. The Gendarmerie are steadily supplanting local police forces. The necessary legislation is sailing through Parliament, despite our lack of a majority. The forint is steadily losing value. Our private polls show that anti-Roma sentiment remains strong and is increasing. The Pannonia Brigade is proving profitably disruptive. But it is all happening very slowly. There is a danger of a sympathy backlash on the Roma question. And there are obstacles at the national security service. We are working on clearing those. But I am worried that we might lose momentum. I think we should seize the moment and move to stage two as soon as possible."

"I tend to think that it would be a mistake to rush things now. What exactly do you have in mind?" asked Sanzlermann.

"The Reichstag Fire," said Hunkalffy, clipping the end from a cigar.

"You want to burn down Parliament?"

Hunkalffy leaned forward, his voice enthusiastic, waving the unlit cigar. "Not exactly. But the Reichstag Fire gave Hitler the excuse to declare a state of emergency, suspend civil liberties and arrest political opponents. The delicious irony is, of course, that the Nazis almost certainly started the fire themselves. Marinus van der Lubbe was executed for an arson he did not commit. A similar outrage would help us move quickly to stage two. What do you think Reinhard?"

Daintner said: "It is possible. Carpe Diem. But where is our van der Lubbe?"

Hunkalffy looked at his watch. "In the hotel lobby, hopefully."

The telephone rang. Hunkalffy picked up the handset. "Yes, send him up. Thank you."

\* \* \*

Alex stood on his balcony, enjoying the breeze blowing in off the river. The night air smelled fresh and sharp, with a watery tang. His jaw and stomach still hurt and his arm ached, but he was slowly feeling better, if only thanks to the powerful painkillers the doctor had prescribed. But what would have happened if Mubarak had not been there? If they, whoever 'they' were, the ones paying Yuri, had tried once, they would certainly try again. Alex looked down at the street. The elderly man who sold flowers on the corner was finally packing up his folding stool and plastic table. Two Romany boys pushed a shopping trolley along the pavement, a third standing inside, all laughing uproariously. He envied the youths their freedom and innocence. He envied them their parents, too. A now familiar longing surged through him. He had tried for some time to prepare himself for his grandfather's death. Miklos was in his eighties, after all. But Alex had not expected to lose him like this. He missed him more than he had ever imagined possible.

Alex went back inside and switched on state television. A male newsreader announced that all demonstrations were banned until the end of the election campaign, in response to what he described as "the shameful events today, when hooligans, saboteurs and anti-national elements attempted to assassinate the Hungarian Prime Minister and caused the cancellation of the election rally of Mr Frank Sanzlermann." The screen showed the fighting at the rally, and cut to a shot of Hunkalffy with blood streaming down his face. "It is still to be decided if pre-arranged election events will be permitted to take place," the newsreader said.

Alex laughed out loud. Throwing a can of drink at the Prime Minister was hardly an assassination attempt. But the earlier footage of the Gendarme attack on the protestors outside the Yugoslav embassy still nagged at him. He thought he had seen Peter Feher, but why would he be there? And who was the blonde woman? He had tried to call Peter but could not get through. Aniko Kovacs appeared, sitting in a comfortable armchair, surrounded by three guests. She was now hosting her own chat show. The woman's rise was unstoppable. Kovacs introduced the trio: Csaba Zirta, the Interior Minister; Balazs Noludi, the overweight, glum-faced editor of *Magyarok Ébredjetek!* and Krisztina Varga, the former Minister of Justice.

Varga spoke first. "I think we all understand what happened at Heroes' Square today," she said, her voice cold and determined. "One by one, this government is stripping away our basic rights and freedoms. The violence we saw today was a provocation, deliberately organised."

Csaba Zirta began to protest when Noludi shouted: "Horseshit." He leaned forward and pointed at Varga, his jowls wobbling. "You are the provocation. You and the traitors and those who would sell-out our nation, the liberals and cosmopolitans, the dirty agents of New York and Tel Aviv, of international finance capital," he exclaimed, his voice shrill, his mouth flecked with spittle. "But we will not stand by as our homeland is turned into a bargain basement."

Varga handed him a paper handkerchief. "Calm down, Balazs. We already are a bargain basement – for the Volkstern Corporation and KZX Industries."

Noludi balled up the paper handkerchief and threw it in Varga's face. Alex watched in amazement. Krisztina Varga was one of the most popular and respected politicians in the country. She had modernised the legal system and brought in new safeguards for human rights. Which were now being rapidly rescinded, so she knew what she was talking about. And now she was saying that the government had organised the violence. Why? The answer was another question – the oldest and most useful: who benefits? Then it quickly made sense. The government instigates riots so that it has an excuse to crackdown on violence and suspend civil liberties.

He picked up his telephone. No messages. He tried to call Natasha again. It still didn't work. He looked at the handset's screen. There were no bars where the signal indicator usually had four or five. That was strange. Strange and worrying, especially when he really needed to contact her.

He looked back at the television. Varga's eyes blazed. "You always were a fool, Balazs Noludi. A useful idiot. You were a useful idiot for the communists and now you do the same job for Sanzlermann. They will chew you up and spit you out, once they have done with you," she said, her voice contemptuous.

Kovacs looked around the studio, her face panicked. The screen went blank and cut to a commercial. A line of chorus girls, dressed in white, red and green, exhorted the audience to 'be patriots and buy Patriot Bonds' to a backdrop of 1930s nightclub music. The screen then cut to shots of Zagreb, Bucharest and Bratislava. "Coming soon to Croatia, Romania and Slovakia," a deep male voice announced. "The investment of a lifetime."

The doorbell rang. Alex walked over to the flat entrance and opened the door.

Natasha said: "You're looking for me."

\* \* \*

Sanzlermann stood in the bathroom of his hotel suite, scrubbing his hands as hard as he could. The tap was open to its maximum and scalding water gushed over the black marble washbasin, splashing over the Italian tiled floor, filling the room with steam. He methodically worked the nailbrush up and down each finger, under the nails and across both sides of his palms. He rinsed his hands and stared at them. They were raw and red and he sighed with satisfaction. He looked longingly at the soap dispenser again, paused, but turned away.

He ran through the day in his mind as he dried himself on a thick white towel. Hunkalffy was a typical Hungarian, he thought. Passionate, impatient, always thinking in the short-term, and no sense for the bigger picture. Still, his idea of accelerating the programme had a certain élan. It needed some thought but probably could be done, with considerable benefits, if it worked. The weirdo Daintner was as enigmatic as ever. If he had any choice in the matter he would have sacked him months ago, if only because of his bizarre colouring. But it had been made clear that the Presidency of Europe was a package deal, and Daintner was an integral part of it. And the man did have brains, he had to admit.

Sanzlermann looked at his watch. Almost 11.00pm and it had been a long day. Hunkalffy and Daintner had finally left and taken the hideous Gypsy with them. Imagine, he thought, he had actually shaken his hand. It was all he could do not to rush to the bathroom and scrub himself clean there and then. He shivered at the feel of the dark, rough palm and his fingers on his. Perhaps he should wash his hands just once more, to make sure.

A memory flashed into his mind: he was eight years old at the children's home in Carinthia. It was a sunny Sunday afternoon and he was sitting in the waiting room, dressed in his best shirt and neatly-pressed shorts while the nuns ushered in his only visitor, the man he called "Oncle Klaus". Sister Evangelina had called Frank's name. He walked forward, hoping Oncle Klaus had brought him another toy or book when she screamed at him, pointing at a dirty mark on his shirt. He held out his hand, trying to stop it shaking. The ruler slammed into his palm, leaving a red weal that did not heal for days. Oncle Klaus had not returned for three weeks.

He smeared antiseptic ointment over his hands and walked through to the lounge, naked under his bathrobe. He poured himself a brandy, sat down on the sofa and picked up the hotel telephone. "Room service, please," he asked, smiling with anticipation.

## SEVENTEEN

Natasha stood in the doorway, staring at Alex's bruised and scratched face and his bandaged arm. "What happened?"

"I was attacked, in the Rudas."

"Why? Who did it? Are you OK?"

"I'm fine. It was two thugs. They thought I had something they wanted. Do you want to talk about this here? Come in, please." She hesitated. "It's OK. I don't bite," said Alex.

Natasha walked inside, taking in the grubby decor, boxes of books and rickety furniture. At least he had cleaned up the kitchen, Alex thought. "The nicest bit is the balcony," he said.

"I'm not here for the views, Alex. What's going on? It's eleven o'clock at night. You've been beaten up. Kitty told me you think I'm in danger. I tried to call you but your telephone is switched off."

"It's not switched off, it's dead."

He handed the digital recorder to Natasha. She looked at the machine. "Somebody attacked you for my recorder?"

"It's not yours." He showed her the KZX logo on the bottom.

She weighed the machine in her hand. "I dropped mine during the interview. I must have picked up the wrong one. Daintner had the same model, to record Sanzlermann as well."

"So it's Daintner's. That explains it. It's encrypted. There are two sound files but I can't open them. And they know about you. The people who attacked me in the Rudas asked if you had it. That's why I wanted to find you. You may be in danger."

Natasha shrugged. "I can look after myself. We have another problem." She opened her bag and took out the USB stick from

189

Sanzlermann's press pack. "I'm such an idiot. I meant to tell Kitty not to use this. It's the most basic rule: never, ever put an unknown USB stick in your computer. I went back to the office to get my things and it was still there, in Kitty's desktop. It's loaded with a Trojan Horse. You click on the video file for Sanzlermann's speech and it launches a hidden data extraction programme. I think it's forwarded the contents of all the computers on our network back to a server in Germany, probably in Munich."

Alex sat down. "Everything?"

"Every word file, every email, every password."

"Can we get it back?"

Natasha shook her head. "It's gone. And even if we got it back, they would have archived and copied all the information by now."

Alex brought his laptop over to the kitchen table. Natasha looked him up and down. "You look pale. Sit down Alex. I'll make us some tea," she said.

He sat down and watched her bustle around the kitchen. It was a long time since a woman had made him anything. Zsofi was even less domesticated than he was. He saw Natasha looking at the photograph of him and Azra on the wall, but sensed that she was determined not to ask about it. She brought two cups of tea to the table. Alex connected his computer to the digital recorder. The software opened, as it had when Alex had first tried to open the encrypted files. Natasha moved the cursor over the graphic buttons and pressed 'play track 1'. Silence. "Access denied" the screen flashed up. "Enter your password."

"How can we open it without a password?" asked Alex.

"We use a dictionary attack."

"A what attack?"

"A programme that uses every word in the dictionary as a potential password, with different number combinations added on. But the recorder may be programmed to shut or wipe the data after several unsuccessful attempts, which would make things much more difficult." She paused and sipped her tea. "There is another option. I wonder . . ." she said, reaching for the laptop and turning it towards her. She quickly pressed several keys on the keyboard.

A few seconds later the recorder blinked and flashed.

"Try it," she said, nodding at Alex's laptop. Two new icons had appeared.

Alex moved the cursor onto an icon and clicked. A familiar console opened, offering play, stop, fast-forward and reverse. He pressed track two and jumped forward to the middle.

"Miss Hatvani, you now have a scoop," Sanzlermann said. "Our policy now, which I am pleased to make public here, is that everyone in Europe be fingerprinted."

Natasha pressed pause. "See, he really said that."

"I know. That's why we published the story. What was the password?"

She smiled. "Password."

"I don't understand."

"It was the default, issued when it was manufactured. The password was still 'password'. Nobody had changed it. It's amazing how often that works."

She pulled her chair closer to the table. "We could be pro-active here."

"How?"

Natasha took out her laptop from her bag, and a USB stick. "There's a Trojan horse on this USB stick. The same one that was on Sanzlermann's. I've added a keystroke logger, which records everything he does on his keyboard. The CEO of KZX is Dieter Klindern. We need him or someone whose computer is networked with his to open an email from us with the Trojan Horse and keystroke logger disguised in an attachment. It will then start trawling *their* archives and send everything back to us, hopefully including Klindern's system passwords. I'm sure most of his emails go through his secretary. Can you get her name and email address?"

"How do you know all this stuff?" asked Alex.

"My ex-boyfriend was a computer security engineer," she said lightly. "He taught me."

Alex was surprised at the pang of jealousy he felt. He reached for his laptop and looked up the KZX website for the telephone number of the headquarters, clicked on his internet telephony programme, and dialled the number. Natasha nodded approvingly. "Good. Internet telephone calls are much harder to trace. You won't leave a number on their records."

Alex spoke in brusque, formal German. "Good evening. This is Dr Braun, at the research division of KZX pharmaceuticals. We urgently need to send some information to Dieter Klindern. Yes, I understand you cannot give me his private telephone number. But you can supply me with the name of his secretary and her email address."

He paused while the guard explained why that would also not be possible.

"Your name is?" Alex snapped. "I will contact your superiors first thing in the morning. I doubt very much you will still be employed by this time tomorrow."

Alex began scribbling. "Yes, yes. Thank you."

He turned to Natasha: "muller.gabriella@kzx.de. But won't she check who sent the email?"

Natasha inserted her USB stick into her laptop. "Of course. I'll fix it so it look like it comes from dieter.klindern@kzx.de. The subject line will say 'Your pay and conditions'. She will read that. The email will automatically erase itself from her inbox once it has been opened."

"How long will it take till you start getting the information back?"

"As soon as she opens the attachment. Hopefully tomorrow morning," she replied, rapidly typing as she opened and closed a series of windows and programmes.

She sat back. "OK, it's gone."

"I'm impressed. Very. Can you get into the *Budapest News* computers? I'm locked out of the network and there's a lot of my notes and contacts details there."

"Didn't you back them up at home? Or on the web?" Natasha asked.

Alex shook his head. Natasha reached across the table for his laptop. He smelled shampoo and a musky soap.

"I can get your files back. But you must back up your data, offsite. I'll open a webmail account for you where you can also store documents. What name do you want it in?"

"Mine, I suppose."

"No. You don't," she said, shaking her head. "That's the whole point. Think of something less obvious. My webmail address is Pushkin2000."

He looked over at the photograph of Miklos, Ruth and him at Lake Balaton, which now stood on the kitchen window ledge. "Langos1980."

"That's cute. I'll set it up to always use https. The 's' means it's secure as the emails are encrypted. If you log on from an internet café or from another computer just make sure the address is 'https://webmail.com'. Then nobody else can read your emails. Not even me." She turned and smiled tentatively at him. "Unless you are sending them to me. Now you need a password. A mix of letters, numbers and symbols is most secure."

Natasha looked away as Alex tapped in Miklos-F*1922.

"You have to remember the password each time. Don't use the autofill option on the browser. How paranoid are you?" she asked, cupping her tea in her hands and sipping.

"After today, very," he said, enjoying the slow thaw in the atmosphere.

"The best way to send an anonymous message is to go to an internet café and use newspaper websites to forward articles on. You can attach a note to the article with a fake name. You don't need to give a sender's email address, just the recipient's. But it has to be quite short."

Alex smiled knowingly. "But what if the newspaper website wants you to register? Then you wouldn't be anonymous."

"Good. Now you're thinking. Register with a false name and personal details, or go to a website which has free log-ons for websites that require registration. If the newspaper website sends you an email with a link to confirm your registration, use a disposable email address." She paused and stared at Alex. "Why didn't you tell me you had been sacked?"

"You didn't give me a chance."

She blushed. "Sorry. I was upset." She looked down at her cup. "Haven't you got something stronger than tea?"

Alex stood up to fetch a bottle of wine. Things were definitely looking up, he thought, when the doorbell rang. He groaned inside. It was almost midnight. There was only one person who came over at midnight. He didn't move. The doorbell rang again and again.

Natasha gathered up her coat and bag. "You've got another visitor. A very persistent one. Don't worry, I'm going," she said, the warmth in her voice rapidly evaporating.

Alex got up and opened the door. Zsofi stood there with a bunch of flowers. She gasped when she saw him and threw her arms around him. Natasha appeared as Alex tried to disentangle himself. Zsofi stared at her and held tighter onto Alex. He opened his mouth to try and explain to Natasha, but the sinking feeling in his stomach told him there was nothing he could say.

"Have a nice evening, Alex," Natasha said coldly, and walked out.

It took Alex twenty minutes to get rid of Zsofi. Seeing Natasha in his flat seemed to make her even more determined and amorous. This time he gathered her belongings – toothbrush, make-up and a few clothes – packed them in a bag and guided her out of the front door.

By now Alex was exhausted, but he realised that he had not yet played the first track. The recording quality was less clear. There was much more hissing and background noise, as though it was being made surreptitiously.

The familiar tones of Attila Hunkalffy sounded through the speakers: "I think you should stop worrying. Interior Minister Zirta has promised that the police investigation will be quietly wound down. Miklos Farkas is gone. The case will soon be closed."

Alex clicked on the pause button. He sat still for several seconds. Had he heard correctly? He felt nauseous and his hand was shaking. Who was Hunkalffy talking to?

The recording moved on. Rattling cups, things being moved around the table. The voices faded and were drowned out. He turned up the volume.

". . . think he knew the plan. The Directorate is very concerned. If he had told his grandson, the journalist," he heard Frank Sanzlermann say.

More rustling, the clink of china and cutlery. Sanzlermann again. "Maybe we should take care of him as well."

Alex clicked the pause button again. *Him?* Him is me, he thought. Anger turned to fear. What if the flat was bugged? Then they would know that he was listening to the recording. Maybe they would really try and 'take care of him'. Alex walked around his flat, and checked that all the windows and the door were properly locked. Zoran, Mubarak's security adviser, had that afternoon installed an impressive new deadbolt lock on the front door, that shot steel bars in four directions, straight into the wall. Even a hand-grenade could not blow the door off now, he promised Alex, before offering to sell him one for twelve euros. Alex had declined, but had accepted a pepper spray.

Alex plugged his headphones into the recorder. Hunkalffy, this time. "Frank, Frank, we can't go around 'taking care' of everyone inconvenient. Alex Farkas is a foreign national, and a reporter. It would look pretty suspicious if he 'had an accident' so soon after his grandfather died. There would be questions, unwelcome publicity, embassies would be involved."

"*Ja, ja*, you are right," Sanzlermann said.

The discussion moved onto tactics in the election campaign, and a breakdown of the latest opinion polls, before Sanzlermann spoke again. "Update me please on the Roma Reduction Programme," he said.

"Initial trials of the drug Czigex have proved very effective," said an unknown voice with a thick Mittel-European accent. "Czigex is based on research carried out by German scientists in 1943 and 1944. It is the first genetically engineered, racially profiled drug in the world. We are medical pioneers. Slovak authorities have proved very cooperative. So much so that they wanted to extend the programme to the whole country immediately, although we have persuaded them that a slow, steady expansion will bring much greater benefits in the long term. Of course we are meeting some resistance from so-called human rights groups, troublemakers and the Roma themselves. But we have also been greatly aided by the disorganisation and factional infighting of Roma organisations, if that phrase is not a contradiction in terms," the voice continued to guffaws.

Alex put the recorder down, feeling shaken. Virgil's voice echoed in his head: "Not with the killing rooms, but with pills." He rewound to Sanzlermann saying: '. . . think he knew the plan. The Directorate is very concerned. If he had told his grandson, the journalist." What was the Directorate, and what plan was Sanzlermann talking about? Was there more than Czigex? Other plans? Maybe that was why he had been attacked in the Rudas.

It was nothing to do with the KZX digital recorder. They wanted the 'plan', whatever it was, and thought Alex had it. Had Miklos known about the 'Directorate'? But then why hadn't he just told Alex? Perhaps because the information was too dangerous. Or because he knew that Alex would start digging and put them both in danger. Alex smiled as he remembered how Miklos loved to quote one of Henry Kissinger's aphorisms: "The presence of paranoia does not prove the absence of plots.' Alex stopped smiling. Or perhaps Miklos had been about to tell Alex everything. Which was why he had been killed.

"Try and be a little bit Hungarian," Kitty Kovacs had once advised him. "Think laterally." All he had was the testimony that he had found in Miklos' book about the Soviet Union, *Seventy years of Progress*. The book lay on the coffee table. Alex picked it up, and flicked through to the title page. The word *Seventy* was underlined. It was now 2009. Seventy years ago was 1939. What had happened in 1939? The Second World War had started. Alex's heart beat faster and goose pimples rippled up and down his arm. Was Miklos telling him that there was some kind of link between 1939 and 2009? Or that seventy was significant? He grabbed Miklos' testimony and counted down to the seventieth line: "*. . . his face, well illuminated by the flickering Flame of a nearby candle, looked as though it contained a terrible secret hidden under the surface.*"

The letter 'F' in the word flame was in capitals. A mistake, or a hidden meaning? But what – only a candle could reveal the truth? A secret hidden under the surface? Alex picked up the folio. He ran his fingers over the cheap grey paper. He held it up to the light. Nothing visible. He read line seventy once more; *the flickering Flame of a nearby candle*. What if the paper *had* been treated, and there was something under the surface, which needed the heat of a flame, or a candle, to release it? He looked around the flat, his excitement rising. He didn't have any candles. The lamp. Light bulbs released heat. He removed the shade from his reading lamp, and held the paper over the bulb. The paper warmed. Shadows formed, which slowly became letters.

*   *   *

Natasha lived with her mother on Rottenbiller Street, in the unfashionable part of District VII. She arrived home just after midnight to find an ambulance outside the entrance. She sprinted up the stairs to their second floor flat. The front door was open and the lock was hanging out from the splintered wood. She dropped her bag and rushed into the lounge. A paramedic tended to her mother, as she sat in her wheelchair, smiling bravely when she saw her daughter. Books covered the polished parquet floor, the antique dining chairs and table had been upended, plants emptied and their earth tipped out over the Persian rugs. A tall blond man, well dressed in corduroys and an expensive overcoat, walked around the flat, taking notes and photographs. Natasha rushed to her mother and hugged her slight frame.

The paramedic closed his blood pressure meter and turned to Natasha. "We'd like to take her in overnight, but she refuses. It was chloroform. She'll feel a bit woozy, but she should be fine tomorrow. Her heart is steady and her blood pressure is OK. Keep her warm."

Irina held Natasha's hand. "Don't worry. I'm just shaken up. Two men pushed their way in. They had ski masks and put something over my mouth. I passed out. But nothing seems to be missing. I called the police when I woke up." The tall man walked over and shook Natasha's hand. He had buzz cut blond hair and inquisitive blue eyes behind fashionable rimless glasses.

"Can I see some identification, please?" Natasha asked.

He handed her his warrant card: Captain Jozsef Hermann, Criminal Intelligence.

"Does the criminal intelligence department normally concern itself with burglaries?"

"In this case, yes, Miss Hatvani."

\* \* \*

Alex poured himself some more coffee. It was almost dawn but sleep was impossible. He picked up Miklos' testimony and read through the hidden text again, its letters faint on the other side of the thin paper.

*My dearest grandson,*

*I am almost certain that if you are reading this, I will be dead. How strange to be writing such a sentence. Clever of you to remember how I always told you to keep the book about 'Seventy years of the Soviet Union' and its achievements, as a 'family heirloom'. But you were always a clever boy. (And I hope you don't mind that I used the most common 'home-made' invisible ink to write this!) I will be dead because Nazism was defeated militarily, but the Third Reich never truly died. It metamorphosed into the Fourth.*

*I do not mean that Jews are again being herded onto trains. On the contrary, German and Austrian politicians cannot spend enough money to restore the synagogues that their fathers burnt down. Rather, the Nazis realised that military supremacy over Europe was no longer feasible. And no longer necessary when they could triumph on the new battleground: the economy. Kapital über alles. The giants of German industry, the steel barons, car manufacturers and electronics makers rapidly adjusted to the new post-1945 order. The managers who diligently served Albert Speer, Nazi*

*Minister of Planning, and Walter Funk, Nazi Minister of Economics, the companies who ran slave labour operations at Auschwitz, the doctors who performed hideous experiments in the camps and found new posts at German universities, all these easily learnt the language of democracy.*

*Small pieces in the jigsaw, but where is the evidence, I hear you ask. I will tell you what I heard and saw that evening of November 9 1944 at the Savoy, and you can make up your own mind. The plan was simple. None are more hard-headed than bankers and industrialists. There was no nonsense about 'wonder weapons' to change the course of the war. The most senior man proclaimed: "Our battlefields will be the meeting rooms of banks and industries, our weapons not soldiers and guns, but balance sheets and currency markets."*

*How was this achieved? The Nazi party went underground, funded by German banks and industrialists. Massive amounts of capital, looted gold, works of art, stocks and shares stolen from the Nazis' victims, were exported through Swiss banks, or were held as security against loans. The funds, suitably laundered, were used to purchase vast stocks of land, agriculture, industry and companies across Europe, North and South America. Funds generated by these ventures were used to set up front companies around the world. These operations began trading with their unwitting foreign business partners.*

*Once Germany was rehabilitated, these front companies set up subsidiaries in Germany itself. The new German companies started buying up more and more firms, steadily increasing their economic power, and so the old-new empire was born. Or rather, reborn. Special attention was paid to the media, to set the political agenda, and influence economic policy. Politicians and opinion formers across Europe were bought up en masse, encouraged to support and propagate the idea of 'European Unity', and free trade, with no barriers. Sceptics and opponents were dismissed as 'dinosaurs' or – black irony – 'nationalists'. As Walter Funk had predicted in 1942, "common endeavour" and "economic freedom" will be the new Europe's watchwords, in a continent-wide free trade zone.*

The organising body, co-ordinating the political, financial and economic plan, was called the 'Directorate'.

With the base established in Germany and Austria, the next stage was to take over Europe's economies. The financial power of the Directorate gave it great influence, especially as the world economy became more globalised. Millions of marks, dollars or euros could be moved with the touch of a button. But a major obstacle remained: each European country still had economic autonomy, through controlling its own currency and its national bank's ability to set interest rates. The answer: remove that autonomy and impose a single currency unit, under the control of a single financial institution. The key is the Federal Monetary Authority. The establishment of the FMA, and its growing economic and political power is perhaps the most remarkable achievement of the Directorate so far.

The FMA will soon control the economies of twenty-eight countries, once the eastern and central European nations join the euro-zone. Once in, each member state must surrender the ability to set its own interest rates. Interest rates will instead be decided by the bank's President and his cronies. Sovereign nations will lose all power to decide their own economic policies, and so will become vassals of the FMA. Only a few politicians, in Britain and Scandinavia, have spoken out against the power of the FMA. But such is the Directorate's power over the media that they are mocked and marginalised.

All this is in line with Walter Funk's plans, for Europe's national economies to be first "brought under control", their internal worth then "stabilised" and their external value, meaning their worth against the dollar or other currencies, "standardised". What is that, if not a prophecy of a unitary currency, now called the euro? Over the decades I have watched the Directorate steadily increase its power and influence. The plan, written in 1944, was recorded in a document. I saw a copy of it and read it through several times, one night when I was working at the Savoy. Aladar Nagy had obtained it. I can recount here what I remember, but I don't know where the actual document is, or even if it survived. The Directorate's most powerful members are the Volkstern Corporation and KZX Industries. Frank Sanzlermann's election campaign, as you doubtless know, is almost entirely funded and organised by KZX and the Volkstern Corporation.

Now I almost hear you asking, my dear grandson, 'Why didn't you just tell me this?' Well, in a way, I am. I had planned to, preferably in person, but I was waiting for the right moment. But a lifetime of reading the runes still steers me towards subterfuge. (And perhaps it's not so bad to make you work a little!) I could, I suppose, have left this testimony with a lawyer or a friend, but I did not want to entrust it to intermediaries. I wondered often if my suspicions were merely the paranoid beliefs of an old man who lived through too much. I could, I knew, convince you of a pattern, but not more. After so many years, perhaps the Directorate had become flabby, its members concerned only to have a comfortable life and a new BMW.

And then I remembered the name of the man who spoke at the November 9 dinner so long ago in 1944: Friedrich Vautker. Whose son, Heinrich, has been appointed President of the Federal Monetary Authority. That, my beloved grandson, is what I wanted to tell you. Heinrich Vautker's appointment is the signal for the Directorate to begin its final takeover. I fear they have somehow discovered that I was present at that fateful evening in 1944. My telephone clicks and buzzes. Some ancestral sixth sense warns me of danger. So be careful, my dear Alex. If they come for me, I will take my own life, rather than reveal to them what I want to tell you. I still have the pills I bought so many years ago in the ghetto. I hope I will finally be reunited with your grandmother. I have been thinking for a while now that perhaps the time has come. Nothing has ever filled the void her death has left in my life. Forgive me if you can.

Live well, my dear boy, and I hope you find happiness. You know that I love you like a son, especially after the tragic death of your parents, and always will. Wherever I am going I will be looking down on you. One last thing – I remember seeing a very pretty girl in your office, when you took me there on a visit. She had a Russian *name, I recall. If an old man can give you a bit of advice, she was looking at you in a certain way . . . your loving grandfather, Miklos.*

Alex sat with the papers in his hand until the sun rose, the tears streaming down his face.

## EIGHTEEN

The doctor was holding an X-ray up to the light when Alex walked into Peter Feher's hospital room. "I will leave you now, Mr Feher. You'll live. Nothing is broken, although you have suffered some nasty bruising to the bone. Your heart is in reasonable condition, blood pressure a little high, and I strongly suggest that you immediately stop smoking those," she said, gesturing at a packet of *Munkas*, next to Feher's belongings on the table. "You must rest, and eat properly. Your daughter should bring you food, as it would be more nutritious than the hospital's meals."

Alex had finally got through to Peter Feher and discovered that he was in hospital. He had brought flowers and a container of soup from a nearby café. It was just as he had thought. He had seen them together on television. The blonde woman was sitting by Peter Feher's bed, holding his hand. He knew the old man had an eye for the ladies, but he was old enough to be her father.

"Alex, this is my daughter, Cassandra," said Peter.

She stood up to shake hands. "Mr Farkas. I've heard a lot about you. I am very pleased to meet you. I am sorry for your loss."

Alex looked back and forth in confusion. He *was* her father.

Feher gestured at Alex to sit down. "And why shouldn't I have a daughter? You look like you should be here not me. What happened?"

"I got into a fight. I'm fine. Really. Why didn't you tell me you had a daughter?"

Feher pretended not to hear and ate his soup. He dozed off and Alex and Cassandra went out to the corridor. They sat down in a corner on two rickety plastic chairs, by a coffee machine. The smell of disinfectant mixed with stale cigarette smoke. A metal ashtray, perched precariously on a metal stalk, overflowed with cigarette butts. The ambulance had brought Feher to the nearest hospital, in the heart of the Eighth district. It was a grubby building with an underlit entrance. The floors were lined with cracked linoleum and the walls a bilious shade of green. Patients and visitors alike wore cheap acrylic jumpers and stone-washed denim, or sports suits.

Alex dropped some coins into the coffee machine. It gurgled, spat, and eventually dispensed two cups of murky brown water. He handed one to Cassandra.

"Thanks. I'm sorry about your job. I liked your newspaper." She was surprised to find herself blushing as she thought of the Farkas family summer villa at Lake Balaton.

"How do you know I lost my job?" asked Alex, his voice puzzled. He had not told Peter yet.

She wrote a mobile number on the back of a business card and handed it to him.

Alex looked down at her job title and back at Cassandra. "You're a spy."

She smiled enigmatically. "The Volkstern Corporation and KZX's activities are a matter of national security. As is your grandfather's death."

"How?" asked Alex, putting her card in his wallet.

"We don't believe the country's most famous dissident was killed in a random burglary."

"Neither do I. So who killed him?" asked Alex.

"We don't know. We're trying to find out."

"My mobile phone keeps breaking down. Is that you?"

Cassandra shook her head and pulled her chair forward. "Alex, there has already been one death in your family. We don't want any more. You are of interest to several organisations. So buy yourself a pay-as-you-go mobile, *not* registered in your name. Better, have someone buy several for you, with cash. Throw them away every few days, and burn the SIM cards."

"Thanks for the advice. Cassandra, it's great to meet you, but . . ." Alex said.

"What do I want?" she replied, finishing the sentence for him. "Our interests coincide. Maybe we can trade information. We know about your trip to Slovakia. You found out more in one day than we have been able to for weeks."

"Thanks. And in return?" he asked, grimacing at the bitter coffee.

She paused. "The men in leather jackets, starting fights at the rally, you saw them?"

"The television news kept switching back from Krisztina Varga and the demonstrators to the violence. A not very subtle attempt to link them together."

"Yes. Hunkalffy hates Varga. He thinks she is a traitor. Those men were nothing to do with Varga," she said, dragging deeply on her cigarette.

"And who are they?"

"They work for the Security Service. The Actions Directorate, department V. It's a rogue operation."

From: pushkin2000@webmail.com
To: langos1980@webmail.com
We need to talk. Can you be at the usual place at 3.00pm?


From: langos1980@webmail.com
To: pushkin2000@webmail.com
OK.


Natasha was staring out of the window at a corner table. He sat down in front of her. Her face was drawn, her eyes red-rimmed. She did not stand up to kiss him hallo.

Sani, the proprietor, appeared. "Coffee?" he asked.

Alex nodded.

"*Meleg szendvics?*"

They both declined. Sani headed back to the counter. The coffee machine soon made a loud gargling noise. Natasha lit a cigarette, and took rapid, shallow puffs.

"You were right last night, about being in danger. I should

have listened and gone back immediately," she said, describing the burglary, the ambulance and the police.

"I'm really sorry, Natasha."

"Why do British people keep saying they are sorry? It's not your fault."

"I got you into this," he replied, feeling guilty.

"No, Alex. I got myself into this. I just didn't realise that it might involve my mother."

"Why is she in a wheelchair?"

"She was with Anton when Hunkalffy ran him over. She broke her back. She can't walk. And please don't say you are sorry. At least she is still alive."

"Where is she now?" asked Alex.

"She's gone to stay with her sister in the countryside. She's safe there."

"And you?"

"I'm sleeping at Kitty's," she said, as Sani brought two coffees.

She looked pale and vulnerable, he thought. He resisted a strong urge to reach out across the table and hold her hand. He was feeling quite vulnerable himself. His head was still full of Miklos' secret testimony: *I think perhaps it is time.* He remembered his grandfather as a wry and lively character with a courtly charm – gossiping with Peter Feher, laughing at the idiocies of politicians, pouring himself a glass of red wine, flirting genteelly with his lady friends. Alex had not realised the depths of his inner mourning. *Forgive me if you can.* He bit his lip.

A sallow-faced, balding man wandered in. He had a hang-dog expression, and wore a cheap fake leather jacket. He took a good look around the empty café as he smoothed back his thinning black hair. He sat one table away from Alex and Natasha. Alex looked at her as if to ask if she knew him. She shook her head, and caught Sani's eye. She flicked some imaginary ash away from the table cloth.

Sani walked up to the man. "That table's reserved."

"Fine. I'll sit somewhere else," he said, getting up to move.

"No you won't. They are all reserved."

"What are you talking about?" he demanded indignantly. "This dump's completely empty. There's not another customer in sight."

"We're closed, for a private party," said Sani, walking to the rear of the café. He opened a door to reveal a small back room wreathed in smoke. Several tough looking men sat around a Formica table, slapping cards down, shouting in Hungarian, and knocking back shots of *palinka*. The conversation stopped suddenly. "Is there a problem, Sani?" asked one.

"I don't know," he said, nodding at hangdog. "Is there?"

He glared at Sani and left.

Alex looked admiringly at Natasha. "Impressive."

"I told you. He looks after me," she said. "*Köszönöm*," she mouthed at Sani. The trace of a smile flickered across his craggy face as he polished the counter.

"I played the other track," said Alex.

"What's on it?" she asked, alert now.

He sipped his coffee. She had a right to know. She was in as deep as he was, now.

"Hunkalffy and Sanzlermann are discussing the death of my grandfather. I think they organised it. Do you really want to hear this?" he asked, quietly.

Natasha looked shaken. "Yes."

"They also discuss possibly 'taking care' of me. And the 'Roma Reduction Programme', based on a genetically engineered, racially profiled drug called Czigex, now being piloted in the Novy Marek area, to stop Gypsies having children, before being put into use across Slovakia, and who knows where else. You were right."

She leaned forward. "Czigex. The plastic packet we found in Teresa's house. That fat man took it from us. Why would Hunkalffy and Sanzlermann kill your grandfather?"

Alex considered his answer. "If I tell you, you will think I'm crazy."

"Try me."

He explained in detail what he had found, his grandfather's hidden testimony, the meeting at the Hotel Savoy in 1944, the

Nazis' post-war plans and the work of the Directorate, the introduction of the euro, all coming together now as Europe elected its first President.

She stirred her coffee in silence for several seconds. "Do you believe it?"

He chewed his lip. "I don't know. On one level it seems too incredible to be true. But when you look at what's happening around us and what we saw in Novy Marek . . . I do know I want to find out more." He paused. "Will you help?"

She looked straight at him. "Yes."

"Good. Here's your new mobile," he said, passing her a cheap pay-as-you-go handset. Mubarak had sent over half a dozen untraceable mobiles that morning. "Don't use your old one anymore. My new number is programmed in. Edith Leclerc is holding her first election rally tomorrow afternoon. At the City Park, near Heroes' Square. I'll meet you outside the Yugoslav embassy at 3.00pm."

Natasha finished her coffee. "I'll be there."

\*   \*   \*

Alex checked the address again that Kitty had given him for the Sotto Voce nightclub: number six, Gabor Street. Kitty had called him earlier that evening, demanding that he come out to meet her and her friends. Natasha had gone to bed early, she told him. He had arranged to meet Kitty at Sotto Voce at 10.00pm. He looked up and down the dark narrow alley. This was Gabor Street, but not a nightclub in sight. Gabor Street was a few blocks from the grandiose Opera House, but was dark and dilapidated. Fragments of once grandiose balconies hung perilously from the fin-de-siècle buildings, held on by rusting iron bars. A Trabant rusted away on the corner, long abandoned by its owner, washed out flyers for massage parlours and cheap English lessons crammed under its windscreen wipers.

Alex stopped in front of a matt-black door, emblazoned with a tiny rainbow flag painted above a narrow eyehole. There was no indication which was number six, but this had to be the place. Number four, on one side, was a twenty-four hour 'non-stop turbo solarium'. A young woman baked an unlikely shade of orange sat in the electric blue entrance hall, carefully plucking her eyebrows. Number eight was a grocery shop, closed and shuttered.

Alex knocked on the black door. A metal flap slid back and two blue eyes peered out.

"Hallo, dear. What can I do for you?" asked a camp male voice.

"I've come to meet some friends," said Alex.

"Lucky them. You'd better come in."

The door opened and he stepped inside. The gym-toned doorman had dyed blond hair and was dressed in a skin-tight white nylon t-shirt and black leather trousers. He looked Alex up and down and smiled. "Welcome aboard. That's a thousand forints, including your first drink."

Alex handed over the money and stepped into a perfect reproduction of a 1920s Parisian brothel. The walls were dark red, with matching drapes running from floor to ceiling. Even the light-bulbs were red. Low chairs were arranged around coffee tables. Edith Piaf crooned smokily in the background. Two middle-aged men dressed in businesses suits sat cosily in the corner over a flickering candle. They held hands and giggled as they poured each other generous slugs of red wine. A crop-haired woman in an army vest and combat trousers sat alone at the bar, eating cocktail cherries, and drinking pink champagne. Several private rooms led off from the bar area, and a staircase stretched into the basement. Alex reached for a door handle.

The doorman took his hand away. "I don't think you want to go in there. Not on a first visit. Are you looking for someone? It's mostly regulars up here, so have a check downstairs. Or you can always buy me a drink," he said, winking.

Alex looked at his watch: 10.15pm. "Thanks, but I'm meeting someone," he said, and walked down the perilously narrow iron staircase into the packed cellar. A wave of heat, cigarette smoke and alcohol fumes hit him. Couples of every gender combination gyrated on a tiny dance-floor in the corner, while a 1970s disco ball shot beams of coloured light back and forth across the walls and over the ceiling. Barry White thundered across the room.

Alex weaved through the crowd, until he spotted Kitty at a corner table, a few metres from the small stage. She waved him over, as she put a fresh bottle of champagne into an ice-bucket. She was wrapped in a black latex mini-dress and held hands with a slender, waif-like youth. A candle on the table illuminated a face of enchanting beauty: slanting eyes that shimmered like a cats', high and delicate cheekbones and bee-stung lips, all crowned with spiky, auburn hair.

Kitty and Alex kissed hallo, and she poured him a glass of champagne. Alex held out his hand to the youth, who smiled beguilingly.

Kitty smiled sweetly. "This is Esmeralda. She's from Barcelona. She's my Spanish teacher."

Alex tried, and failed, not to stare. "Esmeralda, a pleasure to meet you." Her hand was cool and dry. Esmerelda smiled graciously and inclined her head, her green eyes holding his as she stroked Kitty's hand. Something brushed against his knee under the table.

He turned towards Kitty, flustered. "I didn't know, I mean, that you were, er . . ."

"Learning Spanish?" she cut in, laughing. "I just started. *Hola!* Alex, you're so sweet. Didn't you guess by now? It's fun to have all those advertising executives chasing me. But I like girls." Kitty leaned over and breathed in his ear. "*She* likes both," she said, waving at Esmerelda.

The pressure grew against Alex's knee. Esmeralda looked at him, put her arm around Kitty and whispered in her ear.

"No, no. We can't. He's my *friend*," said Kitty, playfully pushing her away.

"We can't what?" asked Alex.

"She's making rude suggestions," said Kitty.

Alex smiled. "Such as?" Esmeralda winked at him.

"I think you have got quite enough on your plate," said Kitty sternly.

"What do you mean?" he asked, taking a large swallow of the champagne.

"If you want to invite a girl out for dinner, then try not to let her see you kissing someone else," she said, her voice barbed.

Alex blushed. "It was a *goodbye* kiss. On the cheek. We were breaking up. It's finished. She's gone to live in Vienna." With her husband, he almost added.

"How finished?" asked Kitty, arching her eyebrows.

"Finished, finito, over and done," he said, decisively.

"So finished that she turns up at your flat at midnight with flowers. It looks like the evening was just starting. At least part two. Why don't you just fit a revolving door? You need to improve your timing. It's best to get the first one out of the building before the second arrives."

"Is that why you invited me here tonight, Kitty? To give me a hard time?"

"You deserve it." Her face softened. "A bit. You know I love you both dearly. And I believe you. But I have to consider everyone's best interests."

Barry White faded out, as the Weather Girls proclaimed that it was raining men. The dance floor erupted in a mass of heaving bodies as the disco ball spun even faster. Alex poured some more champagne and leaned back in his chair.

"Which are?" asked Alex.

"Trust me and be patient. It will all work out in the end. Now let's watch the show."

A burst of Madonna's *Like A Virgin*, a blaze of spotlights, and a six foot tall transsexual encased in a stars and stripes satin bustier under a peroxide wig paraded on stage to wild cheers.

"I hope that song's not dedicated to *me*," she exclaimed to roars of laughter. She launched into a high-kicking voice-over medley of Madonna classics while perfectly-muscled young male dancers gyrated back and forth across the stage. "Thank you, darlings. How lovely to know that there's still a place for us, in this awful wicked, universe!" she proclaimed, shooing the dancers off-stage, taking a bow to rapturous applause.

"Are we awful?" she asked the crowd, as she strode back and forth.

A mumbled yes.

"Are we awful?" louder now, determined to get the right answer.

"Yes!"

"Are we dreadful sinners, debauched and depraved?"

"*We are, we are*!" the audience roared.

"Not too loud now, my darlings, or maybe," her voice dropped to a whisper, "the *Gendarmes* will come and pay us a visit."

A crescendo of boos, jeers and catcalls. She stepped back, hitched her dress up and adjusted her breasts. "And now, it's dedication time." She pulled out a crumpled piece of paper. "Ildiko. It's your birthday. And have we got a present for you!"

Shrieks and squealed protests erupted from the other side of the stage. A hugely embarrassed young woman, in her Saturday night best, her cheeks glowing red, was pushed onto the stage. The singer launched into a husky version of Happy Birthday, à la Marilyn Monroe, dedicated to the birthday girl. By the end of the song she was gyrating merrily with one of the male dancers. Ildiko climbed down to loud cheers. The doorman appeared and began emptying the ashtray at their table. "Enjoying the show?" he asked Alex.

Kitty motioned for him to sit down. "Laci, have a drink with us."

"Yes, fabulous. I didn't know about this place," said Alex, making a space.

"We like to keep it that way. Discreet. Especially at the moment. I like the male dancers best," said Laci, taking a sip of champagne and gesturing at the stage. "They do private shows."

"Not my taste, really, but thanks."

"That's not what I meant," said Laci. "You're a journalist, aren't you? Kitty told me."

"Yes."

"You would be surprised at some of the people who book our boys."

"Like who?"

"People who shout the loudest about family values, for example."

Alex sat up straight. He listened carefully as Laci whispered in his ear.

## NINETEEN

Alex woke from a deep sleep, blinked, looked round in confusion and grabbed his watch. It was 1.00pm. He had crashed out in his clothes on the sofa in front of the television. The rumble in his stomach was a reminder that he had not eaten properly for days. His arm throbbed as he sat up and rubbed his eyes. The television was still on and he turned up the volume. He was due to meet Natasha in two hours outside the Yugoslav embassy, on Andrassy Avenue. Edith Leclerc's rally was scheduled to start at 3.30pm, in the nearby City Park, just behind nearby Heroes' Square. There was time enough to eat something, shower and get dressed.

The BBC newsreader announced that the European Parliament was sitting in an emergency session after six bombs had exploded inside Châtelet metro station, Paris's main transport hub, at the height of the rush hour. The bombs had been timed to explode sequentially as the panicked crowd fled from tunnel to tunnel. More than two hundred had been killed, and many hundreds more injured. The tunnels had compressed and funnelled the shockwaves, causing appalling injuries to those caught inside. The entrance halls had collapsed and hundreds were still trapped in the wreckage. The authorities had tried to evacuate the area but were unable to control the panicking crowds. Dozens more had been killed in the ensuing stampede. Right-wing parties were demanding the immediate internment of all asylum seekers, and that they should be returned by force to their country of origin, and the re-introduction of the death penalty. Riots had erupted across Paris, as mobs attacked mosques and Islamic cultural centres with firebombs. A national state of emergency had been declared and all major cities placed under curfew.

The screen showed rescue workers in bulky white suits with respirator units, clambering onto station entrances which were now piles of rubble. Newspapers and scraps of clothes blew in the wind, and sirens wailed. Dazed and bloodied survivors staggered out, crying and sobbing. All roads out of Paris were blocked. An aerial shot showed cars jammed nose-to-tail on the Périphérique, covering every lane and the hard shoulder. The Immigration Liberation Army had claimed responsibility. The screen showed Hasan Al-Ajnabi, the ILA leader, standing in front of a map of Europe. A crossed swords emblem marked the site of each attack so far, Rome, Berlin, Vienna and Paris. "One capital at a time. Many more to go. Nowhere is safe. The ILA has only just begun its work," said Ajnabi, his black eyes gleaming above his sharp, hawk-shaped face. The President of France had reconvened the government in Avignon.

The news bulletin moved to Strasbourg.

"Will the election for Europe's first President continue after today's outrage in Paris?" the reporter asked the spokeswoman for the European Parliament, an earnest Dutch woman.

"Of course," she replied briskly. "European integration is far too deep-rooted to be derailed by a small group of extremists."

Alex showered quickly, dressed and made himself an omelette. The news from Paris was horrific. But the ILA was more than a "small group of extremists". Its attacks were planned and coordinated with increasing precision. The reprisals would spin out of control, almost as if somebody wanted to start a race war. He switched on state radio while the eggs sizzled. First more details of the bombs in Paris, then domestic political news. In the interests of freedom of speech, the announcer said, Prime Minister Hunkalffy had passed an executive order rescinding the ban on the so-called symbols of tyranny: the communist red star and the Arrow Cross emblem.

Alex listened closely as he ate. Al-Ajnabi had his crossed swords, now Hunkalffy had his Arrow Cross flag. Banners, badges and emblems, these were the brandings of fear and terror, every one meticulously chosen. Hunkalffy too was sending a message, however cleverly cloaked in the simultaneous legalisation of the red star. And finally, the announcer said, the Pannonia Brigade was calling for more members to assist in its new duties as an auxiliary police force. The Brigade would be working closely with the Gendarmerie.

He dressed, locked his flat and walked down Karoly Boulevard to Deak Square. Gendarmes stood outside the Great Synagogue on Dohany Street, turning away visitors. The synagogue, Europe's largest, had recently been restored with great fanfare. A hand-written sign said it was closed for "technical reasons". He took the yellow line metro to Heroes' Square, still processing the morning's news as the small wooden carriages creaked and rattled along the wide, shallow tunnel. The cars were covered with advertisements for the Patriot Bond or pictures of Sanzlermann. Many of the passengers were young, heading to Leclerc's rally. A smiling teenage girl handed him a campaign leaflet and Leclerc badge. The carnival atmosphere evaporated as the metro pulled into Heroes' Square station. Gendarmes and Pannonia Brigade squads lined the platform. Several brandished Arrow Cross flags. Others pointed video cameras at the passengers as they stepped from the train.

The cameramen openly focused on those wearing badges or holding banners supporting Edith Leclerc. A middle-aged man with straggly grey hair and tortoiseshell glasses held his hand over the lens when the camera-man approached. "Dirty fascists," he shouted. Two Gendarmes immediately dragged him away. He protested and tried to wriggle free. Alex watched as a Gendarme swiftly tapped him on the crown. He collapsed, a thin rivulet of blood trickling down his head. The Gendarmes moved forward, banging their truncheons against their riot shields. The passengers looked nervously at each other, and filed silently out of the station. Alex's hands began to sweat as a familiar tension gnawed in his stomach.

*The Muslim prisoners are lined up against the wall. They do not look like soldiers, just young and middle-aged men, dressed in jeans or sports suits. Some are still in their teens. They stare at Alex, their eyes burning and pleading, desperately hoping that his presence can somehow save their lives. The Serb commander struts up and down, his massive paunch distending his black combat fatigues. He pulls off his ski-mask. An almost tangible fear ripples through the prisoners. He is notorious, a poet-turned-killer, a sycophant first of Tito, now of ultra-nationalism.*

*He walks up to an elderly man and presses the pistol against his head. "Where is your Allah now, Turk?" he demands. The Muslim begins to pray, "La-illah illa Allah, wa Muhammad rasul Allah, there is no God but Allah, and Muhammad is the prophet of Allah." The poet-killer presses the trigger and the Muslim's head explodes. He flies back against the wall, leaving a crimson smear as he slides to the floor. "Ooops, my trigger finger slipped," says the commander, laughing out loud. The prisoners on either side of the dead man shake uncontrollably.*

*The paramilitaries pass a bottle of plum brandy from hand-to-hand, as they laugh and joke. The hot summer air fills with the smell of human waste. The bottle is passed to him. He takes a swig. The drink sears his throat and he coughs. A paramilitary slaps him on the back, laughing. A bus arrives. The men are herded on board at gunpoint. "See, reporter, how humane we Serbs are with our prisoners," the commander says to Alex, his deep-set eyes dull and unfocused. "We even provide transport for them. Don't follow us."*

*Alex had waited, hiding in the remains of a burnt-out house. The shooting had started about half an hour later, the crackle of the guns echoing across the valley, mingled with screams and cries. First the long fusillades of machine gun fire, the screams and pleas, then the snap of single pistol shots. He hid in the house until dusk, and walked through the forests to the field. The men and boys lay scattered like broken rag dolls.*

This is how it starts, thought Alex, as he stared at the Gendarmes and the Pannonia Brigade. Setting neighbour against neighbour, first with words and uniforms, then with knives and guns. Or newer, more scientific, methods. The images flashed through his head: the burning packet of Czigex in Novy Marek; Sanzlermann's election posters; corpses in the Bosnian field; his grandfather dead, his ghetto diary. Miklos, he now knew, was the first victim, Vince Szatmari, the second. He had stood by and watched in Bosnia. He would not stand by now.

Natasha was waiting outside the Yugoslav Embassy as a police helicopter clattered overhead. Even in jeans and a long out of fashion Afghan coat she still looked like a model, Alex thought ruefully. He really had the worst timing in the world. Kissing Zsofi's cheek on Margaret Bridge when Natasha ran by and then, just as it looked like she might still be interested, there was Zsofi again – knocking on his door at midnight. Never mind, he told himself determinedly, there were more important issues at stake.

"Did you see the Nazis at the station?" she asked.

He nodded. "They got what they wanted. So far."

They crossed Dozsa Gyorgy Street and walked through Heroes' Square. Natasha handed Alex a USB stick. "Here are your files from your office computer. Back them up please. And

the Trojan Horse is delivering. Gabriella opened the email this morning at 8.20am. Her computer is connected to Klindern's. There is a key-stroke logger built in to the Trojan Horse, which recorded their passwords and sent them back to me. I've got them all."

"That's brilliant. Where are they?" asked Alex as he put the USB stick in his pocket.

"In here," Natasha said, tapping her head. "But if you want to get into the KZX computer we will need to move fast. We should try tonight as they are bound to find the Trojan Horse eventually, and that will trigger a security alert. They will change all the passwords. We need a safe place. Not your apartment or Kitty's. Unless you have other plans."

"No. I don't. I'll find somewhere," said Alex, as they walked into the park.

Metal fences ringed the rally area. Police checkpoints at three entrance points controlled entry and exit. A queue stretched back several hundred metres. "Peace, tolerance and diversity," proclaimed the backdrop banner over the large wooden stage. The centre-piece was a giant photograph of Edith Leclerc flanked on both sides by a montage of multi-cultural Europe: children of every shade of white, brown and black played together, while a multi-national orchestra posed with instruments. A ring of Gendarmes surrounded the stage.

"Come on, we're not waiting in line," Alex said and led her to the centre checkpoint. Police and Gendarmes carefully checked identity cards, writing down every person's name and identity number. Any questions about the intrusive checks were met with a curt reply about 'security procedures' and 'terrorism alert'. Anyone protesting was arrested. Many were turned away. Others left the entrance queue once they saw the checks. A Pannonia Brigade cameramen steadily swept his camera up and down the line. Alex and Natasha walked to the front.

"Press," Alex said to a policeman at the entrance, showing his and Natasha's press cards.

The policeman looked Alex up and down. He had a wide Asian face and blinked repeatedly as he examined their press cards. "Cover for me, will you, Pisti," he asked, turning to the nearby Gendarme. "I've got two troublemakers here. You two, over there," he snapped.

Alex began to protest when he interrupted. "Just come with me. There's nothing to worry about," he said, his voice low and reassuring as they walked into the park. He stopped by a clump of trees. Alex saw that a rip had appeared in the corner of Leclerc's picture behind the platform.

"I know your names. I read your interview with Sanzlermann. I'm going to pretend to be radioing headquarters to check you out," the policeman said.

Alex looked at the policeman. "Is there something you want to tell us, officer?"

"Yes. We don't like this. We don't like it at all. People have a right to demonstrate, to vote for whoever they want. That's why we brought down the communists. The Panonnia Brigade, those hooligans, are now going to be an auxiliary police force. What a joke. The Gendarmes are taking more and more of our duties. Half of them haven't even been trained. Csaba Zirta is posting an election 'liaison officer' to every police station. To discuss security issues raised by the campaign, supposedly. But every one is from Sanzlermann's party. There's nobody from Leclerc's side. This is nothing to do with police business. They are using us. You understand?"

The policeman looked up to see the Gendarme walking towards him. "They're clear. Go on, on your way," the policeman said, looking meaningfully at Alex.

They walked into the enclosure and stood at the front. A multi-cultural children's folk dance troupe left the stage to enthusiastic applause. The smell of roasting chestnuts and burnt leaves wafted across the rally. There were barely 200 people in the crowd. Long queues snaked back almost to Heroes' Square. Edith Leclerc took the stage fifteen minutes late. She stood in front of the microphone, a stout, matronly figure, with gold-rimmed glasses and coiffured grey hair, dressed in a sensible navy skirt. Her bodyguards stood on either side of the stage.

"My fellow Europeans, I am so happy to be in Budapest. *Jó estét kívánok mindenkinek*, I wish you all a good evening," she proclaimed, in a clear tenor voice, triggering a ragged cheer. "Excuse my pronunciation, but now in the new Europe we have so many new languages to learn. These are trying days for us. Our dream of a peaceful, tolerant continent is turning into a nightmare. The tragic news from Paris overshadows our gathering. We mourn for those killed, and pray for the injured."

Alex watched the rip in the banner behind the stage spread further down. The torn parts flapped in the wind. Leclerc turned round, and waved at one of her officials to try and fix the tear. "There are those who would wall off our continent against the rest of the world, who have a vision of an exclusively white, exclusively Christian Europe – I don't have to tell you who they are – they are wrong. Their ideas are based on hate, and prejudice," she proclaimed, as the crowd murmured its assent.

"Should we condemn all immigrants because of a few extremists? Of course not. Their actions, as terrible as they are, can never justify this, for example," she said, gesturing at the Gendarmes in front of the stage, and the outer ring of police, still painstakingly checking identity papers of the last die-hards, determined to attend the rally. "For there is a time when protection becomes intimidation, and our hard-won freedoms are sliced further and further back, until they no longer exist," she continued, her voice rising in strength and passion. "When sinister and unaccountable interest groups, powerful economic and political forces seek to control our fates."

Alex sniffed. Wisps of grey smoke curled out from underneath the platform. The rip in Leclerc's banner spread down, tearing it into two pieces. A flap of banner fell onto her face, and she stumbled in confusion, scrabbling to remove the sheet. Smoke poured from under the platform. Anxiety rippled through the crowd. People began to point at the smoke, and edge backwards. Flames licked at the wooden boards, spreading along the platform. Leclerc's bodyguards rushed forward, peeled away the torn banner and escorted her off the stage. Natasha looked anxiously at Alex. He grabbed her hand and led her away from the burning platform, as the crowd scattered in all directions. Sirens wailed, sounding louder by the second.

\* \* \*

Father Fischer watched attentively as Natasha attached the mobile telephone Alex had given her to her laptop computer. It was 10.00pm and she, Alex and the priest were ensconced in his office at the back of the church. Alex picked up a DVD box next to Father Fischer's desktop computer. The lurid orange cover showed a racing car tearing round a grand prix track. "Ultimate Speed," Alex read out loud. "You are the driver in the fastest, most exciting dare-devil 3D graphics computer car race game yet."

The priest smiled bashfully. "God moves in mysterious ways." He poured three cups of coffee and handed one each to Alex and Natasha.

"At more than 200 kilometres an hour," replied Alex, smiling as he put the box down and accepted the coffee.

Natasha looked up. "We're ready," she said, ignoring Alex's quip. "You do know that hacking into the KZX computer is illegal, Father?"

"Against man's law, yes. Against God's, I think not. Can they find us?"

"Good question." She picked up the handset. "Every telephone has two unique identifying numbers. The networks can use these to locate any handset in the world – where there is network coverage – to within fifty square metres or so. In two or three seconds. The handset can also be used as a microphone to bug a room, even as a camera, if it has one, to take secret pictures of what the user is doing."

"That doesn't sound very secure," said the priest.

"It's not. But anyone watching us needs to know which handset we are using. If it was paid for with cash, ideally somewhere without a CCTV camera, by someone who cannot be connected to us, it's untraceable. It's just one of millions of mobile phones. Isn't it, Alex?" she asked.

"That's what I was told."

Father Fischer looked troubled. "What if someone is watching you, knows where you are, and then gets the network to identify all mobile handsets in that immediate area? Couldn't they make the connection?"

Natasha shook her head as she opened her internet browser. "They might be able to work out that we are here and using these handsets. But they cannot trace what we are doing on the internet because we are using a proxy server relay. At least not immediately."

Father Fischer shook his head, puzzled. "A what?"

She looked up from her laptop. "I'll explain. Whenever you log onto the internet you connect to your internet service provider, which gives your computer an identifier from its own list of internet addresses. An expert can see that we have an address from a Hungarian ISP and can guess we are connecting from nearby."

Alex and Father Fischer listened, engrossed, as Natasha continued. "The proxy server relay anonymises us. It encrypts our data and routes our connection through a network of covert servers around the world. It's like a continually evolving chain. Each server only knows the one it receives the data from and the server it forwards the data to. Nobody knows the whole path. So theoretically nobody can track us. Theoretically. But nothing is 100 per cent certain."

"Impressive. How do you get these programmes? And who writes them and makes them available?" asked the priest, drinking his coffee.

"People who believe in the free exchange of information," said Natasha. "You can download them from the internet."

Natasha typed 'www.kzxindustrie.de' in Firefox. The screen filled with a picture of two children, one European and one Asian, playing happily together. "Bringing Health and Happiness to the World," the website proclaimed. A flashing banner announced: see our new Croatian, Hungarian, Slovak and Romanian language websites. The screen showed a panning shot of the company headquarters in Munich, a collection of white, low-rise buildings, surrounded by landscaped Japanese gardens. Young executives bustled through the pristine, modern corridors. An options menu popped up at the side of the window. Social Responsibility; Our Global World and Corporate History.

Natasha turned to Alex and the priest. "So far we haven't hacked KZX, just looked at their website through a proxy computer. That's public information. The hacking part is when we illegally enter KZX's *internal* computer system. Once an unknown machine tries to enter, it will trigger an alert, and attempt to trace the intruder."

Father Fischer nodded. "You said theoretically nobody can trace us. But if we are online long enough . . ."

Natasha said: "Nothing is 100 per certain. The proxy server relay has vulnerabilities and a company like KZX will have high security, and links with law-enforcement agencies. We have the passwords, so that should buy quite a lot of time. But once we get to the really restricted material, there will be super-strict controls. The KZX mainframe may be able to sense that someone is in and using a proxy server, which will almost certainly trigger an alarm. At that stage we won't have very long. Ready? Because now we're going to break the law."

"Please start," said Father Fischer.

The cursor moved to the log-in window, which asked for a user name and password. Natasha typed 'KlindernD2009', followed by a series of numbers and letters. The screen showed: "Welcome Dieter Klindern." A row of folders appeared entitled 'Internal Document Directory'.

Alex read through the folder titles. "Acquisitions and holdings." Natasha directed the cursor to the list.

"Please enter your second-level password," the screen flashed up. Natasha tapped in 'walterfunk'.

"Access permitted. Please enter your third-level password. The security department has been alerted."

"We are in, but they are investigating who we are," said Natasha. She typed in 'Savoy1944'. "So we had better be fast."

The screen pulsed and flashed: "The security department requires that you re-validate your identity, using your fourth-level password. You have fifteen seconds."

Natasha looked round at Alex, her hands in the air. "I don't have a fourth-level password."

"Type 'heinrichvautker'," said Alex.

"Who?" asked Natasha.

Alex pushed Natasha's hands out of the way. The clock showed nine seconds. He tapped out the letters. Two seconds left. The screen flashed up: "You have now entered the Directorate restricted archive. Your connection is being monitored by the security department."

The screen filled with industries, companies, banks, agricultural combines, newspapers and radio stations, across central and eastern Europe. A sub-menu offered 'governments'.

"Go to governments. Hungary, Croatia, Slovakia and Romania," said Alex. Natasha moved the cursor, highlighted the four and clicked. The download bar crept forward painfully slowly.

"That's the proxy server. It slows the connection," said Natasha.

A police siren howled in the distance. The download bar crept forward.

"One more, Natasha, please. Back to 'Acquisitions and Holdings'. Try KZX pharmaceuticals," he said.

"Please enter your sector-specific password" a new window requested.

Natasha typed in 'novymarek'.

The screen filled with a picture of Romany children, playing in the dirt of an unpaved street, entitled 'The Poraymus Project'. A list of files appeared, dated by decade.

"The what project?" asked Natasha.

"Poraymus. It's a Romany word. It means the 'great devouring', the Gypsy Holocaust. How much can you get?" asked Alex.

Natasha looked worried. The siren sounded louder by the second. "I don't know, three or four at the most. I don't think we have much time. They shouldn't have traced us this quickly."

"So let's speed up. Take 1940s, 1980s and 2000–2008."

Natasha's hands flew across the keyboards. The download bar slowly filled. The police siren stopped. A pulsing blue light revolved through the windows. A knocking at the church's door sounded through the church, polite, but insistent.

Father Fischer rose. "I can only delay them for a minute or two. Hurry. Hide somewhere."

More knocks sounded, louder now. The file bar approached the half-way mark.

Alex stared at the download bar, digging his nails into his palms, willing it to go faster. It crawled along to the seventy-five per cent mark. Natasha sat tensed and hunched. "Come on, come on," Alex muttered, looking repeatedly at the door. He could hear Father Fischer greeting the policemen.

"Sorry to bother you, Father. This is very awkward, I know," a voice explained. "But we are looking for Natasha Hatvani and Alex Farkas and I think they are here."

Father Fischer began to protest when the officer cut him off. "With all respect, before you say anything, Father, I *know* that they are here." Rapid footsteps echoed through the church.

Natasha looked up at Alex. "We could try and make a run for it," he said, knowing it was hopeless. The download bar reached 100 per cent.

"Where?" Natasha asked, as she frantically copied the KZX files onto a USB stick.

"You wouldn't get very far," said a half-familiar voice. A dapper figure with short blond hair and designer glasses walked in.

"Good evening, Captain Hermann. How did you find us?" asked Natasha, smiling brightly as she scratched her neck and dropped the USB stick down the back of her t-shirt.

He pointed at her handbag. "Good evening. It wasn't difficult. Empty it, please." She tipped the bag up over the table. The Magyar Mobile handset tumbled out.

Natasha covered her face with her hands. "I don't believe it. It's been in my bag all the time. I completely forgot about it. It even has GPS. I'm really sorry, Alex. We may as well have put marker beacons on our heads."

Captain Hermann picked up the handset. "I'll keep this. And the USB stick, please," he said, holding out his hand.

Natasha blushed, scrabbled around behind her waist and handed it to him.

"Thanks. Now pack up your laptop and get out before the Gendarmes get here." He sat down and reached for the game controller in front of the priest's desktop computer. "Father Fischer and I have cars to race."

# TWENTY

From: pushkin2000@webmail.com
To: langos1980@webmail.com
Good morning. Sorry about last night. It makes a change for me to almost get us arrested . . . Interesting how our friend keeps turning up. Otherwise, see below URL. V. funny.

The other material I'll print out for you.

Alex sat up in bed, his laptop resting on his knees. He clicked on the link and opened a video on You Tube. Someone calling themselves 'Cosmopolitan' had uploaded three video clips. The first one spliced together news clips of the Gendarmes and the Pannonia Brigade jerkily marching forward and then backwards to the Bangles' song, 'Walk Like an Egyptian'. The second showed Frank Sanzlermann speaking at his Budapest election rally morphing into Charlie Chaplin's Hinkel in the 'Great Dictator', as Chaplin-Sanzlermann strutted up and down, spitting, waving his arms and gesticulating. The third was the funniest: Hunkalffy's face had been dropped onto the singer in Mel Brooks' 'The Producers'. Cosmopolitan had even re-recorded the song with a new chorus. Instead of "Springtime for Hitler and Germany", Hunkalffy sang: "Springtime for Hunkalffy and Hungary, *Magyars* are happy and gay" as he danced across the stage. It was 8.30am and the clip had already been viewed more than 4,000 times. Alex laughed out loud at Hunkalffy's prancing, still chuckling as his mobile rang.

"What's so funny?" asked David Jones.

"I'll send it to you. It's a video mash-up. It's brilliant."

"Good. You do know you are famous now? Or maybe infamous is a better word."

"What do you mean?" asked Alex, sipping his coffee.

"Let me read you the front-page story of today's *Ébredjetek Magyarok!* by your friend Balazs Noludi: 'Who is Alex Farkas?' he asks, although you would think he would know by now. Anyway, I quote: 'This so-called journalist writes the foulest lies about Hungary, claiming that racism is rising against Roma and Jews and portrays us as puppets of Frank Sanzlermann. We true Hungarians ask – why do we allow this rootless cosmopolitan to live among us and abuse our goodwill and hospitality? We call on true patriots to closely monitor this intruder and to inform us of his latest offences, our patriots' understandable outrage may have consequences,' and so forth."

Alex laughed out loud. "Thanks for the heads-up. I must be doing something right then. I'll take a look on the website," he said, and hung up.

He logged onto the *Ébredjetek Magyarok!* website. Just as David had said. There was a photograph of him with the caption: 'Alex Farkas/Wolf: An enemy of Hungary?' The name change was a classic smear tactic, a coded suggestion that his real ancestry was Jewish. Why didn't they just write: "Alex Farkas: Jew" – at least that would have some intellectual honesty. A separate long article by Balazs Noludi again reheated the false allegations – which Noludi himself had invented – that Miklos had been an AVO agent. It was pathetic, thought Alex. The thought-crime of being 'anti-Hungarian', smearing the dead and barely coded anti-Semitism – Noludi and his cohorts had proved most diligent students of communist propaganda techniques.

A separate story trumpeted the Pannonia Brigade's new duties as auxiliary police. Brigade members were now training to 'monitor traitors, anti-Magyar elements and national enemies'. The brigade was launching a new website, where supporters could send in information about Israeli investors and their business activities. Alex opened the other email in his inbox.

From: kittykitty@webmail.com
To: langos1980@webmail.com
Ha! There is no escape. I have your new email address. Just checking you are coming to Ronald's leaving dinner tonight. EVERYONE will be there.

  K xxx


Ronald Worthington had hired a private room at Crusoe's, an upmarket restaurant, for the 'mother of all leaving dinners', to blow the paper's secret slush fund. Alex typed a brief one-line reply that he would be there, and looked forward to seeing EVERYONE.

Alex sat back in his bed and replayed the previous night in his mind. What was Captain Hermann's part in this? He had been at Keleti station when Alex and Natasha travelled to Slovakia, and Natasha had told him that the policeman had been at her mother's flat after the burglary, but had refused to say why or what he was looking for. He was clearly very intelligent, and spoke perfect English. And had every reason to arrest them last night but let them go. His new mobile rang again. It was Isabelle Balassy, the press secretary at the British Embassy. He had last seen her at his grandfather's funeral. And how did she know his new number?

"Alex, how are you? You'll have seen the papers this morning?" she asked.

"Isabelle. Thanks for calling. Yes, I have."

"Can we meet this afternoon? The Muvesz Café at 4.00pm?"

"Fine with me," Alex replied.

"Where did we say again, Alex?"

Alex frowned, puzzled. "The Muvesz Café, at 4.00pm. That's right, isn't it?"

"Perfect," said Isabelle. "See you there."


\*   \*   \*


Cassandra Orczy read through Voter's latest report. It was shorter than his previous one, but in line with his other despatches. The Hunkalffy/Sanzlermann plan was going to schedule. Numerous opposition MPs had been arrested on spurious charges of tax avoidance, after emergency legislation had been rammed through Parliament removing their immunity. The headquarters of the Liberals had been seized under a compulsory purchase order. An obscure law firm had suddenly produced documents that the entire block had once been owned by a pre-war subsidiary of KZX. The building, next door to the Hotel Bristol, was now tipped to be the regional headquarters of KZX Industries. The Pannonia Brigade was planning to march through Budapest's Gypsy quarter in District VIII to protest against 'Gypsy Crime' and call for apartheid between Roma and non-Roma.

The Hungarian Patriot Bond, launched the previous week, was a runaway success. 'Hot money', cash chasing short-term economic growth, was pouring in from Germany, Austria and Switzerland, buying up government bonds, residential and commercial property. Plans were far-advanced to simultaneously launch the 'Patriot Bond' in Croatia, Romania and Slovakia within the next month. According to Voter, the next stage of the plan would focus on the media, especially during the run-up to voting in the Presidential election. The government had re-employed technicians trained under communism to jam the BBC and Voice of America. Foreign stations would not be openly blocked. Instead cable satellite and internet providers would suffer a series of 'technical problems'. Hunkalffy was also pushing for arson attacks on newspaper print works – to be blamed on criminals – and criminal prosecutions against troublesome journalists for not yet-legislated offences such as 'defaming the head of state', and 'making false accusations'. Hunkalffy's ideas were meeting internal opposition, Voter reported. There were mutterings that Hunkalffy was too personally and emotionally involved to see the 'big picture'. His decision to legalise the Arrow Cross flag, described as "a propaganda gift", had caused particular anger.

Orczy sipped her coffee and lit a cigarette. It was frightening, depressing and valuable information. But what was she going to do with it? She picked up the one paragraph memo that had been circulated that morning.

From: Director, Hungarian State Security Service
To: All department chiefs
All four branches of the HSSS: Intelligence gathering, Operations,
Counter-Intelligence and Analysis are to be merged into the new National
Security Department of the Gendarmerie. This will take affect within one
week. I regret that no jobs or positions currently held can be guaranteed,
but all employees are welcome to apply for positions with the NSD.

The decision itself was not unexpected, but she was still shaken
by the speed of the announcement. She thought she had a day or
two at the most. She reached for the telephone.

\*    \*    \*

Alex looked around for Isabelle as he stood in front of the Art-Deco
cake display case at the Muvesz Café. The café, on Andrassy
Avenue, was a Budapest institution. Powdered dowagers perched
on Beidermeyer chairs gossiped under a gilded ceiling, as white-
booted waitresses glided back and forth, balancing trays of drinks
and cakes. The smell of burnt coffee, chocolate and tobacco was a
comforting mix. He saw Isabelle at the door and stepped forward,
nearly bumping into a buxom waitress. She deftly raised her tray
and stepped around him as Isabelle walked in.

"Good afternoon, Alex," said Isabelle, as they kissed hallo.

"Over there?" he asked, gesturing at a quiet table in the corner.

"Not there, come with me," she said, as she led him to the very
centre of the café.

He winced as she held his left arm. It was healing steadily, but
was still very sore. Isabelle usually chose a discreet spot, far from
other customers, for their occasional meetings. Now she led him
right to the centre, visible to everyone. But she was often full of
surprises. Isabelle was in her early thirties, he guessed, an appealing
mix of English rose from her mother's side and vivacious Hungarian
from her father's. The Balassy family had fled Hungary in 1956 for
London, where her parents had met and where she was born, and
then moved to New York. Her parents divorced when she was

sixteen and she opted to stay in Manhattan with her father. Her long, wavy, auburn hair was pulled back in a pony-tail, highlighting her large brown eyes and wide, full mouth. She wore a black turtle neck jumper under a close-fitting burgundy jacket and skirt that highlighted her slim but curvaceous figure.

A few months earlier, at the end of a wine-sodden dinner at the ambassador's residence, Alex and Isabelle had found themselves alone in a deserted cloakroom. After several minutes of memorably erotic kissing, she had broken away from him, claiming that she never mixed business with pleasure. Now they met for a drink and dinner once a month or so. They subsumed any lingering attraction in trying to extract information from each other while giving as little as possible in return. Alex had experienced similar probing questions from various British 'liaison' officers in the Balkans, and was fairly sure Isabelle worked for MI6.

A pale, earnest looking young man sat at the table behind, reading *Ébredjetek Magyarok!*. As Alex and Isabelle sat down he put his newspaper aside, and took out a notebook.

Isabelle called the waitress over and ordered two coffees, before looking at Alex. "Ask me, in a loud clear voice please, what will happen if you are expelled from Hungary?" she said, in her mid-Atlantic accent.

Alex looked puzzled. She smiled encouragingly. "Go on, just as I told you. Loud and clear."

"Miss Balassy," said Alex, in his best BBC newsreader voice. "Can you please tell me what will happen if I am expelled from Hungary."

The young man began scribbling. The waitress brought his coffee, which he ignored.

"Certainly, Mr Farkas. Her Majesty's Government will regard this as a grave breach of diplomatic practice. The London correspondents of *Ébredjetek Magyarok!*, Hungarian Television and the Hungarian state news agency will all be immediately declared *persona non grata*. They will barely have enough time to pack."

The eavesdropper scribbled frantically in his notebook. She spoke again. "Let me be crystal clear about this. They will be expelled, and their operations closed down by special government order. And we will encourage our allies both within and outside Europe to follow suit. Including the United States. Now ask me what will the consequences be if something, let us say, untoward, should happen to you?"

Alex leaned back in his chair, so that the scribbler could hear better. "Could you please explain what would occur if I met an unfortunate accident?"

The eavesdropper sat poised and listening, pen resting on his notebook.

"Her Majesty's government is most concerned that members of her press corps be able to function freely and without hindrance. Especially British citizens. We know that figures closely allied to Attila Hunkalffy are behind *Ébredjetek Magyarok!*. We are also in possession of certain *personal* information about Prime Minister Hunkalffy and Mr Frank Sanzlermann, that we have not released."

She paused, to give the eavesdropper time to take his notes. "But should anything unpleasant occur to you, or any other foreign correspondent, we would immediately release that *personal* information to the world's, and, I emphasise, the world's press."

Isabelle leaned over the table to the young man taking notes. "Did you get that all down?"

The note-taker looked startled, then alarmed. He packed up his notebook, threw a thousand forint note on the table, and bolted.

Alex turned round to watch him scuttle out of the door. He grinned. "What personal information?" he asked, remembering Laci the waiter at Sotto Voce.

"I can't tell you that. Unless you sign the Official Secret Act, and I don't think that would help your career. But they know what we are talking about. There is something else."

"What?" asked Alex.

"Istvan Matonhely."

"The Pannonia Brigade leader. What about him?"

"Matonhely has just opened a bank account with one million euros. Paid in cash."

\* \* \*

Crusoe's private dining room was a glass-walled peninsula jutting over the artificial lake around the Vajdahunyad Castle, in the City Park. The water glimmered in the night, reflecting the candles on the table, and the full moon. Soft lamps cast a yellow light on the castle's ornate towers and balustrades. It was almost midnight, and Ronald's leaving party was in full swing. There were eight of them sitting around the table: Alex, Kitty, Natasha, Edina, Euan Braithwaite, and a couple of advertising sales staff.

Alex sat next to Edina Draskovitz and Euan Braithwaite. She wore a dark blue Mandarin silk top and matching silk trousers and looked surprisingly feminine. Flush with success over his new job as a sports reporter for Reuters, Euan was recounting how, as an enthusiastic novice journalist, he had travelled to Albania after the NATO air strikes. He had promptly been kidnapped by the Kosovo Liberation Army. The KLA fighters had marched him through the mountains to their hideout, before threatening to shoot him as a Serb spy.

"How did you escape?" asked Edina, her face resting on her hand as she stared up at him.

"We talked about football. I interviewed Maradona years ago. They wanted to shake the hand that once shook Maradona's hand. After that, they said I was free to go," said Braithwaite, turning pink under her gaze. He took a long swig from his beer. "The commander even drove me back to the nearest NATO checkpoint."

Their laughter resounded around the room when the background jazz faded away and the lights dimmed. Four skinny Romany men carried an enormous woman in on a Sedan chair, lined with purple brocade, and golden tassels that swung from side to side. She emerged and glided forward into Crusoe's private dining room like a ship setting out to sea. All conversation stopped as she looked around the room. Glasses just raised were held in mid-air. Lit cigarettes were left unsmoked. She was wrapped in a voluminous dress of purple velvet, her neck adorned with gold chains. A single dark red rose was perched behind her ear, its colour perfectly matching her lipstick. Her deep set black eyes were almost oriental, set above high cheekbones. It was a strong and handsome face, with a generous, curved nose and thick lips above several rolls of flesh that flowed from her chin to her abundant neck. She stared imperiously at the diners and the handful of waiters, as though everything was to her satisfaction.

Kitty Kovacs slid onto the seat next to Alex. "That is a whole lot of woman," he said, reaching for another bottle of wine.

"Too much for you. Too much even for me, I think," she said, laughing.

Alex smiled. "Where's Esmerelda?"

"Back in Barcelona." Kitty looked in Natasha's direction. She was deep in conversation with Ronald Worthington. He loudly promised to make her 'chief barmaid-in-chief', once he opened his new pub. "Why don't you go and talk to Natasha?"

Alex drank his wine. "I don't think so, Kitty. She can see where I'm sitting." *If an old man can give you a bit of advice, she was looking at you in a certain way . . .*

Kitty smiled. "So you have learnt to be a little bit Hungarian."

A hiss and howl of feedback echoed around the room, followed by Ronald Worthington's booming voice. "Ladies and gentlemen, if I may have your attention."

Ronald was dressed in a cream linen suit, a maroon fez perched on his head, which kept slipping down the side of his pate. The four Romany sedan-chair bearers set up their instruments behind him: an accordion player, two violinists and a trumpeter. He pushed the fez back into place, as he took the microphone:

"Jamila, the Gypsy Queen of the Night, and her mini-orchestra."

A cheer and clapping. The musicians looked around and bowed. Ronald offered Jamila the microphone, which she waved away with a look of disdain.

She looked out over the room, sang a long, single note that filled the room. Even the waiters stopped in their work and stood still, listening.

"Shine my star," she sang, "Shine my star, for you are the light of my heart."

The first violinist slowly teased a tune from his instrument, jammed under his neck, and the second soon joined him. Alex watched the hairs on his arm stand to attention. A powerful feeling, poignant and intense, rippled through him. The wind whistled through the shack in Novy Marek. He saw Natasha looking at him in the dark as Teresa sang. He turned to Ronald.

"I heard that you liked this song, old chap," said Ronald, wiping the sweat from his forehead, "so I asked her to sing it especially for you."

Alex looked up. Natasha briefly glanced at him, and turned away, mouthing the words in time with the singer. The trumpeter took up the tune, and the accordionist joined in. Jamila reached behind her ear, and threw him the rose, which he caught with a flourish.

Kitty turned to him. "Why don't you go outside on the balcony?"

"Why? It's cold out there," he said, handing her the rose.

She shook her head. "Thanks, but that's for someone else. Go. Outside. Alex," she ordered.

He put the rose on the table and walked onto the terrace. He leaned against the fence, staring at the water. Fractured shapes formed and broke on the surface as it rippled in the breeze. The night air was cool and refreshing. The door opened.

She was standing next to him, lighting a cigarette. "You didn't reply to my email."

"I knew I would see you here tonight."

She smiled. "I like Ronald. He's helped me a lot," she said, looking out over the pond.

"He has. And you've helped me, very much," said Alex, moving nearer. His arm brushed against hers. "At least tonight there aren't any policemen around. We won't get arrested."

"That depends," Natasha replied.

He turned to face her. "On what?"

She stared at him. "On what we do."

Alex watched the breeze shape her dress against the curve of her waist and the rise of her breasts. He took the cigarette and flicked it into the lake. It sparked briefly when it hit the water, hissed and floated away. Her eyes were huge in the dark. She licked her lips, once, lightly.

"You shouldn't smoke. It's bad for your health," he said, moving closer to her. She stood still, and seemed to lean towards him. Alex continued: "Exercise is better. Running is the best. Plenty of fresh air on Margaret Island."

A half-smile played on her lips. "And girls."

He touched her face and she turned to him, her eyes shining. Alex drew her closer, her arms snaking around his neck as she opened her mouth to his.

## TWENTY-ONE

They sat up in bed, watching the sun rise over the city. His every sense was fine-tuned. A trail of tangled clothes led from the flat's entrance: his coat, her coat, his shirt and trousers, her dress, brassiere and knickers tangled in his underwear. They had fallen on each other. Urgently at first, as if to make up for all the time they had spent on the journey. She met him, push for push, her nails raking his back, her legs locked around him until she cried out his name. He felt her ripple inside, felt his pleasure grow, spreading through him until it erupted, and he moaned hers in reply. They had rested for a while, tracing patterns in each others' sweat, whispering shy confidences, and made love again, more slowly, savouring every touch and taste.

The sky slowly lightened, turning from black to maroon to blue as the hum of early morning traffic sounded in the distance.

"What if I am imagining the whole thing?" asked Alex, biting his lower lip. "Maybe there is no conspiracy, just the rough and tumble of politics in hard times. Why shouldn't Hunkalffy be Prime Minister? He is an elected MP."

He bit down harder. "Or Sanzlermann be President of Europe if people want to vote for him? That's democracy. People can choose their leaders. I'm obsessed. Like Hillary Clinton, and her 'vast right-wing conspiracy', out to get Bill."

Natasha leaned closer and touched his mouth. "Stop. Then who killed your grandfather?"

Alex shrugged. "I don't know. Robbers."

"Robbers with a paint-brush and a pig's head?"

"Robbers who wanted to make the robbery look like something else. Who knows why?"

"And Vince Szatmari?" she asked, pulling the quilt up around them.

"It was a hit and run. They happen. People get killed on the roads every day."

"Yes. Like Anton," she said, swallowing hard.

Alex drew her to him. "Don't. That wasn't your fault."

"I jumped aside. I saved myself first," she said, her voice cracking. Her eyes filled with tears. "Maybe I could have pulled him out of the way. And my mother. . . ." she said, burying her face in his shoulder.

"Everybody would do what you did. We escape from danger. It's a natural reflex."

He let her cry silently for several minutes until she raised her head. He handed her a tissue and she loudly blew her nose, smiling bravely.

"I'm sorry. It's OK. Really. I just torture myself thinking about it. I can't help it. I was there." She turned and looked at him, her eyes wet. "You're breaching all my defences. I'm not used to this."

Alex smiled and squeezed her hand. "I'm glad."

"Are you?" she asked, her voice intense, her eyes holding his.

"Yes. Very."

"So am I." She kissed his cheek. "What were we talking about? Your fertile imagination. But what about the burglars at my mother's flat? The burglars who didn't steal anything. And Captain Hermann? He obviously thinks something is happening. And your *friend* Isabelle," she continued, digging a fingernail into Alex's leg.

"Ouch. She's not my friend. She's a spy. But really, we don't have any proof. It's all circumstantial. A Nazi plot to take over Europe. But how do we know? Where's the evidence?"

"It is all around us. Hunkalffy is dismantling democracy. Like the governments in Romania, Croatia and Slovakia. The hatred against Gypsies. Czigex. The Pannonia Brigade. A Gendarme raid at Kultura ten minutes before you were supposed to meet Miklos. Miklos and Vince Szatmari's murders. The files we got from the KZX computer."

"It's not enough," said Alex, chewing his lip. "We need more."

"More. Yes, that's a good idea," said Natasha, sitting astride him and kissing him deeply.

The telephone rang, waking him. Alex looked at his watch: 10.00am. "Put her down and switch on your television," said David Jones.

"Put who down?" asked Alex innocently. Natasha stirred and wrapped herself around him. She opened a sleepy eye. He smiled at her and put his finger on his lips.

"Reuters knows everything. You should be at Heroes' Square. Both of you. I've just sent two reporters, a photographer and a camera crew up there. The Pannonia Brigade is inaugurating its first battalion: a thousand members."

"Thanks. I'm on my way."

"There's more. After the inauguration the Brigade is marching to the Eighth District, to protest about 'Gypsy crime'. There's going to be trouble. I'm going there with a photographer. Your ex-photographer, actually, Edina Draskovitz. I'm thinking about giving her a job."

"You should. Thanks for the update. What would I do without Reuters?"

"Stay in bed all day, you lazy sod."

"That was my plan, actually. Say hi to Edina for me. See you later."

He pressed the television remote control. Aniko Kovacs appeared, reading the morning news, the end of an item about the Pannonia Brigade. "And so we encourage all true Hungarians to show their support for the Pannonia Brigade at Heroes' Square today, and accompany them to Budapest's biggest nest of crime. Meanwhile, Prime Minister Hunkalffy and his friend Frank Sanzlermann, soon to be the first President of Europe, this morning greeted the leaders of Croatia, Slovakia and Romania. Presidents Zorvajk, Hrkna and Malinanescu arrived in Budapest to show their support for

Mr Sanzlermann, and to attend the gala opening of today's exhibition at Parliament," she said.

The screen showed Hunkalffy and Sanzlermann standing on the tarmac at Budapest airport, shaking hands with the three leaders as they stepped off Sanzlermann's red, white and black campaign aeroplane. Kovacs outlined how the exhibition was entitled "The Life and Times of Four Anti-Bolshevik Heroes: "Hungary's Admiral Miklos Horthy; Croatia's Ante Pavelic, Romania's Martial Ion Antonescu, and Slovakia's Father Josef Tiso, all wartime leaders and Nazi allies. The exhibition was designed by a subsidiary of the Volkstern Corporation. The highlight was a virtual reality room where visitors could don suits and goggles linked to a computer and pretend they were on the battlefield, engaged in combat with the Red Army.

Alex's old mobile phone beeped to alert him that a message had arrived. It was a video file. He picked up the handset. Natasha sat up next to him as he opened the message. There was no sound. The first few seconds showed a dark, poor-resolution image of Alex, Natasha, Mike Jakub and Svetlana Todorova crowded together in Novy Marek, in Teresa's house. It was followed by a shot of Alex entering his apartment building. The next sequence showed a pig being dragged into a field. The animal squealed and struggled as it was held down. Blood gushed as a knife sliced through the pig's throat and it shuddered in its death throes, sending a red spray across the camera lens. The last frame showed the pig's head, on a plate, in front of a man's legs in blue pyjamas. The sender's number was blocked.

Alex dropped the handset, breathing hard to stop himself from throwing up. Natasha picked it up and replayed the video. "Alex, you aren't imagining anything," she said, holding his hand until it stopped shaking.

*   *   *

Cassandra Orczy leaned back in her office chair and entered her computer password for the second time, a complicated series of letters and numbers that was randomly generated and changed every week. "Access denied" again. She tried once more, carefully checking the sequence was correct. Her computer would lock after three failed attempts. The screen went black, and a small panel declared "Unauthorised Access Attempt: Security Alert." Cassandra sat back and sipped her coffee, and smiled as she looked at her white Zsolnay porcelain cup. If she wanted a gold-rimmed one now she would definitely have to buy it herself. She looked around the room with nostalgia: the framed quotation from Sun Tzu, the filing cabinets, the chipped desk, its in and out trays both empty, the coffee machine on her desk. She checked the drawers once more. All empty. There was nothing to show that anyone had ever worked here. The view was what she would miss most of all, she mused, as she watched the Danube flowing by.

The door flew open and two burly men in black uniforms marched into her office. Each wore caps emblazoned with a logo showing the letter 'H' inside a 'C'.

"Didn't your mother teach you to knock before you enter a lady's room?" she said, as they walked around her desk.

"I didn't know we were," sneered one. "Nice view. Shame it's wasted on communist scum. But not for much longer."

"Which rock did they find you under?"

"The Volkstern Corporation security department."

"We already have a security department. And we don't need protecting, especially not by the Volkstern Corporation's thugs. So get out of my office." She pressed a button under her desk.

The Volkstern guard sat on Cassandra's desk and grabbed her breast, squeezing it hard. She winced in pain. "Don't fuck with us," he said. "You've got two minutes to get your shit and then we escort you from the building." He threw a black plastic rubbish bag on her desk.

"I don't need that. There's nothing here. Ok, you win. I'll go quietly," she said, her voice conciliatory as she tried to twist away. "Please let go of me. It hurts and you've made your point."

The guard dropped his hand.

"Would you like some coffee?" Cassandra asked sweetly, picking up the pot on her desk.

The guard grunted no. She emptied half the pot over his groin. He gasped in agony and grabbed at his trousers, falling to the floor. The second guard spun on his heels and lunged at her. Cassandra threw the remaining coffee in his face. He screamed, reeled backwards and banged against the wall, clawing at his face. The door opened and four well built men walked in, looking alert and dangerous.

Cassandra said: "OK, they're all yours." The four grabbed both Volkstern guards, pinned their arms behind them and slammed them to the floor. Cassandra knelt down and whispered near their ears. "Now you tell your masters this: don't fuck with *us*."

\*   \*   \*

Twenty squads, each of fifty Pannonia Brigade members, marched in military formation up Andrassy Avenue towards Heroes' Square. Each squad leader held the Arrow Cross flag. The square was ringed with Gendarmes. The squads wheeled and turned as they arrived in the square, lining up as though on a parade ground. Csaba Zirta, Interior Minister, stood on a raised platform, at the northern end of the square, flanked by priests from the Catholic, Lutheran and Calvinist churches. A banner draped the length of the platform proclaimed: "No to Gypsy Crime and no to Cosmopolitan Speculators." The banner was emblazoned with two red circles with a line through them: one superimposed on a picture of a caricature of a Romany man, the other over the Israeli flag. One by one the Guard members walked up to the podium, shook Csaba Zirta's hand and were blessed in turn by the priests.

\*   \*   \*

Jozseftown, Budapest's largest Romany quarter, stretched north of the Great Boulevard into the heart of the Eighth district. Its dark, narrow alleys were a world away from the trendy bars and cafés of nearby Andrassy Avenue. The dilapidated apartment blocks were untouched since the 1930s. Romany families with five, six, even more children were crammed into dank one or two room flats. Many shared a bathroom and toilet with other families. Electricity and gas supplies were pirated, but no inspectors came calling here. The locals called it *Nyolcker*, pronounced 'n'yolts-care', a shortened, slang version of the Hungarian for 'Eighth district'. But despite the poverty and squalor, *Nyolcker* buzzed with life and vitality. Life was lived on the streets here. The squares were usually crowded with children playing football, teenage rappers, gossiping housewives and unemployed men smoking and reading the day's newspapers. But today *Nyolcker* was empty and eerily silent.

The gate to *Nyolcker* was Rakoczi Square, an open park, stretching back from the Boulevard, flanked by Jozsef Street on one side and Berkocsis Street on the other. In a half-hearted attempt at community improvement, the local council had installed a giant bank of television screens in the park, which now showed non-stop campaign advertisements for Frank Sanzlermann. The Pannonia Brigade had announced that it would march down Andrassy Avenue, along the Great Boulevard and through Rakoczi Square into the two side streets to "reclaim Jozseftown for true Hungarians" and "clear out the Gypsy criminals". The whole area had been sealed off. Frustrated television crews argued in vain with the Gendarmes as they stopped journalists from following the Pannonia Brigade along the Boulevard.

Alex and Natasha cut through the back streets to meet Mike Jakub, David Jones and Edina. They stood at the top end of Jozsef Street, fifty metres from where it met the Boulevard. The four journalists and Mike walked out into the middle of the street. Mike and Alex clambered onto a roof of a battered Lada and looked across the road. Mike pointed at the Gendarmerie buses parked across the other side of the Boulevard. Gendarmes milled about dressed in helmets and full body armour. This part of Budapest was usually crowded with traffic at mid-morning, but was empty now. A squad of Gendarmes stood on a corner staring back at them. The sound of the Pannonia Brigade marching down Andrassy Avenue echoed in the distance. The Brigade was almost at Oktogon, where Andrassy Avenue met the Boulevard. It would take the Pannonia Brigade about ten minutes to get to Rakoczi Square. The bank of television screens showed Sanzlermann and Hunkalffy drinking beer and singing, with their arms around each other.

"Ready?" asked Alex.

"Of course," said Mike, grinning.

Cassandra Orczy sat in the far corner of an internet café not far from Parliament, and logged onto her webmail account. Webmail offered a holding folder for draft emails. The drafts folder was one of the internet's worst kept secrets: it offered a secure communication channel for everyone from spies to terrorists. Back in the Cold War spies had used dead-letter drops to communicate: a chalk mark on a wall meant that something was hidden in an agreed place, a beer can by a tree, nothing to report.

In the cyber-age emails were far faster and more efficient, but unfortunately for those who wanted to keep their communications private, they left a permanent data trail. Instant messaging was more secure, but not foolproof. Emails could be encrypted but that itself tended to draw the attention of security services and others. Computer to computer internet telephony was almost impossible to tap, but anyone nearby could listen in to the actual conversation. It was useless for internet cafés. But the drafts option of web-based email was almost perfect. The email stayed in the equivalent of a 'holding' file, and as it was not sent, there was no data trail to track. All that was needed was for both parties to have the password to the account. No-one had yet worked out how to monitor email drafts, although Cassandra had heard that the Israelis were making great progress. Either way, only one other person had access to her account: 'Voter.' She opened her drafts folder:

Dear Mummy,

I'm really getting fed up with all these family rows. Grandma keeps fighting with Auntie and says she is sorry she ever came here. Auntie says Grandma should have stayed at home. Grandma says she thought

Auntie had everything under control. There's even talk that another cousin, that I've never heard of, is coming to sort everything out. Meanwhile our French cousin is making lots of new friends, which is making everybody jealous. Plus there's the big family party at home this afternoon, for all the other relatives that have just arrived.And they are already squabbling all the time. Families!

Much love, Maria.

She read the draft again, slowly. 'Grandma' was Sanzlermann. 'Auntie' was Attila Hunkalffy. The 'French cousin' was Edith Leclerc. The 'family party at home' was the exhibition inauguration at Parliament, for the 'other relatives', the Presidents of Slovakia, Croatia and Romania. The arguments were good news, and gave her something to work with. But who was 'another cousin, coming to knock their heads together'?

\* \* \*

The Pannonia Brigade was about 200 yards away, marching in formation along the Grand Boulevard, when the television screens on Rakoczi Square flickered and went black. Sanzlermann and Hunkalffy were replaced by Jamila, the Gypsy queen of the night. Her powerful voice soared across the streets. As Jamila sang, the Romany women poured out of the apartment blocks, their bright headscarves and floral skirts a blaze of colour on the freezing winter day. Grey-haired grandmothers, plump middle-aged housewives and teenage girls, some carrying babies on their arms, all rushed forward to the end of Jozsef and Berkocsis Streets. They formed a line across the streets and along the top end of Rakoczi Square, linking arms, blocking the Pannonia Brigade's path into *Nyolcker*. Many of the women carried saucepans and frying pans. As the Guard marched nearer they began to hit the pans, at first randomly, and then in a steady beat. Across the other side of the Boulevard the Gendarmes readied for action, putting on their helmets, unsheathing their riot sticks, and loading their CS-gas guns.

Alex, Natasha and David Jones watched as Mike Jakub climbed back onto the Lada at the top of Jozsef Street, a loudhailer in his hand. Edina stood nearby, firing off pictures.

"Welcome to *Nyolcker TV*," Mike said, gesturing at the bank of television screens. "As you can see, we have prepared a real Gypsy welcome for you," he continued, triggering laughter from the women. "We are broadcasting live over the internet. We have a dozen cameras covering the whole area." Jamila vanished, replaced by pictures of the police across the street, now watching themselves on the screens. "You can watch it at nyolcker.com. We are also uploading to You Tube and Google Video. So whatever you do next, remember the whole world is watching."

The Pannonia Brigade arrived and spread out along the Boulevard, past Jozsef Street and Rakoczi Square to Berkocsics Street, the men standing three or four deep, a few feet in front of the Romany women. The Pannonia Brigade commander huddled with the Gendarmes' captain. The Gendarme shouted and gesticulated, telling him to send the Pannonia Brigade to break through the line of Romany women. The Pannonia Brigade commander pointed at the television screens. The screens switched back and forth between the two men arguing with each other. The Pannonia Brigade commander shook his head in disgust and walked away. The Brigade fell back, the men forming squads and marching back down the Boulevard. The Gypsy women laughed and jeered, banging their saucepans and frying pans as hard as they could.

## TWENTY-TWO

The rusty device was mounted on a wooden plinth in a glass case. Alex read the label: "Cogwheel and tubing from a water pump used in the first Budapest municipal effluent treatment plant. Circa 1887." Housed in a riverside warehouse, the city's Museum of Water Treatment and Sewage was far from the tourist trail, on the fringes of the Ninth district, the rough working class area than ran along the Pest side of the Danube. Alex was the only visitor. He looked at his watch. Cassandra Orczy had told him to be here at 1.00pm. It was now 12.50pm.

Natasha had gone to have lunch with Kitty Kovacs. He smiled as he imagined their conversation, as she updated her on all the news. Not only about her love-life but how Mike and the *Nyolcker* women had seen off the Pannonia Brigade. David Jones had already put out a Reuters story, headlined "Romany women face down Hungarian Fascists", with Edina's pictures. The blogosphere was ablaze with follow-up reports and comments. He was meeting Natasha at Parliament that afternoon for the inauguration of the Volkstern Corporation exhibition. He felt warm and happy. He replayed the night in the cinema of his head, over and over again. His mind lingered on a picture of her moving against him, her back arched, her mouth open and her eyes locked onto his. He brought his fingers to his nose and inhaled. He could still smell her: delicate sweat, rich evening perfume and a metallic feminine tang.

He turned round as a clatter of high heels resounded through the empty room. "You look different," said Cassandra, eyeing him up and down. "Like the cat who got the cream."

247

They shook hands, and she unbuttoned her coat.

"I'm enjoying myself. This is a fascinating place," said Alex dryly. "How is your father?"

"That's why I like these museums. Obscure, out of the way but always interesting. My father is much better, thank you. He's back at home. Ordering his wife around and generally terrorising everybody."

"His wife?" asked Alex, looking quizzically at her.

"My mother was not his wife. She was someone else's wife. It was all a long time ago."

"Not that long ago," he said.

She smiled. "You're very charming. Let's walk and talk. I've brought something for you. A token of good faith. I expect something in return."

They stopped in front of a delicate medieval engraving of the course of the Danube, with all its tributaries, every one now vanished under the city.

She handed Alex a copy of the memo from the head of the Hungarian State Security Service, announcing that it was to be merged with the Gendarmerie.

Alex read it carefully. A major story. An internal coup, in effect.

"Can I keep this?" he asked.

"That piece of paper means that I am no longer employed. There is no point in me applying for a job with the Gendarmerie, not that I ever would."

"What are you going to do now?"

"I, and several of my colleagues, have, let us say, gone freelance. Let's go for a walk. What have you got for me?"

The river was running high, an oily scum swirling on the grey waters. A plastic bottle bobbed and twisted in the current. Alex said: "We know what KZX is doing. It's called The Porajmus Project, named after the Romany Holocaust. It's based on Czigex, the world's first genetically engineered smart racial drug. For female Romany patients only. Take one capsule after meals, with water, and . . ."

"You will never have another child?" asked Cassandra.

"Exactly. And take a look at this." He took his mobile and played the video clip he had received that morning.

Cassandra blanched. "*Jézus-Maria*. That's hideous." She sat down on a nearby bench, reached into her bag and took out two photographs. "Are these the Roma that you met in Novy Marek?"

He sat down next to her. 'Yes. Why?"

"Alex, I have bad news. Teresa Sandori and her husband Virgil died in a fire two days ago. Their house burnt to the ground in five minutes. The Slovak authorities blamed it on 'faulty wiring', and a pirated electricity supply."

Alex felt sick. The bench was cold and hard against his back. He saw baby Mario resting against Teresa's shoulder, and the pride in Virgil's eyes as he explained how he would stay with his 'little dove', even if they would have no more children. Had he had done this? Would they still be alive if he had not talked his way into their house, pried open their lives?

"Are you sure? How do you know it was them?" Alex asked.

"We received a report about a fire there. It included the photographs taken for Teresa and Virgil's identity cards."

"They had a baby," said Alex.

Cassandra shook her head. "I'm so sorry."

"Were they murdered? Was it arson?" asked Alex.

Cassandra nodded slowly, her voice grave. "We believe so, yes."

"Teresa and Virgil are dead because they spoke to me," said Alex, in a low monotone.

Cassandra said nothing for several moments. "No, Teresa and Virgil are dead because someone killed them. Not you. You can't torture yourself over this Alex."

Alex stared at the river. "Tell me about the Directorate."

Orczy started with surprise. "How do you know about that?"

"So it does exist."

Cassandra looked at the water rushing by. "Very much so. Unfortunately." A police motorboat roared down the river towards the Chain Bridge, its blue lights flashing. She sat for several moments. "We think the Directorate was formed towards the end of the war, in Budapest. There was a meeting attended by high-level German industrialists, bankers and economic officials. It's somehow tied into the European Union and the adoption of the euro."

"The evening of November 9 1944, at the Hotel Savoy," said Alex, as he pulled out a photocopy of Miklos' hidden testimony. *"Our battlefields will be the corridors of banks and industries, our weapons not soldiers and guns, but balance sheets and currency markets . . . The Nazi party went underground, funded by German banks and industrialists. Massive amounts of capital, looted gold, works of art, stocks and shares stolen from the Nazis' victims were exported through Swiss banks, or were held in their vaults as security against loans,* and so on. It's all here. I think I know more about the Directorate than you."

Cassandra turned in surprise. "Where did you get those papers?"

He handed the sheets to Cassandra. "It's my grandfather's secret testimony. Miklos was at the Savoy that night. He was a waiter. There was a drunken dinner. I think he was going to tell me everything. There was an actual document from 1944 setting out the whole plan and how the Directorate would work, but Miklos destroyed it. The Nazis loved paperwork, so there must be other copies. That's why he was murdered. That's why Vince Szatmari was killed, because he found out their plans. Set up a puppet government and take control of the economy. Then drastically devalue the forint, so Directorate front companies can buy every Hungarian asset for next to nothing. Siphon off the profits, close the companies down and absorb them into KZX and the Volkstern Corporation. Hungary is a trial run. Then they will do the same in Croatia, Slovakia and Romania. Sanzlermann is the front man. Hunkalffy, Dragomir Zorvajk, Dusan Hrkna and Cornelius Malinanescu are just stooges. And then the Czech Republic and Poland, and the Balkans."

Orczy peered at the spidery writing. She read through the papers slowly, turning them over one by one, nodding to herself. "We think the Directorate is meeting again. Next Sunday, November 9, election day. A private dining room is booked at the Hotel Savoy. Volkstern security staff are already taking the walls, floors and light fittings apart."

"But you could get someone inside," said Alex immediately.

"Who?" she asked. She saw his expression and smiled wearily. "Don't be ridiculous."

*Alex watches Azra pray, her lips moving quickly as the Bosnian Serb soldier drags her away, drunk and laughing. She sees him, parked on the other side of the checkpoint, safe on the Croatian side of the border. Azra turns towards him and mouths his name. An iron hand clamps his arm as he moves for the car door. "You can do nothing," his interpreter hisses. "Nothing. They will kill you without thinking, just for fun, and claim it was Muslim terrorists." The soldier and Azra vanish into the woods. He can no longer see them. A scream, an animal howl like nothing he had ever heard, and a single gunshot. He should have gone to her. He should have gone. He gets out of the car and throws up at the side of the road.*

Azra, Miklos, Vince; Teresa, Virgil, Mario – the names resounded in Alex's head. The list was getting longer and longer, he thought grimly. "I could be a waiter. You can get me in."

Cassandra shook her head. "They will kill you."

Alex moved closer to her. "Only if they find out who I am," he said, his voice intense. "We both want the same thing: to expose the Directorate. You need someone on the inside. I need to get inside, to infiltrate the dinner. Then I can find out how the Directorate works, who are its members, what are its plans. I need to be there, to see it first-hand. It's the last part of the story."

She looked again through Miklos' secret testimony. "The story. Still the reporter."

Alex stared out at the river, seeing Azra's anguished face. "Yes, I am. That's what I do."

"If, *if*, we did send someone in, why should it be you?"

"This started at the Savoy with Miklos in 1944. It ends there with me now."

"And you would share everything you know with us? And whoever else wanted to know? You can write your article but you would also be working for us. Doesn't that bother you?"

Alex rolled his teeth over his lip. "Yes, it does. But I wouldn't have any choice, would I?"

Cassandra put the copy of Miklos' testimony in her bag and looked hard at him. "No. You would not. And there's no guarantee we could get you out to write anything."

She smiled ruefully to herself, and searched in her handbag. A distant roll of thunder sounded and the sky turned dark. "Meanwhile, there's something else you should have."

"What?"

"This," she said, handing him a photograph of a villa on the shores of Lake Balaton.

## TWENTY-THREE

A cold winter rain fell on the window of the Number 2 tram as it trundled along the riverbank towards Parliament. Alex checked his watch. Just after 2.30pm. Less than half an hour and he would be with her again. The carriage was crowded with shoppers going home from the market at the Freedom Bridge. A short, stocky bald man with a determined expression rummaged through a bag of potatoes. He wore a thin denim jacket, acrylic jumper and brown polyester trousers, and held the potatoes between his thumb and forefinger, reciting the price of each.

His voice rose steadily in volume as he addressed the carriage, until he was shouting, "How can I feed my family? How can we live like this?"

He turned to an elderly woman wrapped in an expensive, black wool coat. She was reading *Ébredjetek Magyarok!*, a prim hat perched on her neat grey hair and a fur stole around her neck.

"Dear Madame, do you know I have worked for thirty years? I have three children and a wife and we have not eaten meat, even a piece of sausage, for two weeks," he said.

"Look Madame, I work in a factory," he continued, showing her his grubby palms and grimy nails. "Every day, for nine hours. But we eat potatoes. The Prime Minister rides in helicopters, while we eat potatoes. Can you explain to me why?"

The woman shook her head disapprovingly, tutted and turned away, burying her face in her newspaper. The bald man fell silent, and bent low over his shopping, holding his head in his hands. A plump Romany woman in an orange floral skirt, with a child on her knee, patted him on the back, and mumbled some words of

253

comfort. The tram stopped in front of the Hotel Bristol. A skinhead strutted on board, dressed in a shiny black bomber jacket. He stood next to the Romany woman, wiping the surface of his black jacket with his hand and sniffing contemptuously.

"Dirty Gypsy. Filthy, filthy," he said. He prodded the baby with a thick, stubby finger. The baby began to cry. "Breeding like animals. Everywhere you look, Gypsies, foreigners and Jews."

The Romany woman tried to hunch into herself. She gathered her baby closer, but it kept crying.

"Shut your brat up, or I will do the job for good," the skinhead said. He jabbed the baby again with his finger. It howled even louder. The carriage fell silent, and the wheels rattled, as the tram passed the Hungarian Academy of Sciences. A large banner over the entrance proclaimed that it had just been renamed the National Academy of Hungarian Intellects. Alex looked around the carriage as the skinhead contined abusing the Romany woman, the anger rising within him. A silver-haired man wearing glasses shrugged his shoulders, turned away and looked out of the window. Alex caught the eye of the bald man with the bag of potatoes. He tucked his shopping under the seat and stood up. He raised his eyebrows and looked at the skinhead.

Alex nodded. He punched the skinhead in the stomach fast and hard, sending him stumbling back. "Why don't you shut up? Or are you only good for hitting women and children?"

The skinhead's face contorted with anger as he struggled to get his balance. He lunged at Alex, his fist clenched. Alex tried to dodge the blow, but it caught him hard on the left shoulder. Pain shot down his wounded arm. He gasped and kicked the skinhead as hard as he could in the shins. The skinhead cried out in surprise as the tram lurched around a bend in the tracks. He lost his balance, hopping and stumbling towards the door.

The bald man jumped forward and neatly kicked him in the small of his back, sending him flying face first down the carriage steps. The skinhead tried to get up, swearing and flailing in his fury. The bald man smiled as he leant over him and grabbed the neck of his jacket. He slammed his face against the window. The tram stopped.

The doors opened and he threw the skinhead out onto the pavement, his expression dazed as blood dripped from his nose. The bald man emptied his bag of potatoes over him, before getting back on the tram.

"Thanks," Alex said, trying to catch his breath, and rubbing his shoulder. "This is for the potatoes," he said, taking a banknote from his pocket.

"No, no, really. I couldn't. It was worth every forint," the bald man said, waving away the money, standing straight and smiling as they shook hands. The elderly woman glared at them from behind her copy of *Ébredjetek Magyarok!* and shook her head, muttering to herself. The Romany woman clapped her hands with delight.

"Wait," the man said, "let me give you this." He pulled out a crumpled sheet of paper from his jacket pocket and handed it to Alex.

"PUT AN END TO FEAR – JOIN THE MARCH FOR FREEDOM," the handbill announced in large black letters. Alex read on:

We will no longer be afraid
We will no longer stay silent
We will no longer be terrorised
March with us on Sunday November 9, European Presidential election day.
Meet outside the National Museum at 6.00pm.

A small line of type leaflet said "Support the Hungarian Freedom Movement." www.szabadmagyarorszag.hu/ www.freehungary.hu/ www.freiungarn.hu/.

Alex thanked him. Hungarian revolutions always started at the National Museum, or nearby. In 1848, the dashing poet and national hero Sandor Petofi had stood on its steps and read a manifesto calling for freedom from Austrian tyranny. In 1956, the uprising against the Russians had begun outside the National Radio headquarters, on neighbouring Brody Sandor Street. The walls were still pockmarked with bullet-holes from the street fighting. Both revolutions had ended in defeat. But what was the Hungarian Freedom Movement?

Alex pocketed the leaflet as the tram trundled towards Parliament, where Attila Hunkalffy was hosting Sanzlermann, Dusan Hrkna, Cornelius Malinanescu and Dragomir Zorvajk at the opening of the exhibition commemorating the region's leaders during the Second World War. A giant green, red and white Hungarian flag hung from the Gothic crenulations of the Parliament roof, down to the very top of the entrance. The Magyar ensign was flanked by the Slovak, Romanian and Croatian flags. A long maroon carpet stretched down the steps from the Parliament entrance, between the brace of stone lions that guarded the ornate doors, into the stately grace of tree-lined Kossuth Square. Lajos Kossuth, leader of the brief 1848 Hungarian revolution against the Habsburgs, looked on silently from the marble plinth where he was immortalised in stone. Metal barricades and a line of Gendarmes kept the crowds back. Most held paper flags, miniature versions of those draped across the Parliament façade.

The blast wave hit the tram side-on.

The carriage's windows blew in, hurling shards of glass across the passengers. The carriage wobbled once, tried to right itself, and slowly toppled over. The boom of the explosion echoed across Parliament Square. A second, perhaps two, of silence and then the screams and moans started.

Alex lurched backwards as the carriage fell on its side, lost his balance and tumbled onto the floor, glass raining down around him. Debris thumped onto the carriage, a staccato barrage of scraps of metal, lumps of brick and concrete. He slid across the floor and banged his head on a chair stanchion, stunning him for a few moments.

He opened his eyes to see the Romany woman hunched over her baby, looking from side to side, her eyes wide with terror. The elderly woman was still sitting in her chair, hat and fur stole now gone. She looked puzzled as she stared at the ground, now next to her head. A human hand fell through the smashed window and landed with a thwack on her copy of *Ébredjetek Magyarok!*, spattering crimson on its pages. She screamed and threw both down the carriage.

The rain was falling hard now, pouring through the broken windows. Pale rivulets of watery blood ran down on the carriage. The howls of ambulance sirens and the clatter of police helicopters sounded in the distance. A phalanx of Gendarmes charged onto the square from the nearby Ministry of Justice. "It is forbidden to move from where you are or to attempt to leave the area," the leader announced through a loudhailer. "This is now a closed emergency zone. Stay where you are. Medical help is on the way."

Alex struggled to his feet. A powerful smell of burning rubber and roasting meat filled the carriage. He saw the bald man was splayed out, face down, blood pouring from his head. He moved to help him, but something felt dislodged in his head, and there were two of everything. A cut above his head was bleeding, and his hair was full of glass splinters. He blinked and squeezed his eyes, grasping a handrail for support. The world slowly came back into focus. Panic and anguish surged as he climbed out of the shattered window. Where was she? He pulled out his mobile telephone, and punched out her number. Nothing. He looked at the screen: no network service available. He slid down the carriage wall and stumbled out onto the square.

Smoke was pouring out of the front of the Parliament. The flags draped over the entrance had been shredded by the blast, their meagre remnants still smouldering. Cars were burning, exploding one by one with a dull crump as the petrol tanks ignited. Only the feet remained of the lions guarding the entrance. Mangled remains of metal crash barriers were scattered across the square. A lunchbox lay open on the ground, next to an apple and a carefully-wrapped sandwich. The blast wave had stopped the clock by the Ethnographic Museum that faced Parliament at 2.52pm. He could see dead bodies splayed by the Parliament entrance. Fragments of body parts and severed limbs were scattered across the car park. A portly man screamed for help as he stared at the bloody stump of his knee.

Tourist buses from Romania and Slovakia had been blown across the square, slammed into lampposts, sagging as though they had been punched. A police car had been turned over by the blast. It slowly span on its roof, a dead policeman suspended upside down by his seatbelt. His radio screeched urgent instructions. Alex stumbled across the charred grass, trying in vain to get a signal on his mobile telephone.

Ambulances converged from all directions. He felt his hearing fade in and out. Sodden scraps of paper flags floated down the gutter. He almost walked into a young woman with short dark hair laying face down on the grass. "Natasha," he cried as he turned her over. He sagged with relief and shame when he saw a round, pale face. He turned his face upwards to the rain and staggered across the grass towards the Parliament's entrance. He swayed on his feet and his legs turned to rubber. The world wobbled and turned black.

*　*　*

Dieter Klindern leant back in his armchair in Sanzlermann's suite and smoothed down the sleeve of his black silk Nehru jacket. The chairman of KZX Industries was a trim, handsome man in his early sixties, with close-cropped steel grey hair and pale blue eyes. He wore half-moon glasses above a long nose, thin, colourless lips and small, neat teeth. The room was dark, the curtains drawn against the cheerless winter dusk. A silver coffee pot and a tray of cakes sat untouched nearby. Hunkalffy and Sanzlermann sat in front of him, on two hard-back chairs, like errant schoolboys caught cheating in an examination. The two men glared at each other. Reinhard Daintner sat a few metres away, silently watching. Klindern could barely control his anger.

"A *bomb*. How imaginative," he sneered.

Hunkalffy opened his mouth to speak. Klindern cut him off. "Please do not interrupt me, Prime Minister. I prefer to finish my sentences myself." Hunkalffy lowered his head.

Klindern continued: "And do not misunderstand me. I am hardly concerned about the loss of life a few hours ago. If you wish to arrange the deaths of your own citizens that is your own affair. What does concern me is that your little freelance operation, which as you well know should have been cleared with the Directorate, may now place more than seventy years of work in jeopardy," continued Klindern, his voice rising as he poured himself a cup of coffee from the jug and cups arranged on the table next to him.

Klindern let the silence stretch out, and banged the jug down hard on the table when he had finished pouring. Hunkalffy and Sanzlermann jumped as the cups and saucers rattled in protest. "And you couldn't even get the timing right. Dragomir Zorvajk is in hospital, with a stomach full of shrapnel. A big child, too distracted by your ridiculous exhibition to leave in time. Unlikely to be with us for much longer, the doctors say."

He walked over to Hunkalffy and Sanzlermann. "Because of your bungling, our whole southern flank is threatened."

Hunkalffy sat silently. Klindern circled around him. "Do you have any idea what you have done? The destruction of Yugoslavia was one of the Directorate's greatest achievements. It took decades of work, of careful planning. We spent millions, hundreds of millions, used up diplomatic favours and political capital from Washington to the Vatican to achieve a centuries-old dream: an independent Croatia, Christian, Catholic, cleansed of its Serbs. A permanently grateful client-state, with a coastline full of warm-water ports. Our launch pad into the Balkans, our *drang nach süd* to the Mediterranean, even Africa. At the helm, Dragomir Zorvajk, young, handsome, a sports hero, veteran of the homeland war. Untouchable, adored by all, a leader who could never be questioned. Thanks to you, now flat on his back in a Hungarian hospital, his stomach shredded, and unlikely to make it through the night."

Klindern paused and stirred his coffee. He jabbed his finger at Hunkalffy. "You, of all people, should know that there are enough ways to manipulate an election. Almost as imaginative as setting Edith Leclerc's stage on fire, and blaming it on an 'arson attack'. And this ridiculous 'Pannonia Brigade'. The whole world is laughing at your storm troopers, beaten back by Gypsy housewives. *Aaach.*

Plus, this absurd campaign against the foreign press by your media lackeys. You merely make heroes out of these diletanttes. What were you thinking? Do you ever think? We made you, Hunkalffy . . ." said Klindern. He paused silently for several seconds. "There are already several within our organisation calling for *severe* sanctions to be taken against you."

"But, I mean, the bomb was his idea as well," Hunkalffy said, pointing at Sanzlermann. "A big bang outside Parliament, a few days before the election, would give us the perfect cover to ensure the right result. We have even arrested the ILA's supposed leader in Budapest. There could be no better alibi for the biggest crackdown since the collapse of communism. Your own words, Frank," said Hunkalffy, turning to Sanzlermann.

Sanzlermann turned to Hunkalffy indignantly. "You little shit."

Klindern banged his fist on the table. "*Idiots!* You know nothing about the ILA." The two men fell silent. Daintner walked over to the DVD player under a wide-screen television.

"Track one, please," said Klindern. Daintner pressed the remote control.

The player whirred for a few seconds. The screen filled with a pin-sharp image. Moans and sighs echoed around the room. Sanzlermann was leaning back against the sink in the toilet cubicle of his executive jet, one hand pressing hard against the closed door. His eyes were closed in pleasure. A male steward knelt in front of him, his head rising and falling. Klindern watched the figures moving on the television screen with an expression of cultivated distaste, as though he had found a fly under one of his fingernails.

Sanzlermann paled and sat silently. Hunkalffy smirked.

"That is bad enough," said Klindern. "But this is far worse. Track two, please."

Daintner pressed another button on the remote control. The screen showed Sanzlermann engaged in energetic sexual congress with a full figured young woman of remarkable gymnastic ability in his bedroom at the hotel suite. They slid around the bed, switching positions, flipping each other over from side to side with practised ease. But it was clear that while her body was engaged, her mind was not. She was scanning the room even as she moaned and writhed under him. Klindern gestured to Daintner, and the screen froze.

"At least that one is a woman," said Hunkalffy, grinning.

"*Shut up*!" snapped Klindern. "Do you know what a honey-trap is, Frank?"

"When one side uses a sexually attractive woman to ensnare a target, either for purposes of blackmail or to extract information," he said miserably.

Klindern said: "You are positively dripping in the stuff."

## TWENTY-FOUR

Alex opened his eyes, blinking repeatedly as his surroundings slowly came into focus. He was lying on his back between crisp white sheets in a narrow iron hospital bed. An air-conditioner hummed in the background. The room was dark, cool, and smelled of antiseptic. His left arm had been bathed and bandaged with a fresh dressing. He carefully moved his head from side to side. A jolt of pain shot through his face, as though a steel bar was implanted through the bridge of his nose. His skin felt like he had been thoroughly sandpapered and his left side ached, from his shoulders to his toes. A single window showed a night-time pavement, and occasional glimpses of car tyres, ankles and shoes.

Cassandra Orczy sat on a chair by his bed, watching the television news with the sound turned off. He struggled to sit up but she gently pushed him back down against the sheets.

"You have to rest for several days, the doctor said. You're suffering from mild concussion, bruising, grazes and they took a lot of glass out of your skin. But you'll live."

He lay back on the hard pillow. "Where is she?"

"You should be proud of yourself. You and ten other foreign journalists have been declared *persona non grata* in Hungary. You are all to be arrested and then expelled as a punishment for 'damaging the reputation of the government'. But you aren't going anywhere for a while."

Alex gripped the bedstead. The metal felt cold against his hands. "Where is she?" he demanded, his voice rising. "Is she dead?"

"No, she's not dead. She's fine," Cassandra said, her voice exasperated. "She was late, and by the time she left for Parliament Square the bomb had already gone off."

"Thank God," he said, sagging back as the relief coursed through him. "When can I see her?"

"You can't."

"Why not?"

"Because, dear Alex, you're dead," she said, smiling sweetly, as she leaned forward to smooth down his sheets.

"I don't feel very dead."

"That's what it says in the newspapers, so it must be true. You were killed in the bombing today." She handed him an eight page emergency edition of *Magyar Tribün*, published that evening. A short news story on page three said that his remains had been identified.

"Four paragraphs. Is that all? And no picture," said Alex, indignantly.

Cassandra pulled the chair closer to his bed, her blue-green eyes unblinking. "This isn't a game, Alex. You want to infiltrate the Directorate. So your best alibi is that you are dead. Here's the proof," she said, tapping the newspaper. "It's up to you. You're in a safe house but you are not a prisoner. You can leave whenever you want. But you won't get any help from us getting into the Savoy. In fact, we just might tell them that you're coming."

She looked older, he thought. She was pale, her hair had lost its lustre and there were new lines on her face. He said: "You wouldn't do that."

"Try me. This operation has started now, Alex. Some very serious people are involved, not just in Budapest. People whose time you don't waste. I had to persuade them that you could do this. So make your mind up. Are you in or out?"

He stared at the pattern of cracks in the ceiling. He saw a spider, perhaps an octopus. Her hands pulled him closer as they moved together, their legs entwined, her breasts sliding across his chest, their skin slippery with sweat, her tongue against his. Natasha thought he was dead. She was mourning him and he was here, alive.

A wave of guilt burst through him. He raised his fingers to his nose and inhaled. Hospital soap. The antiseptic smell suddenly overwhelmed him. He saw the bodies outside Parliament, in the field in Bosnia, the broken limbs, the bloody clothes, the sightless eyes. He was injured. He was lucky to be alive. His heart pounded and his breathing turned ragged.

Cassandra looked at him, alarmed. "You've gone white. I'll get the doctor. You're in shock."

He shook his head and forced himself to breathe slowly and calmly. "It's OK, I'll be fine. Really. It's just a reaction. Just give me a little time." She handed him a box of tissues and left the room. He cried silently for several minutes, the tears draining the torment from his system, and lay back, exhausted. She returned with tea and a tray of sandwiches.

Alex accepted a cup. It was hot, sweet and very reviving. "Thanks. I'm in. But at least tell me where she is."

"Safe in the countryside with her mother. We have someone watching them."

He moved on the bed, trying to get comfortable. "How did I get here?"

"Isabelle Balassy brought you. She found you on the grass, put you in her car and talked her way through the checkpoints. She said her car was sovereign British territory. She also had a pistol in her glove compartment, which may have helped. I told you to lay still," she said, moving the pillows to support him as he sat up. She turned up the television volume. "Satellite stations aren't working at the moment. 'Technical difficulties', supposedly. Internet providers are down as well. Hungarian state television is broadcasting continuous news. The Immigration Liberation Army has claimed responsibility. But no sign yet of Hasan Al-Ajnabi's usual video tape."

Aniko Kovacs wore a black jacket, and black blouse with a red, white and green neck scarf. The Hungarian, Croatian, Romanian and Slovak flags hung in front of her desk. She read the news in a low, sombre tone. "The death toll in today's terrorist attack has now risen to forty-eight, with another ninety-seven injured, many critically, including Croatian President Dragomir Zorvajk. Responsibility has been claimed by the Immigration Liberation Army." The screen showed Hunkalffy standing on the wrecked Parliament entrance looking grim and determined, Frank Sanzlermann at his side. Dusan Hrkna and Cornelius Malinanescu stood at a respectful distance, hands behind their backs. Smoke still drifted from Parliament and the charred remains of cars.

Kovacs continued: "Prime Minister Hunkalffy has declared a temporary state of emergency to ensure that Sunday's Presidential election takes place in conditions of peace and security. The following restrictions are in force with immediate effect. All public gatherings of more than four people are banned; a curfew is in force between midnight and 6.00am. A period of 'campaign silence' is also imposed to prevent the further inflammation of national passions." A piece of paper was slid across her desk. She read: "We have just learnt all citizens are required to take part in Sunday's election. For reasons of security citizens will be required to show their completed ballot papers to a Gendarmerie officer, who will then stamp it, and their identity cards, before the paper is placed in a secure box."

The camera cut to Sanzlermann standing outside Parliament. "We stand foursquare behind our friend and ally Attila Hunkalffy, at this time of national tragedy. We extend our deepest sympathies to Hungary at this time of national mourning. This terrorist atrocity will be avenged." Malinanescu strutted forward and opened his mouth to speak, but was replaced by a shot of Edith Leclerc, standing outside the Hotel Bristol.

A scrum of reporters surrounded her, shouting questions. "I condemn utterly this cowardly attack," she declared. "But I cannot continue to campaign under these conditions. I do not withdraw my candidacy, but I have no option but to return to Paris. I will not legitimise these restrictions on basic freedoms by remaining here. As terrible as this bomb attack was, I do not believe there is any need for a state of emergency, curfew or so-called 'campaign silence'. Democracy should be strong enough . . ." she said as the screen went blank.

Aniko Kovacs suddenly appeared, looking from left to right. She touched her earpiece. "Dear viewers, our apologies for our technical difficulties. We now go live to the arrest of the ILA leader in Budapest."

The screen showed a terrified Mihaly Lataki being dragged into a van by two Gendarmes.

\* \* \*

Klindern looked at Hunkalffy and Sanzlermann with distaste. "Reinhard, track number three please," he said, gesturing at the DVD player.

Daintner pressed the remote control. A young woman with long, wavy, light brown hair walked into the headquarters of the State Security Service on Falk Miksa Street. Daintner said: "Here is your Eva. If that is her real name, which I doubt. Current whereabouts unknown."

Sanzlermann sat with his head in his hands.

"First the flight attendant. Now this," said Klindern, his voice cold. "As far as our recordings show, you told her something about Sunday's meeting. But there is too much background music. So why don't you tell me?"

Sanzlermann muttered. "Nothing, I promise, nothing."

"Tell me what you said, or you will have cause to regret it."

"That there will be an important dinner here on Sunday night, with VIPs from all over the world, to watch the election results. Half the staff know. It's hardly secret."

"I told him she was trouble, but he wouldn't listen. He can't stop following his prick. All the way to the State Security Service," said Hunkalffy, triggering a look of hate from Sanzlermann.

Klindern turned to Hunkalffy, his eyes glittering, his sun-tan now glowing with anger. "And what are you following, *Prime Minister*?"

Hunkalffy looked startled. Sanzlermann sat up straighter and smiled warily.

"This hotel episode is probably manageable. Even if the video footage was somehow leaked we could blame the stress of the campaign, hold a tearful press conference, have Dagmar pledge her love. It might even boost our support in the end. Mea culpa, human frailty, a man under terrible pressure, etc," said Klindern. "But this, this *display*. . . . Reinhard, track four please."

The screen showed Hunkalffy sitting naked on a leather armchair in the Prime Minister's office, in front of a coffee table. Empty champagne bottles were strewn across the floor and liquid slopped over the table edge. Hunkalffy leaned forward and loudly sniffed up a line of cocaine off an antique mirror, before sliding it across the table to two naked women, one blonde, the other brunette. He handed the blonde a 500 euro note. She rolled the banknote into a thin tube and snorted up the drug, while the brunette watched hungrily. Her eyes wide with excitement, the blonde walked over and sat on Hunkalffy's lap. He opened a fresh bottle of champagne and tipped it over her breasts. She writhed with pleasure. The brunette quickly snorted up the last line of cocaine and walked over to Hunkalffy. He guided her head to the blonde's chest.

Klindern chopped his hand through the air. "Thank you, Reinhard. That's enough."

Daintner ejected the DVD and handed it to Klindern. Hunkalffy sat rigid, his face beetroot, his hands gripping the side of the chair. Daintner's mobile rang and he turned away to take the call.

"Do you think we aren't watching you?" demanded Klindern. "That we don't know what you do in your office? *In your office*. What a fool you are. Cocaine and whores."

Daintner hung up, walked over to Klindern and whispered in his ear.

"*Damn*!" Klindern exclaimed, thumping the coffee tray so hard the liquid sloshed over the table. "Zorvajk has just died. You pair of idiots."

Sanzlermann scratched furiously at his raw red hand. Hunkalffy stared sullenly at Klindern.

"Sadly, we still need you both. For now. But any more blunders," Klindern said, holding the DVD, "and this disc will finish you both. Your marriages, careers, everything. Imagine how many hits this would get on an internet video-sharing site."

Hunkalffy stood up, his face dark with fury. "Then do it."

"What?" demanded Klindern, amazed. "What did you say?"

Hunkalffy walked across the room to Klindern. "I said, do it. Post it all on the internet. And then what? One, I will deny it, and say it is a smear, manufactured by Leclerc's supporters using computer tricks. And you will have to support me," he shouted, his boiling anger barely controlled. "Two, Sanzlermann's campaign will certainly be damaged. But where will that leave you and your friends, Herr Klindern? Weakened. Very weakened. Voting is just a few days away. There is no time to find a replacement candidate or move the election to another country. We are your only options. My private life is my own affair. My lovers are my business. If you choose to make them public, then be prepared to take the consequences."

Klindern laughed. "Attila, Attila, that fiery *Magyar* spirit will definitely get you into trouble one of these days. There were those who said you would have made a better candidate than poor Frank here. I'm beginning to think they were right. Sit down, Prime Minister, have some coffee," he said, his voice conciliatory.

Hunkalffy shook his head and returned to his chair. Klindern stopped laughing: "Nonetheless, we do have a credibility problem. Leclerc has returned to Paris. You have declared a state of emergency. You have closed down satellite television and internet providers. There are already mutterings in Brussels that the election should be postponed and rethought. That would be a disaster. The Directorate specifically chose Hungary as you assured us everything was under control. That does not appear to be the case."

Hunkalffy asked calmly: "What do you want me to do?"

"It is vital that Sanzlermann takes power in an election that is seen to be legitimate, not through a campaign of state-sponsored intimidation," said Klindern, his voice hardening. "Rescind the state of emergency and the new laws, carry on with the plan, but ensure that this appears to be a contested election, not an exercise in rubber-stamping."

\* \* \*

Alex sat up in bed, examining the land registry deeds for a large lakeside villa on the outskirts of Balatonfured, once a favourite resort of the Austro-Hungarian aristocracy. It was his first morning in the safe house and Cassandra had just given him the papers. They were newly issued and listed him as the owner. The house, she explained, was built by Miklos' grandfather, Alajos, at the end of the nineteenth century. Alex knew about the family's factories on Csepel Island, and the mansion on Andrassy Avenue. He half remembered hearing about a villa at Lake Balaton, and this must be it. Alex – and Miklos while he was alive – had long given up all hope of meaningful compensation for the lost Farkas economic empire, let alone repossession.

After the collapse of communism, Hungary had not restituted individual properties but had issued compensation coupons. There were too many vested interests to do otherwise. Hundreds of thousands of Jewish homes, shops, factories and businesses had been taken over, often by former friends and neighbours, many later appropriated by the state. It was a rare issue on which all sides of the political spectrum agreed: the leader of the Social Democrats lived in a mansion in the Buda hills whose owner had been killed at Auschwitz. As had the owners of the villas now housing the headquarters of the Liberals, Conservatives, Hunkalffy's party, and numerous government and business offices.

What was lost was gone forever, except, it seemed, this villa. Why? Alex wondered. And quite how Cassandra was in a position to give it to Alex was unclear, but the deeds were proof enough. It was all there, in black and white, with the requisite stamps. He picked up the photograph she had given him, and stared at the grandiose entranceway, its path curving through landscaped gardens. The house must be worth hundreds of thousands of pounds. What was he going to do with it?

He imagined himself as a gentleman of leisure, cultivating the grounds, while Natasha spent her days having dresses fitted and her hair styled. It was a pleasurable if unlikely vision. Why would she ever want to see him again, when she found out he was alive? The prospect was profoundly depressing. He chewed his lip so hard it almost bled, determined not to think about her, when he heard a knock on the door. It opened slightly, and he saw Isabelle Balassy peeking around, holding a large bunch of purple tulips.

"Are you receiving visitors yet?" she asked.

"Of course. How many of you are there?" asked Alex, his spirits brightening.

She walked in, followed by a wiry olive-skinned man, carrying a bottle of *szilva palinka*. He had a shaved head, a pierced nose and a smile that lit up a room.

"Just two. It's only a flying one to see if you are still in one piece. I'm glad to see you are. I'll find you a vase for the flowers," she said, kissing his cheek, her hair brushing against his skin.

"*Shalom, habibi,*" said Ehud, shaking his hand. "How are you feeling? We were very worried about you."

Alex stared at the Israeli. "Much better, thanks. Ehud, what are you doing here?" he asked, although the answer was already forming in his mind.

"Kultura has been closed by the tax police, so I have some free time. I'll be back in a couple of days." Ehud put the bottle of *szilva palinka* down on the bedside table. "Get better."

\* \* \*

He was locked inside a filthy train at Keleti station, and she ran alongside as it pulled out, waving frantically at him. He tried to open the door but it was jammed shut. She was crying and shouting his name, banging on the window, as he pulled harder and harder on the handle. But the door wouldn't open, the train speeded up and she disappeared into the distance. Alex awoke suddenly, possessed by a longing so powerful it was physical. His head was full of his dream, his hands were clenched tight, and this time he could not wish his yearning away. He ached to see Natasha, and knowing that she was probably not far away made it even worse. Guilt and longing surged inside him. He saw her grieving over him, yearned to wipe away her tears, to tell her he was still alive. He tried to remember her smell, her taste, the feel of her skin against his.

After three days in the safe house Alex's body was recovering well but his mind was in turmoil. He slept poorly, agonising if he was doing the right thing. He knew he had fallen in love with Natasha, but then why had he sacrificed her so easily? He had already visualised their reunion countless times. He would knock on her door, she would open it, too stunned to say anything. Or he stood there silently, just staring at her beauty. Every version ended the same way, in a hurricane of clothes and passion. He could walk out of the safe house whenever he wanted. So why didn't he? Partly, he told himself, because of his moral obligations, and the simple desire for revenge: for the deaths of Miklos, Vince Szatmari, Teresa, Virgil and Mario. Partly because he wanted to blow open the Directorate, stop the Poraymus Project and even, if he could, bring down KZX and the Volkstern Corporation. But there was something else that drove him, he admitted in the long sleepless hours, perhaps the most powerful hunger of all, the same yearning that had driven him to risk his life in Bosnia and Chechnya: to break the story and see it published under his by-line. And this time he would actually make the news, instead of just reporting it.

He switched on the television news to break his chain of thought. The morning anchor on CNN, an ebullient gay man, was about to interview the US Secretary of State about the European Presidential election. A knock on the door sounded and he turned down the volume.

Ehud walked in, carrying a tray of humus, kebabs, salads and pita bread. The smell was mouth-watering. "Breakfast, *habibi*," he said, in his strong Israeli accent. He put the tray down on the table next to the bed. Alex thanked him, smiling with pleasurable anticipation. The food at the safe house was quite as bad as at any Hungarian hospital.

"It's from your favourite restaurant. I saw your friend Mubarak there," said Ehud.

"You know each other?" asked Alex, as he filled a pita bread with humus.

"Of course. For many years. He's very angry and upset that you were killed," Ehud said, trying not to laugh. "We get on very well.

We are one of his best customers."

"Who's we?" asked Alex.

Ehud ignored the question. He turned up the volume. The Secretary of State, a former ambassador to the European Union, was outlining the United States' strong concerns about what he called "sustained human rights abuses against the Romany minority" across eastern Europe.

"If they are so concerned then why don't they do something about it?" asked Alex.

"Maybe they are." Ehud stared at Alex for several seconds while he chewed, looking first at his left side, then his right. He shook his head and exhaled through his nose. "I don't know. You are an amateur. We have no time to train you properly. The security will be extremely high. The worst thing is you have a personal stake in this. I don't see how it can work."

"Then make it work," said Alex.

"You know why they are letting you do this?" asked Ehud, taking a piece of pita bread and wrapping it around a large piece of kebab.

"Because I'm clever and brave?" Alex said, sardonically.

"No, *habibi*. Because for them you are disposable," he said, eating the morsel in one bite. He poured some *szilva palinka* into two tea cups. "*L'chaim*," he said, as they clinked cups. "So let's make sure you are not."

Alex switched channels to state television news. The screen showed a muddy village in eastern Hungary. Motorcyclists rode up and down the pot-holed main street, Arrow Cross flags streaming from the back of their machines, while the residents looked on nervously. Alex and Ehud watched silently as the reporter explained how the village's Gypsy quarter had been sealed off by the Gendarmes, while they searched for a "notorious gang of criminals".

The camera showed frightened Romany families huddling together, while the Gendarmes turned their homes inside out, hurling their meagre possessions into the street. A biker roared up and conferred with the Gendarmes. They pointed to a breeze-block shack with a tin roof. The biker rode to the gate and carefully reversed his motorbike into the open entrance. He revved his engine harder and harder, and huge plumes of exhaust fumes billowed into the shack. A teenage Romany boy staggered out, holding his younger sister in his arms. Both were coughing and crying. The Gendarmes grabbed the girl, beat the boy to the ground and threw him into their van.

Alex was filled with a cold rage. He squeezed the cup in his hand so hard the handle broke off. The cup fell to the floor, shattering into tiny shards. Ehud gripped his shoulder, his voice tight and determined. "Their day will come. Soon, Alex. I promise you."

They spent hours rehearsing Alex's legend, his fake biography, its details supplied by Cassandra. Ehud asked him the same questions again and again until the answers came automatically. He was Jozsef Zenta, forty-eight, born in Szeged, southern Hungary. He had a genuine identity number, tax number and address card. He was a waiter, divorced. He liked to cook, eat and drink and go fishing on the river Tisza. He was grey-haired, overweight, wore glasses and walked with a mild stoop. A make-up artist came in to dye Alex's hair and fit a fake moustache. A prosthetics expert fitted him with a rubber stomach. His long eyelashes were trimmed. He had brown contact lenses and removable cheek implants to make his face look fatter and rounder. Lifts in his shoes altered his posture, making him lean forward slightly. An optician brought a selection of low diopter glasses that would not alter his eye-sight too much.

"By the way, what do you think of the Hunkalffy government?" Ehud asked.

"It's part of a conspiracy to establish economic hegemony through puppet governments."

Ehud drummed his fingers on the table. "Economic hegemony and puppet governments. Is that what they are talking about in Szeged?"

Alex blushed. "Well, between you and me, this lot are just as bad as the last one, ain't they. All they do is line their own pockets and steal as much as they can. Still that's what politics is about isn't it? Got to look after yourself and your family, that's the most important – whoever wins it won't make any difference," he said, blurring his words and running them together.

"OK. Walk please," instructed Ehud.

Alex strolled across the room, confident and alert, taking in his surroundings.

"No. Slump a little. Act the part."

Alex curved his shoulders and shuffled slightly. "Better," said Ehud.

At the end of the day Alex looked in the bathroom mirror. A grey-haired, overweight middle-aged man, with old-fashioned tortoiseshell glasses and bad posture, stared back.

"*Tov*. There's one thing that will help you," said Ehud.

"What?"

"Psychology. People see what they expect. You'll see tomorrow. We are going to a funeral."

"Whose?" asked Alex.

"Yours, habibi," said Ehud, smiling broadly as he slapped Alex on his back.

## TWENTY-FIVE

Bandi Polgar stood on the roof of the Art-Deco apartment block on the corner of Kossuth Lajos Street and Ferenciek Square and studied the streets below with a practised eye. The Hotel Savoy, on the other side of the road, was built on a corner and occupied half a city block. The famous corner café, on the ground floor, looked out onto Kossuth Lajos Street and Ferenciek Square. The Gendarmes had erected three lines of fences to seal off the area. The first, in front of the pavement, stretched around the hotel's two sides. The second line, forty metres away, ran parallel with the first. A single television crew from the state channel, Gendarmes and security guards milled around in the empty space in the middle.

A third set of fences sealed off Kossuth Lajos Street from the north, Free Press Street, which led to the Elizabeth Bridge from the south, and all the side streets. Gendarmes controlled the checkpoints in each cordon. The crossroads, usually one of the city's busiest intersections, was now eerily empty and quiet. The fences were made of sections, twelve feet high and ten feet wide, built of grey metal rods welded to a steel frame. They had wide feet, long sliders on the right side and metal sleeves on the left. The international press milled around in the area between the second and third cordon. Bandi spotted CNN and BBC camera crews. The journalists wore green vests marked 'Press' and many carried helmets and gas-masks. A tall American photographer was even wearing a flak jacket. Smart guy, he thought to himself. If all went well, they were about to get the story of a lifetime. Either way, it was going to be a night to remember.

It was 7.00pm, a chilly winter evening, with a sharp breeze blowing in from the Danube. Thankfully, it was dry. The roof had an excellent view. Large crowds were pouring down Kossuth Lajos Street and up Free Press Street and the side streets – all to be blocked by the fences and Gendarmes. The Elizabeth Bridge was so jammed with protestors no traffic could get through. So far the crowd's mood was spirited but determined. They waved excitedly at the helicopter circling overhead. The fences were bedecked with Hungarian flags, ribbons and flowers. Bandi rested his mobile telephone on the balcony railing. He took numerous pictures and uploaded them to a secure photo-sharing website.

He lit a cigarette while he waited for confirmation that the pictures had arrived. All he wanted nowadays was a quiet life, to run his chain of non-stop flower shops. But fate, it seemed, kept conspiring against him. Bandi was a powerfully-built ethnic Hungarian from Vukovar in Croatia, with wiry red hair, strong features and unusually large hands. Back in 1991, he had fought in the Croatian army trying to hold his hometown against the invading Serbs, escaping with minutes to spare before it fell. After further service in Croatia and Bosnia, he then went AWOL, smuggling his fiery Serbian wife Vesna and their three children across the border into Hungary and applying for refugee status. Bandi's military experience made him of special interest. After two weeks of debriefing, all five were made Hungarian citizens. He received a substantial soft 'loan' to start his business and buy a house. There was a price, the glamorous blonde female official at the concrete office block on Falk Miksa Street had explained: every now and then Bandi would be available for 'special assignments'. If not, he could return to the front. Bandi paid willingly.

His last mission was in Belgrade in October 2000. If Slobodan Milošević was to be overthrown by the CIA, MI6 and their new Serbian 'friends', then Budapest needed to know as much as possible. When, after several attempts, the Belgrade crowd had successfully stormed the Parliament, Bandi was in the first wave. He still had a crooked nose and scar on his left eyebrow to prove it. Many valuable lessons about urban street fighting had been learnt that day. He drew deeply on his cigarette and watched, alert now, as a paunchy, middle-aged man in a light brown overcoat walked towards the first Gendarmerie checkpoint. If he got through and made it inside the Savoy he would probably last two hours, perhaps longer if he was lucky, according to their gaming scenarios. Bandi wished him well, whoever he was, for as far as he could judge it was little better than a suicide mission. Maybe not, he hoped, if the plans worked. The Gendarmes' security looked tough and efficient. But so was his team.

\* \* \*

Alex waited for the denunciations, the shrieks of outrage, as he walked towards the checkpoint. His heart thumped and he wiped his hands on the thin raincoat Ehud had given him. "Him, officer, that one over there," someone would surely scream, "He's wearing a disguise. A spy! An infiltrator!" He waited for the Gendarmes to rush over and club him to the ground, pull off his moustache, rip open his shirt. He felt someone tap him lightly on the shoulder. Not yet, please, he said to himself, not yet, I haven't even got inside the hotel. He turned around.

"Jozsef?" Natasha asked tentatively. "We met at the funeral. Alex's funeral. I'm . . . I was his girlfriend, I suppose."

He smiled shyly and tried not to stare. She looked more desirable than ever. She was wearing her Afghan coat, jeans and knee-high boots, with a wide scarf wrapped around her head. Sadness had etched a stark beauty on her face. Guilt and longing churned inside him. "*My* girlfriend," he wanted to shout, and grab her by the hand, tell her everything, and flee from Budapest as far and as fast as possible. The funeral, at the Jewish cemetery, had been mercifully brief. Peter Feher, David Jones, Mubarak, Isabelle Balassy, Natasha, Kitty, Edina, Ronald Worthington and several other former *Budapest News* staffers had all attended. Ronald and David had delivered a rather touching eulogy. Alex had gone with Ehud, who had warned him it would be difficult and unsettling but was absolutely necessary. Alex had to believe he was Jozsef Zenta, for if he didn't nobody else would. Shut down your emotions, instructed Ehud, as they walked in. He tried, but he had never imagined how hard it would be to watch his friends mourning his death when he was alive and well, and standing just a few yards away. And how wretched he would feel.

Ehud had insisted that he introduce himself to everybody as an old friend of Alex's. The first one will be the most difficult, Ehud told him, and then it will be easier. Don't worry, he murmured deadpan, everyone thinks you're dead. Alex had practised speaking in a hoarse whisper, with a lisp, to disguise his voice, using lots of street slang. He said hallo to Kitty first, excusing himself with a long-winded explanation about his sore throat. Ehud was right. She and the other mourners were polite and friendly, but not overly interested in the chubby, nondescript man from Szeged. It worked, although when he shook hands with Natasha he felt himself blush bright red as he rambled on about his bad throat. She smiled kindly, which only made him feel worse. After the prayers Peter Feher had invited him to join everyone at the Margaret Patisserie, where he had arranged a private room. Alex declined. Peter had winked at him.

Alex said: "Yes, I remember, of course. You're also a reporter."

"It's a big story today. What are you doing here?" she asked, lighting a cigarette.

"I'm a waiter. I'm working in the hotel tonight," he said hoarsely, gesturing at the Savoy.

Natasha blew a plume of smoke to one side. "You shouldn't be working if you're still sick."

"I know, but I need the money." Alex's heart thumped even faster and he bit his lip. The best disguise, the most practised legend, he knew, was meagre defence against a woman's intuition.

"Will you do something for me, Jozsef, when you have finished work?" Natasha asked.

He smiled uncertainly.

"Call me please. I'd love to know what happened inside, with all those important people."

"Gladly. It was nice to see you again," he said, walking off.

"Jozsef!" Natasha called.

He turned back, and looked at her questioningly. She handed him a card. "How can you call me if you don't know my number? Here it is."

\*　\*　\*

Bandi watched the man in the light brown overcoat present his papers, pass through the two Gendarme checkpoints and walk towards the Savoy's entrance. It looked like he was in. Time to go to work. Bandi's toughest guys were waiting in a safe house, and dozens more were spread out in the streams of protestors converging on the Savoy from all directions. His team was far outnumbered by the Gendarmes, but would hopefully soon be leading something unstoppable: the crowd. Each of his boys carried a mobile telephone loaded with maps, GPS, still and video cameras. The handsets automatically mashed-up the photographs and video clips they uploaded with a street map. A button on the map marked each upload which, when clicked, opened it up. Information was everything when fighting for control of the streets. His teams could all report vital tactical developments to each other in real time.

The handsets were also linked to a live video feed from the city's CCTV network. Everything ran through a secure satellite connection, linked to a central control room somewhere downtown. Quite who was controlling that he didn't know. That information, a slim American in a blue button-down shirt, had told him, was "above his pay grade". Bandi flicked rapidly through the camera locations: Kossuth Lajos Street, Free Press Street, the Elizabeth Bridge and both sides of Ferenciek Square all showed a steady flow of protestors heading towards the Savoy crossroads. His handset buzzed twice. The first was confirmation that his photographs had been successfully uploaded, the second that a 'blogbeep' had arrived. Blogbeeps were sent through a micro-blogging service that simultaneously uploaded messages of up to 150 characters to a linked group. It said: "Gendarmes reinforcing on Petofi Sandor," a street that led onto Ferenciek Square. Bandi tapped out: "We are on," and pressed send.

The telephone buzzed again. He opened the photograph website and clicked on a shot of two Gendarmerie vans on Petofi Sandor Street. Gendarmes milled around, dressed in full body armour, carrying heavy plastic shields. Bandi's pictures of the crowds, the fences and the Gendarmerie checkpoints, the weakest link in their lines, were already uploaded. Another photograph appeared, of two dozen motorcyclists, sitting on their motorbikes, in a square not far from Kossuth Lajos Street. They were drinking and shouting at passersby. Good, thought Bandi, we've been waiting for you.

*　*　*

Alex walked into the Savoy's entrance. So far, so good, Jozsef, he thought. Meeting Natasha had been as unexpected as it was unsettling. But he couldn't allow himself to think about her now. The important thing was that he was inside. The Gendarmes had checked and double-checked his documents, but they had worked. The Savoy's black and grey marble lobby, with its Art Nouveau lamps and deep leather armchairs, was usually crowded with guests and hotel staff. Tonight it was hushed and tense. The reception staff had been replaced by Volkstern Corporation security in black uniforms.

A guard holding a clipboard barred his way. "You are?" he demanded.

"Jozsef Zenta," replied Alex, handing his papers over again. "I'm a waiter for the dinner. Last minute substitute, someone got sick. It's all arranged with Istvan Nagy, the dining manager."

"Empty your pockets and walk through this, slowly, then stand here," said the security guard, ushering Alex through a metal detector as he looked at the papers. The machine whined as the guard checked Alex's papers. Alex reached into his jacket.

"*No! Put your hands up!*" shouted the guard. More security staff appeared, looking at him menacingly. Alex began to sweat. "It's just a few coins," he said, breathing hard. The guard reached into his pocket and took out some small change.

The guard ran a handheld metal detector over Alex's front and back, and up and down his arms and legs. It remained silent. He

280

pulled out a small device, the size of a handheld radio, from his pocket. He waved the device over Alex. It stayed silent. Nodding, he thoroughly frisked Alex, checking every limb, his armpits and groin. His hands quickly skated over Alex's stomach. He looked puzzled, and then began poking and kneading. Alex squirmed in protest. The guard's fingers felt like gun barrels.

"Shirt off," he grunted.

"Pardon?" asked Alex.

"Are you deaf? Take your shirt off."

The guard looked at the tightly-strapped corset that was wrapped around the false stomach.

"I've got a hernia, you know. Do you want me to take this off as well?" asked Alex, indignantly, pointing at the corset. He looked at his watch. "I'm supposed to start serving in a few minutes. Or shall I tell them that I'll be late?"

The guard handed his papers back and waved him on disdainfully. "OK fatso, get to work."

\*　\*　\*

Alex, Istvan Nagy and five other waiters lined up outside the entrance to the Presidential suite. Two more armed guards frisked them, before ushering them through another metal detector, and finally into the dining room. The Beidermeyer furniture had been waxed and polished. Dim light-bulbs glowed in the crystal chandelier. A table had been set for sixteen, with solid silver cutlery, crystal wine and water glasses and antique porcelain place settings. Berlin cabaret music from the 1930s played in the background. The air was already filling with cigar smoke. Alex helped the other waiters quickly set up the bar in the corner, and poured wine, schnapps and champagne into glasses. He stepped out and circulated with his tray of drinks.

The guests drifted in; fourteen men and two women. The youngest looked to be in his late forties, the oldest, a pensioner in a wheelchair. Hrkna was there, together with Malinanescu, Daintner, Hunkalffy and Sanzlermann. All as sleek as seals, thought

Alex, shiny, prosperous and satisfied, as though the world was theirs by right. They talked in low voices, with the easy arrogance of those whose wishes are always met, and quickly. Dieter Klindern chatted animatedly with the President of the Volkstern Corporation, Sylvie Krieghaufner. Krieghaufner was a well-preserved blue-eyed ash-blonde of a certain age, dressed in a shimmering black silk dress. She was smoking a long, slim panatela. The skin above her cheek-bones was drawn unnaturally tight, Alex noticed. Her forehead was virtually unlined and her lips too large for her narrow, bony face, which gave her a rather equine look.

Malinanescu walked over and introduced himself to Krieghaufner, bowing low and kissing her hand. Klindern looked on, with an expression of amused condescension. A petite, elderly lady stood slightly aside from the others, watching carefully as she sipped a glass of mineral water. She was dressed in an old-fashioned green tweed jacket and skirt, her hair wound tight in a bun.

Krieghaufner caught Alex observing them and nudged Klindern, muttering something that made him laugh. Both looked at Alex. He blushed and turned away. He tried unobtrusively to eavesdrop on the conversations as he circulated, without much success. Once he had served the drinks he could hardly stand there listening. He heard the words "Czigex", and "the Gypsy problem," but the two silver-haired men with loud voices were on the other side of the room. "Who would have thought the Jews would turn out to be such fighters," another proclaimed. Otherwise it was scraps and snippets: names of Swiss banks, newspapers and television stations recently acquired and politicians now declared to be 'good friends of ours' prompting a quip from Sylvie Krieghaufner that "so they should be, they cost enough".

For a man who might soon be President of Europe, Sanzlermann did not look very happy, Alex thought. And where was the much-vaunted chemistry between him and the Hungarian Prime Minister? The two men seemed to be doing everything to avoid each other, and could barely conceal their mutual distaste, sitting far apart, at opposite ends of the table. The talk moved on to ski resorts, European politics, the last U.S. Presidential election. The dinner passed quickly. Goose liver followed by beef tenderloin with roast potatoes, then dessert – pancakes with flaming brandy. Alex lit the hot spirit, as Nagy poured it over the line of plates before each was presented. The first tot of brandy ignited with a whoomp. He barely jumped back in time so that his fake moustache was not set on fire. The grey-haired lady ate little, and waved away dessert.

Alex looked up to see Reinhard Daintner watching him. Daintner worried him. Alex had met him two years ago, when he had interviewed Sanzlermann as a rising star of Austrian politics. He knew Daintner was extremely intelligent and those pale eyes caught everything. Did he remember him? Or even know? Of course not, Alex told himself. How could he? It was a ridiculous idea. Focus on the task at hand.

Once the plates were cleared, the waiters were dismissed. The doors were closed, and the waiters retreated to the hotel's basement kitchen to construct a feast from food cooked but not served. They sat noisily helping themselves to the beef, goose liver and vegetables, pouring each other generous glasses from the half-drunk bottles of wine.

Istvan Nagy, a chubby, bald man, was clearly relieved that the dinner had gone smoothly. He wiped the sweat from his shiny forehead with a white napkin. "Have a glass of this," he said, handing Alex a glass of twelve year old Cabernet Sauvignon.

Alex sipped disconsolately. The rich, velvety wine was vinegar on his tongue. Here he was, in the same building as the Directorate, even serving their food, and all he had discovered was that a Prime Minister, two current Presidents, and a probable future one were having dinner with some German industrialists and a Swiss lady. He pushed a piece of beef around his plate.

The telephone rang. Istvan Nagy nodded. "Yes, Mr Daintner. Of course," he said. He looked at Alex. "Go up. They need someone to serve drinks. Daintner asked for you."

## TWENTY-SIX

All conversation stopped as Alex entered the room. A plasma screen showing an illuminated map of Europe covered half of one wall. Sylvie Krieghaufner stood by the display with a pointer.

"Is this such a good idea, Daintner?" asked Hunkalffy, pointing at Alex.

"With all due respect, Prime Minister, would you prefer to serve yourself, and the Directorate with drinks all night? We have a lot to discuss and we will be here for several hours. As long as we speak German he will not understand a word, other than 'give me another', or 'bring me'." Daintner turned to Alex. "*Nicht wahr?*"

"*Bitte? Ich verstehe nicht,*" said Alex, looking worriedly at Daintner.

Daintner waved Alex away. Alex walked over to the bar, and began filling glasses. His skin tingled with anticipation. He was in. He was about to find out the Directorate's plans. The question was, how would he get out? He couldn't imagine that they would let him walk out of the front door. He could only hope that Ehud, Cassandra and the other 'serious people' involved had planned for that. Meanwhile, *be a waiter!* He removed dirty glasses, topped up half-full ones and replaced full ashtrays with empty ones.

Sylvie Krieghaufner resumed her presentation. "The growth of satellite television and the internet has allowed our control of public opinion to evolve far faster than we had anticipated. Acceptance of European integration, and the dissolution of sovereignty, have provided economic opportunities of which our predecessors could never have dreamt. Voters wish to believe they are making independent choices. And we wish them to believe that too. Especially as we control the Euro-sceptics. These expensive gentlemen for example," she said, tapping the screen.

The screen showed faces of well known Euro-sceptic MPs in France, Germany and Britain.

She stopped for a moment and drank from a glass of water. A new map highlighted eastern Europe. "Let me return to the area where we have recently concentrated most efforts: the post-communist countries. There we have enjoyed remarkable success. Both governments and private owners have queued up to sell historic newspapers and publishing houses for a pittance. Where the staff have proved resistant to the new European reality, the publication has been closed. Governments have placed no restrictions in our setting up private television stations. We believe we have found the perfect environment for the synergy of our business and political interests."

Alex watched discreetly from the bar, trying to memorise as much as he could. Krieghaufner touched the screen again. "And finally a picture of our holdings." The regional map returned. "White are newspapers, blue, radio stations, red, television." A sea of multi-coloured lights pulsed. There was barely a centimetre of free space. "The Volkstern Corporation owns over eighty per cent of newspapers, local and national television stations, in these countries," she continued as the lights pulsed. Flushed and excited, Krieghaufner sat down to handshakes and congratulations.

The quiet was broken by the steady tapping of a pen on a wine glass. The lady in the tweed suit looked down at her notes. "Frau Krieghaufner, it does not demand much imagination to purchase some ramshackle newspapers and television stations. Especially when the funds are provided for you. We in Zurich were promised far more than this for our investment."

Klindern quickly interjected, his voice emollient. "And you will have it, Frau Schmidt. The Directorate will soon wield economic power that until now was beyond all our imaginations."

"Explain, please," demanded Schmidt.

"We are going to take over the internet," Klindern said, as casually as he might order a second cup of coffee.

\* \* \*

Bandi watched intently from the roof as the crowd poured down the main roads and the side streets towards the Hotel Savoy. Elegant housewives from the Buda hills and their lawyer husbands marched alongside factory workers from the grim industrial districts at the end of the metro-lines; pierced and tattooed trendies from the bars of District VII linked arms with noisy football fans, while stout farmers from the countryside handed out apples and pears. An elderly lady in a bedraggled fur coat held a framed sepia photograph of a young man, inscribed 'David: 1930–1944.' Two blind sisters in their Sunday best tapped out a path with white sticks, proudly rejecting offers of help. A trio of Gypsy musicians played marching tunes on their trumpets. Stallholders were selling hot coffee, sandwiches, beer and Hungarian flags. The numbers were looking good, Bandi thought. If it carried on like this in another half an hour or so, they should reach critical mass.

The floor show artists from Sotto Voce triggered loud cheers. Three six foot tall transvestites, dressed in leather basques and lederhosen, waved rainbow flags and pouted. "Come out of the closet, Frank," shouted one, to a chorus of hoots and whistles. "And let's have some fun!" Bandi laughed out loud when his mobile telephone buzzed. The message said: "Bikers heading towards Savoy." The bikers' aim, he guessed, was to pass through the fences across Magyar Street, and roar up and down in the open area in the middle between the two cordons, taunting the protestors while protected by the Gendarmes.

"*You're* not going anywhere," he muttered to himself, as he rapidly tapped out his instructions.

\* \* \*

Schmidt raised her eyebrows. "The whole internet? How?"

Klindern smiled. "Initially, only in our current areas of operation. Firstly, some brief context. Internet search engines are the most comprehensive information resource the world has ever known, and are becoming ever faster and more efficient. They catalogue people's needs and desires, hopes and fears. In one month last year, the five leading search engines recorded almost ten billion searches. The best part is that these searches are carried out voluntarily. They record what people really want. Once collated and analysed, they will provide an unprecedented source of economic, medical, social and financial information."

Schmidt nodded. "And how do we get this information?"

Klindern stood up and tapped the plasma screen. A web browser appeared in Hungary's national colours of red, white and green. The top left column said: "kzxsearch.hu." He continued: "Stage one: the kzxsearch web browser, with a built in search engine. This is kzxsearch.hu. Each country will have its own native language browser, kzxsearch.ro for Romania, kzxsearch.de for Germany and so on. Every user of the kzxsearch browser has his own identifying number and tiny programme, called a 'cookie', built into the browser. The browser records and categorises every web search, every website and every page visited."

A picture flashed up of a good-looking, well dressed young man. "Meet Janos Horvath. A salesman, in his mid-twenties, with typical interests: girls, travel, partying, clothes and cars. The cookie records his internet habits. It co-ordinates that information with our internet service providers and kzxcompanies to provide personally targeted advertising. Kzxsearch also allows us to monitor his political activities, should he regularly visit, for example, so-called human rights or civil liberties organisations."

Klindern tapped the screen. Hungarian language advertisements, for singles holidays, cars, glamour magazines and designer clothes, each personally addressed to Janos Horvath, appeared down the right hand column. "Our initial trials have shown that personalised advertising is surprisingly effective. The mere use of someone's name breaks through the angst and loneliness of modern life. The user feels wanted, if only by advertisers."

"So now we are in the social work business. Very touching," said Schmidt sardonically. "And why will anyone use kzxsearch, rather than Yahoo or Google?"

Klindern smirked. "Because we will offer free, high-speed internet accounts on our internet service providers to anyone carrying out a minimum number of searches a month through kzxsearch. As well as recording every web site visited, the ISPs will store every email sent. The cost of this offer will comfortably be covered by the profits the Directorate's subsidiary companies will make from additional sales from the targeted advertising. We predict that in two years sixty-five per cent of internet users will sign up for a kzxsearch account. That is stage two."

A faint glimmer of a smile formed on Schmidt's mouth. "Impressive, Herr Klindern. You are thinking ahead. We appreciate that. What is stage three?"

Klindern inclined his head. "Thank you. You may be aware that computing is increasingly moving away from personal machines to the 'cloud'. Cloud computing means two things: data banks and programmes that can be operated remotely. It's the same principle as web-based email, but with word processing and spreadsheets and so on. Soon you will be able to do all your work from any computer. Actual machines are physically vulnerable. They can be stolen or break down. Even a spilt cup of coffee can be disastrous. Without back-up data is lost forever. The cloud has no such vulnerabilities. It can be accessed from anywhere, by personal computers, of course, but also by mobile telephones, PDAs, even internet-enabled watches. The physical personal computer will soon be redundant."

Schmidt scribbled rapidly in her notebook, before looking up. "And how will you take control of the this 'cloud'?"

Klindern sipped his cognac. "We will build our own. It follows automatically from stage two and kzxsearch: all data on internet users will be held centrally on our servers. We are writing new software programmes for email, word-processing, spreadsheets and so on that our subscribers will be obliged to use, which will give us full access to all their data. Memory storage technology is racing ahead. Our software developers are also working on new data mining programmes. Control of the cloud will give us a full social, political, medical and financial profile of every European Union citizen. We will know what they are writing to their boss, to their lover, how they are making money, what they are eating and drinking, what they are *thinking*." His voice rose with excitement: "We will not only know what they want, we will be able to decide it for them. *This* is the Directorate's vision: cyberspace – the ultimate *lebensraum*."

Klindern opened his mouth to continue when the sound of screeching tyres and crunching metal sounded through the room.

\* \* \*

Natasha was interviewing an elderly male protestor in a shabby suit when she heard the low rumble of motorbike engines sounding louder and louder. She quickly thanked the man, ran down Kossuth Lajos Street and sprinted up a side alley, holding her notebook. She was right. The bikers were a hundred metres away, roaring down the narrow road. Their leader, a fat man in black leather, with a long, greasy beard, was riding a low-rider vintage Harley Davidson, with chopper handle bars. A large Arrow Cross banner trailed from the bike's makeshift flagpole.

The Gendarmes were moving the fence at the top of the side street aside, to let the bikers through, when a plastic bag burst fifty yards in front of them. A puddle of treacly motor oil rapidly spread across the road, spattering the pavement and the bottom of Natasha's jeans. She looked up. A teenage Romany boy was grinning from the top floor window of the apartment block behind her. He gestured for her to move into the doorway. She stepped back. Oil bombs rained down, covering the street and pavements with a thick, greasy slick.

Motor oil, again. A memory flashed into her mind: she and Alex tipping a barrel of oil down the staircase at Kosice station. A sharp pang of longing twisted inside her. The Harley Davidson juddered as its rider tried to stop, breaking her reverie. The back wheel slid sideways. The front wheel hit the slick, instantly slaloming from left to right. The rider swore furiously as he fought for control. The oil won. The machine toppled sideways with a thunderous crunch. It scraped along the ground, its rider trapped underneath, screaming and cursing, the Arrow Cross flag entangling itself in the bike's rear wheel.

The biker behind him was riding a sports BMW. He braked hard but it was too late. His wheel touched the slick and he went down flailing. The BMW flew out in front of him and smashed through the gap in the Gendarmes' fence, it wheels spinning as it skidded across Kossuth Lajos Street. A second wave of oil bombs burst along the street, carefully spaced every few metres. One after another the bikers crashed into each other, all losing control as they hit the oil. In less than a minute half the column was down, at least twelve riders dazed or unconscious, their machines careering across the road. The riders at the rear turned round and roared off. A tough looking man on the other side of Kossuth Lajos Street picked up the BMW. He sat on the bike, revved the engine and ripped off the tattered Arrow Cross banners. The crowd cheered.

Natasha stared at the chaos, scribbling in her notebook: the toppled motorbikes, their engines screaming and whining; the shredded Arrow Cross flag; the oil-shiny street; the dazed bikers staggering back and forth, their leathers ripped and filthy; the Romany boys taunting them from the windows. She thought it was one of the finest sights she had ever seen. She took out her mobile telephone and began taking pictures of the chaos. She didn't see the man walk up behind her. She only struggled briefly as he forced the pad against her mouth.

\*　　\*　　\*

Klindern walked over to the window that overlooked the narrow alley where the bikers were crashing into each other. He stared at the pandemonium five floors down and turned to Hunkalffy, his voice tight with anger. "Prime Minister, please explain what is happening in your capital?"

"A group of provocateurs, the so-called Hungarian Freedom Movement, called a demonstration for this evening," Hunkalffy explained, looking around the table for support. Hrkna swirled the wine around his glass, examining its light and colour, Malinanescu studied his fingernails. Sanzlermann seemed transfixed by the display on the plasma screen.

Klindern beckoned Hunkalffy to the window and pointed at the crashed and broken motorbikes below. "What, exactly, is this?"

Hunkalffy paled. "You instructed me to ease the restrictions that we put in place following the bombing. I did as you said."

"I did not expect an outbreak of *anarchy*," Klindern shouted. "Get out, and take control."

The room was silent as Hunkalffy left. Klindern returned to his seat. He paused and took a sip from his cognac. "My apologies. We have talked of the future. But let me take you back to our first meeting here at the Hotel Savoy," he said, acknowledging the man in the wheelchair, who smiled in return. "The founders of the Directorate draw up a four-track strategy: the takeover of political parties and governments; the manipulation of the media; the control of national economies; and, crucially, the police and security services."

Klindern touched the plasma screen with the light-stick. The map of Europe reappeared. Croatia, Hungary, Slovakia and Romania glowed gently. "We have concentrated on these four countries, as our historical allies. Tragically, Dragomir Zorvajk cannot be here with us tonight," he continued, giving Sanzlermann a barbed look. "The Czech Republic and Poland have so far proved less eager to welcome our investments than their neighbours. But we plan a steady expansion once we have consolidated our hold on the centre. I will not now review all of our holdings, as it would take us well into tomorrow, if not the day after. Suffice to say that in each of our four key countries, in terms of controlling economic assets, political parties, and security services, we have made similar progress."

Reinhard Daintner entered, holding a pile of DVDs. He passed one to Klindern. A tiny camera was taped to each box. "Daintner has compiled the full extent of the Directorate's holdings on this disc," said Klindern, opening a box and holding the DVD between his thumb and forefinger. "It can only be used with the camera supplied. Once the disc is loaded into your computer and the camera is attached, it launches a retinal recognition programme. Each disc is numbered and specially programmed. Nobody else will be able to access your information. For your eyes only, as James Bond might say," he said, triggering polite laughs around the table.

Klindern continued. "And now, the man who, more than any other, has kept our ideals alive. SS Colonel Friedrich Vautker."

He gestured at Alex to bring over the elderly man in the wheelchair. Alex stared down at his pink bald head, and his liver-spotted hands as he wheeled him to the front of the table. He considered tipping the wheelchair over and sticking a steak-knife into his chest. He might even succeed, and live for perhaps another five or ten seconds.

Vautker waved Alex away. "In winter 1944, I had dinner in this hotel. The Russian savages were advancing across the continent. But every long dark night must surely be followed by a bright new dawn. Together with our friends in Switzerland, we laid our plans," he said, nodding at Schmidt. "Which have now come to fruition. Our greatest triumph is the introduction of the euro. We once believed war ensured financial hegemony. But now we know that peace offers the best chance for economic domination. Peace, then the erosion, and abolition, of national economic sovereignty, to be replaced by the rule of the Federal Monetary Authority. Safe in the hands of my son, Heinrich Vautker," he said, pausing as the applause rippled around the room.

"This weekend we begin our consolidation of our control of the European Union, when Frank Sanzlermann wins the first round of the Presidential election," he said, gesturing at Sanzlermann, who smiled wanly. "The techniques we have honed here will then be implemented across the continent. The 'Patriot Bond' will draw in millions of euros. When the bond fails to pay the promised interest, its collapse will be blamed on 'international speculators' and the forces of 'finance capital'. I advise you to stay away from synagogues at that time," he said, to laughter. "There will be little opposition, while Europe's attention is focused on the Immigration Liberation Army. Speaking of which, let me introduce our special guest. Daintner," he said, gesturing at the door, and snapping his fingers.

Daintner rose to open the door. A tall, dark-skinned, hawk-faced man strode in. He was dressed in an Italian silk suit and had a soldier's bearing. He looked up and down the table, smiled, and bowed to the audience. There was silence for a few seconds before a ripple of recognition passed through the room. Sanzlermann sat staring wide-eyed. Cornelius Malinanescu blinked rapidly. Dusan Hrkna stood up, waving his fist and swearing.

Vautker's voice was soothing. "Sit down, please, Mr Hrkna. I understand your anger. But sometimes the bigger picture needs to be kept obscure until the right moment. May I present the man known as 'Hasan Al-Ajnabi', leader of the Immigration Liberation Army. Mr Al-Ajnabi is a founder member of the Directorate. We have many allies in the Middle East, keen to protect their countries from the power of finance capital, and its lackeys in Washington."

Vautker gestured at Alex. "A large whisky for Mr Al-Ajnabi," he ordered. Alex tried not to stare. The ILA was run by the Directorate. The Directorate was starting a race war. Brilliant, in its way. Hunkalffy returned to the room as Alex handed Ajnabi his drink.

Klindern asked: "Are the forces of anarchy under control yet, Prime Minister?"

Hunkalffy glared at him. "So far, yes. The motorcyclists crash was a one-off incident. Of course, if you wish to completely disperse the crowd, we could implement the Tiananmen option. But that would not look very good on You Tube, would it?" he said, sarcastically.

Klindern's smile did not reach his eyes. "Attila's little joke," he said brightly.

Vautker tapped his false arm on the table. It made a dull knocking sound. "Gentlemen, please. Let us not squabble on this historic night. I will briefly outline our current situation. Some of our work remains unfinished. The Jews have survived, even prospered. Our project in Iraq was destroyed by the American blunderers, still under the control of the Jewish lobby. But our funding for Israeli universities, Jewish community centres, even Holocaust memorials," he sputtered, "has proved a most useful camouflage and brought us much intelligence. And if the Jews are – temporarily at least – out of reach, the other race-mixers are not."

He grasped the pointer and banged the plasma screen. A Gypsy settlement appeared. Barefoot children scampered in the dirt, mothers hung out washing on lines stretched between dilapidated wooden houses. "Observe, please, the filth and squalor. But soon Europe will be cleansed. Thanks to my personal initiative. The Poraymus Project. The world's first racially-profiled genetically engineered drug. The Gypsy infertility pill. Our pilot project in eastern Slovakia has already brought excellent results. Once launched across Europe, we estimate that within five years the entire Gypsy race will start to decline dramatically in numbers, before eventually dying out," he said, to applause. "You will find details on Herr Daintner's DVD."

Hunkalffy stood up. "No. This is too much." He trembled as he spoke, his hands gripping the table edge.

*He thought about the Gypsy boy every day. It was an accident, just a terrible accident.*

The applause stopped. Klindern asked: "Is there a problem, Attila?"

*The boy and the girl were standing with their mother on the street corner. The girl was beautiful; slim and elegant, like a fashion model.*

Hunkalffy swallowed hard: "A firm hand, tough laws, yes. The Gypsies are prone to criminality. They are wild, anti-social."

*He drove closer to the kerb, just to take a better look at her, but his telephone rang.*

"They must be brought under control. But to wipe them out? No, I cannot agree," Hunkalffy said, his voice growing in strength and confidence.

*The phone kept ringing. He reached down and scrabbled for his handset.*

"He cannot agree," said Klindern, faux-amazed. "Then what did you think we were doing in Slovakia, Attila? Running a trial of a fertility drug?" he said, triggering more laughter.

"I didn't know." Hunkalffy paused and looked around the room. "I am Hungarian, Prime Minister of this country."

*The car's front wheel hit the pavement and bounced forward.*

Hunkalffy stood straighter. "And I am part Gypsy. My grandmother was a Romany."

*The girl jumped out of the way but the car ploughed into the boy and his mother. They flew up over the bonnet, into the windscreen.*

Klindern looked concerned. "Attila, sit down," he said, his voice conciliatory. "It's been a long day. But it's almost over. Relax. Have another drink."

Hunkalffy shook his head, staring straight ahead.

*The glass shattered. The car spun out of control and crashed into a lamp post.*

Klindern reached under the table. He pulled out a pistol with a long, narrow silencer.

Hunkalffy stood transfixed.

*He reversed back into the road. The boy and his mother lay on the pavement.*

Hunkalffy looked at the silencer. Klindern pointed the gun at him.

*He panicked and drove away, tyres screeching.*

Klindern fired three times, the silenced pistol snapping like a children's cap gun.

Hunkalffy slammed backwards against the wall, his shirt flooding crimson.

*He wanted to visit them in hospital, to say he was sorry, to try and make amends.*

The blood bubbled up in Hunkalffy's mouth, running down his jaw. He tried to wipe his face.

*They lay so still on the pavement. He was so sorry.*

He shuddered, and died.

## TWENTY-SEVEN

Bandi nervously lit another cigarette, took a long drag and crushed it out on the roof. He could read a crowd like others read a newspaper and the numbers weren't there yet. The weather had taken a turn for the worse. A biting wind was blowing in from the river, bringing a freezing, driving rain. He picked up his telephone and flicked through the video feed links. He looked at the demonstrators: the exhilaration was fading, the energy dissipating. Some of the protestors were already drifting off. The stallholders selling drinks and snacks were packing up. Several journalists had retreated back to their vans and cars.

He looked closer as he saw several familiar faces walking down Kossuth Lajos Street. He zoomed in. Yes, it was her – the woman who had recruited him at the Falk Miksa Street office, the good looking, well-dressed blonde, wearing a fur coat. She was with two men. One was elderly, and the other. . . . could it be? He zoomed in tighter. He was right, she was holding hands with the Arab guy who had given him his soft loan, 50,000 euros in cash. The Arab was talking to the pretty English redhead Bandi had met once at the Security Service headquarters. But two spies, an old guy and a money-changer weren't enough.

His telephone rang. An American voice said: "Your call, buddy."

Bandi replied: "Ten minutes."

The American said: "Two. Or we shut this thing down."

Bandi said: "Five." He ran back into the building and sprinted down the stairs.

\* \* \*

Klindern pointed the pistol at Alex. "It's over. Come here."

Alex's heart pounded as he walked across the room, trying to remember the moves Ehud had taught him. He quickly looked around as he walked over to Klindern. No help, obviously, but would they intervene? Sanzlermann's hand shook as he poured a large cognac. Hrkna looked unconcerned and lit a cigar. Krieghaufner and Schmidt observed him with amused interest, as though they were watching the premiere of a much acclaimed new play. Al-Ajnabi's eyes glowed with hate.

Klindern ripped off the fake moustache. "Alex Farkas. Not so dead after all, it seems." He held the moustache up to the light. "Did you really think that this," he sneered, "would fool us?"

Alex shrugged, inching towards Klindern.

"Poor Attila. One Gypsy less, at least," Klindern said, keeping the pistol trained on him.

"He died bravely," said Alex, moving closer.

Klindern laughed cynically. "Dying bravely. The Hungarian national sport." He flicked the fake moustache onto Hunkalffy's body, watching it land in a pool of blood.

Alex grabbed the pistol.

He yanked it to the right and forced it upwards hard and fast. He twisted Klindern's hand backward, pushing as high as he could.

The first bullet hit the chandelier, sending shards of crystal flying around the room. The guests dived onto the floor, Malinanescu barging Schmidt aside as he scrabbled under the table. The gun fired again and again, the bullets smashing into the chandelier and the ceiling. Glass and plaster dust rained down. Klindern fought hard for control, punching Alex repeatedly in his chest and stomach. A glancing blow caught Alex on the side of his head. The pain fuelled his fury. He wrenched the pistol sideways with all his strength.

Klindern's fingers snapped.

He let go of the gun and staggered backwards. Alex slid forward and kicked him rapidly and repeatedly in the groin. Klindern threw up and collapsed, writhing on the floor in a puddle of his half-digested dinner. The reek of vomit and cordite fumes filled the room. Alex grabbed Klindern's right arm. He turned it around, elbow facing down, and slammed it over his knee. It broke with a sound like a twig snapping. Klindern turned white and fainted.

Alex jumped up, covering the room with the pistol. Only Al-Ajnabi still sat at the table, drinking his whisky.

Vautker rolled his wheelchair towards Alex. "Finally, you fight."

Alex pointed the gun at Vautker.

"*Bitte*, shoot," said Vautker. "The magazine holds eight bullets. Three for Herr Hunkalffy, and five in the wall and ceiling. Of course, I may have miscounted."

Alex pointed the gun at him and pulled the trigger. It clicked on an empty chamber.

\*    \*    \*

The men looked up as Bandi walked into the cramped apartment, their faces full of anticipation. They laughingly called themselves 'The Dirty Dozen', although Bandi thought of them as twelve Trojan Horses. After sixteen hours of waiting the room stank of bodies and sweat. Its stale air was thick with cigarette smoke, the floor carpeted with junk food wrappers and crushed drink cans. A television flickered in the corner, a naked woman writhing on its screen. The flat was located on the third floor of an apartment block on Kossuth Lajos Street facing the Savoy. Its entrance was blocked off by the first line of security fences. The plan was for Bandi's guys to break out and take down the two lines of fences, while the protestors, urged on by his men on the other side, smashed through the Gendarmes' cordons. They would all then meet up in the middle.

Bandi walked over and pulled out the television plug. The screen went black.

He said: "Party time."

\*    \*    \*

Two security guards frogmarched Alex out of the dining room, his feet scraping along the floor, his wrists handcuffed together. He squirmed as one pressed the muzzle of a pistol into his spine. The lift travelled down into the hotel storage room. The revelry of the other waiters was clearly audible through an open door, just ten yards away. The security guard pressed the pistol barrel harder into his back. "Don't even think about it," he hissed.

They pushed him into a large windowless room and stood holding him. The door opened. Daintner pushed Vautker forward in his wheelchair.

Vautker pointed a Luger pistol at Alex. "This one is loaded." He laughed, a dry cackling sound. "The only question was how long we would allow your pathetic charade to continue. How poignant. Just as he uncovers the dastardly conspiracy, the heroic reporter is tragically killed."

He nodded at the security guards. One gripped Alex's arms, his fingers digging into his wound. The other ripped Alex's shirt open, sending the buttons flying.

"Take it off," Vautker snapped, gesturing at Alex's corset. The guards ripped it off leaving the false stomach sagging pathetically on its straps. Vautker wheeled himself up to Alex and slowly dug the barrel of the Luger into his wounded arm. "Who are you working for?" he asked softly.

"Me. There's only me," said Alex, wincing from the pressure of the pistol.

Vautker wheeled himself backwards and ripped the bandage from Alex's arm. He grabbed his pistol by the barrel, and slammed the butt into the wound. It burst open and blood ran down Alex's arm. The pain was excruciating.

Vautker smiled. "You will talk. Everyone does, in the end."

"Fuck you," said Alex, panting as he sagged against the guards.

Vautker clicked his fingers, and Daintner opened the door. Two more guards appeared, dragging in Istvan Nagy, his hands tied behind him, his eyes wide with fear.

"I don't understand. I don't want to die," pleaded Nagy. "This is nothing to do with me."

"I believe you. You are an innocent, caught up in events beyond your control."

"Yes, yes," gasped Nagy, his eyes full of hope.

"Release him," snapped Vautker.

Nagy stood shakily in front of Vautker. Vautker shot him once in the head. The boom of the gun filled the room. Nagy's skull burst. Blood, bone and brains flew across the room and he toppled backwards.

Alex fought down the bile rising inside him. "Why did you kill him? He was just a waiter."

"I did not kill him." Vautker said, smirking. "You did."

\* \* \*

Bandi and his men sprinted out of the apartment block and spread out along the pavement between the buildings and the first security fence. Each wore a gasmask, a kevlar helmet and vest, and carried several metal cylinders, the size of cola cans. Several carried thick crowbars, four foot long. They split into three squads, two of three and one of six.

The Gendarmes saw immediately what was happening, radioed for assistance, and began running towards Bandi's men. The two groups of three raced left and right towards the Gendarmes. The squad of six jammed their crowbars under the fences and pulled down hard.

Bandi shouted: "Now!"

The two squads of three hurled their stun grenades at the Gendarmes, dropping to their knees and covering their ears with their hands. The fences slid upwards, metal arms shrieking against the sleeves. The stun grenades exploded with a deafening bang and flash. The journalists and camera crews began running through the empty intersection, towards the noise.

\* \* \*

Vautker turned to the security guards. "Leave us now. Undo his handcuffs. Give him something for his arm. I don't want him to bleed to death yet." He kept his pistol trained on Alex as a guard handed him a napkin. "You have some courage and initiative. Like your grandfather."

Alex wrapped the cloth around his arm. "My grandfather? What has he got to do with this?"

"Everything. If it were not for him, you would not be here. I knew your grandfather. Better than he realised. He used to serve me coffee here."

Vautker tapped his left arm. "I left the original outside Kharkov. Your grandfather was always solicitous. A most resourceful man." He sounded almost wistful. "I don't know who he thought he was fooling with those papers. Those wastrels in the Arrow Cross, I suppose."

Alex stared at Vautker. "You knew who he was. Why didn't you send him to the camps?"

He shrugged. "What for? By then one more dead or alive did not matter. I always suspected he had discovered something at the dinner. Some papers went missing and were never found. But poor Miklos, who could he tell? The AVO? The KGB? What would he say? That the Fourth Reich would achieve what the Third failed to? They would lock him up and throw away the key. I found it amusing that he was safe behind the Iron Curtain with a dreadful secret that he could share with nobody. We were safe until 1989, and by then everything was in place."

Vautker stared into space. "I was not in favour of killing your grandfather. He was a witness, one of the last left. A link to the past. He saw first hand how our dreams were born, and how they are now becoming reality. I am sorry that I ever mentioned his name. But those hotheads around Hunkalffy and Sanzlermann would not listen."

Alex pressed the cloth against his arm. "The war ended in 1945. You lost. We won."

Vautker laughed and waved the gun at Alex. "How naive you are. You did not win. Money won. Money always wins. We invaded Poland on Ford trucks. American punch cards helped us solve the Jewish problem. The war was a sideshow, nothing more. Even while our soldiers were killing each other we worked with British bankers in Switzerland, meeting our international financial obligations, paying our debts. The most important thing is to keep the money moving. How did we fund those payments? By looting the banks of the countries we captured. As the Swiss say, 'Gold has no race.' What a beautiful system. *Kapital über Alles.*"

Vautker sat up straight, his eyes shining. "As for now, could we launch the Poraymus project alone? Do you really believe that in their hearts, Europe's leaders don't support us? That they don't approve? Pick up any newspaper. In Italy Gypsy girls drown on the beach and they carry on sunbathing and eating salami, a few metres from their corpses. The Czechs, the Slovaks, the Hungarians have been sterilising their Gypsies for years. The women have Caesarean sections. When they wake up they find the doctors took the baby out and everything else as well. The Poraymus Project is nothing new. It's just more humane and efficient."

Vautker smiled with pleasure, reciting as though reading from a book. "Let us imagine a continent at peace, freed of its barriers and obstacles, where history and geography are finally reconciled. Who said that?" he demanded.

"I don't know," said Alex. Vautker was, he estimated, about two metres away.

"Valéry Giscard d'Estaing, drafter of the EU's constitution. Now try this ... 'It is not very intelligent to imagine that in such a cramped house like that of Europe, a community of peoples can maintain different legal systems and different concepts of law for long'."

"I have no idea," said Alex. He could leap onto the wheelchair and try to grab the gun. Vautker could not walk. But Daintner was fit and mobile. And how would he get out of the hotel? But anything was better than dying down here.

Vautker smiled. "Adolf Hitler. His dream: one continent, one government, one legal system, one unit of currency. And now it's about to be realised."

The door opened and Alex's plan evaporated. A security guard walked in, carrying a slim young woman in an Afghan coat. She was unconscious, her hands tied behind her back.

\* \* \*

The stun grenades burst open with a sharp crack. The Gendarmes fell back, temporarily blinded and deafened, staggering in confusion. Bandi gripped the fence as his men levered it up. It creaked, groaned, rose until the arms slipped out of their sleeves, and fell back with a crash. Bandi and his team raced through the gap. They now faced the second line of fences. They had, he reckoned, about thirty seconds to bring it down before the Gendarmes arrived.

The men moved seamlessly into formation. The squad of six sprinted up to the second line of fences and jammed their crowbars underneath, while two groups of three covered the spaces to the side, stun grenades at the ready. The Gendarmes gathered fifty yards away, wary now of the stun grenades. The fences rose, slid back, and rose again. The Gendarmes loaded their rubber bullet guns, knelt and took aim.

Aniko Kovacs and the cameraman ran towards Bandi. She thrust a microphone in his face. He saw out of the corner of his eye a Gendarme marksman kneel and take aim at him.

"Are we live?" he asked.

She was almost speechless with excitement. "Yes. Who are you?"

Bandi lifted the gas mask from his mouth to speak: "Patriots."

The rubber bullet bounced off his helmet, knocking him sideways. Kovacs reeled back as a rubber bullet bounced off the ground and hit her shoulder. She recovered, stood her ground and continued broadcasting: "We are live here at the Savoy where an unknown group of men is trying to bring down the fences around the hotel. The crowd is advancing from four directions. The Gendarmes are firing tear gas and rubber bullets. The people are taking control of the streets."

Bandi righted himself and looked over at the cordon. Rubber bullets bounced off the bars as it rose, slipped, rose again and toppled backwards into the empty space. The adrenalin pumped. The familiar rush kicked in. Bandi sprinted to the gap in the second fence, shouting "Forward, forward," Kovacs doggedly running after him.

Bandi's team followed him into the vast empty space at the crossroads of the four main roads. CNN and the BBC crews raced towards them, as rubber bullets pinged off the buildings. Bandi's men quickly split into formation, as the six in the middle attacked the fence that blocked off Kossuth Lajos Street. The crowd on the other side stood transfixed and then surged forward. Bandi could see his guys weaving through the protestors to get to the fence. The protestors quickly grasped what was happening and began to lift the metal fence higher and higher.

Two squads of Gendarmes advanced. Bandi's two teams of three hurled their stun grenades. The fence rose and toppled back towards the crowd. The line was breached but the Gendarmes stood their ground. They lifted their riot shields and deflected the stun grenades into the crowd. The flashes were blinding, the noise thunderous in the crowded space. Screams and shouts of fear and pain resounded. The protestors ran in all directions.

The first group of Gendarmes dropped to their knees, aimed and fired steady bursts of rubber bullets at Bandi's men. The second launched salvo after salvo of tear gas into the crowd. Bandi's men charged forward at the Gendarmes, weaving from side to side as the bullets bounced off their kevlar vests and helmets. The street resounded with the bang of the stun grenades, the crack of the rubber bullets and the shouts and screams of the crowd. A dense cloud of tear gas rolled down towards the Danube.

\*   \*   \*

Vautker laughed and pointed his pistol at Natasha. She lay on the ground on her side, unconscious, breathing steadily. "Does she know about Azra? Azra Mehmedovic, taken to her death, right in front of your eyes, with your pockets full of dollars, and your UN press card. Yes, we know all about Azra, and your pathetic emails to her family, offering them money. She risked her life for you. All your promises to get her out, lies. More empty words in a life built on them. But they didn't want your blood money, did they? Did you think of Azra, that night when you got your prize? I am sure you got a pay rise. Was it worth it? Is this worth it?" he asked, waving his foot at Nagy's body.

Alex felt an old, familiar shame. "I did my job. I reported what I saw. Reporters cannot get involved," he said, knowing how hollow the words sounded.

Vautker wheeled himself closer to Alex.

"You were just doing your job. Some of my friends tried that defence. It didn't work then and doesn't work now. What are you doing here, if you cannot get involved?" he sneered.

Daintner lit a cigarette. Vautker coughed as the smoke drifted over him. "Daintner, you know I cannot bear cigarette smoke. And this is hardly the time for cigars."

"My sincere apologies, sir," he said, crushing the cigarette out on the floor. Daintner handed him a folded linen napkin.

Vautker opened the napkin with one hand, wiped his mouth and continued. "Tell me who you are working for. Or I will kill her," he said, pointing the gun at Natasha.

Alex stared at Vautker. "Nobody. I was working alone," he panted.

"I warned you," said Vautker. He pointed the Luger at Natasha.

\*     \*     \*

Bandi rapidly processed the scene of chaos, his breath wheezing through his gas mask. The crowd was pouring down Kossuth Lajos Street through the gap in the fences and surging forward from the Elizabeth Bridge. But it was splitting into clusters, some fleeing from the violence towards the river, others retreating behind the colonnade on Kossuth Lajos Street. The Gendarmes were trying to close the gaps in the first two lines of fences. The air was thick with the stench of tear gas. The street filled with the sound of retching and coughing. The football fans smashed open a fire hydrant. Water erupted, and the protestors washed the tear gas from their faces as it cascaded down. The Gendarmes formed a line across the entrance of the hotel, arms linked, in front of the concrete barricades. Bandi watched a tall, heavily built priest with a wet cloth wrapped around his face pick up a can of tear-gas which had landed on the Sotto Voce float. He leaned back with an athlete's poise and hurled it at the line of Gendarmes. It landed right in the middle, spinning tear gas in every direction and triggering loud cheers.

Bandi's mobile telephone buzzed. Reinforcements were coming. And more.

\*　\*　\*

The shot was thunderous in the small room. The bullet smashed into the wall by Natasha's foot. Vautker shouted: "That was your last chance. Next time I won't miss. Who is helping you? Who else knows about the Directorate? The Russians? The British? The Israelis?"

"Nobody. I told you. I am working alone."

"*Liar!*" screamed Vautker. "Did you think you would earn your salvation here tonight? Vindicate yourself? Azra is dead because you sat and watched. So you enter the lion's den, and reveal the villains to the world. Settle your account with your conscience, and by the way, pick up another prize along the way. A nice plan if it had worked. Except it did not. Daintner, please."

Vautker handed his gun to Daintner. "Cover him," he instructed. He wheeled himself over to where Natasha lay on the floor. He pulled out a syringe from his pocket and held it up to the light. He pushed the plunger. A thin stream of clear liquid spurted from the tip of the needle.

Vautker turned to Alex. "A muscle relaxant. KZX Pharmaceuticals own the patent. The Americans use it on Death Row. She's already unconscious. A further dose will kill her. She will suffocate. But first she will wake up and you can see her choke to death. Who is your contact?"

Alex paled. "What is to stop you from killing her anyway, if I tell you?"

"Nothing. But at least you won't have another death on your conscience. This is not a college debate, Farkas," said Vautker.

He gently inserted the needle into her arm. Natasha stirred and murmured.

"*No!*" screamed Alex.

\* \* \*

The steady chug of a diesel engine echoed down Kossuth Lajos Street. Hundreds of heads turned as one to watch the giant armoured bulldozer rumble up the centre of the road, spewing exhaust fumes in its wake. Thick, curved metal screens protected the body, the wheels and most of the cabin, except for a small gap through which the driver could see. The bulldozer lumbered up to the line of Gendarmes. They stared straight ahead. The driver tooted twice on his horn. The crowd laughed, taunting them.

\* \* \*

Alex watched Vautker's thumb move towards the plunger. "Wait. *Wait.* I'll tell you. I'll tell you everything," he said, his voice frantic. Vautker's finger hovered over the needle.

\* \* \*

The bulldozer roared forward. The Gendarmes ran in every direction. The bulldozer's giant blade slammed into the fences, pushing them aside and crushing them. It reversed, changed its angle of attack and roared forward again.

Bandi ran into the centre of Kossuth Lajos Street, urging the crowd on.

"*Forward, forward!*" he cried, as first dozens, then hundreds followed in his wake, pouring through the space between the two lines of fences. The driver revved his engine again, and the protestors cleared a path as he faced the last line of Gendarmes at the Savoy's entrance.

The Gendarmes aimed their guns at the protestors. One raised his weapon and fired repeatedly into the air. The crowd fell silent as the gunfire echoed across the streets.

The commander raised a bullhorn to his mouth. "These are live rounds, not rubber bullets. You have ten seconds to disperse, or we will open fire."

\* \* \*

Vautker turned purple and made a sound like a blocked pipe being cleared. He waved his hands, clutched his throat, and slumped forward in his wheelchair.

\* \* \*

The sound of motor exhausts echoed from four directions. Police buses smashed a path through the fences and stopped in front of the Savoy. Dozens of policemen in full body armour, carrying machine pistols and stun grenades, spilled out and formed a line in front of the Gendarmes.

The helicopter circling overhead flew in lower, the powerful under draft sending caps and hats flying across the street. Police commandos abseiled down ropes, landing in front of the Gendarmes, guns at the ready.

The Gendarmes looked at their commander. He touched his radio earpiece and listened for several seconds. He shook his head. They lowered their guns.

The crowd roared and cheered.

The Gendarmes stood aside.

The bulldozer tooted its horn and lurched forward, smashing its way through the concrete barriers at the Savoy's entrance. The crowd poured through, shouting and laughing.

\* \* \*

Daintner walked over to Natasha. Alex jumped to protect her, but Daintner waved him away. He checked her breathing, undid the bindings on her wrists and walked back to Vautker. He opened one of Vautker's eyes. It looked out, unseeing. Alex stared as Daintner checked his watch.

Daintner said: "Don't touch the handkerchief. The solution is supposed to work in two minutes, but it appears between three and four is more accurate."

Daintner picked up the syringe and stuck the needle in Vautker's arm. He pressed it down steadily until the syringe was empty. Vautker twitched several times and lay still.

"Who *are* you?" asked Alex.

"Let us say. . . ." Daintner paused. "That I am a concerned voter."

"But how did you . . . who are you working for?"

"Goodbye, Alex," said Daintner as he walked out.

\*　\*　\*

Natasha stirred. She sat up unsteadily, blinking and looking around in confusion.

"Jozsef?" she asked, leaning back against the wall, trying to get her balance.

Alex took off his glasses, walked towards her and crouched down. "No. It's me."

Natasha stared hard at him. "*Alex?* How? Am I dead?' She looked at her hands. "I can't be, because my wrists really hurt."

He shook his head. "No, you are definitely not dead."

Natasha slowly processed her surroundings, flexing her fingers. "Are you dead?"

"No," he said, smiling widely as he moved nearer to her.

She slapped him hard around the face. "Then what was I doing at your funeral?" she shouted, her eyes blazing. "*Bastard! Liar!* I cried for you. How could you do that to me?" She raised her hand again. "No. *No.* Stay away from me."

Alex caught her wrist, and pulled her towards him as she pummelled him. He held her tightly, breathing in the smell of her, his hands in her hair. The blows slowed, then stopped.

"I'm sorry," he said, after they broke apart. "I had to do it like this."

Natasha wiped her eyes, trying not to smile. "You owe me. You really owe me."

"I know."

"A joint by-line."

He nodded.

"With my name first."

Alex grinned ruefully and helped her up. They walked to the door where a large envelope was rolled into the handle. He reached for it, but Natasha knocked his hand out of the way. She grabbed the envelope and carefully took out a dozen sheets of aged, grey paper.

"What is it? Tell me," Alex demanded, reaching for the papers.

Natasha stepped back triumphantly, holding the documents out of reach. She showed him the top page. The title said: "The Budapest Protocol."

## TWENTY-EIGHT

## BUDAPEST NEWS SPECIAL EDITION

### HUNKALFFY, SANZLERMANN
### FOUND DEAD BY DANUBE
Police seek 'Directorate' leadership
as take-over plot exposed

**By Natasha Hatvani and Alex Farkas**

Police forces across Europe are searching for Dieter Klindern, head of KZX Industries, and Sylvie Krieghaufner, president of the Volkstern Corporation, following the discovery of the bodies of Frank Sanzlermann and Attila Hunkalffy on the banks of the Danube.

Interpol has issued a warrant for their arrest on charges of murder. Budapest police said that Sanzlermann, front-running candidate for President of Europe, and Hungarian Prime Minister Hunkalffy both appeared to have been killed by multiple pistols shots. The politicians' deaths follow the aborted first round of voting for Europe's President on Sunday night. It is not clear if or when the European Presidential election will now take place. A spokesman for the European Union said: "We are considering all our options but remain firmly committed to the principles of European unity and integration."

These have been some of the most tumultuous days in modern European history. Sanzlermann, the right-winger tipped to be Europe's first President, was the front-man for a shadowy cabal of German and Austrian industrialists, backed by Swiss banks, the *Budapest News* can reveal. The decades old plan to take over Europe was recorded in a document known as the 'Budapest Protocol', drawn up at the Hotel

311

Savoy in November 1944 in the last days of the Second World War, and reprinted in this newspaper.

The document, hidden for more than sixty years, details the secret plans of the Nazi leadership to go underground and prepare for the Fourth Reich – an economic, rather than a military empire. The Directorate set up an international network of front companies funded by looted Nazi assets. As the German and Austrian economies were rebuilt after 1945, the Nazi funds were steadily repatriated and used to buy up other companies and banks. The Directorate soon controlled large sectors of the European economy, concentrating on manufacturing, media, pharmaceuticals and industry. Since the collapse of communism in 1989, the Directorate has focused on the post-communist countries, where weak institutions and widespread corruption have eased its covert takeover.

The introduction of the euro and the abolition of national political and economic sovereignty allowed the Directorate to manipulate governments and economies across the continent. The election of Frank Sanzlermann as European President would have been the culmination of the Directorate's plan. The post was given wide powers over economic and foreign policy, with a veto over new legislation after intense lobbying from Germany and Austria against strong British opposition.

"This was a sinister plot with decades-old roots, that would have allowed the Directorate to hijack the whole process of European integration," said Istvan Kiraly, former communications director for Sanzlermann, who is now working on a book about the campaign. Kiraly's revelations of how the Directorate operated are to be exclusively serialised in the *Budapest News*.

The Directorate controlled the extreme nationalist governments in Croatia, Hungary, Slovakia and Romania. Its takeover of eastern Europe was to have been sealed at a dinner at the Hotel Savoy in Budapest. The dinner was also attended by Hungarian Prime Minister Attila Hunkalffy, Slovak President Dusan Hrkna, and his Romanian counterpart Cornelius Malinanescu, together with senior German and Austrian industrialists and Swiss bankers. Hunkalffy's last weeks in office were marked by an authoritarian clampdown and repeated human rights' abuses.

The *Budapest News* can also reveal that the Directorate planned to wipe out Europe's Romany population through 'Czigex' a genetically engineered 'smart drug' that induces infertility among Romany women. Czigex, which has already been used in eastern Slovakia, is based on the notorious experiments conducted by Nazi doctors in the concentration camps.

The astonishing revelations have sent shock-waves across the world. French President Jean-Luc De Rouen said: "We did not fight the Nazis only to discover that they had secretly won the Second World War. We are reconsidering our future in the European Union." The future of the euro may be in doubt after its value plunged by thirty per cent overnight against the dollar, and over forty per cent against the pound sterling.

High ranking members of the Directorate are believed to hold senior positions in key committees in Brussels and Strasbourg. Its head was Gerhard Vautker, an eighty-eight year old former SS officer, known as 'the Colonel', who was found dead in Budapest on Sunday night. His son, Heinrich Vautker, last night resigned as President of the Federal Monetary Authority, citing 'personal reasons'. Presidents Hrkna and Malinanescu were both arrested on their return home. Budapest police also announced that George Smith, regional editor in chief of the Volkstern Corporation's media arm, had been arrested in connection with the murder of Vince Szatmari.

Hundreds of thousands demonstrated on Sunday night in downtown Budapest in a protest organised by the Hungarian Freedom Movement (HFM) against the Hunkalffy government and Frank Sanzlermann in a display of 'People Power' not seen since the toppling of Slobodan Milošević in October 2000. Police commanders refused to arrest the demonstrators after an armed stand-off with the Gendarmerie. "When Hunkalffy called for help, the response mechanism was blocked," Hungarian intelligence sources said. The leadership of the HFM is unknown. A statement delivered to news agencies announced its dissolution, but warned, 'Our work is completed for now, but we remain vigilant.'

# Adam LeBor

*Business: Euro expansion plans now in question, page 14*
*Property: Directorate collapse set to trigger price boom, page 16*
*Media: How Alex and Natasha got the story, page 18*
*Society: Former Farkas family Balaton villa to be "Miklos Farkas Summer Home for Underprivileged Children", page 24*

## APPENDIX ONE

## The Red House Report

This book is a work of fiction, but was inspired by a genuine US intelligence document, known as the 'Red House Report', reproduced on pages 328–331. Dated London, November 27, 1944, the report was compiled by the G-2 section of SHAEF (Supreme Headquarters Allied Expeditionary Force) that dealt with economic warfare, and was sent to Cordell Hull, the US Secretary of State. It details the "plans of German industrialists for post-war operation", specifically: patents, financial reserves, the export of capital and the strategic placing of technical personnel.

The source was an agent of the French Deuxième Bureau, or military intelligence, who had worked for the French on German issues since 1916 and was in close contact with German industrialists. On August 10 1944 he attended a meeting at the Maison Rouge hotel in Strasbourg, France, where numerous senior German industrialists and Nazi officials discussed their plans for underground activity after Germany's coming defeat. Among those reportedly attending were representatives of Krupp, Volkswagen, Messerschmitt and Rheinmetall. The meeting was presided over by SS Obergruppenfuhrer Dr Scheid, who declared that the war could not be won and German industry should take steps in preparation for a "post-war commercial campaign". Each industrialist was instructed to make quiet contacts with foreign firms "without attracting any suspicion", and prepare the ground for borrowing "considerable sums from foreign countries after the war". Such talk was high treason, and any ordinary Germans who expressed such sentiments would likely find themselves very quickly inside a Gestapo cell. But as businessmen, the Nazi leaders at the Maison Rouge were nothing if not practical.

A smaller meeting followed, where even more sensitive matters were discussed. The report recounts: "At this second meeting it was stated that the Nazi Party had informed the industrialists that the war was practically lost, but would continue until a guarantee of the unity of Germany could be obtained." The industrialists were instructed to prepare themselves to finance the Nazi Party, which would be "forced to go underground". At the same time the German government would allocate "large sums" to industrialists to establish a "secure post-war foundation in foreign countries", while "existing financial reserves in foreign countries must be placed at the disposal of the [Nazi] Party so that a strong German empire can be created after the defeat."

The instructions to export as much capital as possible ran directly counter to Nazi policy and laws, but by summer 1944 Germany's realists were already planning far ahead. The exported funds were to be channelled through two banks in Zurich, or via agencies in Switzerland which bought property in Switzerland for German concerns using a Swiss cloak, for a five per cent commission. The report notes: "Previously exports of capital by German industrialists to neutral countries had to be accomplished rather surreptitiously and by means of special influence. Now the Nazi Party stands behind the industrialists and urges them to save themselves by getting funds outside Germany and at the same time advance the party's plans for its post-war operations." Partners of German companies in the United States were considered especially important, which is not surprising, as before the United States entered the war in 1941 there were extensive links between the American and German business establishments, especially in the oil and chemical industries.

I found the Red House Report in 1996 while I was researching my book *Hitler's Secret Bankers,* which investigated the extent of Swiss economic collaboration with the Nazis and the role of Swiss banks in laundering looted Nazi gold and financing the Nazi war effort. The report was one of numerous intelligence documents declassifed and released in the United States after Jewish organisations such as the World Jewish Congress and others filed Freedom of Information requests. The intelligence reports poured out, revealing a secret history of economic warfare – and, perhaps, future planning. It is a curious feeling to hold a copy of the Red House Report in your hand. The papers are typewritten, the edges of the letters fading. The language is dry, factual, without adjectives. For the purposes of *The Budapest Protocol* I simply switched the meeting to the fictional Hotel Savoy. But beyond a novelist's caprice are more fundamental questions: did the meeting take place; did the Nazis' plan a fourth, economic Reich, or as the document records, "a strong German empire"? And did they build one?

Some things we do know. The Maison Rouge hotel still exists. The level of detail in the report, the strong endorsement of the reliability of the source in the report's covering letter, the fact that it was sent to the Secretary of State, and most of all, that the plans outlined in the report fitted in with known Nazi policy objectives mean that the meeting almost certainly took place. It's also noteworthy that the Nazi industrialists met in Strasbourg, the capital of the French province of Alsace, on the German border, where Germany had traditionally had strong economic interests. The Red House Report was definitely read in high places.

In his 1946 book, *Germany Is Our Problem,* US Treasury Secretary Henry Morgenthau advocated a de-industrialised Germany, in part to break the economic power of the German industrial conglomerates that had financed and profited from the Nazis, most of which soon rebuilt themselves and even now remain household names. It seems Morgenthau knew of the plans for a new economic empire outlined in the Red House Report and the plans to export capital. "These funds will be at the disposal of the Nazis in their underground campaigns (but the industrialists will be repaid by concessions and orders when the Party candidates come to power)," he wrote. "Two Swiss banks through which operations may be conducted were named and the possibility of acquiring a Swiss dummy at five per cent was noted."

The Nazis always placed high importance on economic assets hidden in neutral countries and their potential use in the future. In November 1945 the British section of the Allied Control Commission for Germany found a secret circular written in September 1939 by the German Economics Ministry. It contained instructions to all German Foreign Exchange Control Authorities (Devisenstellen) on how to protect and camouflage their assets abroad. The instructions were considered "state secrets" and only forty copies of the memo were made. Point II/1 on the camouflage of foreign enterprises instructs:

> It is of great interest that the camouflage be effective and successful in order to enable these companies to act as far as possible as bridgeheads for German trade in the future. The camouflage the companies must undergo is to be carried out in such a manner that they can be <u>authenticated as independent foreign enterprises</u>. [underlined as in original]

The document continues:

> The actual influence in the new foreign firms must be secured by effective <u>economic</u> and <u>personnel</u> measures. Special attention is to be paid to the <u>selection of persons</u> for appointment as managers of the newly created foreign firms. . . . Of course any participation of <u>Jewish</u> foreigners in camouflaged German firms has to be avoided.

All of this perfectly accords with the plans laid out in the Red House Report. Sixty-five years after Dr Scheid and the Nazi industrialists met at the Maison Rouge hotel, the record of their discussions still makes for intriguing, if not unsettling, reading.

## APPENDIX TWO

## Sterilising the Roma

In February 2009, a Hungarian Romany woman finally won an eight year legal battle for compensation after a coercive sterilisation. The woman, known as AS, had been sterilised by doctors at a hospital in a small town in eastern Hungary. Her case was taken up by the European Roma Rights centre, which is based in Budapest, and represents an important victory for Romany human and reproductive rights. AS was admitted for an operation to remove a dead fetus in January 2001. She was asked to sign forms giving her consent to this, and to sterilisation. However the doctors did not explain to her the procedure, the risks or the consequences of being sterilised.

Hungary and its neighbours are now members of the European Union, which brings the responsibility to treat all citizens equally. AS's legal victory follows a decision by the Hungarian government in 2008 to amend the Public Health Act to ensure that all patients give informed consent to sterilisation. But for many in the region, especially among the notoriously conservative medical professions, modern notions of equal rights do not extend to the Roma. The practice of coercive sterilisation predates the change of system in 1989 and reaches back to the communist and Nazi era. It is one of the most radical examples of the institutionalised discrimination that the Roma face: the removal of the right to reproduce.

Even in the early years of the twenty-first century, there were numerous reports of coercive sterilisations in Hungary, Slovakia and the Czech Republic. I have met several victims myself.

319

In February 2003, together with my friend and colleague Peter Green, I travelled to a small village near the city of Presov, in eastern Slovakia. We were investigating reports by human rights and Romany activists that dozens of Gypsy women had been sterilised without their consent. What we found was both shocking and profoundly depressing: levels of poverty and deprivation usually seen in the developing world and a clearly delineated, officially sanctioned – if not orchestrated – de facto policy of apartheid between the Roma and their neighbours.

The non-Roma half of the village was clean and tidy, its spacious houses built of brick and concrete and painted white. The Roma were confined to draughty hovels of wood and earth, which they had built themselves, on the outskirts of the settlement. They had no heating, electricity, gas, water or proper sewage disposal. Barely clothed children scampered through mud and ice, and dogs nosed around household waste. The Roma lived like this not because they wanted to, but because the local council refused to register them as residents. With no recognition of their status – especially important in the post-communist countries' Kafkaesque bureaucracies – officially, they did not exist. They could not vote in local or national elections. Their children could not go to school. The local council refused to provide any municipal services. There was even a separate wooden church for the Roma to worship in.

Inside one of the hovels we met Zita. She was twenty-three, and like many Roma, illiterate. Like almost all Romany women, she dreamed of a large family. For Roma, the family is of supreme importance, the axle on which their world turns. During the Nazi Holocaust, which the Roma call the "Poraymus" or great devouring, Romany families furiously resisted being separated. The Nazis decided it was easier to let them live – and die – together. They even had their own family compound in Auschwitz, from where some were selected for medical experiments. In early 1998 Zita gave birth by Caesarean section to her second child, a daughter. Still groggy, she was presented with a piece of paper to sign by a nurse. She told us: "They gave me a paper to sign, but I don't know what it said because I cannot read or write. I was in pain after the operation. My signature is three crosses and I signed with that. After the operation, a nurse came and explained that I will not have any more children. I felt very bad. I started to cry."

Zita's case mirrors that of AS in Hungary and is typical of a policy of coercive sterilisation of Romany women, according to investigators from the Centre for Reproductive Rights, a New York-based human rights group. The centre's report, based on a three-month investigation, was published in March 2003. It detailed about 110 cases of coerced or forced sterilisation in Slovakia as well as a policy of medical apartheid. Romany women were segregated in wards, waiting rooms, toilets, washing and dining facilities. They were often subjected to verbal or physical abuse and were denied access to their medical records. Their hospital files were often stamped with an "R". Many Romany women are vulnerable, poorly educated and have no concept of their legal rights. Zita's husband, Krystian, told us: "I know 100 per cent that she has been sterilised. I lived with her for eight years and now, five years after that operation, she cannot have children. They think the Roma are devils and they can do what they want with us."

We also met Maria, who like Zita, can no longer conceive. Maria, then twenty-nine, was also illiterate and has seven children, which is not uncommon in Romany families. Before giving birth in early 1998 by Caesarean section, she, too, was handed a form to sign. "They put a pen in my hand, took my hand and helped me to sign the paper. They didn't tell me what I signed. I had an operation, but I don't know exactly what it was. Now I have found out that I cannot have children. I started to ask what was going on, but I do not speak Slovak very well and I don't know how to ask a Slovak doctor what has happened to me." Medical records held by Barbora Bukovska, a lawyer and human rights activist, confirm that Maria was sterilised at the age of twenty-four.

From the village we travelled to Presov hospital to hear the other side of the story. A doctor there showed us a grisly catalogue of photographs of still-births and deformed fetuses. These were the reason why the hospital carried out so many Caeserian sections and sometimes had to remove wombs and ovaries as well, he argued.

Dr Marian Kisely, the head of obstetrics, told us that they had never sterilised a Romany woman against her will. "It is always done for medical reasons and with the agreement of the patient. There were cases when we had to perform an emergency hysterectomy because the mother's life was in danger."

As a new young democracy, then about to join the European Union, Slovakia was and is sensitive about its image. Forced sterilisation of an impoverished minority was not the public profile it sought. Questions were being asked in international organisations, by human rights groups and an embarrassing fuss being made. But in Slovakia, like its neighbours, old communist-style reflexes still prevailed. The Romany women asked us to print neither their surnames nor even the name of the village for fear of retribution from the state. We had already heard several stories of how agents of the Slovak secret service had harassed activists for supposedly bringing the country's name into disrepute. Some officials even threatened the activists with prosecution for failing to report a crime, that is, the sterilisations, on time to the police. What was bringing Slovakia's name into disrepute was not the activists, but the failure by the new democratic government to stop the decades-old policy of sterilising Romany women.

\*    \*    \*

As the case of AS shows, Slovakia has no monopoly on ill-treatment of the Roma. Similar scenes of poverty and squalor can be found across post-communist Europe, from the Baltics to the Balkans. In Hungary, between seven and eight per cent of Hungary's population of ten million are Roma. Here too many live in conditions of grinding poverty and endemic unemployment, exacerbated by the global economic recession and the slow down in the construction industry, where many Roma formerly worked.

In 2005, two years after I travelled to Maria and Zita's village, governments in central and south-eastern Europe launched the Decade of Roma Inclusion, at one of Budapest's glitzy riverside hotels. Many of Mittel-Europa's great and good were there, including George Soros, numerous Prime Ministers and high-ranking officials. There was plenty of grand-standing, fine speeches and stirring declarations of the need to fight for equality and against discrimination, all of which have had little, if any, practical effect. None of Hungary's post-communist governments have tried to meaningfully tackle the Roma's appalling living conditions and lack of economic opportunity. In parts of eastern Hungary Roma poverty is now so dire that some are reduced to stealing potatoes from the gardens of their neighbours, many of whom are little better off themselves.

With poverty comes crime and rising social tension. At the end of 2008 Hungary created its first national police force to combat crimes against Roma, after a spike in attacks. Fifty officers were investigating seventeen unsolved cases in the last two years, all involving guns, Molotov cocktails or hand grenades. Two Roma died in the north-eastern village of Nagycsecs, shot dead trying to flee their house after it was firebombed. A man and a woman died after a grenade was thrown through their window in the southern city of Pecs, and their children were injured. Three Romany houses were firebombed and three shot at in summer 2008, although nobody was injured. In February 2009 a Romany man, Robert Csorba, and his five year old son, Robika, were shot dead trying to flee their burning house after an arson attack. The attackers reportedly lay in wait outside their home in the village of Tatarszentgyorgy, central Hungary, before opening fire with hunting weapons.

These deaths in particular caused widespread revulsion and horror. They galvanised public opinion and thousands of mourners attended the funeral of Robika and his father, including representatives of the main political parties. Romany activists and politicians said the Csorba killings and the other firebombings were racist attacks and claimed that a 'death-squad' was targeting Gypsies. As of early April 2009 nobody had been arrested in connection with the killing of Robert and Robika Csorba. The police said they were pursuing multiple lines of enquiry.

It's also possible that these murders were examples of the growing trend of Roma on Roma crime. Romany society is plagued by thuggish money lenders who target poverty stricken individuals and provide loans at 100 per cent interest, triggering a spiral of debt. Not all of the Roma's problems are due to external factors. The failure to develop a dynamic communal leadership, and social mores that in many families value early marriage and children over education and a career are increasing the Roma's marginalisation. Many human rights workers or social activists working can recount how bright young Romany school students, especially girls, are forbidden from going to college, and are married off while still in their teens.

The growing prejudice against Roma and their worsening social conditions are exacerbating a disturbing sense of disconnection from mainstream society and its laws. There are frequent reports in the Hungarian media of Romany mob attacks on drivers involved in car accidents and on the police who attempt to mediate. Eight Romany men are on trial in the eastern city of Miskolcs after a horrific murder in the village of Olaszliska, northern Hungary. A driver who hit a Romany girl, lightly injuring her, was dragged out of his car by a mob and beaten to death in front of his two young daughters. Understandably, hideous events like the Olaszliska lynching cause widespread fury and disgust: both at the perpetrators and the failure of the police to protect ordinary citizens.

The beneficiary of this is the far-right in Hungary, which is growing in both strength and confidence by focusing relentlessly on what it calls 'Gypsy crime'. Jobbik is even calling for the re-introduction of the Gendarmerie, the national police force that was dissolved after the Second World War. That is unlikely, but it's increasingly clear that the dire situation of the Roma, growing racism, the worldwide economic downturn and the Roma's dislocation from mainstream society are all the necessary ingredients for a social explosion in the making.

## APPENDIX THREE

## Staying Anonymous on the Internet

Send an email or visit a website and you may as well tell the world. Emails are insecure, can be instantly forwarded *ad infinitum* and live forever. Under EU law your Internet Service Provider is already required to keep a record of your browsing habits, including every website you visit, for two years. The government now wants to set up a comprehensive database of all internet usage including details of where and when emails were sent – although it says it will not include their contents. Can we believe them?

Encrypted and secure communication methods that were previously the preserve of governments and intelligence services are now easily available to anyone with an internet connection. They are free, downloadable and reasonably easy to use.

- Internet telephony programmes are very difficult to tap when used computer to computer. Unless you are a person of interest to the authorities, they are probably secure enough for sensitive conversations, providing that the room is not bugged. Chat and instant messaging however are not secure and some countries, such as China, have added filtering software to prevent discussion of sensitive topics.
- Be aware that every email you send can include the IP (Internet Protocol) address of your computer and of your Internet Service Provider (ISP), which identifies it. These are contained in the email's headers and can be easily found with the view/headers buttons on mail programmes. Tracing programmes available

on the internet and tracing websites can use the IP address of the computer and/or of the ISP to find the sender's physical location.

- Using https rather than http in Gmail (this can be set as default) keeps your webmail encrypted between your browser and Gmail's servers. Gmail, unlike some other webmail providers, does not include your IP address in email headers. For higher levels of security GNU Privacy Guard allows you to encrypt, send and store email and data, with a digital signature. Those wary of sending any emails because of the data trail they leave can use the drafts folder on any free webmail service as a continually updated message board for anyone with access to the account.

- Guerrilla Mail provides instant, free, disposable email addresses. These are also very useful for websites that ask you for an email address so they can send you a link to click on before they will allow you access.

- The IP address that identifies your computer leaves a trail across cyberspace as you surf the internet. Tor, the onion router, disguises this and allows you to surf anonymously. It encrypts and bounces users' web requests through a series of routers around the world. Think of it as a cyber-cell system, where no single router knows the whole path of your data request. Tor is free and is usually bundled with Privoxy, a web go-between that requests and forwards data. Both can be configured with the Firefox browser. Numerous companies also offer commercial services to anonymise your computer's web-surfing and provide anonymous emails.

- Manage your cookies. Cookies are data stored on your computer by the websites that you visit. They may be useful, such as passwords, for example. But they may also be used for "data-mining" purposes, to track how much time you spend on a website, which links you click on, and so on, giving advertisers valuable information about your personal interests. Browsers now include the ability to turn cookies on or off, or manage them individually.

For more information on secure cyber-communication go to:

Electronic Frontier Foundation: www.eff.org

Tor: www.torproject.org

Global Voices Online: www.globalvoicesonline.org

Frontline Defenders: www.frontlinedefenders.org

Citizen Lab: www.citizenlab.org

# APPENDIX FOUR

# RED HOUSE REPORT

RED HOUSE

Secret

Mr. Klaus

No. 19,489  London, November 27, 1944
BY AIR POUCH

Economic Warfare (Safehaven) Series: No.

Subject: Transmitting Intelligence Report
No. EW-Pa 128 by G-2 Economic
Section, SHAEF, regarding plans of
German industrialists for post-war
operation.

SECRET
For Department, Treasury and Foreign Economic
Administration.

The Honorable
The Secretary of State
Washington, D.C.

Sir:

I have the honor to enclose Intelligence Report
No. EW-Pa 128 by G-2 Economic Section, SHAEF, dated
November 7, 1944, describing the plans of German
industrialists for the post-war resurrection of Germany.
Among the topics dealt with in this report are: patents,
financial reserves, exportation of capital, and the
strategic placing of technical personnel.

Respectfully yours,
For the Ambassador:

John W. Easton
Lt. Colonel, F.A.
Economic Warfare Division

Enclosure: Intelligence Report.

(Original and hectograph to Department)

JBW:jmc

# RED HOUSE REPORT *continued*

Enclosure No. 1 to despatch No. 19,469 of
Nov. 27, 1944, from the Embassy at London,
England.

S E C R E T

SUPREME HEADQUARTERS
ALLIED EXPEDITIONARY FORCE
Office of Assistant Chief of Staff, G-2

7 November 1944

INTELLIGENCE REPORT NO. EW-Pa 128

SUBJECT: Plans of German industrialists to engage in
underground activity after Germany's defeat;
flow of capital to neutral countries.

SOURCE: Agent of French Deuxieme Bureau, recommended by
Commandant Zindel. This agent is regarded as
reliable and has worked for the French on German
problems since 1916. He was in close contact
with the Germans, particularly industrialists,
during the occupation of France and he visited
Germany as late as August, 1944.

1. A meeting of the principal German industrialists
with interests in France was held on August 10, 1944, in
the Hotel Rotes Haus in Strasbourg, France, and attended
by the informant indicated above as the source. Among
those present were the following:

Dr. Scheid, who presided, holding the rank of
S.S. Obergruppenführer and Director of the
Hecho (Hermsdorff & Schonburg) Company
Dr. Kaspar, representing Krupp
Dr. Tolle, representing Rochling
Dr. Sinderen, representing Messerschmitt
Drs. Kopp, Vier and Beerwanger, representing Rhein-
metall
Captain Haberkorn and Dr. Ruhe, representing Bussing
Drs. Ellenmayer and Kardos, representing Volkswagenwerk
Engineers Drose, Yanchew and Koppshem, representing
various factories in Posen, Poland (Drose,
Yanchew and Co., Brown-Boveri, Herkuleswerke,
Buschwerke, and Stadtwerke)
Captain Dornbusch, head of the Industrial Inspection
Section at Posen
Dr. Meyer, an official of the German Naval Ministry
in Paris
Dr. Strossner, of the Ministry of Armament, Paris.

2. Dr. Scheid stated that all industrial material
in France was to be evacuated to Germany immediately.
The battle of France was lost for Germany and now the
defense of the Siegfried Line was the main problem. From
now on also German industry must realize that the war
cannot be won and that it must take steps in preparation
for a post-war commercial campaign. Each industrialist
must make contacts and alliances with foreign firms, but
this must be done individually and without attracting any
suspicion. Moreover, the ground would have to be laid on

329

# RED HOUSE REPORT *continued*

-2-

of penetration which had been most useful in the past,
Dr. Scheid cited the fact that patents for stainless steel
belonged to the Chemical Foundation, Inc., New York, and
the Krupp Company of Germany jointly and that the U.S.
Steel Corporation, Carnegie Illinois, American Steel and
Wire, and National Tube, etc. were thereby under an
obligation to work with the Krupp concern. He also
cited the Zeiss Company, the Leica Company and the Hamburg-
American Line as firms which had been especially effective
in protecting German interests abroad and gave their New
York addresses to the industrialists at this meeting.

3. Following this meeting a smaller one was held
presided over by Dr. Bosse of the German Armaments Ministry
and attended only by representatives of Hecho, Krupp and
Roehling. At this second meeting it was stated that the
Nazi Party had informed the industrialists that the war
was practically lost but that it would continue until a
guarantee of the unity of Germany could be obtained. German
industrialists must, it was said, through their exports
increase the strength of Germany. They must also prepare
themselves to finance the Nazi Party which would be forced
to go underground as Maquis (in Gebirgeverteidigungsstellen
gehen). From now on the government would allocate large
sums to industrialists so that each could establish a
secure post-war foundation in foreign countries. Existing financial reserves in foreign countries must be
placed at the disposal of the Party so that a strong German
Empire can be created after the defeat. It is also
immediately required that the large factories in Germany
create small technical offices or research bureaus which
would be absolutely independent and have no known connection with the factory. These bureaus will receive
plans and drawings of new weapons as well as documents which
they need to continue their research and which must not be
allowed to fall into the hands of the enemy. These
offices are to be established in large cities where they
can be most successfully hidden as well as in little
villages near sources of hydro-electric power where they
can pretend to be studying the development of water
resources. The existence of these is to be known only
by very few people in each industry and by chiefs of the
Nazi Party. Each office will have a liaison agent with
the Party. As soon as the Party becomes strong enough
to re-establish its control over Germany the industrialists
will be paid for their effort and cooperation by concessions
and orders.

4. These meetings seem to indicate that the pro-
hibition against the export of capital which was rigorously
enforced until now has been completely withdrawn and
replaced by a new Nazi policy whereby industrialists with
government assistance will export as much of their capital
as possible. Previously exports of capital by German
industrialists to neutral countries had to be accomplished
rather surreptitiously and by means of special influence.

# RED HOUSE REPORT *continued*

-5-

Now the Nazi party stands behind the industrialists and urges them to save themselves by getting funds outside Germany and at the same time to advance the Party's plans for its post-war operation. This freedom given to the industrialists further cements their relations with the Party by giving them a measure of protection.

6. The German industrialists are not only buying agricultural property in Germany but are placing their funds abroad, particularly in neutral countries. Two main banks through which this export of capital operates are the Basler Handelsbank and the Schweizerinsche Kreditanstalt of Zurich. Also there are a number of agencies in Switzerland which for a five per cent commission buy property in Switzerland, using a Swiss cloak.

8. After the defeat of Germany the Nazi Party recognizes that certain of its best known leaders will be condemned as war criminals. However, in cooperation with the industrialists it is arranging to place its less conspicuous but most important members in positions with various German factories as technical experts or members of its research and designing offices.

For the A.C. of S., G-2.

WALTER K. SCHEINN

G-2, Economic Section

Prepared by

MELVIN M. FAGEN

Distribution:

Same as EW-Pa 1.
U.S. Political Adviser, SHAEF
British Political Adviser, SHAEF

331

# SELECT BIBLIOGRAPHY

Readers interested in further investigating the themes of *The Budapest Protocol* may find the following works of interest.

Bank for International Settlements, The, *The Bank for International Settlements and the Basle Meeting*. Basle: BIS, 1980.

Barsony, Janos and Agnes Daroczi, *Pharrajimos: The Fate of the Roma During the Holocaust*. New York: International Debate Education Association, 2008.

Black, Edwin, *IBM and the Holocaust: The Strategic Alliance between Nazi Germany and America's Most Powerful Corporation*. New York: Crown Publishing Group, 2001.

Borkin, Joseph, *The Crime and Punishment of I.G. Farben: The Startling Account of the Unholy Alliance of Adolf Hitler and Germany's Great Chemical Combine*. New York: Free Press, 1978.

Braham, Randolph L. *The Politics of Genocide: The Holocaust in Hungary*. New York: Columbia University Press, 1981.

Fonseca, Isabel, *Bury Me Standing: The Gypsies and their Journey*. London: Vintage, 1996.

Garlinski, Jozef, *The Swiss Corridor: Espionage Networks in Switzerland during World War II*. London: J. M. Dent & Sons 1981.

Higham, Charles, *Trading With the Enemy: An Exposé of the Nazi-American Money Plot 1933–1949*. London: Robert Hale, 1983.

Jeffreys, Diarmuid, *Hell's Cartel: IG Farben and the Making of Hitler's War Machine*. London: Bloomsbury: 2008.

Laughland, John, *The Tainted Source: The Undemocratic Origins of the European Idea*. London: Little, Brown, 1997.

Lee, Martin, A. *The Beast Reawakens: The Chilling Story of the Rise of the Neo-Nazi Movement*. London: Little, Brown, 1997.

LeBor, Adam, *Hitler's Secret Bankers: How Switzerland Profited from Nazi Genocide*. London: Balazs and Schuster, 1997.

LeBor, Adam and Roger Boyes, *Surviving Hitler: Choices, Corruption and Compromise in the Third Reich*. London: Balazs and Schuster, 2000.

Liegeois, Jean-Pierre, *Gypsies: An Illustrated History*. London: Saqi Books, 2005.

Linklater, Magnus, Isobel Hilton and Neal Ascherson. *Klaus Barbie, The Fourth Reich and the Neo-Fascist Connection*. London: Coronet Books, 1994.

Loftus, John and Mark Aarons, Mark, *The Secret War Against the Jews: How Western Espionage Betrayed the Jewish People*. New York: St Martin's Press, 1994.

Simpson, Christopher, *The Splendid Blond Beast: Money, Law and Genocide in the Twentieth Century*. Monroe: Common Courage Press, 1995.

Radnoti, Miklos, *Foamy Sky: The Major Poems of Miklós Radnóti*. Budapest: Corvina, 2002.

Porter, Anna, *Kasztner's Train*. London: Constable: 2008.

Szep, Erno, *The Smell of Humans: A Memoir of the Holocaust in Hungary*. Budapest: Central European University Press, 1994.

Turner, Henry Ashby Jr., *German Big Business and the Rise of Hitler*. Oxford: Oxford University Press, 1985.

Zsolt, Bela, *Nine Suitcases*. London: Jonathan Cape, 2004.

## Donations

Part of the proceeds from the sale of *The Budapest Protocol* will go to the Medical Foundation for the Care of Victims of Torture.

The Medical Foundation for the Care of Victims of Torture is the only human rights organisation in the UK dedicated solely to treating survivors of torture and organised violence. By 2008, in over two decades of work, it had received almost 50,000 requests for help from individuals, families and children from around the world, struggling to come to terms with the trauma of torture and the instability of living in exile. Responding to the many and complex needs of survivors involves caring for their emotional and psychological welfare, and ensuring that their practical and legal needs are equally addressed in helping them to rebuild their lives, while advocating on their behalf to ensure the UK honours its obligations to people fleeing persecution.

REPORTAGE PRESS

REPORTAGE PRESS is a new publishing house specialising in books on foreign affairs or set in foreign countries; nonfiction, fiction, essays, travel books, or just books written from a stranger's viewpoint. Good books like this are now hard to come by – largely because British publishers have become frightened of publishing books that will not appeal to a mass-market audience.

At REPORTAGE PRESS we are not averse to taking risks in order to bring our readers the books they want to read. Visit our website: www.reportagepress.com. A percentage of the profits from each of our books goes to a relevant charity chosen by the author.

Our DESPATCHES series brings back into print classic pieces of journalism from the past.

You can buy further copies of *The Budapest Protocol* directly from the website, where you can also find out more about our authors and upcoming titles.

REPORTAGE PRESS